BOO

A NOVEL

RENE GUTTERIDGE

WATERBROOK
PRESS

FOR MOM AND DAD

Boo
Published by WaterBrook Press
2375 Telstar Drive, Suite 160
Colorado Springs, Colorado 80920
A division of Random House, Inc.

The characters and events in this book are fictional, and any resemblance to actual
persons or events is coincidental.

ISBN 1-57856-573-1

Published in association with the literary agency of Janet Kobobel Grant, Books & Such, 4788
Carissa Avenue, Santa Rosa, CA 95405.

Library of Congress Cataloging-in-Publication Data
Gutteridge, Rene.
    Boo / Rene Gutteridge.— 1st ed.
      p. cm.
    ISBN 1-57856-573-1
   1. Fiction—Authorship—Fiction. 2. Novelists—Fiction. 3. Indiana—Fiction.
4. Tourism—Fiction. I. Title.
    PS3557.U887B66 2003
   813'.6—dc21

                           2003007287

Printed in the United States of America
2003—First Edition

10 9 8 7 6 5 4 3 2 1

What People Are Saying About
Boo
by Rene Gutteridge

"Rene Gutteridge's new book is a darling story with a rare blend of love, intrigue, and laugh-out-loud humor. It will tickle your funny bone, but even more important, it will make you think about how often we try to force our notions of God's will onto everyone else. Don't miss this one!"

—Colleen Coble, author of *Without a Trace*

"Ever wonder what a horror writer must think and feel when he's off the clock? Ever wonder if he might have a soft side, a caring side that writes tender poetry in his dark lonely mansion? Ever wonder what might happen if one day he was redeemed? Gutteridge doesn't give up on anyone in this story. Her fast-paced plot (where new faces pop up like pneumatically rigged spooks in a funhouse) and her crisp dialogue won't let you stop reading, and she certainly doesn't give away the ending until the last page, where Boo finally gets to—okay, okay, I won't give it away either. But hurry up and get started. And, oh yeah, bring a blanket, a box of tissues, and lots of cat food."

—Chonda Pierce, comedienne and author of *It's Always Darkest Before the Fun Comes Up* and *On Her Soapbox*

"I understand Ms. Gutteridge has a professional baseball player in her family tree. Not surprising. This is Major League storytelling that has the crowd on its feet."

—Michael O'Connor, author of *Sermon on the Mound*

"Rene's characters jump off the page and invite you to be part of their lives. I just wanted to curl up with my cat and live in Skary, Indiana. What a fun and cozy read!"

—Kristin Billerbeck, author of *Blind Dates*

It was a balmy afternoon—

Balmy? No. Cloudy.

It was a cloudy afternoon—

Cloudy or balmy?

It was a—

It was *what,* for crying out loud?

It was a— It was a—a—sad. Sad, sad day. The worst day ever.

A sad day? Weather isn't sad.

It was a sunny day—

Yes, start out sunny. You can't go wrong with sunny.

...a sunny day and...

Scratch the weather. That's cliché. Are you cliché now? After all this time? You can't come up with a better beginning than a weather report? Start over.

A dark shadow of evil, one so fierce it threatened to destroy all in its path, loomed over the partially cloudy horizon.

That's good. A dark shadow of evil. Is evil a shadow? What is that dark shadow? What is the evil? Think, think, think—

The evil can only be seen when there is light, because shadows only exist when there is light. In the dark it is hidden, inching forward over the landscape like a thick, black ink, fearing exposure by the rotation of the earth, waiting for the light to reach it again.

What is the evil? Must establish the evil. It is invisible without its shadow. It is exposed by the light because one can see its shadow. It sits on the edge of a tiny town, ready to drown it. Torture it like an overpowering storm. What is it? What has a shadow but can't be seen?

Who cares? Why do you care? What is this? Nothing. Absolutely nothing. Just like you. You're absolutely nothing. A smudge of an existence.

...waiting for the light to reach it...

Don't wait. You can't afford to wait. You are dying a slow death, and you know it. You are writing formulas and fabrications and fuddle. Yes, fuddle. People hang on every word you write, and you never think twice about what it is you've said, or how you've said it, or why you've said it.

It's over. This is over. It's all over. Not another word exists in you. Not one more single description. Not an ounce of fascinating character. Not one brief moment of brilliance.

Not a glimmer of light.

CHAPTER 1

MISS MISSY PEEPLE shuffled down the gravel hill as fast as her callous, fungus-ridden feet would let her go. She could feel her ankles swelling. She hadn't moved this fast in years. But she had news that would shake up her little town of Skary like they'd never been shaken before. This was comparable to the news her sister, Sissy, had delivered almost thirteen years ago. At seventy-two, poor Sissy had slipped on some gravel and hit her head on a slab of concrete on her way to tell the important news. But she had made Missy proud. She had managed to utter in her dying breath the words that would have the town talking for years: Dr. Schoot and Nurse Wintery were having an affair. She'd given her life for the sake of Skary.

But this old maid had news that might raise Sissy from the grave.

Missy huffed and puffed her way down Scarlet Hill, maneuvering her cane this way and that to keep herself from tumbling to her death. It was a balmy day—oh, perhaps not balmy, but sunny and slightly warm for this late in the season, and Missy was sure she was actually breaking a sweat.

The clock tower rang out proudly that it was noon, and only a few hundred feet in front of her Missy could see the folks gathering for lunchtime at the community center. Her lungs seemed to collapse further with each breath she tried to take. But she must keep going. Quite frankly, she'd rather die than not tell all.

She made her way onto the sidewalk, where her shoes glided more easily but for the crack here or there. She managed to avoid those so as to not break her deceased mother's back. Howard the barber stood outside his shop smoking a stinky cigar and reading the weather report from the newspaper.

"Those dumb weathermen! Look at how bright the sun is shining today, and they're saying here that it's going to be cloudy! What do they know?"

"Not now, Howard! Not now!" Missy spat as she scooted past him, clubbing him in the foot with the end of her cane. "I must get to the center. I've got news!"

Howard laughed heartily. "What is it this time, Missy? Dr. Twyne's cloning pigs again?"

Missy scowled and gave Howard a nasty wave of her hand. Her news was too pressing to go back and argue with Howard about the pig cloning, though she *did* have proof of that, no matter what anyone said.

Fifty yards to go and her arthritis kicked in. She managed to scoop an aspirin from the bottom of her purse, chew it up, swallow it, and never miss a step. She always did like that bitter taste.

Half her bun was falling down, her nylon stockings were barely holding up, and her polyester floral dress was sticking to several parts of her body by the time she managed to shove her way through the line into the center and make her way to the small platform that held the American flag the way an athlete holds a trophy.

She thumped the microphone needlessly. It always stayed on. No one knew how to turn it off. But it gave a high-pitched shrill of a sound that hunched backs and raised hairs. Missy Peeple smiled authoritatively as everyone turned to see what was going on.

"Excuse me, excuse me," she said, hushing the already quiet crowd. Her brows arched, and her eyes narrowed. "I have a very important announcement to make. One I think everyone will be interested in hearing."

She glanced around the room, pleased to have everyone's attention. She liked attention. She craved it. And at eight-seven years old, she was just about to hit the pinnacle of her life. She said a little prayer. Not to God, but to Sissy, hoping she was somewhere watching this monumental event.

"It's a little hard to explain." Wolfe Boone's long legs didn't quite fit between the pews, and as he struggled to cross and recross them, his big foot hit the wood with a *thud*.

Reverend Peck tried hard to look calm and serene and pastoral as he sat next to Wolfe on the third row of the middle pew. His hands were folded neatly in his lap. He nodded his head understandingly. He smiled soothingly. But inside, his organs were beating like a cha-cha band. Everything was rattling, including his mind, as he tried to remember the last time he'd had a conversion. Seventeen years, if he remembered right. And certainly nobody famous! It was Dr. Schoot who had converted on his deathbed after years of drinking and carousing.

Reverend Peck nodded and patted the tall man on the shoulder. "Take your time."

"Well, you see," he began, "I was sitting up at my house, you know, the one up there on the hill that overlooks the town? And I was starting my new novel. And I didn't really know what I was going to write about. I wasn't worried. I just thought I'd start writing…"

Reverend Peck thought to himself that Wolfe Boone's voice was softer and less deep than he expected. He spoke properly, with a tinge of a British accent. And though his hair was tousled and long over the ears, he was a good-looking man, probably in his late thirties, early forties. Reverend Peck had seen him from time to time in the grocery store and at a restaurant here and there. But he'd never spoken to him. Wolfe Boone always looked as if he didn't want to be spoken to.

"I had this silly notion of an evil that had a shadow but was invisible. And that's where I get all my best ideas. Silly notions. And so I just began writing, but then I stopped. And I realized I was very sad inside. Do you know that feeling? Just empty. Just dead."

Reverend Peck nodded and smiled. He wondered if he should call him Wolfe, or Mr. Boone, or Boo. That's what they'd called him for years. Boo. It was a fitting nickname for the man who had made the town of Skary famous, the man no one really knew.

"Sure. I understand completely."

"Yes, well, so I'm feeling quite dead inside and really more than dead if there is such a thing, and I'm looking out my window, and from my window I can see the steeple of your church. So I walked down the pathway around the hillside and down to your church and here I am." He cleared his throat. "I know I'm babbling. I'm a better writer than I am a speaker."

Reverend Peck studied the man's eyes. He always did that before talking to someone about God. It helped him remember how precious the human soul is. "Please don't worry about being awkward around me. I'm here to help."

Wolfe Boone nodded and then seemed to have nothing more to say.

Reverend Peck filled in the silence. "So this is your first time in the church?"

"Yes." Wolfe Boone threw his hair back out of his face. "I've wanted to come before. Many times." He shrugged. "I just haven't." He looked Reverend Peck directly in the eyes. "Someone has led me to this decision today. And Reverend, I don't want to wait any longer. What must I do to be saved?"

Ainsley Parker splattered the ketchup across the fries in the perfect manner to make the things look "bloody." She had never thought French fries looked liked fingers, or ketchup looked like blood, but "Bloody Fingers" was the most popular dish at The Haunted Mansion restaurant, as much as she despised it. Kids would roar with laughter while pretending to be cannibals. Grownups weren't much more mature about it.

She waited impatiently for Chef Bob to finish the order of Queasy Quesadillas, a frightful invention of cheese, red tortillas, smashed green chilies, and a pasty black bean sauce made to look like something horribly disgusting, but no one really knew what. It didn't matter. If it was grotesque, it was popular.

A familiar scent that was not from the kitchen caught her nose. Garth Twyne. His cologne always beat him into sight. "Here comes lover boy," murmured Marlee Hampton as she picked up her own order.

"How much rejection can one guy take?" Ainsley moaned.

She heard Garth cross the floor in a strut caused by too-tight Wranglers. "Ainsley!"

She turned and watched him make his way to the counter near where she stood.

"Garth. Don't you have some dying horse to save?"

"That was yesterday. Saved Herbert's horse, you know. Three more minutes and the horse would've been a goner. Herbert was so grateful he said he's adding me to his will. The doctor saved the hay—I mean the day!" He laughed and snorted. Ainsley held her breath in order not to smell the aftereffects of his lunch.

She laughed to herself: In almost every conversation she had with Garth, he somehow had to mention that he was a doctor. She assumed the complex came from the fact that his brother, Arnie, was a real M.D., and Garth was just a vet. He'd been kicked out of medical school for incompetence, which surprised no one. Arnie had gone on to be a surgeon in Indianapolis. Ainsley glanced back at the kitchen to see what was taking Chef Bob so long with the quesadillas.

"So I'm assuming you haven't heard the news."

"What news?" she said into the kitchen. "Bob? Where are those quesadillas?"

"Missy Peeple just made the announcement at the community center."

"You're cloning pigs again?"

"That's not funny, and no, it was something far more important."

Garth's tone was grave enough for Ainsley to actually turn around and pay attention to him. "All right, what was the news?"

Garth smiled widely, his yellow teeth crooked and dull. "Guess."

Bob finally sent through the quesadillas. "Garth! You're so annoying!" Ainsley snatched up the order and carried it to her table. Garth followed closely behind.

"What? I'm just trying to have a little fun."

"I'm not in the mood." Ainsley smiled at her customers, out-of-towners, she guessed, by the way they marveled at the restaurant's horror paraphernalia. "Here are your Queasy Quesadillas, your Bloody Fingers, an order of Slime Balls, four Vampire Sodas, and one Screamy Potato."

The teenage boy's eyes were wide with delight. "Does Wolfe Boone come in here any?"

Ainsley tried to hold a steady, polite smile. "Occasionally."

The girl chimed in. "What's he like? Is he scary?"

"Oh, he's everything you would imagine him to be," Ainsley recited. The questions were endlessly the same.

"What does he usually order?" the father asked.

"Mad Cow Meatloaf."

"Is that really his house on the top of the hill?" the wife asked.

"Yes."

The boy tried to reach the fake eyeball floating in his soda. "I bet he's mean. He's mean, isn't he?"

Ainsley had little patience for all this. The last person in the world she wanted to discuss was Wolfe Boone. He was the very reason she had to wear vampire teeth and dress like a ghoul. He was the very reason this town was nothing more than a tourist trap for the dark side. The very thought of him made her sick to her stomach. Conflicting emotions passed through her heart as she thought of her Aunt Gert, battling cancer, suffering as her mom had. Gert was the reason she stayed in this town, the only reason she stayed at this restaurant. Before it sold its soul to the devil, The Haunted Mansion was a quaint diner called Sylvia's. Her mom and aunt's favorite. She stayed and worked here out of principle but nothing else. She adjusted her vampire teeth so she wouldn't sound as if she had a speech impediment.

"Is there anything else I can get you?"

They all shook their heads, and Ainsley returned to the counter, Garth following so closely she could hear him breathing. She turned around. "Garth! Give me some room, will you?"

"You're a little snippy today."

"Are you going to tell me the news or not?" Ainsley wiped her hands on her apron and eyed the couple in the corner waiting to be served. "It's the busiest time of the day, you know."

Garth's eyes narrowed, and a wicked little grin crept across his thin and crusty lips. He dropped his voice to a whisper. "Wolfe Boone gave his life to the Lord Jesus Christ."

Ainsley looked hard at Garth with a fierceness she could hardly control. "Is this some sort of sick joke?"

"Not according to Missy Peeple. Said she was watering the flowers at the church and heard him talking to Reverend Peck about the whole thing."

Ainsley shoved her hair out of her face. "What does she know?"

"This makin' you angry, darlin'?"

"*He* makes me angry in general, and you know it."

Garth snickered under his breath. "You're cute when you're mad."

"You'll have to excuse me. I've got customers waiting." She tried to smile at Garth politely. Her mom had told her always to be polite, even to people she didn't like. And she knew Jesus had mentioned that once or twice himself.

Ainsley walked past Garth, took the couple's order, and then stepped outside the back of the restaurant for her fifteen-minute break. Could this be true? Missy was by far the most accurate and experienced town gossip, but it was easier to believe Garth was cloning pigs.

A yellow cat purred its way through her legs, wrapping its tail around her ankles. "Shoo!" she instructed the cat, who hurried off to the garbage cans.

She'd been a Christian nearly her whole life. That's why she despised what that man had done to her wonderful little town. What had once been a nice, quiet, simple town was now a haven for all that was gruesome, horrid, and monstrous. All because of him. How could a man like that change? For real?

She looked up to the sky. If he was faking it, then God would know. *God knows everything and brings all evil into the light.* Ainsley smiled with that small reassurance. A cold north wind blew in suddenly, and she shivered and wrapped her arms around herself. Just a moment ago it had been sunny. But now dark, heavy clouds filled the sky.

A storm was coming.

CHAPTER 2

"AMEN."

Wolfe Boone opened his eyes. He half expected to see angels and white light hovering above him, but instead the church had actually seemed to darken while they prayed. He looked at the reverend, who was smiling. The reverend glanced outside.

"Looks like some clouds have rolled in."

Wolfe nodded but found himself speechless. Though the windows didn't gleam with supernatural light, something was astoundingly different. The change was on the inside, however, and though he couldn't be certain, he expected he looked just the same on the outside. Still, there was a remarkable tranquility inside his spirit, nearly unexplainable for a man who could describe just about anything. He chewed at his fingernails as he pondered this.

He also pondered evil. He'd met money and fame while writing of ghosts and goblins and devils and demons. And while most critics of his genre would argue that he was as evil as the characters he developed, Wolfe Boone had always sensed that in a war between good and evil, good would always win in the end, that good and evil were not mutually equal enemies. He knew evil to be weaker and believed it depended on manipulative and seedy tactics to stay in the game. Though it was meaner and darker than he'd ever imagined, it was powerless against the Life that now resided in him.

And as he processed the forgiveness he'd just received and the new life he'd been given, he felt as if wisdom had replaced whatever intelligence he possessed. Life was not the same.

"You have a lot to think about," the reverend said, and Wolfe blinked away his thoughts. "How do you feel?"

Wolfe rubbed his hands together. His mind contained a vast number of words, and he could pick any one of them as if flipping through a dictionary, but only one word seemed completely appropriate: "New."

The reverend nodded and grinned. "The Bible says you are a new creation now. The old has gone. The new has come." The reverend looked down at his hands, as if trying to find a way to describe something. He then said, "You will find that your perception has changed. Things will look different now than they did before." His eyes were filled with light and peace. "And all that you regretted in your life is buried. A new life has been given to you."

Wolfe managed to smile at the reverend despite the fact that he felt he could cry. He did it intentionally. He knew he could appear serious and brooding, which many people mistook for dark and creepy.

The reverend returned the smile and stuck out his hand for Wolfe to shake. "I'm glad to know you. I'm so glad you came here today."

"I'm glad too," Wolfe replied, shaking his hand firmly.

The reverend stood suddenly. "How about some lunch?"

"Lunch?"

"Yes. How about you and I have lunch together?"

Wolfe stood too. He'd never eaten lunch with anyone in this town before.

"We better hurry," the reverend said, ushering him out the door. "The wind's blowing something furious in."

They stepped outside into the wind and made their way down the hill into the town. Wolfe towered over the gentle and meek man beside him, but somehow the reverend seemed to stand a little taller. A swelling of pride filled Wolfe's heart as he accompanied the reverend. He had a new friend, and that was nothing short of a miracle.

"Haunted Mansion restaurant okay?" the reverend asked as they made their way along the sidewalk.

"Sure."

"I like their Thrilled Cheese sandwich." The reverend glanced to the bushes, which rattled as he and Wolfe walked by. "Shoo! Outta here!" A couple of frolicking cats bristled, then moved deeper into the bushes, out of sight. "Those cats!"

Twenty yards away from The Haunted Mansion, Wolfe began to notice the strange looks from people. Howard the barber raced outside, nearly tripping over himself as they went by. Everyone else stopped to watch them walk along the sidewalk together.

"What's going on?" Wolfe asked the reverend.

"I don't know," the reverend whispered back.

By the time they arrived at The Haunted Mansion, a small crowd had gathered, and even the strong wind couldn't carry away the deafening silence.

"Come on," the reverend said, nudging Wolfe into the restaurant, almost shoving him through the swarm of people. When they got inside, Wolfe heard a fork drop and saw guests at their tables staring and gawking. Looking at Wolfe, he said, "Don't you worry about a thing. We're going to sit down here and eat our lunch. I don't know what's going on, but we'll get to the bottom of it."

Wolfe stared at his brown boots. The unconventional witty side of him wanted to shake his head violently from side to side and scream like something out of *The Exorcist,* but more than a few elderly people were nearby, and that might cause a scene not even he could write. Of all these people, nobody knew him. They'd created him, so to speak— an image of him, anyway. But they didn't know him. They didn't know he could be funny. They didn't know he liked old black-and-white romantic movies. And he suspected they didn't want to know him. They'd created a tourist town around who they wanted him to be, and just by the stares he was getting while standing next to the reverend, Wolfe realized suddenly that his new spirituality was going to rock a few boats.

Then it began. The twitch. It was a twitch. Then an itch. The eyes would water, and then it would be out of his control. He imagined it was violent in nature because of his size. He was six foot four. And if he tried to hold it in, he feared his brains might blow out of the back of his head. But oh how he wished he had a proper sneeze. Not dainty. Just not…well…

"AAAAAHHHHHCCCCCHHHHHOOOOOOOO!!!!!!" At least a dozen people ducked. A woman screamed, something fell with a loud *thud,* and everyone turned to see a little old lady passed out on the ground.

But no one was helping the woman. Instead, they were all staring at Wolfe, their faces white as ghosts.

"Excuse me," Wolfe managed, wiping his nose and sniffling. He looked at the reverend, who, although visibly astonished, didn't seem as frightened as everyone else.

Wolfe stepped forward, and the crowd parted. He bent down next to the old woman who was starting to come to. "Ma'am? Are you all right?" Her eyes fluttered, and she nodded a bit.

Someone bent down to help the woman and give her a drink. Wolfe stood, and the reverend guided him away from the crowd. "Come on. Let's sit over here."

Wolfe sat with his back to the crowd. He was used to the stares. When he would come into town, people tended to stare. Usually no one approached him, though, and he was able to go about his business fairly normally. What was different this time? Was it because he was with the reverend?

The reverend glanced at the crowd, his face red. "Those people," he mumbled. Even so, his eyes reflected compassion.

Wolfe tried to smile. "Well, I suppose they expected to see my head spin and you-know-what fly out of my mouth."

The reverend lifted his eyebrows, then cracked a smile, and before long they were having a good laugh.

"I guess the next gossip will be that I'm performing exorcisms!" the reverend chuckled. Then his laughter subsided. "Don't you worry about what happened back there," he said. "We're going to sit here and enjoy our lunch. Get to know each other. If I can flag down a waitress, we'll get ourselves started with something to drink."

Wolfe knew who their waitress would be. They were sitting in her section, the one she'd had for the past five years. Before that, she'd been in the smoking section near the windows on the east side of the restaurant.

Wolfe could still feel the stares in the silence, and he sank into his seat. He might be a new creation, but apparently no one knew that yet.

The wind blew even colder, and Ainsley tilted her head as it swept past. It chapped her cheeks and took her breath away. She loved the fall. The oranges and yellows and reds that painted the countryside made her want to curl up on the couch in front of a fire and read a good book. It was hard to find a good book anymore, though. The only bookstore in town stocked its shelves with tales of witches and ghosts. She checked her watch. Her break was over.

Inside, she noticed the kitchen was quiet and empty. What was going on? It was still the lunch hour. Why wasn't anyone back in the kitchen cooking?

"Bob?"

She peeked through the order window to find a crowd standing near the door of the restaurant. As she rounded the corner, she ran into Bob.

"Well, that was eventful," Bob said as he made his way back to the grill. "Now I'm five Queasy Quesadillas and two Bacon Boogers behind." Ainsley followed him.

"What's going on?"

"A sighting of our resident horror novelist." Bob slapped two patties of meat on the grill, and they sizzled and spattered. "He's eating lunch with the reverend right now."

Ainsley gasped. "What?"

"I guess Miss Peeple was right on the money," Bob said, flipping one patty into the air, then the other. He grabbed four pieces of bacon and put them next to the burgers. "I guess he's officially converted, breaking bread with a man of the cloth and everything."

Ainsley left the kitchen and walked through the swinging doors.

The crowd was beginning to disperse, and Marlee was making her way toward Ainsley. "They're eating lunch together!" Marlee said in an excited whisper. "Over there!" She pointed to the corner of the restaurant. "They're in your section."

Marlee stepped aside so Ainsley could see. Sure enough, there they were. In the corner. In her section.

"Don't you think that means the man's given his life to the Lord?" Marlee whispered, pretending to wipe the counter in front of her.

Ainsley folded her arms. "I don't know," she said. "I know Reverend Peck. He's as genuine as anyone can be. Maybe *too* genuine. Maybe he's being taken advantage of." Ainsley glanced at Marlee, then threw her a dishtowel. "You might want to try wiping the counter down with a *rag*, not your hand." She had to laugh. Marlee always got caught up in such things.

"Oh." Marlee shrugged in embarrassment. "Sorry. I'm just in shock. I mean, who'd have thought Boo would become, you know, saved?"

Ainsley's hands were now on her hips. "I just can't believe it. There's something going on here. The man has single-handedly destroyed this town with his ghost-and-goblin nonsense. I'm not going to let him destroy the faith by pretending to be something he's not."

"How do you know it ain't for real?" Marlee asked, turning to pick up the order Bob called through the window.

Ainsley suddenly realized she was the only waitress available to wait on the two. It was well known by the restaurant employees that Ainsley Parker refused to wait on Wolfe Boone. She was always tactful about it. She simply asked another person to do it without making a scene. But she was afraid that she might say something rude or distasteful. She despised Wolfe Boone and everything he stood for. She knew God had told her to pray for her enemies, and she did that occasionally, but soon her emotions would succumb to outrage, and she'd find herself unable to pray at all. Over the years she had learned to live with it. But she was certainly never happy about it.

She glanced up to see the reverend waving her over. Finding another waitress nearby to wait on them was futile. All were busy, including

Marlee, who was showing two middle-aged tourists how she secured her Elvira wig to her real hair.

The reverend was still waving, so Ainsley held up a polite finger and smiled, indicating she would be with them in a moment. She caught her breath and adjusted her vampire teeth.

Every time she'd prayed for Wolfe Boone, she had prayed for him to leave town. Except once, when in frustration over God's seeming unwillingness to remove the monster, she had prayed, "Well, if you're not going to kick him out of here, then save the rotten scoundrel!" The prayer was sincere only because she was desperate, but now as she saw him sitting with Reverend Peck, she wondered if that had been the prayer God had wanted from her all along. She swallowed hard, took out her order pad, and tucked the stray hairs of her ponytail behind her ears.

Well, God is certainly in the miracle business. And if that man has turned from his wicked ways, I might as well have seen the Red Sea part.

The reverend nodded and then looked at Wolfe. "Looks like our wait-ress is on the way. Ainsley Parker. Do you know her? Sweet girl. I always like to sit in her section because she gives me free refills on my soda."

Wolfe stared at the table and shook his head. "I doubt it will be her," he said quietly.

"Why's that?"

"I don't think she's too fond of me."

The reverend folded his hands on top of the table. "Ainsley? Oh, she's fond of everyone. Sweet, sweet girl. I've known her since she was born." Wolfe looked up to see his eyes sadden. "Buried her mother when the poor girl was just seven. But she's grown up just fine. The Lord's taken care of her." He paused and said, "Just like the Lord's going to take care of you."

Wolfe smiled at the reverend and was about to say something when he heard, "Good afternoon. What will you have today?"

Ainsley Parker stood at the end of the table, smiling a little but looking only at the reverend.

"Good afternoon, Ainsley," the reverend said cheerily. "I'll have two Thrilled Cheese sandwiches."

"Extra cheese, right?" she winked.

"Yes." The reverend looked at Wolfe. "And this is my friend Wolfe Boone. Have you two met?"

Wolfe's heart pounded in his chest as he met her eyes. They were the most beautiful shade of green he'd ever seen. He hadn't ever been close enough to see her eye color before. Her blond hair was in a ponytail, and he loved that, especially when it swung from side to side as she walked. And though it seemed forced, at least she was smiling. The very fact that she was standing there taking his order was, he was quite sure, a minor miracle.

"And for you?"

"Um. Meat."

"Meat?"

"Oaf. Loaf, I mean." Wolfe clinched his teeth in frustration. He was an oaf if there ever was one.

Ainsley shook her head. "You want what?"

He swallowed and tried to control himself. "I'm sorry. The meatloaf."

"The *Mad Cow* Meatloaf?" She said it with emphasis, as if trying to make a point, but he didn't know what that point might be. So he just nodded. "You want Swamp Mud or Screamy Potatoes?"

"Yes." He felt a bead of sweat roll down the side of his face.

"Both?"

"No."

"None? Substitutes cost a dollar."

"No, I mean. No...the uh, yes, I want the uh...Swamp Mud."

"Fine. And Gory Green Beans or Creepy Corn on the Cob?"

"Green beans."

"The *Gory* Green Beans?"

Wolfe glanced worriedly at the reverend, who hadn't seemed to notice anything unusual. "Yes."

Ainsley's pencil tapped against the edge of the table. "Yes. So you want the ones smothered in the black, slimy sauce that looks like something might reach up out of it and strangle the daylights out of you? Those are the ones? Because we don't have just plain green beans here anymore, cooked in a little bacon grease, served with real butter."

Her delicate face, twisted into a little scowl, revealed a temper that amused him. Her vampire teeth lost their hold for a moment and fell crooked in her mouth. She dropped her eyes and pushed the teeth back into place. A small smile crept onto his lips. "And a water."

"Water." She scribbled it down. "That's about the only thing that's still served normal around here." She looked at the reverend and smiled sweetly. "And strawberry soda for you, I know. With a twist of lime. And no ice."

"That's my girl," the reverend said. He took her hand and patted it. "You've always taken good care of me."

"I'll be back with your order," she said to him, then glanced at Wolfe with a less enthusiastic expression. She turned on her heel and left.

"You okay, son?"

Wolfe looked up and realized the reverend was staring at him. He wiped at his forehead and found it covered with sweat. He quickly grabbed his napkin and blotted. "I'm fine." He smiled. "Just thinking I should get my teeth done up like that," he said, referring to her vampire teeth.

The reverend leaned forward and then glanced toward the kitchen of the restaurant. "Yessiree, that Ainsley. She's a sweetheart." He grinned at Wolfe. "And pretty, too."

"She certainly is opinionated."

"That's the way her daddy raised her. To think on her own. To know who she is." The reverend smiled at the thought. "Yep. Sheriff Parker's the only one who's had that little lady's heart for thirty years. Guess the right man hasn't come along yet." The reverend held Wolfe's gaze a moment longer than necessary, then folded his napkin in his lap. "Or maybe he has and she just hasn't realized it."

Wolfe laughed out of sheer embarrassment. He wasn't exactly sure what the reverend was alluding to. Surely becoming a Christian hadn't rendered him hopelessly transparent.

"So Wolfe," the reverend said after a brief silence, "tell me about yourself."

Relief caused him to smile. It wasn't his favorite topic of discussion, but anything beat the current one.

Wolfe climbed the gravel hill that led to his two-story house. His two German shepherds, Goose, the dark-eyed male, and Bunny, the blue-eyed female, leapt off the porch and greeted him with their usual enthusiasm. He'd forgotten that they'd been outside when he left. He squatted down and let them lick his face, then stood and briskly walked the rest of the way to his house, amused by the sudden "bounce" in his step. For the first time in as long as he could remember, he felt good inside. He felt a peace, unexplainable but present. And a hope, for nothing in particular but well-defined nevertheless. The new creation concept that the reverend had explained made perfect sense to him, and for a man who never believed in too much of anything, this was something he could hold on to.

He left his shoes on the porch and walked inside his home. He'd called it his sanctuary before, but today the description held less meaning, for the reverend had told him the Lord now lived inside him. Yet it radiated a certain warmth, as if a welcomed and favorite houseguest was nearby in another room, perhaps preparing tea or reading a good book. He fell into his favorite overstuffed leather chair and kicked his feet up onto the ottoman. Across the room, sitting neatly on the bookshelf, was a Bible. He'd used it many times, but never for personal study or growth. He knew the words well, but now they held new meaning.

Picking up the phone next to him, an antique passed down from his grandmother, he dialed Alfred's personal line.

"Good afternoon, Wolfe," Alfred said as he answered the phone. Alfred always answered Wolfe's calls, and thanks to caller ID, always knew when he was calling. The phone scarcely rang at Wolfe's house; he had no need to screen calls.

"Hi, Al."

"It's sitting on my desk, my friend. It's here! All warm and cuddly underneath a nice, hardbound cover. Boy, there's a lot of buzz about this one. More than I can remember on any of your other books. Being shipped around the world even as we speak. I know you never care about your covers, but this one is a dandy. It's blood red with this shadow in the background, and you can barely see a—"

"I need to know something."

Alfred paused. "Oh?"

"Chapter three, two paragraphs down. What color are her eyes?"

A longer pause was followed by a nervous cough and then Wolfe could hear the sound of pages being flipped through quickly. "Eye color? You're wanting to know your character's eye color?"

"Blue or green?"

"Is it important to the story line or something?"

"It's important to me."

More pages were flipped and then Alfred said, "A dazzling, iridescent green, the kind that glows like the dewy grass at dawn." Alfred cleared his throat. "Nice line. Is, um, everything okay?"

"Thank you, Alfred," Wolfe said, smiling. "That's what I needed to know."

Wolfe hung up the phone and rested his head against the back of the chair. He smiled at the thought of her green eyes, that she had come close enough to him so he could see their color. He'd guessed right. As he closed his own, that was the only picture that filled his mind.

AINSLEY HUMMED AS she pulled carrots out of the refrigerator. She always hummed when preparing a meal. It seemed like something Martha Stewart would do. Humming added to the allure of it all, though tonight's meal was nothing special, just homemade chicken noodle soup and a salad. And her hum was strained because she didn't really feel like doing anything other than stewing about the day's events.

She paused for a moment to wonder if Martha would cut the carrots julienne style and decided she would. As she sliced, her thoughts turned to him. *Him.* A tinge of guilt stung her heart as she thought of how she treated him. It wasn't like her to be rude. The harder she thought, the faster she chopped, until suddenly her index finger was stinging. She looked down to find blood trickling down her skin.

"You okay, honey bunny?"

Her father was in the doorway, smiling as he removed his coat and hat. "Hi, Daddy," Ainsley said with a faint smile. "I just cut myself."

Her father went to a drawer in the kitchen and then brought her a Band-Aid. "Let me see."

Ainsley removed the dishtowel from her finger, and for a moment she could see the cut before the blood streamed again. "It's not too bad."

She washed her hands, wincing at the sting, then allowed her father to wrap the Band-Aid around the finger. Seeing that the cutting board and knife were clean, she went back to chopping carrots.

"What's for dinner?" She heard him sit down at the kitchen table and then heard the predictable rattling of the newspaper as he turned to his favorite page...the comics.

"Just some soup and a salad. I'm cutting the carrots julienne style for the soup."

She could hear her father chuckle. "Is that how Martha would do it?"

"There's a proper way to do things, Daddy. People make fun of her, but she's the best at what she does." She heard the chuckle again and chose to ignore it. He could not fully appreciate why the linen closet items were stacked neatly and secured together with a satin ribbon. Or why the bed sheets in every single room smelled of baby powder. Or why the pumpkin pie was always firm and slightly spiced. She sighed at the burden of being underappreciated, as was Martha, but she had too much on her mind to dwell on it. She could truly think of only one thing: Wolfe Boone.

She never called him Boo, as the townspeople lovingly did. No, he wasn't likable enough to have a pet name, though she had a few choice names of her own for him, kept quiet only because she knew God wouldn't approve.

She mulled over her first encounter with him, then became sullen over the fact that it was nothing like she had imagined. Through the years, over and over in her head, she had imagined what she would say to him if she ever got the opportunity. She practically had the speech memorized, as well as a rebuttal for nearly every excuse he was bound to make. She even had a few clever insults to choose from, any of which she could use as she turned on her heel, her nose in the air, and walked away, hoping all the carefully crafted words and phrases she used would make some impact on how he lived his life.

But instead she ended up serving him meatloaf…with a smile, no less!

She had to give herself a little credit; she certainly hadn't imagined their first encounter including Reverend Peck. That threw her.

She also didn't take into account how good looking he happened to be. Not that it made much of a difference. Evil comes in all forms. But she guessed she'd never really gotten an up-close look at him, or maybe she just liked her own vision of a man with dark, glassy eyes and sunken features. But his eyes were a soft brown with specks of yellow, and they captivated her more than she cared to admit. "He could certainly use a haircut, though," she muttered. Her father looked up. Had she said that out loud? He went back to his paper, and she continued to cut carrots.

Besides, no matter what he looked like, she still refused to believe the man that virtually wrecked Skary, Indiana, could now be a servant of her Lord.

"Ouch!"

Ainsley felt blood running down her thumb.

"Ainsley?" Her father was now by her side, holding her hand up in front of his face. "You cut yourself again?" His eyebrows raised with worry.

Ainsley took her hand away and ran her thumb under some water in the sink. "It's just a small cut. It won't even need a Band-Aid." She scolded herself. Martha could talk, look at the camera, and chop, all at the same time, and *she'd* never cut herself.

"Are you okay?" Her father walked around to her other side, trying to make eye contact.

"I'm fine." She smiled to try to reassure her father. But she knew her father could read her well, and a smile wasn't going to deter him if he felt something wasn't right. She quickly went back to the cutting board and scooped the carrots into the pot of soup. "It'll be ready in a little while."

Her father's large hands turned her around, and she could tell by the straight line of his lips underneath his bushy mustache that she wasn't going to get away with anything. "Ainsley Marie. This is your father you're talking to. I know when my little girl is troubled. Now, before you end up cutting off your entire hand, let's sit down and talk."

Ainsley scratched her head and sighed. She really needed to be tearing the lettuce—never chop, always tear—for the salad. And she hadn't even washed the other two heads of lettuce, because every proper salad should have a minimum of two but preferably three kinds of lettuce. However, before she knew it, she had plopped down at the kitchen table and was staring into the face of concern.

"Now," her father said with sternness, "I want to know. Did someone hurt you today?"

"No, Daddy. It was—"

"Did someone say something mean to you? Did someone hurt your feelings? Or take something of yours? Was a customer rude to you?"

Ainsley waited for her father's questions to end, silently praying that someday his overprotectiveness would stop. It didn't help that he was the town sheriff. It was like having the perpetual big brother with you on every single date. Not that she could really complain about that, since she hadn't been on a date in—well, longer than she wanted to admit. Then again, her best prospect was Garth Twyne, and he held out little hope for ever being anything more than a good after-hours joke.

"Honey, you look so sad," her father said. "Tell me what happened. Whoever it is, whatever they did—"

Ainsley held up her hands. "Daddy. It's nothing like that." She swallowed and propped her head up on her hands. "It's just something I heard today."

"Oh? What'd you hear?"

"It's about the, uh, you know, the crazy guy. The spook." Her father frowned in confusion. "Wolfe Boone." She rolled her eyes at even having to say his name.

"What about him?"

"Well, apparently he had this big conversion or whatever you want to call it, and apparently Miss Peeple witnessed it, and apparently he's turned his life over to God, and apparently now he's some sort of Christian or something." By the time she was done explaining, her arms were folded against her chest and her eyebrows were closing together in a scowl.

Her father smiled in surprise. He never kept up with the town gossip. "Boo's turned his life over to the Lord?"

"*Apparently,* Daddy. Didn't you hear me say *apparently?*"

"What makes you think he didn't?"

Ainsley stood and grabbed a head of lettuce, tearing the pieces off with a fury that Martha would never tolerate. Thief, her father's cat and quirky sidekick, jumped on the counter. Ainsley scowled at him, and he purred with indifference as he made his way around her lettuce pile and over to the next counter. "Off, Thief!" Her voice quivered in anger. She wasn't really mad at the cat, though he had an annoying habit of thinking he was human. "Well, it was just so *perfect*. I mean, having lunch with Reverend Peck, just to show the town how *great* he is now. How *spiritual.* It takes more than breaking bread with the pastor to change, you know."

Her father's eyes were bright with bewilderment. "He had lunch with Reverend Peck?"

"*Yes.* At The Haunted Mansion, of all places. What does that tell you? Huh? HUH? It's some sort of ploy. Some sort of—I don't know, marketing scheme or something. Who knows? Who knows what kind of nonsense a deranged mind like that can think up?"

"Ainsley, Ainsley," her father said with a short laugh. "Whoa now. I think you're jumping to conclusions here."

"*Me?*" Ainsley almost dropped the mutilated head of lettuce. "I'm not jumping to conclusions! Everyone else is. By assuming that he's gotten saved just because Miss Peeple, Miss-Garth-Clones-Pigs-Peeple, said so."

"Well, he was seen with Reverend Peck."

"That means nothing. Absolutely nothing." She turned to a new head of lettuce, a wonderful Ruby Red. The colors were nothing short of fabulous, as Martha would say. She carefully tore each piece, mindful not to make them too big because one should never have to cut a piece of lettuce down to the proper size while eating a salad.

"Ainsley, dear, I know you mean well. And I know you've not agreed to what has happened to this town in the past few years."

"Oh, by that you mean that you can't walk down Main Street without feeling like you've died and gone to H-E-double-toothpicks?"

"Honey, you're being harsh. Boo's work has done wonders for our economy. People from all over the country, even the world, come to our little town of Skary just to visit. So it's catered a little to a horror novelist. What's worse? That, or that our town would become nonexistent, which, as you know, was about to be the case before Boo came to live here."

Ainsley felt her nostrils flare. "So everyone says. I think God could've just as easily done something big, some sort of miracle to save our little town. Instead, the devil decided to have a little fun with us." She turned to her father. "Daddy, I have to wear vampire teeth and a black cape just to get a job here." She knew she was being a little overly dramatic, as she could probably just go the next county over to work, but she was trying to make a point.

Ainsley set the lettuce down and rejoined her father at the table. He took her hand and stroked it. "You must give the man the benefit of the doubt. If he has indeed changed and become a Christian, then shouldn't we be thanking the Lord? And isn't that an answer to your prayers?"

"So you've forgiven him for the Thief incident?"

Her father's bright expression diminished ever so slightly at her words. "Well, I had to do that a long time ago. God tells us to do that. Besides, it's still unclear exactly what happened." He studied Thief as the cat moseyed around his ankles and over to the food bowl.

"It's not *that* unclear. He calls animal control to take your cat to the shelter because he *says* Thief was having a little fun with a girl cat on his property, which is ludicrous because everyone knows Thief is neutered."

"I know, I know. Who knows what he thinks he saw? That was a year ago, and I let it go."

Ainsley looked long and hard at her father, then down at the table. "You're right, Daddy. As usual. You're right. Who am I to judge so quickly? If it's genuine, then we'll know. And if it's not, then God will know, and that's what matters." She glanced up at him. "Right?"

"That's my girl."

She shrugged. "I actually talked to him today."

"Oh?"

"He sat in my section at the restaurant. He ordered meatloaf."

"Well, what did you think? Was he nice?"

"I guess. I don't know."

"Well, what was your impression of him?"

Ainsley thumped her fingers against the table. "Hard to say. We didn't have much of an exchange, other than the order."

"And?"

"He was handsome."

"Handsome?"

Ainsley nodded and watched her father stand and go to the kitchen counter, taking up where she had left off with the lettuce. "Well. That's interesting. Of all the attributes a person can have, you pick up that he's handsome?"

"Daddy, it's no big deal. I'm just stating a fact. I've seen him a lot, but I never noticed that about him before."

"You're right about Miss Peeple. She misses the mark quite frequently. I mean, Garth Twyne cloning pigs is just one example. One of many examples."

"Daddy—"

"I'm just saying, you have good instincts about people. You always have. If you think something fishy's going on with this *supposed* conversion, then I think you need to go with your gut. You received those instincts from me, you know."

"Daddy!"

"The man creates fiction and fables for a living. I wouldn't put it past him to be making this up too."

Ainsley threw her hands up and laughed. Her father glanced over his shoulder with a frown. "What's so funny?"

"You are. I'm going to be an old maid because of you."

"Me? It's your fault that nobody's good enough for you. And besides, who will take care of me if you're not here?"

Her smile faded. His tone was light, but there was so much truth to it. She slumped in her seat and thought of the impossibility of her leaving town. *Once* an impossibility. Until six months ago. When she had made up her mind. With finality. As soon as her Aunt Gert passed away, she would leave Skary, go somewhere far away from the burdens of family and the indecency of what had happened to the town her mother had adored so much.

Ainsley stood to help her father with the salad. "Give me the lettuce. You're tearing the pieces too big. Grab that knife and chop the celery, will you?"

Her father obeyed, and for a few moments they prepared the dinner

in silence. She tried not to think about Aunt Gert. She hated the idea
that she would pass on soon, and she hated the idea she had made Aunt
Gert her gatekeeper. But nevertheless, it was reality, and along with the
decades of responsibility she felt for taking care of her father, Aunt Gert
was the only other reason Ainsley stayed. She shook her head and looked
at her father. "All I said was that he was handsome."

"OUCH!"

"Daddy!" Ainsley grabbed his hand and found a small trickle of
blood on his index finger.

He snatched his finger away and sucked on it. "Could you just stop
repeating that?"

"You'd better leave the chopping to me." Ainsley took the knife
away from him with a smile. "And what about 'the benefit of the doubt,'
Daddy? Didn't you just tell me I should give him 'the benefit of the
doubt'?"

Sheriff Parker went to the Band-Aid drawer. "That was before I
knew he was handsome."

Missy Peeple thumbed through the pages of the book. She'd never read
or even touched a Wolfe Boone book. The cover of *Black Cats* was bright
red, with a dark shadow of a cat at the corner. His name was in large let-
ters, and the title was much smaller, centered at the bottom of the cover,
nearly obsolete, as if to say, "Wouldn't anyone read a Wolfe Boone book,
regardless of the title?"

She had to admit, out of all the books he'd written, this one sparked
her curiosity more than the others. After all, just the title somehow
insinuated that the book might be at least loosely based on the town. For
nine years an odd phenomenon regarding the population of cats had
plagued Skary, and no one could explain it. A shelter had to be set up
just to manage the problem, and though most everyone had their animals spayed or neutered, the problem still had not gone away.

Missy's knobby fingers glided over the small embossed title as she considered the implications of Mr. Boone's conversion. And a strategy, too. Yes, her mind was always thinking of strategy, no matter the circumstances.

Ever since their little town inherited Boo, nothing had been the same. Their tourism capital couldn't be rivaled within three hundred miles, and it had more than tripled in the last five years alone.

And so she sat in her rocking chair, alone in her dusty old house, dark though it was bright and sunny outside, and rocked back and forth, forming a plan. A sketch of a plan really, for she knew she needed more information. Information was a deadly weapon, and the more she had, the more she would have to modify her plan. But few people knew how flexible Missy Peeple could be.

First, she knew, in order to acquire more information, she would need help. So her mind sifted through possible accomplices. She'd have to be careful. This was going to require a lot of subtlety. A lot of finesse. Her "accomplices" would operate only on a need-to-know basis. There was nothing more dangerous than the wrong person with the right information.

Her eyes narrowed with determination. People were foolish to reason that this little conversion of his would not affect the comforts of this town. She would be an unappreciated hero for her efforts to save Skary and its prestige, its fame, its wealth.

She could remember driving back and forth down Main Street at the ripe old age of seventy-one for thirty minutes, seeing nothing more than a dog on the sidewalk. Now Skary was vibrant. Flourishing! Perhaps only she had eyes to see that, once again, Skary was on the brink of becoming a deserted old town that nobody in the world had heard of.

Not if she could help it.

Perhaps her tactics would be frowned upon by some who thought angels came to sing to them in the morning. But those people had no common sense, much less a regard for the sacredness of reputation, namely, the reputation of this town.

The first piece of information she must acquire was the identity of the person responsible for the man's conversion. Aside from God, that is. She needed a name. She had her suspicions, but she needed to know for sure who had felt obligated to share the good news with this man.

And keep that person at bay.

Then she needed a plan to return Boo to the way he was.

She turned to the last page of *Black Cats* and read the acknowledgments. Who was Boo close to? Who mattered to him? Though a little blurry even through her glasses, Missy Peeple was able to make out the name of a man that she knew immediately would be very helpful in her crusade. She snapped the book shut.

The first person to unwittingly join her cause.

There would be more.

Wolfe had imagined, and he had quite an imagination that stemmed all the way back from his childhood, that as he walked the neatly swept sidewalks of Skary's main street, people might thoroughly welcome him, or at least smile and wave. After all, he felt so different inside. Surely everyone else could sense it.

But instead, on this chilly early morning, he found people staring at him through their shop windows, their noses pushed up against the glass, as if they knew something he didn't. He even tried to wave a few times, thinking perhaps people just weren't used to seeing him venture into town any farther than the grocery store and The Haunted Mansion. But only one person waved back, an elderly man who seemed to have such poor eyesight he probably couldn't make out who he was waving at. And a black cat took a little interest in him as he passed by a music store.

So Wolfe kept walking, pondering the mystery of all that had taken place a few mornings back. How thankful he was to know the reverend and to feel accepted. As he swept his tangled hair out of his eyes, he almost smiled at the idea of what everyone must be thinking. For years, thirteen to be exact, he'd stayed a recluse in his house on the hill, pretending to be oblivious to what was happening down below in the town. He didn't want to know. But he knew.

He'd always been comfortable being by himself, but as he realized just recently, he'd so secluded himself that he'd actually become lonely. Really lonely. And the fulfillment that came with writing successful horror novels had ended long ago. These days, he just followed the formula that worked, all the while wondering if there was something more to life.

Now he'd found it.

This morning, he vowed to put an end to his loneliness. He passed by the town's pet shop, which he noticed had a sale on vampire bats. Then his mind shifted to Ainsley.

He'd found comfort over the years in just watching her. He loved to watch her. She was kind and warm to people. She made direct eye contact when she spoke. She grinned at everyone, even the ones who didn't grin back. She was a breath of fresh air in a world that didn't have time for people. And she was everything he'd always wanted to be.

Now maybe he had a chance at being that.

A plump woman careened into his thoughts, and before he knew it, he'd knocked her over, or she him, he wasn't sure. All he knew was that he was lying face-up on the sidewalk, with a leather purse over his face.

Before he could think to remove it, he found himself blinking up at a bright and chubby face. His head was pounding a little from hitting the sidewalk, but he managed a small smile in return, the first pleasant exchange he'd had all morning. Then a firm grasp took his hand, and he was up on his feet, staring at a woman who almost matched his height.

She grinned from one rotund cheek to the other, blinking abnormally fast with her hands clasped together, her heavy leather purse hanging from one of her arms. "Oh my! I am ever so sorry. I never do watch where I'm going." She laughed and shook her head.

"No, it's my fault," Wolfe offered, even though he didn't even know what happened. "I was in deep thought and not paying attention."

One mittened hand suddenly hit her chest, right at her heart, and at first by the stunned expression on her face, Wolfe thought she was having a heart attack. But then he realized it was just astonishment.

"I hate to be a bother," she said, staring at him as if he were a pile of gold, "but...well...can I have your autograph? I've read all your books.

They scare the tittle out of me, to tell you the truth, and I've never wanted to bother you before because I know you must get a million— no, probably a billion—people asking you for your John Hancock, but since I near killed you here in the middle of Main Street, maybe I should just ask you now?"

Wolfe chuckled. "Sure. Do you have a pen?"

The woman frowned. "Oh dear. No. I don't have a pen. But I do have a nice tube of Streetcar Red lipstick and a napkin. Will that do?"

Wolfe swallowed. He guessed it would have to. "Okay."

She grinned again. "Oh, good. Then it'll look like blood."

"Blood?"

She fished into her purse and came out with the tube. "Here." She handed him a folded napkin too and Wolfe tried to figure out how he was going to sign his name with a tube of lipstick. He decided just to go for it. After all, the woman was so intent.

"There you go," he said, handing it back to her.

"Thank you! Thank you! I'm such a big fan. This is so exciting." She held the napkin delicately. Then she looked back up at him, her eyes filled with a deep sincerity. "The name's Melb. Not with an *a*, like Melba. Just Melb. Melb Cornforth. But if you accidentally call me Melba, it's okay because I'm used to it. It's so stinkin' confusing I don't blame you. Melb's a stupid family name, on my father's side, and for the sake of tradition they gave it to me. Shoot, I probably shoulda just gone by Melba and made my whole life easier. I swear sometimes I think I'm gonna go insane just trying to explain the whole thing." She sighed and tried to smile. Wolfe thought she was one of the most peculiar people he'd ever met. "Maybe I am insane and just don't know it. The thing is, I'm concerned about the rumor."

Wolfe blinked, trying to follow the woman's rambling. "I'm sorry?"

"It's just a rumor, isn't it?" She clasped the handles of her purse and held it awkwardly against her chest. "I'm your biggest fan."

Wolfe shook his head, trying to be gracious and kind to the one person who seemed to be taking an interest in him. But she kept shifting topics, and he had not the slightest idea what she was talking about. "I'm sorry, I just—"

She was pulling something out of her purse, and the next thing Wolfe knew, her hand was in his face holding a small business card up for him to see. "See? I've been a proud member since 1992."

Wolfe squinted to see what the card said. THE OFFICIAL WOLFE BOONE FAN CLUB. MELBA [with the A scratched out] CORNFORTH, PROUD MEMBER SINCE 1992. He smiled at her and said, "Oh. How nice."

"Yes, so you can imagine how concerned I am about the rumor." She took a couple of steps backward, as if something about him startled her. "I'm not one to gossip, you should know. I don't listen to all that nonsense. When I go to get my hair fixed, I'm going to get my hair fixed. Not for any other reason, if you catch my drift. Listen, I'm all for going to church. I go to church every single Sunday, have since I was born. In fact, my mama took me to church when I was only two days old, and back then that was a no-no because of all the disease and such. But church is important, and I have nothin' against it."

Wolfe scratched his head. Did this have something to do with what had happened at the church? He bit his lip, trying to decide what to say. But he didn't have a chance to say anything, because Melb kept talking. "It's just that so many of us read your books. And so many of us *count* on those books. I've already got a copy of *Black Cats*. You see what I mean? It's important. It would be life-altering if something were to happen and you stopped writing." Her eyes were suddenly fierce with emotion.

Wolfe began to piece things together. Somehow she knew about his new faith. He tried to reassure her with a smile. "Melb, you must understand. I have no plans to stop writing."

"Oh! Thank heavens!"

"I just plan on writing different things."

Melb's face dropped as if a weight were pulling her skin down. "Different?"

"Sure. I've always appreciated literature, and I hope to write a few classics of my own." He grinned at the thought of it, but Melb was not grinning back.

"Classic literature? Are you out of your mind? You can't write classic literature!"

"Well, I'm sure it'll take some practice, but I hope to accomplish—"

"I can't sit in bed at night under my covers with a hot cup of tea and read some historical coming-of-age story. I need *suspense!* I need *murder!* I need *evil!*" She lost her breath, and the color drained from her face. Both fists sat on her large hips—her purse now swinging—and she seemed to be snarling ever so slightly. "Do you hear me, mister? It's not fair. It's simply not fair to reel me in like some helpless fish, only to slice me open with the news you plan to get righteous!"

Wolfe must have had a shocked look on his face, because Melb's expression suddenly seemed softer, and she patted him on the arm. "You're just brilliant the way you create those characters. They draw me in, you know? I can relate to them. I feel their pain." Her eyes grew distant as she ruminated. "And I don't know how you do it, Mr. Boone, but you write those female characters of yours like no one I've seen. It's almost like you're inside the female head or something." She smiled at him. "Sometimes, I swear it's like I know them. Like they're familiar to me, almost as if you're writing about someone I know."

Wolfe cleared his throat, and in the cool of the morning he suddenly felt very warm. "Well, Melb, it was nice to meet you. I must get going now."

Melb blinked but nodded graciously. "I understand. I'm sorry to have kept you here so long. Listen to me, rambling on like some lunatic out of one of your books." She placed a mitten on his forearm. "Just promise me, Mr. Boone, that you'll keep writing those horror novels. Promise me."

Wolfe looked down at her, tried to smile, and could say nothing more than "Have a nice day." He moved past her and kept walking down the sidewalk, never looking back, though he could feel her staring at him. He couldn't promise her that. In fact, he could almost promise just the opposite. He'd spent years dabbling in the dark side. Now he felt completely drawn to the light.

Missy Peeple's cane tapped the concrete as she stood in a darkened corner of the street, a cubbyhole perfect for hiding and waiting. The chill in the early morning air seemed to reach down her throat and squeeze the oxygen out of her lungs, but she wouldn't be deterred. Not by that grumpy Old Man Winter. Nosiree. Besides, he couldn't hold a candle to Missy. Though she had two layers of mittens on, her hands felt like ice cubes. Her nose dripped in perfect unison to the tapping of her cane, which she amused herself with momentarily, but then she grew bored with it.

"Where is that woman?" she spat.

Just then a large shadow extended itself past the small nook she stood in, and Missy recognized it immediately.

"Hello?" a voice called.

"In here!" Missy Peeple reached out, just as Melb came into view, and pulled her into the nook.

Stumbling in, Melb was breathing hard and holding her chest. "My goodness! You scared me half to Hades, Miss Peeple. You shouldn't just reach out and grab someone like that!"

"If you wouldn't read all those horror novels, you wouldn't be so paranoid all the time," she scolded. She wiped her nose with her mitten and narrowed her eyes at Melb. "So what did you find out?"

Melb shook her head. "It's true, I'm afraid. I didn't really get a straight answer from him, but from all indications he doesn't plan to continue what he's doing."

Missy Peeple growled from deep within her throat, and Melb took an astonished step back. "I felt a little bad about this, Miss Peeple," she said after a moment. "I don't much like to deceive people, even though I was quite curious myself. Still, I wasn't completely honest with the man about why I was asking him all those questions." She leaned against the wall opposite Miss Peeple. "He's quite a handsome fellow, I have to say. And has good manners, too. He's not at all scary like I thought he'd be. From that picture on the back of his books, you'd think the poor fellow was mean as snot. But I guess you shouldn't judge a book by its cover." She chuckled, and then her smile faded as she glanced up at Miss Peeple. "Anyway, I don't know what I'm going to do now. I've tried other horror novelists, but they just don't seem to have the depth and insight that Boo has."

Missy finally grew tired of hearing Melb speak, and so she said, "Melb, you really must try those romance novels."

Melb's eyes widened. "Romance novels?"

"Why yes. The heaving bosoms. The hairless-chested men. Oh, the romance. Blah blah blah. You might be surprised how truly scary they can be."

"Oh?" Melb chewed on the end of one of her chubby fingers. "Well, I have to admit, my favorite part of Boo's novels are the romances, even though usually one or both die in the end, but still..." Her eyes grew blissfully distant at the thought.

"They're quite addicting you know. Now, hurry along. We can't be caught hovering in the shadows. People will start talking, and the last thing I need is to be the center of the town's gossip." She smiled tensely at Melb. "Good work."

"Oh, uh...thank you." Melb started to leave and then turned back and said, "Miss Peeple, what do you plan to do with this information? I mean, you're not going to, um..."

"It's out of sincere concern," Miss Peeple said to Melb. "And what I plan to do with the information is save this little town from complete and utter devastation."

Melb's eyes were wide as she nodded. "Oh, of course."

"But," Missy warned, "you mustn't tell a soul about this. Do you understand?" She leaned forward. "Most people abuse information they have, Melb. They gossip, pass it around like a platter of cheese. Information is important, but it must remain in the right hands."

Melb smiled and patted Miss Peeple on the arm. "Well, it's good to know that it's in the right hands then." She clutched her purse and stepped back onto the sidewalk. "Have a good day."

Missy nodded and said, "See you at church, dear."

CHAPTER 4

AINSLEY DABBED ON a little lipstick, just enough to give herself some color. She thought about mascara but decided against it. Lipstick. Mascara. Blush. No reason to give anyone a chance to speculate. The little town was nice but fickle. Besides, her daddy always told her she had a natural beauty, and all the makeup just covered it up.

The chill in the air made her decide on her plum-colored turtleneck and the fall vest she'd made last year. It had a dazzling pattern of leaves on it. She'd gotten the pattern from the *Martha Stewart Living* magazine. She carefully put it on and admired herself in the mirror for a moment before whisking her hair up into a high ponytail and trotting downstairs. Her father was at the table finishing his breakfast.

"How were the eggs, Daddy?" she said, kissing him from behind. She'd poached them perfectly, the old-fashioned way. She'd made a batch of pumpernickel bread last night for breakfast, but also to give the house a warm autumn smell. She loved the way pumpernickel smelled.

"Fine, sweetheart." He handed her his plate and took a swig of her freshly squeezed orange juice. Then he looked at her with his head cocked to the side. "Lipstick?"

"Just a little, Daddy. Besides, I'm a grown woman, and I think I can pull off a little makeup, don't you?"

Her father shook his head but thankfully was too late for work to argue. "Gotta go, sweet pea."

"I'll see you tonight," she said with a wave. "Be careful out there."

Her father put his badge on and then his winter jacket. "Thief!" he called. The cat pounced off the kitchen counter and escorted him outside to his cruiser. Ainsley stood at the door and waved as the two got into the car. Thief's black fur bristled in the cold air as he jumped into the passenger's seat. Ainsley watched them leave before quickly cleaning up the breakfast dishes. So often she just wanted to leave them there until later, but there was hardly a circumstance she knew of that allowed for that kind of slop. It took her only five minutes. She took a dish out of her freezer and set it in a box by the front door.

She sprayed air freshener in the entryway before grabbing her coat off the rack and tying her hand-knitted scarf around her neck. She pulled on her gloves, grabbed the box, and headed out the door.

Her body shivered a little as she set the box in her trunk. The morning bore the first real chill of the fall, and it had quite a bite to it. The stack of logs for the fireplace was low, so she went around back to get a few more. She piled them on and then adjusted the array of pumpkins she had lined up and down the porch stairs. The porch needed a good sweeping, but she didn't have time. She had a lot to do before getting to work.

She climbed into her car and let it warm up for precisely ten minutes while she read her daily devotional. By then her hands had warmed up well enough for her to fill in the blank spaces for her thoughts about it at the bottom of the page.

Then she headed to Mrs. Blythe Owen's home. She left her car running so it would stay warm and gathered everything she needed. She walked up the sidewalk to her home and made a mental note to pull up her fall flowers come winter.

She knocked softly on the door and called, "Mrs. Owen? It's Ainsley."

She heard a muffled "Come in," and opened the front door to find Mrs. Owen in her La-Z-Boy recliner, knitting a blanket.

"Ainsley, come in, come in," Mrs. Owen beckoned.

"I brought you my beef and mushroom pie," Ainsley said, putting the dish in her refrigerator. "It has instructions on how to heat it up." She walked into the living room where Mrs. Owen was knitting. "Now, I know you get in a hurry and like it to cook faster, but it must stay on 350 for two hours or the noodles will dry out."

"Thank you, dear," Mrs. Owen said. "You know how I love that dish of yours."

"How are you doing?"

"Oh, the arthritis isn't liking this cold weather, you know," Mrs. Owen complained. "My hands are so knotted up I can barely hold my needles." She shook her head. "But thank God for a warm house. Seems to be a nip in the air today."

Ainsley smiled and patted her on the shoulder. "There is." She squeezed the old woman's hand warmly and after a little more chitchat assured her she'd visit on Thursday.

Hurrying out to her car, she checked that off her list of things to do and then went to McCauley's, the town grocery store that had been renamed Gobblin's, a stupid play on words that was supposed to be scary and insinuate the "gobbling" of good food. Ainsley refused to acknowledge the name change, though, and always referred to it as McCauley's, named for its three generations of owners.

Inside, she took her sack of coffee beans to the meat counter. Barney, the butcher, greeted her with a hearty smile. "Hi there, young lady."

"Hi, Barney." She handed him the sack of beans.

"Finely ground, right?"

"Yes sir."

She never knew why they ground the beans at the meat counter, but that was just the way it was. She had her own coffee bean grinder at home, because she never made coffee from anything but freshly ground beans, but it was small and took a long time with this amount of beans. She admired the thick cuts of beef and pork, thinking to herself she should make her pork loin specialty sometime soon. Behind her she heard a customer complaining about the fact that everyone in town seemed to be out of allergy medicine. It happened a lot in a town that had a cat-to-human ratio of twenty to one. Barney returned with the beans, perfectly ground.

"Thank you," Ainsley said, and waved at him as she hurried out of the store. She drove seven blocks, turned down Parsley Street, and stopped at Mr. Laraby's home. She didn't bother to knock. He was nearly deaf and, to Ainsley's relief, didn't own a shotgun.

"Mr. Laraby?" she called loudly.

The old man appeared from the kitchen carrying a bowl of cereal. He startled as he saw her from the corner of his eye. "Ainsley!"

"Hi, Mr. Laraby. Sorry to scare you."

"What, dear?"

"I said, sorry to scare you."

"Well, stare all you want. I get my good looks from my mother's side." He winked and shuffled to the kitchen table.

Ainsley laughed, shook her head, and gave him the ground coffee beans. He peaked inside the sack. "Oh! Thank you! What a treat!"

"I know you like them freshly ground."

"What, dear?"

"I said, I know you like your beans freshly ground."

"I seem slightly round? I've been retaining water lately, I guess." He looked down at his stomach.

"No, Mr. Laraby. *Freshly ground.*" She pointed to the sack. "Your *coffee beans.*"

"Oh." He grinned and Ainsley kissed him on the cheek.

"I have to go," she said properly, though she doubted Mr. Laraby heard.

He waved at her and thanked her again for the coffee. Back in her car, she checked that off her list. Just one more stop to make. She turned up the heater and radio. As busy as she was this morning, there still remained one thing—more accurately, one person—on her mind. And nothing, not even some good old gospel tunes, could drown him out.

He opened the door to Sbooky's, what appeared to be a charming little bookstore on the corner. A large handwritten sign on the front of the door said, "No cats allowed." The first thing he saw upon entering was a gigantic poster of himself hanging from the ceiling. He rolled his eyes and regretted even opening the door. But before he could turn around, a young man with greasy hair and a slight case of acne nearly jumped over the counter at him.

"No way!"

Wolfe could only stick his hands in his pockets and shrug. He guessed he could've predicted this.

"Dude! No way! I can't believe you're in the store. My manager's on break. But he's going to die. He went to get donuts and coffee."

"I see," Wolfe said, looking around the store. He noticed immediately that it was overstocked with horror and suspense novels, every kind imaginable. His, of course, lined the front shelves with cardboard promotional displays.

The kid was beside himself with excitement. He pointed to the front of the store. "Got all your books, man. Every single one. Read all of 'em too. Every single one. People come from all around the country to buy one of your books from *this* store. They sell 'em at every store that carries a book, but it means something to people to get it here."

Wolfe tried to smile. "I've never been here before." He looked around the store and noticed that at least in the back there seemed to be something other than horror.

"No way! Well, welcome to Sbooky's. Get it? *Sbooky's?* With a *b* instead of a *p* so it's got the word *book* in there but it sounds like *Spooky's*."

Wolfe nodded. "How clever."

"Yeah. It used to be 'The Book Nook,' but that's kind of boring, don't you think?"

Wolfe shrugged. "I don't know. Sounds nice to me."

"Yeah, but since we became Sbooky's, our sales have gone through the roof." Before Wolfe knew what was happening, the young lad had hopped back over the counter and was now holding a Polaroid. "Say cheese!" The flash went off, and Wolfe squinted, dazed and dizzy. "Thanks, dude. We'll hang this on our wall and tell everyone." The kid then said, "So, why are you here, anyway?"

Wolfe blinked off the bright light around his corneas and said, "Well, I'm looking for a book."

"I can help you there."

"Okay. I'm needing something about God. Not the Bible. I already have one. But a book about God. Do you know what I mean?"

The kid's eyes widened in confusion. "Oh. Uh…yeah…no, actually."

"You know, something on the deeper spiritual life." Wolfe tried to remember a title the reverend had mentioned.

"Ah. Gotcha." The kid bounced down an aisle and returned with a book in hand. "Here ya go."

The title read, *Spirits Around Us.* He handed the book back to the kid. "Um, not exactly. I'm looking more for something about knowing God better. A theological book, I guess you could say." Ah. Yes. He remembered. "*Mere Christianity* by C. S. Lewis."

"A theo-what?"

Wolfe shook his head. "You don't have any books here about God?"

The kid shrugged and picked at his face. "I dunno. I mean, we got a lot of books about Satan." He sort of smiled and looked away.

Wolfe sighed. "I can see that. Tell you what, I think I'll just browse."

"Okay. Take your time. And if you need any help—"

"I know where to find you."

Wolfe removed his coat, deciding to head to the back corner. At the very least it promised to give him a small selection of good literature.

Ainsley stepped lightly along the sidewalk, happy that fall had arrived and winter would soon be here. Fall and winter were her favorite seasons. She loved to roast chestnuts on the open fire, something not many people knew how to do. Martha had shown her four winters ago. Before that, she'd been stuck roasting marshmallows, which wasn't terrible, just not very sophisticated.

She waved or smiled at all she passed. She didn't know everyone in the town by name, but she recognized nearly everyone by face. Only three weeks until Thanksgiving. They always had a big Thanksgiving at her home. They'd invite friends and family and feast like they would never eat again. And Ainsley loved every minute of it. Every year she decorated the house to make it warm and inviting, and though she certainly made the traditional favorites, she also liked to surprise the guests with something new and exciting. Last year it was pumpkin crème brûlée. She hadn't decided this year, but she was tinkering with the idea of it being an hors d'oeuvre.

Ainsley waved to the church organist across the street, then entered the bookstore.

"Hey. Welcome to Sbooky's," said the kid as he stood behind the counter, his nose in some gruesome looking book.

Ainsley took off her gloves and hat. "Hi. I was hoping you could help me with something."

He set down his book and said, "Name it."

"I'm looking for a rather rare book—"

"We have a lot of rare books, even some of Stephen King's that are out-of-print first editions, signed by the man himself."

Ainsley tried not to let out a disgusted sigh. "A *children's* book."

"Oh."

"You *do* carry children's books, don't you?"

"Sure. We've got a huge selection of *Goosebumps*."

"The book I'm looking for is called *The Life and Adventures of Santa Claus* by Frank Baum."

The kid, whose nametag read DUSTIN, scratched his head.

"Frank Baum. You know, *The Wizard of Oz?*"

"Oh, yeah, right. Did he play the scarecrow?"

Ainsley willed her eyes not to roll. "*No.* He wrote the book."

"It was a movie. Didn't see it, though."

Ainsley bit her bottom lip. "Yes. But first it was a book. A classic. You should read it sometime." She glanced down at the book in his hand. "It has witches in it."

Dustin's face lit up. "No kidding?" He smiled. "I'll give it a try."

"Terrific. Now, about the book. Do you have it?"

The kid shrugged. "Don't know. You can go look. Should be under the author's last name."

Ainsley turned toward the back of the store and hoped somewhere in the little niche of worthwhile books she would find the one she was looking for.

Wolfe's heart thumped so loudly inside his chest he found himself covering it up with a copy of *Great Expectations* just in case it was actually audible. He couldn't believe the coincidence. Here she was! In the bookstore! Should he talk to her? Pretend not to notice her? Leave? Stay?

The questions flooded his mind in a way that made him dizzy with nervousness. He could see the top of her head making its way through the aisles and toward the back of the store. He wasn't in the children's section, but he was close, and at his height, it was hard to hide behind a display. He noticed suddenly that the palms of his hands were soaked, and as much as he tried to rub them on his pants leg, they weren't about to dry out.

At first she didn't see him. She was standing nearby at the one bookshelf they had for children's literature, her finger running along the spines of the books, intent on what she was doing.

Wolfe thought for a moment about slipping out the other way to the front door. Then he thought he should just go up to her and say hello. But instead, he only stood there and stared, and before he knew it, he was caught doing just that.

Her eyes widened as she saw him, and the heart that pounded so heavily just seconds before now barely fluttered. He found himself holding his breath. Realizing how awkward he must look just standing there staring at her, he tried to smile. It perhaps came out more of a grimace, though, because she didn't smile back.

He swallowed down all the organs that had seemed to push their way up into his throat and said, "Hi there."

Her mouth hung open and her hand dropped to her side, but she recovered quickly and said. "Oh. Hi."

Wolfe took a step forward. "So you come here often?" He barely got the question out before biting his own tongue as punishment for how cheesy that sounded.

Her face remained neutral as she said, "No, actually. I try to avoid this place at all costs." She glanced down at the book he was holding, as if curious, then continued. "Anyway, I'm looking for a rare children's book." Her eyes cut to the shelf next to her. "But apparently it's pretty tough to find any good children's literature in this place."

He smiled and nodded. "I thought it was pretty lucky to find Dickens here." He held up the book. But his hands were so slippery that it fell out of his hand and slapped onto the floor. He stooped down to get it, but lost his balance and hit his head on a rack full of Cliffs Notes, knocking several onto the floor next to him.

He heard her gasp. "Oh! Are you okay?"

He gathered himself and his book and stood up slowly. "Painfully humiliated. But I hear the scar only lasts a few years."

She looked very concerned, but then she went back to looking at books. Wolfe decided it couldn't get much worse, so with great courage he stepped forward, causing her to look up.

"What book are you looking for?"

With apprehension she said, "It's a Frank Baum book." Her lips pressed together. "I don't suppose you even know who that is."

"Of course I do. He wrote *The Wizard of Oz.* Among other things."

A small smile of satisfaction crossed her lips, but then it faded. "Yes, well, I'm looking for a rare children's book he wrote called *The Life and Adventures of Santa Claus.*"

"Never heard of it."

"That's because it's rare."

"Ah."

She swallowed as if to gather herself and then said, "Well, I shouldn't waste my time looking here. All this store cares about—" She stopped suddenly and glanced up at him. Her eyes reflected something different than her demeanor, but he couldn't tell what. "I'm late for work, actually, so I'd better go."

Wolfe tried not to let his face show disappointment. "Okay. Well, good to see you."

"Yes," she replied, then started to walk off. As she passed him she said, "By the way, that's a great book." She pointed to the one he was holding.

"I know. I've read it five times."

She stopped. "You've read *Great Expectations* five times?"

"Yes. I decided I should actually buy it instead of going to the library and checking it out every time."

Though her lips never curved into a warm smile, her eyes reflected a certain sentiment that Wolfe recognized as somewhat friendly. He grinned at her as best he could and said, "Have a good day."

"Oh. Thanks," she said, as if suddenly aware that she was just standing there. "You, too." And then she left.

Wolfe leaned against the bookshelf behind him and sighed in relief. He looked down at the book in his hand. "Thank you, Charles Dickens." Then he made his way to the front of the store where Dude had his nose in a book.

CHAPTER 5

"HERE'S A T-BOONE steak for you," Ainsley said, setting the platter down carefully in front of the young man. "And the Turkey Sand-Witch for you." She smiled at the young woman, whose eyes seemed bright with life.

"Thank you," the girl said.

"Anything else?" Ainsley asked.

The young man spoke up. "We're on our honeymoon," he said. "I'm looking for some fun places to take us. Any suggestions?"

"Congratulations!" Ainsley gushed. "You two look so in love." The couple glanced at each other and grinned. "Well, let me tell you, you're going to have to get out of this town to find somewhere romantic. I'd suggest going about ten miles—"

The man interrupted. "We purposely came here, to Skary, for our honeymoon."

"You did?"

"Yes," the girl answered. "We thought we'd have a lot of fun! We're staying in that little bed-and-breakfast down the road. What's it called?"

Ainsley sighed. "Arsenic and Old Lace."

The girl squealed. "Yes! That's it! It's just the cutest little place!"

"Yeah. Just try not to get murdered," Ainsley replied.

The couple laughed heartily, but Ainsley could only manage to smile mildly. The man said, "We loved all the axes hanging from the ceiling."

"You can't get much more romantic than axes, can you? Can I get you anything else?"

The girl leaned forward on the table. "Do you know him?"

"Who?"

"Wolfe Boone, of course."

"Oh. No. I mean, yes. I mean, not really. Sort of." She closed her mouth to stop rambling, took a deep breath, and finally answered, "I've met him."

"Is he creepy? He looks like he would be."

As much as Ainsley wanted to answer that question with yes, she had to be truthful. "No. Not really. He could use a haircut, but that's about it." She tapped her pencil on her pad and said, "I'll be back to check on you in a bit."

Ainsley found Marlee reading a magazine behind the counter. "Don't you have customers?"

Marlee smacked her gum and didn't look up. "They're fine. They'll yell if they need anything."

Ainsley shook her head and leaned against the counter to take the pressure off her already aching feet. "The point of being a good waitress is that your customers don't have to yell for you, you know."

Marlee smiled and nodded but continued reading about the latest fall lipstick colors.

"I ran into him today."

Marlee looked up. "Who? Garth?"

Ainsley rolled her eyes. "Running into Garth isn't worth reporting."

Her eyebrows raised. "Well, then who *is* worthy of reporting?"

Ainsley swallowed. She didn't mean it *that* way. Did she? "Wolfe Boone."

"Boo?"

"Yeah. At the bookstore."

"The bookstore? He's not known for venturing out much, is he?" She stood upright and closed her magazine. "What happened? Did he seem, you know, converted?"

Ainsley popped her knuckles and frowned. "Look, it's more than what you look like on the outside. Who can say if his heart has changed?"

"What was he doing there?"

"Reading Charles Dickens, apparently." Ainsley glanced over to her latest customers and noticed they both needed a refill on their drinks. She grabbed the tea pitcher, but before she could step out from behind the counter, Bob came through the doors of the kitchen.

"Ainsley, phone call." Bob held the phone up in the air. "They've taken your Aunt Gert to the hospital."

Ainsley walked as fast as she could down the sidewalk toward Sbooky's. She didn't feel like smiling, but she did to those who smiled first. Bob had let her take the lunch hour off, and she had to get to the hospital. She'd visited Gert at home yesterday, spent the evening with her, and knew she did not look good.

Please, God, she thought as she wrapped her scarf around her neck to block the cold wind, *please let me find that little book.*

Once there, she made a beeline to the back of the store and for ten minutes searched the shelves for the little book.

"May I help you?"

Ainsley turned around to find a middle-aged, short and round man standing near her. His eyes were bright and his smile was friendly. "I hope so."

"I'm Hardy Bishop. I own this store. I don't know that we've ever met. I know all my customers."

Ainsley tried to sound pleasant. "Yes, well, I've only been in here a couple of times."

"Oh? Not a big reader?"

"Not of what you sell." Ainsley lowered her head, hoping she didn't sound too crass. But it was true, and she couldn't pretend it wasn't. She looked up at Hardy, who was still smiling, apparently unfazed by the comment. Ainsley took in a deep breath and continued, "I'm looking for a children's book by Frank Baum."

"Ah. Mr. Baum. Yes. I'm a big fan of *The Wizard of Oz.*"

The tightness in Ainsley's chest released, and she even smiled. "You know his work?"

"Why yes." He pulled a book off the shelf. "We always stock *The Wizard of Oz.*"

"I'm looking for a rare children's book he wrote. You see, my aunt, the only relative I have left on my mother's side, is dying of cancer, and this was a book that they shared together as children, and it would just be awfully wonderful if I could find this book for her. She adored it and speaks of it today, but her copy burned in a fire." Ainsley felt her eyes moisten with emotion as she spoke. "It's called *The Life and Adventures of Santa Claus.*"

The bright smile Mr. Bishop had worn only moments before faded with each word Ainsley spoke, until the corners of his mouth drooped with a certain sadness. "I'm sorry, sweet lady," he said. "But you won't find that book here."

"You don't carry it?"

Mr. Bishop shook his head and guided her to the front of the store. "No, it's extremely rare. In fact, I can't say that we've ever carried it. It is a wonderful story, though." He smiled eagerly at her as he made his way behind the counter. "What is your name?"

"Ainsley. Ainsley Parker."

"Ah, Sheriff Parker's daughter, I presume. Well, Miss Parker, let me call someone for you. They own a bookstore that specializes in rare books. They're in Indianapolis." He picked up the phone and dialed the number. Ainsley listened intently and gathered the news was bad. Mr. Bishop hung up the phone and shook his head sadly. "They had one copy. But it sold. I'm sorry."

Ainsley felt a lump in her throat. "Oh my. What terrible timing."

Mr. Bishop nodded. "Apparently went for a pretty hefty price tag, too. The owner of the store said he sold it for more than a thousand dollars."

"*What?*"

"Yes. Apparently it's very sought after. The buyer paid what old Harrison was asking. First edition in prime condition. I guess it was worth it."

Ainsley nodded, trying to hold back the disappointment that

flooded her heart. She had no idea the book was *that* rare. Her voice quivered when she spoke, and she was embarrassed. "Well, thank you so much. You were so kind for going to the extra trouble—"

From the corner of her eye, Ainsley noticed a Polaroid snapshot of Wolfe Boone hanging on the counter. She glanced over at the life-size cardboard replica of him near one of the bookshelves. It was as if she were looking at two different people. The cardboard man she thought she knew well. The small Polaroid man she was beginning to realize she didn't know quite as well as she thought.

"Miss Parker?" the owner asked.

She turned back to him. "I'm sorry. I was just noticing your—uh, never mind. Anyway, thanks for your help."

She had to get to the hospital. She headed back into the cold.

❦

Missy Peeple's crumbling old teeth chattered in the cold, which she supposed helped to disguise her voice, lest anyone would want to know who was *really* calling. She was on hold, but from the little phone booth near the hardware store, she could see Boo leaving the church and walking up the hill to his home. She sighed in disgust. He was spending time at the church. That couldn't be good.

"Are you still holding?"

"Yes, I'm still here," she said, putting a deliberate and hard-to-find chime in her voice.

"I'm sorry to keep you waiting, ma'am. I'll have to take a message. Mr. Tennison isn't available."

"Oh, is that so? If he knew what I had to say, I think he'd be on the phone."

"He's a very busy man—"

"Listen," Missy said. "I've got information. Do you know what information means in a business like yours, deary?"

"Well—"

"Wrong answer. The correct answer is 'One moment, please. I'll get him.'"

A pause was followed by, "Ma'am, I don't know what you think you're doing, but…"

Missy held her breath. She'd only put three dollars' worth of quarters into the pay phone, and the time it took for the little brat to make up her mind had ticked the minutes away. She could still see Boo climbing the hill to his house, carrying a paper grocery sack filled with something. Her curious mind played over what it might be. How could a man of such fame and glory give it all up so easily? And with such disregard for the town that practically made him famous.

"Then I'll leave a message. The message is this: 'Wolfe Boone has become a Christian.' I just thought his editor might like to know."

She could hear the girl writing. "Your name?" she asked blandly, as if it were a prank call.

She paused, wondering if she should indeed gamble and give out her identity. She tried to guess what kind of man this Alfred Tennison might be. How would this news affect him? And what would he do with it? The call in and of itself was a gamble, but she had a feeling, a gnawing feeling, that Mr. Tennison would become quite useful.

"Miss Peeple. That's M-I-S-S," she said calmly, then added her phone number, and just for kicks, gave her address, too. The operator indicated her time was up, so she hung up the phone, just in time to watch Boo shut his front door.

Missy stood and pondered the phone call until something caught her eye. It was Oliver Stepaphanolopolis, the owner of a local used car business. She knew him from church. Had bought a car from him once, back when she was still allowed to drive. He passed Melb Cornforth, who was leaving The Haunted Mansion restaurant. He held the door for her, and she thanked him and continued on. But Oliver stood there and watched her walk down the sidewalk until he realized Thief, the sheriff's cat, was about to make his way inside the restaurant. He shut the door quickly.

Missy Peeple smiled. Greed could make a man do anything. Love could make him do the unthinkable.

She made a mental note of it and then bundled herself up for the walk home.

Ainsley held Aunt Gert's hand as tightly as she could, trying to hold back her tears. Gert was slightly propped up on several hospital pillows, her face pasty and pale, but her eyes as bright as always.

"Dear heart, don't you cry. Why are you crying?"

Ainsley wiped at her tears. "I'm sorry. It's just…they're saying you won't leave the hospital this time." Before she knew it, she was sobbing, her head in the arms of the fragile old woman she was supposed to be comforting.

"There, there," Gert said, stroking her head. "Death, where is thy victory? Where is thy sting?"

Ainsley lifted her head as the tears continued to roll. "But Aunt Gert, you're all I have left of Mom." Ainsley covered her face and continued to cry. "This is so selfish of me! You're the one who needs comfort." She gathered her emotions and tried to smile at her aunt. "You'll get better. I know it. You will."

Gert's lips trembled a little, and she patted Ainsley's face. Then she took a deep breath, as if that single motion drained all her energy. "Some people want to die at home. But I don't. Everyone who would be at home knows Jesus. There are people here at the hospital I can still reach."

"God can always work a miracle."

"Sure He can. But I doubt He will." She squeezed Ainsley's hand. "I know it's hard for you to understand. You're in the prime of your life. Dying seems horrible. But when you're my age, and you've lived through love and loss and pain and joy, you get a little tired, and the idea of leaving this old bag of bones behind and going to be with the Father…well, it doesn't seem all that bad."

Ainsley cried some more, all the while trying to stop herself.

Gert coughed a little and then continued. "You're a bright young woman, full of life. Full of light. I'm so proud of you. And your mother is too. She's up in heaven looking down on you. I'll tell her hi when I get there."

Ainsley laughed a little. "Okay."

"You've got your whole life ahead of you, and I don't want to see you waste any time crying over me." Her gaze focused directly on Ainsley. "Besides, I know when I'm gone, you'll be leaving. You have a whole other world to find out there."

"I'd rather have you. You know that. I'd stay here forever if it meant you'd stay with me."

"I know," she smiled. "This isn't such a bad town, you know. It's not big and flashy, but there's something to be said for—"

"I don't hate this town. You know that. I love it. It holds the dearest memories of Mom. But I hate what it has become. And I think it's time I let Dad go too. For me and for him."

"Yes, well, all things happen for a purpose."

Ainsley stroked Gert's hair. "I wish I could see the good in everything like you do."

"So be happy for me, that the pain'll soon be gone and that I'll be free from all the bad things on this wretched earth." Her eyes looked up at the ceiling, as if she were seeing the very glory of God and His angels. "And old Wilbur's up there. Can't believe it's been twenty years since the old fogy passed on. I'll be glad to see him. He was the love of my life, you know." She cracked a smile. "'Course, he was much more romantic in his younger years. The older he got, the crankier he got. But I still loved him." Her eyes shifted to Ainsley, and she patted her on the arm. "You'll find that someday, you know. The love of your life."

Ainsley laughed out loud and shook her head. "At the rate I'm going, I'll die an old maid. And Daddy is no help. Remember when Oliver Stepaphanolopolis set me up with that nice young man, Billy Hanover, who lived two counties over?" Gert nodded. "Daddy greeted him at the door with a shotgun. There's nothing that kills romance like the idea that your date's father is going to shoot you dead."

"What about that vet? What's his name?"

"Garth?!" Ainsley snorted. "Hah. Never in a million years."

"What's wrong with him?"

"Many things, not the least of which is that he smells like a horse all the time."

Gert laughed, and Ainsley finally realized her tears had dried up. She felt a strange peace and knew God was comforting her.

"Well," Gert said, "you'll find the one. I know it."

Ainsley sat back in her chair. "How will I know? How do you know who is the right person?"

Gert chuckled. "Well, from my experience it's usually the last person on earth that you'd expect."

"No kidding. Why do you say that?"

"Mostly because God has this funny sense of humor. But also because God wants us to find the person that complements us, so when we become one, as they say, we're a whole person. If you marry someone just like you, then when you become one, well, there's too much of one personality, let's just say that." She tried to sit up a little, as if excited about the topic. "You'll find you have a few common interests. Enough so you can get to know each other."

Ainsley listened carefully. Aunt Gert had always been wise, the wisest woman she knew. Still, in her heart she was skeptical. She tried to imagine what the exact opposite of herself was, and the thought scared her to death. Gert laughed, as if reading her mind.

"Don't you worry about it, honey. It won't pass you by. You'll know."

Ainsley blinked and looked at her aunt. "How will I know for sure?"

"There'll be this little flutter to your heart. And when you look in his eyes, you'll see a little sparkle, and it'll tell you that he has eternity in mind."

Ainsley shook her head. "You're going to have to be more specific, Aunt Gert. By flutter, do you mean a little hiccup in your heart rhythm, like when you've had too much caffeine? Or more of a *thump, thump,* like when you've had the daylights scared out of you? And I'm sorry, but seeing someone's eye sparkle with thoughts of eternal love seems a little hard to read. Maybe they're just standing near a light bulb or something."

Gert chuckled heartily, gasped for some breath, and then patted Ainsley's hand. "Dear, you've always been such a thinker. Just like your mom."

"I know. I overanalyze everything, don't I?"

"Not a bad quality," Gert said. "Just not very romantic."

"No one's ever accused me of being overly romantic. I've got it in me, but I'm much more practical."

"You're perfect just how you are," Gert said reassuringly. "And whoever it is God has for you will be perfect too."

Ainsley sighed as she thought of the monumental task of finding the right person. "Well, I hope God doesn't use his sense of humor on me. I hate surprises."

Gert closed her eyes. "Oh, dear heart. Don't ever say that out loud." She looked toward the ceiling and pointed upward with a shaky hand. "He's always listening."

CHAPTER 6

WOLFE SAT NEAR his bay window as evening absorbed the light of the day. He loved watching the sun set, especially from his old house on top of the hill. He'd fixed himself a fresh cup of coffee and felt more relaxed than he had in years. He continued to be amazed by the unexplainable peace he felt inside his heart. Though there was nothing really tangible about his conversion, his spirit confirmed its truth and authenticity. And now, as he watched the glorious colors of the evening sky stretch themselves in every direction, he knew he watched the paintbrush of God on the canvas of earth.

The stars twinkled early this time of year, and so he released the blinds of the window and went to sit by the fire he'd started. In the small drawer next to his favorite leather chair, he took out his private collection of poetry. It was a thick journal, full of the very depths of his soul. Many nights he would spend writing. Other nights he would spend poring over years' worth of these kinds of writings. No one even knew he wrote poetry. It was the most private thing he did.

Tonight he turned back several months and read a poem he'd written on a warm spring evening. It amazed him how such colorful words could explain such dark despair. It was an uncomfortable read, to say the least. He hadn't realized how very depressed he was, how dismal his soul. Hope was not to be found in these pages. He closed the journal and smiled at the thought of how much hope he had now.

He pulled out his favorite pen and decided to write his very first poem as a new creation. The feelings that pulsed through his heart were nearly indescribable, and for a long moment he could only try to find in his vocabulary a somewhat accurate description of the state of his soul.

Finally, the words came...

Ah, that my soul would breathe for the very first time in my life.
As if the air of the heavens has filled my lungs,
That the oxygen of the Spirit feeds my blood.

Wolfe read and reread the words, content with their meaning and content to be able to write from his heart.

The phone rang, startling Wolfe. It rarely rang, and almost never in the evenings. Who could be calling?

"Hello?"

"Wolfe! Glad I caught you."

Wolfe sat back down in his chair. "Alfred? What are you doing calling so late?"

"Late? My friend, this is not late. One in the morning is late."

Wolfe smiled. "True. But you've always been such a nine-to-five person. Is something wrong?"

A pause from Alfred seemed to indicate that something was wrong. Although his voice remained cheery, Wolfe knew differently. "No, no. Nothing's wrong. Um...how are you?"

"I'm fine. Why?"

"Why? It's just a question, Wolfe. I'm making extremely polite conversation here."

"I know. That's what scares me," Wolfe said, sitting up in his chair and then leaning forward, propping himself up on his knees. "I can't remember the last time you asked how I was doing."

A heavy and disgruntled sigh filled the earpiece on Wolfe's phone. "I'm just wondering—your next book. Have you an idea yet?"

"What next book?"

He could almost hear Alfred's teeth grind together. "What next book? What do you mean, 'what next book?' There's always a next book."

"I don't know, Al. I'm not sure there's going to be one. Soon, anyway."

His voice trembled nervously. "The whole world sits and waits for your books to be published. You can't just quit."

"I'm just figuring a few things out."

"Look, if it's about money, we can talk."

"It's not money."

"What then?"

"Alfred, I have to go now."

"Why?"

"I've got things to do."

"Like what?"

"I'm writing."

"You are?"

"Yes."

"Oh." There was a long pause, and then Alfred said, "Something horrifying?"

"I imagine to you it would be. Good-bye, Alfred. Oh, and I'll call you soon. We do need to talk."

"We do?" Alfred gulped. "It's true…"

"What's true?"

"Call me soon."

Wolfe hung up the phone and leaned back comfortably into his chair. It felt good to have the power over himself. Before, the life, the writing, the words…they all seemed to have power over him.

Wolfe sipped his coffee, trying to finish the poem he'd started, but he found himself dwelling on the beautiful face and voice of Ainsley Parker. The more he thought of her, the more aware he became of his heart beating inside the walls of his chest, until finally he had to stand and try to get a perspective, in particular that Ainsley Parker wasn't interested in giving him the time of day.

Still, he had a new hope in life, and that hope extended to the long-unrelenting feelings he'd had for this woman. For the first time, the idea of loving her seemed magically possible.

Wolfe paced the length of his living room, his shadow from the fire long and lean against the hardwood floors of his home. He paced and paced until finally he stopped and mumbled, "I have to talk about this to someone."

His hands rested on his hips, and he stared at his feet. Who in the world was he going to talk to?

Like an artist, Marlee painted a pink strip of blush from the corner of Suzy's mouth to the top of her temple, and then repeated the task on the other side. "Oh, honey, you look just like that Gwyneth Paltrow!"

"I do?" Suzy asked with glee.

"Oh yes. I just need to do your eyes, and then watch out, baby! The men will come knocking tonight!"

Ainsley sat on the couch and watched with half-interest as her friend tried to turn every lovely face in the room into someone who looked as if they belonged to a circus. She only attended Marlee's Mary Kay parties out of obligation to her friend. Her gesture inevitably ended up more trouble than it was worth. She never bought anything, and then she would have to scrub her face raw before she went home to her father.

She smiled as Jenny, Suzy's sister, passed by on her way to the kitchen. Jenny gave her a polite nod. Ainsley knew she probably seemed like a snob, as if she felt too good for the town. But it wasn't that at all. In fact, she had never wanted to live anywhere else—pre-horror days, anyway. And the disappointment people were bound to see in her eyes came from many sources, not the least of which was that she was lonely. She wondered how many people who never gave a second thought to marriage were married, and how many who had wanted it their whole lives were alone.

Jenny returned from the kitchen. "Beautiful, darling, beautiful!"

Marlee was painting a hideous green across Suzy's small eyelid. "You're next," she told Jenny. "Who would you like to look like? Julia? Or someone more classic, like Marilyn?"

"Julia! I want to look like Julia Roberts!" She approached Marlee, studying Suzy's face. "Do you think you can do that?"

"Of course," Marlee gloated. "I can do anything with this makeup. It works miracles, but *only* if you have the right product."

Jenny rocked on her feet. "Can you make me have that real wide smile and those real white teeth?"

Marlee was now lining Suzy's eyes as if the poor woman didn't have an eyelash to be seen. "Sure. It's all in the lipstick and lip liner. I'll show you how." She glanced back at Ainsley. "And Ainsley, who do you want to look like? Julia too? Or maybe Gwyneth."

Ainsley smiled, but inside she didn't know why making each other over like Barbie dolls was supposed to constitute a fun evening with friends. Maybe a part of her hated that she still felt bad about wearing makeup. "I'd like to look like a wife with two kids who's been married for ten years and been in love every single day of it."

Her friends turned to look at her. Marlee said, "Well, I've got a nice coral color that would look terrific with your blond hair."

Ainsley laughed and went to the table they'd filled with snacks. Marlee had provided pretzels. Suzy, cheese puffs. Jenny, Doritos. Ainsley had spent an hour making a rolled, puffed pastry filled with Portobello mushrooms, cream cheese, and fresh spinach. The platter was nearly empty. She nibbled on a pretzel.

Jenny was looking at all the different colored eye shadows. "I've never met anyone who wanted to be married as badly as you," Jenny said. "And it's not as if you haven't had the opportunity."

Suzy had one eye closed but was looking at Ainsley. "It's true. Every guy I know wants a date with you. You're just too picky."

Ainsley shrugged. "I'm not going to settle, be married and divorced in a year just so I can have that big wedding I always dreamed of."

Marlee shook her head as she lined Suzy's other eyelid. "Honey, you're just such a dreamer. You expect the love of your life just to show up on your doorstep and knock."

Knock, knock.

The girls turned to the door. Suzy giggled. "Expecting anyone, Marlee?" Jenny asked.

Marlee shook her head. "Not that I know of."

"I'll get it," Ainsley said.

She strolled to the door imagining for a moment that perhaps fate had delivered the man of her dreams to the doorstep on this cold fall evening. But then, it would be odd for fate to deliver the dude to someone else's doorstep. Still…her heart swelled with anticipation as she opened the door.

It deflated as quickly. "Garth." She glanced back over her shoulder. The girls laughed but went back to their business. She stepped outside and shut the door behind her. "What are you doing here?"

"You're not going to let me in?" Garth gestured. "It's freezing out here."

"It's not my house for one thing," Ainsley said. "Besides, it's a girls' party, and you're no girl."

Garth shivered. His teeth were chattering and his lips started turning blue. Rugged and weathered he was not. Ainsley felt mildly sorry for him but decided he'd leave sooner this way.

"What are you doing here?" she insisted.

"I came to check on you. To see if you're all right."

"I'm fine," Ainsley frowned. "Why wouldn't I be?"

"I heard you ran into Boo today. At the bookstore."

"So? How do you know that anyway?"

"It's not important," Garth said. "What's important is that my little lady is okay."

"I'm not your little lady, and why in the world wouldn't I be okay?"

"The guy can be pretty creepy from what I hear, and I thought he might've tried to scare you or something."

"Why would he do something like that?"

"I dunno. Because, you know, that's what he does for a living. He scares people."

"Garth, for heaven's sake, he was there looking at books, just like any normal person."

Garth frowned in contemplation. "He's still a weirdo. I mean, converting to Christianity on a whim, trying to make everyone think he's 'changed.'" Garth used his fingers to form quotation marks.

"Look, he was a perfect gentleman, and I don't know where you're getting the idea that he wasn't." She felt a growl crawling up her throat.

Garth crossed his arms and peered down at her. "A perfect gentleman. Sounds like you two hit it off."

"You're so annoying! You know that, don't you?" She looked away as she finished her thoughts. "By a perfect gentleman, I meant that he was polite and courteous. You should take a few pointers," she said and glanced up at him. "Why is it any big deal that I ran into him at the bookstore anyway? And why is it any of your business?"

"It's my beeswax because I care about you, Ainsley," he said, trying to make his eyes look steamy and sultry. "Someone has to look after my innocent little kitten."

"I can look after myself," Ainsley said, opening the door and stepping back inside. "You should go home. You look as pale as death." She slammed the door, causing the girls to turn around.

Marlee smiled. "Was that the love of your life knocking?"

Ainsley fell onto the couch with a grunt. "You know good and well that was Garth Twyne."

Marlee shrugged, adding more blush to Suzy's already bright pink cheek. "Maybe it's fate," she said.

Ainsley stared up at the ceiling. "Or a terrible omen."

"Maybe we wouldn't hit it off. Maybe we're not meant to be. But I can't help thinking that we're supposed to be together. That we're meant for each other." Wolfe paused and looked into her pale blue eyes. She sat there quietly, motionless, as if understanding every word he spoke. "I mean, there's no reason why we can't at least get to know each other, right? What's the harm in that? And if I'm a new creation, like Reverend Peck says I am, then what I've done in the past should mean nothing, right? From the day I became a Christian, I start new." He sighed and turned, trying to find the right words. "It's just something I feel deep inside, something I've felt from the beginning. Sure, maybe I should've said something earlier instead of dreaming what life would be like if we were together. But now seems as good a time as any, doesn't it? To explore the feelings we might have for each other. I'm not getting any younger, that's for sure."

"Woof! Woof!"

Wolfe turned, throwing up his hands. "I'd expect you to agree with that, Bunny," he said. "Would you just be quiet and let me do the talking? I have a lot to get off my chest."

Bunny's tail thumped against the wood floor and then Goose came trotting in and sat next to her.

"Oh, now you're interested," Wolfe said to Goose, whose own tail joined in the thumping. "Where were you a second ago when I was spilling my guts?" Wolfe sat down on the couch and stared at both his dogs. "How did you two know you were right for each other?"

"Woof!" Goose answered, his chocolate eyes bright with energy.

Wolfe smiled and patted them both on their heads. "You two have it easy, you know. You sniff each other's backside and know it's true love." He laughed as they wagged their tails and then trotted off to their food bowls.

Well, at least he had said it out loud. He'd confessed it to a German shepherd, but at least it was out of his heart, off his tongue, and in the air somewhere, being carried off to bigger and better places.

Wolfe walked to his window and stared down at the tiny town. Its lights twinkled cheerfully, and from where he stood he could actually pick out the house that she lived in with her father. He could also see the church steeple glowing in the single light that illuminated it from below.

With one deep breath, Wolfe Boone decided that he would ask Ainsley Parker out on a date. If she refused, then he would know. For all the years he'd wasted writing silly books about evil creatures, he hoped he could make up for them now and that the years he had left would be filled with joy, laughter, and love.

You sentimental fool.

Knock, knock.

"Woof!"

Knock, knock.

"Woof! Woof!"

Wolfe opened one lazy eye and caught both dogs scurrying out of the bedroom. He heard their claws tapping down the hallway toward the stairs.

Pound, pound!

Was someone at his door? He turned to look at his clock. It was a little after seven. The sun had cleared the horizon already, and the day looked bright and inviting. He'd slept well considering all that was on his mind.

His feet hit the cold wood floor, and he skipped across it until he got to the stairs, which had carpet down the middle. Bunny and Goose were at the front door, whining and looking at Wolfe as if they could make him move faster.

He finally got to the front door and opened it, just in time to see a man walking away. A mail delivery truck was parked at the curb.

"Wait!" Wolfe called.

The man turned around and trotted back up the porch stairs. "Sorry. I know this is awfully early. I just have a lot of packages to deliver, and this one was marked *overnight,* so I figured it was important."

Wolfe smiled as he signed on the clipboard. "You do this for all your customers?"

The man stared at his shoes. "You're right. Stupid excuse. Actually...can I...um... Can I have your autograph? I'm new on this route. And I just couldn't believe I got to deliver a package to your house, and I'm a big fan. This is horribly unprofessional, I know. I'm sorry. I'm just—"

"Sure." He took the paper and pen from the man. "There you go."

"Thank you!" The man handed the package over and ran back to his truck. Wolfe closed the door, keeping the package high enough in the air to avoid the dogs' wet and curious noses. He placed it carefully on the counter and decided to make the morning coffee before he got overly excited.

As the rich aroma filled the house, he leaned on the counter and stared at the little package. It was neatly wrapped in brown paper and even had brown string tied around it. He folded his arms together and sized it up, wondering if this was, indeed, his key to courage.

He'd spent an awful lot of money on it. He sighed and poured himself a cup of joe. Courage didn't come cheap these days.

CHAPTER 7

AINSLEY HELD UP the wreath to show her father. She'd put it together using fall colors and a special dried herb that Martha had suggested on her television program last week. It gave off a warm pine smell and boasted a nice dash of color. At the bottom, she'd skillfully tied a mustard-colored ribbon that pulled the whole thing together. Her father was just finishing his story about how he and Thief had nabbed some juveniles spray-painting Pointe Bridge last night and some other kid who thought it'd be funny to shave the hair off of thirteen cats.

"What do you think?"

"It's beautiful," her father said as he unfolded his morning paper. "You've got real talent in that area."

Ainsley smiled. "Thank you, Daddy. I thought we'd hang it on our door the week of Thanksgiving." She put the wreath down and joined him at the breakfast table. "More coffee?"

"No thanks, honey. I've got to run."

"Before you go," Ainsley said, causing her father to sit back down, "we need to discuss Thanksgiving. It's less than three weeks away, and we still haven't discussed who we want to invite."

Her father nodded. "I know. I need to make a list."

"And get it to me soon," Ainsley said. "I've got a lot of preparation, and I can't wait until the last minute to put these recipes together. I've also got to make the table decoration, and I need to know how many people to expect so I know whether or not to do a centerpiece or a table runner. And I certainly must know how large of a turkey to buy. Plus, if we have a big crowd, we'll need to add a ham, and the glaze takes time, Daddy."

Her father held up his hands and laughed. "I'll have the list to you soon."

"Thank you." She stood and kissed him on the cheek. "Have a good day. We're having tortellini soup tonight."

She helped her father out the door, reminding this man who carried a pistol to be careful on the last step of the porch because the cement was coming loose. He smiled and waved tolerantly, and Ainsley laughed, thinking that he was probably perplexed how he could lose a wife and somehow gain a mother. Thief trotted alongside him obligingly, his tail raised haughtily in the air.

Inside, she cleared the breakfast dishes, happy she was on schedule. She needed to go visit Mr. Lackey in the hospital. She'd bought him a sack of jelly beans, hoping that would brighten his day. She was also hoping to visit Aunt Gert before work, and if she got a move on, she'd be able to make it. Luckily, she wasn't scheduled to come in until lunch.

She threw the last plate in the dishwasher when she heard a knock at the door. She couldn't imagine who it would be this early but figured it was probably Garth, coming to rescue her from some mythical danger.

Knock, knock.

"I'm coming!" Ainsley called. She straightened her shirt and brushed back the wisps of hair in her face before opening the door.

"What in the world?" It was a stupid thing to say to a guest at your doorstep, and Ainsley slapped her hand over her mouth just after saying it, which probably made her look more disgraceful. Still, she couldn't hide the shock of seeing Wolfe Boone standing in front of her.

"What?" he replied, obviously flustered. "I'm sorry, did you say something?"

Ainsley shook her head, finding it hard to form a word on her tongue. In his hands he was carrying a neatly wrapped, small brown package. She also noticed his hands were shaking terribly. She looked back up at him, and he was trying to smile, but he looked more like someone who was trying to pass off stomach cramps.

"Hi. Do you remember me? We met at the bookstore."

"What are you doing here?"

His lips trembled before he spoke, and Ainsley found it excruciatingly painful to watch the man stand there. He barked a laugh twice before attempting to speak, as if he thought it was just as absurd as she did that he was standing there. He glanced down at her with a wince and said, "I'm sorry. I brought you this." He practically shoved the little package at her, then she almost dropped it. He lunged forward, and they hit heads.

"Sorry," he said, rubbing his own forehead.

She tried to smile at him, but she still couldn't imagine why Wolfe Boone was on her doorstep. She looked down at the package. "What's this?"

For the first time, he looked relaxed, sticking his hands in his pockets, rocking back and forth. "It's a surprise."

"Oh." She stared down at it. "You showing up on my doorstep, now that's a surprise." Trying to avoid those deep, engaging eyes of his, she found herself staring at the red spot on his forehead. "So you came here to bring me this surprise?"

"Yes," he said. "And to ask you…um…to ask you…"

Ainsley leaned forward. "Yes? To ask me…?"

His eyes, though naturally serene, danced suddenly with anxiety. "To ask…uh…" He seemed to choke on his own words. "To ask you where you get your hair cut."

Ainsley laughed out loud. "To ask me where I get my hair cut?"

He wasn't laughing. In fact, his face looked full of dread. "Yes. Your hair always looks nice, and I need to find a good barber."

Ainsley couldn't help but be amused, and she knew her smile indicated she was just that. "It's called Foofey's. It's the next county over."

"Oh. Foofey's. Doesn't sound like I'd find a barber there."

Ainsley let another laugh escape. "No, but it's perfect if you need a highlight or a perm."

He finally smiled too and self-consciously ran his fingers through his hair. "I could probably use both, but I think I'll just keep looking for a barber."

"Try Howard. He's a couple of blocks from the community center."

"Thanks." He stepped back then and pointed to the package. "I hope you like it. I have to get going."

"Okay. Bye. And thanks." She couldn't imagine what was in the package.

He turned and walked off, then suddenly spun on his heel and came back. Ainsley barely had time to digest anything when she found herself staring up at him again. And this time, she looked in his eyes.

"There is one more thing."

"Oh?" Her voice cracked.

"I wanted to ask you…out."

"Out?"

"On a date?"

"A date?"

"Yes. You go on dates, don't you?"

"Uh…" Now that was a tricky question. "Uh…"

He nervously rubbed the red spot on his forehead as he waited for an answer, and Ainsley felt sweat peek out at her temples even as she stood in the cold. He wasn't actually asking her out on a *date,* was he?

She finally managed to disengage her eyes from him, and before she knew it, she was saying, "No."

"Oh."

"No."

"I got it the first time."

"You just can't."

"Can't what?"

"You just can't come here and ask me out on a date. Because, you see, I've been angry with you for a long time. I have to wear vampire teeth because of you, and when you come and do something so foolish as to stand here and ask me out on a date, well, then that flies in the face of everything I'm accustomed to. I've despised you a long time, you see, and if I went out on a date then I'd have to forgive you, and I'm just not ready to do that yet, even if you are handsome and do have gorgeous eyes. Do you know what I mean?" She said it as if she'd just explained how to do a box pleat on denim.

His mouth was hanging open, and his eyes were wide with what seemed to be an equal measure of perplexity and hope.

"Close your mouth. You'll swallow a fly."

He did, slowly backed up, and gave a little nod before hurrying off to his Jeep parked on the street. Ainsley watched him go, then stepped back inside the house. She threw back her head at the absurdity of it all. Did Wolfe Boone actually just ask her out? Did she actually just tell him he had gorgeous eyes?

She then realized she was holding his package. She timidly took it to the table, set it down, and stared at it as if it might just do a song and dance. Instead it lay there, perfectly still, beckoning her to open it. It was a charming little package, tied up with string. Hardly anyone she knew used string anymore. The package was addressed to Wolfe, but other than that it had no indication of who or where it was from.

"Well, it's not going to open itself," she mumbled, finding a pair of scissors and then returning to the table. She cut the string with great care, then carefully opened one side and slid the contents out of the package. She took one look at it and burst into tears.

Wolfe's hands shook so hard he could barely hang on to his steering wheel. His Jeep sputtered along, still not quite warmed up. Wolfe was equally numb. He drove the speed limit until he found himself at the church.

Before he even knew it, he was inside, making his way to the basement where the reverend's office was.

"Reverend?" he said quietly.

The reverend was standing at his bookshelf. He turned, a surprised look on his face. "Well, Wolfe! I didn't hear you come in! What a nice surprise. How are you enjoying that sack of books I loaned you?" His pleasant expression turned concerned very quickly. "Are you all right?"

"Don't I look all right?"

"Not really." The reverend laid down a book he was holding and walked toward Wolfe. "Are you sick?"

"No."

"Has someone offended you?"

"No."

"Well what is it? You look terrible."

Wolfe fell into the old sofa next to the wall and said, "I'm in love."

Aunt Gert grabbed a tissue and then handed the box to Ainsley, who grabbed three. "Oh, dear heart, that was so precious. I haven't heard that story in years. It was my favorite, you know."

Ainsley patted Aunt Gert's hand. "I knew how much hearing this story would mean to you."

"More than you know," Aunt Gert said. She had little energy left, but she thumbed through the book, examining the front and back cover, feeling every part of it with her fingers. Ainsley watched with sheer joy, so grateful that her aunt was able to hear that story again. For a long moment, peaceful silence filled the room. Finally, Aunt Gert set the book down on her lap. "Dear, how are you?"

"Me? Oh, I'm fine."

"You look troubled."

"Troubled? How do you know that? I've just been sitting here."

"Now dear, you know I've always been able to sense these things about you. Many times your cute little face gets all bunched up into a scowl, but even when that doesn't happen, when you're trying to hide it, you give off this sort of unmistakable signal."

Ainsley crossed her arms. "Well, apparently I'm giving off some sort of signal that causes really freaky things to happen." She looked at Aunt Gert's inquisitive face. She didn't want to explain that last statement, so she cut off the looming question by asking, "Do you believe in signs?"

"What sort of signs, dear?"

"Signs. Like something telling you something."

"You mean, like a sign from God."

"Sure. Right. A sign from God."

"I believe in those kinds of signs, yes."

"Yeah, well, I think I just got one this morning. And I am *not* happy about it. But I just can't imagine why else God would—" She glanced at Gert. "I just think He's trying to tell me something by doing something else, sort of a reverse psychology thing, you know?"

With her hands gently folded in her lap, Gert's soft eyes met Ainsley's. "Oh, honey, God isn't much into playing games. He tends to be rather forthright."

Ainsley stared at the cold hospital tile. "Why can't He send an angel with instructions, like He did to Mary when she conceived Jesus?"

Gert chuckled. "Well, honey, I think that's because that was one of those important times in history when there could be no margin for error and no room for a human interpretation. We humans always tend to miss the point."

With a hefty sigh, Ainsley nodded. "I suppose that's true. But the absurdity of this man on my doorstep asking me—" Ainsley stopped herself.

"Asking you what?"

"Nothing." She stood and kissed Aunt Gert's cheek. "You look good today. You have some color in your cheeks."

"Oh, that must be the warm rays of heaven growing nearer."

"If you're going to die, could you please be less excited about it?" Ainsley smiled down at her a little. "There are those of us who have to stay here without you, you know."

Gert laughed as heartily as she could. "Oh, you are a woman after my own heart."

"See you tomorrow. Call me if you need anything. And I mean *anything*."

"I will," Gert assured her. "And Ainsley?"

"Yes?"

"Follow your heart, not some sign you're unsure of. All right? God gave you a good heart full of wisdom."

Ainsley just smiled and turned, dismissing her aunt's advice, though she knew better. But how could she possibly know what was best? Ainsley couldn't trust her heart any more than she could trust a "sign."

Outside the hospital, Ainsley sat down on a bench next to a nurse who was puffing away on a cigarette. They exchanged friendly smiles, but then both sank back into their own private thoughts. By the end of the nurse's cigarette, Ainsley knew what she had to do. And she knew one other thing: The sign she'd received this morning was unmistakable.

She held her breath, half out of nervousness, half because of the smell. She stepped carefully across the tile of the small lobby, avoiding the yellow puddles that seemed to be everywhere, apparently from the small black poodle sitting in the corner with its owner.

Ginger, the red-haired receptionist, looked up and flashed a tolerant smile. She'd never liked Ainsley, mostly because Ainsley was the only thing standing between her and a life full of bliss with Garth Twyne.

"Well, well. If it isn't Ainsley Parker, here to bless us with her presence. What brings you to this side of town?"

Ainsley rolled her eyes. 'This' side of town was twelve blocks away from 'her' side of town. "I need to speak with Garth."

"He's busy. He *is* a veterinarian, you know."

"You don't say," Ainsley said, placing her fists on her hips. "Well, it happens to be important, and it won't take much time. Can you get him, please?"

"I don't think so. I'm sure he's in *surgery.* You just don't walk in on a *doctor* in surgery. His patients, *not you,* are his number-one priority."

Ainsley was just about to retort when Garth walked by and saw her through the window. "Ainsley," he said through his typical goofy grin, "to what do I owe this pleasure?" He went around to the door and let her in.

"Hi, Garth," Ainsley said, shooting Ginger a look. "Can we talk?"

"Talk? Ooooh. This sounds serious. Am I in trouble?" He chided like a little boy, and Ainsley felt the usual tension form in her chest, born of aggravation.

"Somewhere private." Ainsley looked him directly in the eyes, trying to get across to him that she was serious about why she was here.

His thin, blond eyebrows rose. "Oh? My day is getting better already. Follow me."

Ainsley dragged her feet as she followed Garth to his office, a small, smelly room with cheap posters of dogs everywhere, not a single cat to be seen. Garth made no bones about it: He hated cats. He would practice on them but not happily, and most people in town finally just got dogs or drove forty miles to Dr. Harold, the next closest vet. And yet amazingly this town still had too many cats.

"Please, sit down," he said, gesturing toward a stained chair in the corner. "May I get you something?" Ainsley wanted to scream at his formality.

"I'd rather stand, thank you." Ainsley watched Garth shut the door and walk to the other side of his desk.

"Suit yourself," he said dryly. He sat down in his own chair with marked emphasis, then looked up at her, clicking the pen in his hand. "So?"

The small of her back grew suddenly damp, and every word she needed to say seemed stuck in her throat. Could this *really* be what she was supposed to do? It had to be. Because the other option was…was no option at all.

"Yes?" His pen clicked faster.

"I, um," she stuttered, trying to sound light, "I…"

"Yes, I have the 'I' part. It's about you. It usually is." He flashed a smile, but Ainsley didn't miss the insult. She supposed years of similar rejection might make one a little less sensitive.

Ainsley tried to smile as she regained control of her flapping tongue. "What I'm trying to say is…is…um…"

"What is it?"

"Yes."

"Yes?"

"Yes."

Garth leaned back in his chair, dropping his pen to the desk. "Yes, what?"

"Yes, to you."

"Yes to me." He shook his head. "I'm not following."

"Yes to your offer."

"What offer?"

"To take me out on a date." The words seemed to echo as if she'd shouted them in the Grand Canyon. She watched Garth carefully. His expression barely changed, except for a small twitch at the side of his mouth, where a smile was trying to escape.

Garth folded his arms across his chest and rocked back and forth in his chair, staying silent and looking Ainsley up and down. Ainsley tapped her foot and threw her arms in the air. "Well, say something, for crying out loud."

The smile finally won over. "I didn't ask you out, Ainsley."

"Of course you did." Ainsley forced calmness. "Two years ago. Don't you remember, right outside the restaurant? It was a cold day." She then forced a smile. "So my answer is yes."

Garth chuckled, then laughed, then snorted, sneezed, coughed, snorted again, wiped his eyes, and then said, "I don't think so."

"Excuse me?"

He leaned back in his chair with agitating calmness. "You can't just come in here, after all this time, and ask me out, you know."

"Ask *you* out? I didn't ask *you* out! You asked me out, you moron! And I'm saying yes!"

"I don't think it's that simple, my little chocolate-covered fire ant."

Ainsley's whole body burned with rage. "Garth Eugene Twyne! For ten years straight you've panted over me like a dog at its water bowl. You've gone out of your way a thousand times to tell me how much you love and adore me. Don't sit there in that ratty little chair of yours now, with that smug little expression on your face, and pretend you don't have any idea what I'm talking about!"

"Well, I do know one thing," Garth said wryly, "You're still really cute when you're mad."

"Forget it," Ainsley said, turning around in his office and swinging the door open, only to find Ginger on the ground with her ear to the floor.

"My contact," she tried. Ainsley stepped over her with disgust and kept walking.

She went through the door that led out to the lobby, this time forgetting about the puddle mines. Her heel slipped on one, but luckily she recovered only to nearly fall face first into another. She continued out the door with the little bit of integrity she had left and went straight to her car.

"Wait!"

Garth came running after her, tripping over his own shoelaces as he hopped the curb and stumbled toward her.

"I said, forget it," Ainsley mumbled. Her face burned with embarrassment.

"No, wait." He touched her arm. "I'm sorry." He stuck his hands in the pockets of his wrinkled doctor's coat. "You just caught me off guard." He stepped back one pace, smiled at her with some hint of genuineness, and said, "Ainsley Parker, will you go out with me?"

Ainsley stared hard into his eyes, and for a moment she thought she heard that still, small voice that had led her through the years, a voice that sounded hesitant. But she decided she was mistaken. Because what she thought she heard it say sounded crazier than what she was about to do, so she looked at Garth and through gritted teeth said, "Yes."

From somewhere nearby, she thought she heard Ginger scream.

CHAPTER 8

"ALFRED?"

The older man smiled up at Wolfe, running his hands through his already slicked-back, dyed-black hair, shiny as oil on leather. "Wolfe. Boy, it gets cold in Indiana, doesn't it?"

"What in the world are you doing here?"

"About to freeze to death," he chattered.

"I'm sorry, come in." Wolfe stepped aside so his old friend and editor could enter. Alfred looked around as he took off his coat and handed it to Wolfe. Wolfe hung it up in the coat closet and joined Alfred in the living room.

"Not too much has changed," Alfred said, glancing at Wolfe. "It's been several years since I was here."

"You don't usually get on a plane and come all the way out to Indiana unless you're seeing dollar signs," Wolfe said with a small smile. "Do you have some sort of news?"

"No, no." Alfred sat down in one of the wing chairs, still looking around the house. "Just missed you."

"Ha!" Wolfe stood above him with his arms crossed. "Try again."

"How about some coffee first? I can't feel my toes."

Wolfe went to the kitchen and filled a large mug, black the way Alfred liked it. He brought it back, and Alfred took the mug. "You remembered."

"And surely you remember how keen a sense of discernment I've always had about you. Why don't you tell me why you're really here?"

Alfred reached into his blazer pocket and pulled out a small, thin box, handing it to Wolfe with a noticeable grin. "To give you this."

Wolfe shook his head as he stared at the little box. "Let me guess. Another pen."

"Not just any pen, my friend. It's a Montblanc."

Wolfe opened the box, and there, bundled in velvet, was a navy pen with the little plastic star on the top of the cap. "How much did this one cost you?"

"Wolfe, it's a gift. You don't ask people what they spend on gifts. But if you must know, it was seven hundred and forty dollars. It's the Friedrich Schiller LE, you know, the great German philosopher and writer—"

"I know who Schiller is," Wolfe said.

"Oh. I had to look him up," Alfred smirked. "Maybe you'll have a pen named after you someday."

Wolfe smiled. "Well, thank you. You're kind to think of me. I'll put it with the other four."

Alfred shrugged. "Every writer needs a Montblanc. It's a sign of greatness. And *you,* my friend, are *great.*"

"Well, I type all my manuscripts on a computer now, but I'll save this for a book signing or something."

"Yes, we have several lined up near Christmas. Don't forget."

Wolfe sat across from Alfred and laid the pen on the coffee table. "Alfred, I don't think you flew all the way from New York to give me a pen, Montblanc, Bic, or otherwise."

"All right," Alfred breathed, setting his coffee down and smoothing the wrinkles in his slacks. "I'm worried about you. All right? Fair enough? Don't you see I'm here because I care? I came all the way here to check on you." His hands flew up in the air and came back down, slapping each knee. "And I had to fly second-class too."

"Why are you worried about me?"

"Hello? Don't you remember the conversation we just had? The one that caused me to book a flight?" Alfred's voice got higher. "The one where you said you weren't sure about your next book. If there was even going to be a next book."

"I'm not liable," Wolfe said. "My contract's up with *Black Cats.*"

"I know you're not *legally* liable, but what about all the millions of fans all over the world who are waiting for your next book? Doesn't that do something to you? Make you feel the least bit guilty?" Alfred took a breath. "You're not going to another house, are you?"

Wolfe stared at Alfred, unable to answer.

Alfred stood suddenly. "Okay, look. Maybe I'm coming on a little too strong. After all, I haven't even given you a chance to explain yourself." He stared into the dark fireplace, then turned to Wolfe. "If it's a nervous breakdown, that's completely acceptable. It happens to the best of the best. It's almost expected. And quite frankly, a breakdown can do a lot for a writer's career. Usually more after they're dead, but that's beside the point. What I'm trying to say here is that we can work through it. Get you therapy. I'll fly a therapist out here, for crying out loud. There are therapists who practice on only famous, wealthy writers. If it's something minor, like a mental block, we can get that fixed. If it's bigger, like some sort of identity crisis, we can work through that, too." Alfred's hands were cupped together as he said, "I'm here for you. What do you need?"

Wolfe smiled, then laughed, then almost cried at the absurdity of Alfred Tennison. Wolfe wondered if he himself had lost perspective like this before last week.

"What's so funny?" Alfred demanded.

"Nothing, nothing," Wolfe said with a wave of his hand. "I'm sorry. I shouldn't be laughing."

"Laughing is good. It's better than crying, although we can work with crying if that's what you need to do to get another book out." Alfred's face was drawn tight with desperation. "Frankly, I feel as if I could weep myself."

Wolfe sipped his coffee carefully, then said, "Al, I'm not having a nervous breakdown. In fact, quite the opposite. I'm finally set free."

"Set free. Set free. Set free from…from…what?"

"Myself," Wolfe said. "It's complicated and simple all at once."

Alfred finally sat back down. "Why don't you explain it to me?"

Wolfe sized Alfred up in a split second and knew this was a man who wasn't going to understand. But the least he could do was try. "It's a relationship—"

"I knew it! That was my second guess. Nervous breakdown was first, but relationship was second. Who is she? Do I know her? It's Babs, isn't it? Babs Tyson?"

"Babs Tyson? Why would you think that?"

"She's adored you for years, Wolfe. You can't say you haven't noticed the glowing reviews she's always given you in the *Times*."

"Well, Al, I can't say I respect a woman who writes positive reviews just to get a date."

"It's good to know we don't like the same kind of woman." His face grew serious. "So who is she? Leave it to a woman to wreck the career of the most famous writer alive."

"I'm not the most famous writer alive, and you didn't let me finish. It's not a woman." Wolfe stood and paced the length of the floor, Bunny and Goose watching his every move, but not more carefully than Alfred. "Alfred, have you ever had a time in your life when you wondered what in the world everything means? Where you stop and ask yourself what your purpose is and why you're alive? I sit up in this lonely old house and write my novels, and they have no meaning. They're just a bunch of words, lifeless on the page, doing no good other than scaring the dickens out of people."

"And making us both millionaires, but I see your point."

Wolfe turned to him. "Do you?"

"Sure, Wolfe. There was a time in my career when I wondered, 'Should I be doing trashy romance novels?' Sure, they sell. But can I really just sit day after day and read the same story line over and over again? *No!* I told myself. I put my foot down and instead decided to sink my teeth into something more moving, like horror. And a good choice it was. Here I am with you, the most famous writer in the world."

"Stop saying that," Wolfe groaned. "It's not true, and even if it were, I'm at a point in my life where I'm a little embarrassed to be known for writing what I write. How can I feel good about making people afraid?"

Alfred stared up at Wolfe. His mouth even hung open a little, as if he were trying to understand a foreign language. "I don't understand."

"Okay, it's like this. There's this girl, and every day she visits old people and takes them things they like. And when they come to her restaurant, she remembers whether or not they like sugar in their tea, and how much sugar, and if they really like mashed potatoes, she'll sneak them an extra serving. She smiles at everyone and has a lot of friends, and she just has this glow, like she's at perfect peace with the world."

"So this is about a woman."

"No. I mean yes. I mean no." Wolfe stumbled to catch his breath. "No. It's about God. Okay? It's about God."

"God?"

"Yes. It is about a relationship. A relationship with God. Where I can talk with Him, pray to Him, be forgiven. Don't you see, Al? Can't you see a difference in me?"

"I'll say," Alfred mumbled.

"For the first time in my life, I feel I have a purpose, yet, extraordinarily, I'm not doing anything but living day to day. I have no objectives. No goals. No *deadlines.* Yet I have this peace. This unimaginable peace, deep within my soul."

Alfred stared at the floor for a long moment before finally saying, "She said you turned religious. I should've known what she meant was you were losing it."

Wolfe locked eyes with Alfred. "Who? Who are you talking about?"

"Nobody." Alfred stood and walked to the coat closet. "Well, I'm glad I traveled all this way to learn you're going to Sunday school now."

"Alfred, wait. Please. Let me explain."

"You've explained, haven't you? What else is there to say?" Alfred pulled his coat on and flattened his collar. He forcefully buttoned it up as if he were standing in the middle of a blizzard. "I'm glad for you, Wolfe. Really, I am. Maybe you can pray that I don't lose my job when I have to go back to the house and tell them that you traded the devil for Jesus."

Wolfe swallowed. As crass as Alfred was, he couldn't have put it better himself. "I'm sorry, Al. I'm sorry you're upset." He followed Alfred to the door. "Thanks for the pen."

Alfred walked down the front porch steps to where his rented SUV was parked. He got in, started it, and without letting it warm up, pulled off without so much as a wave.

"Hi, darling," Sheriff Parker said. He threw his coat on the back of the chair, but Ainsley didn't have time to go hang it in its proper place in the coat closet. After all this time, the man still couldn't understand where coats belong!

"Hi," Ainsley mumbled, squinting in the darkening room as she wrote on the piece of paper in front of her.

"Need some light?" he asked, switching on the kitchen light before Ainsley could protest. "My goodness. Are you wearing blush?"

Ainsley looked up at her dad and nodded slightly. "Yes, Daddy. I'm wearing blush."

"But you're so pretty," he said, sitting at the table. "You don't need anything like that."

Ainsley chose not to let the conversation go further.

"Well, what's the occasion for the makeup anyway?"

She didn't know how to answer. In fact, the words wouldn't even form on her tongue.

"Ainsley?" her father asked a few seconds later. "What's the matter? What are you concentrating so hard on over there?"

She finished writing her thoughts, and then dropped the pencil to the table. Brushing her hair out of her eyes, she slid the paper across the table to her father, who picked it up, found his reading glasses in his pocket, and studied it for a moment.

"'The Top Ten Reasons to Like Garth Twyne'?"

Ainsley couldn't even manage a smile of enthusiasm.

"What's this about?"

She stood and went to the kitchen. She sliced two pieces of bread from the fresh loaf she'd baked earlier and went to the refrigerator to get the sandwich ingredients. "I'm going out tonight. With Garth. I'm going out with Garth Twyne." The words felt heavy on her tongue, and just saying them seemed to suck the life right out of her body.

"Really?" Her father smiled with enthusiasm, as she had expected. Hardly a day had gone by when he hadn't expressed his regrets to Ainsley about her dislike for the guy. In Sheriff Parker's eyes, Garth was the perfect match for Ainsley. He intended to stay in Skary, and he had roots there. He had a stable, well-paying job. Plus, though Ainsley would never say so, Garth kissed up to the man so much her father actually thought himself a world-renowned law enforcer. "After all this time, are you trying to tell me the guy's finally won your heart?"

"No!" Ainsley said as she cut slices of cheese. "I'm simply saying I'm going out on a date." She glanced over her shoulder. "That's what dates are for, right? So the guy can win your heart by wooing and ooing you?"

"Well, pardon me for saying this, honey, but the guy's been wooing and ooing you for years now. What more can he do?"

Ainsley spread her homemade mustard onto the bread. She paused for a moment to smell the garden spices in it. "Mooing and gooing is more like it, Daddy. He's been obnoxious, and you know it. He's not my type for one thing. And he gets on my nerves for another. Not to mention he has no respect for personal space, which becomes more of a problem because I'm pretty sure he only brushes his teeth once a day, and I'd bet money he doesn't even floss."

"Then why are you going on a date with him?"

She laid the thinly shaved chicken breast onto the provolone cheese slices. "It's complicated, okay? But I wrote down a few positive things on that paper."

She heard the paper rattle and her father clear his throat. "Number ten: He grows a garden." She could feel her father staring into her back.

"He feeds all the vegetables to his pigs, but it's a start."

"Number nine: Isn't balding." She heard her father laugh, and she turned around. He was rubbing the top of his head. "That a problem for you?"

"Of course not," she smiled.

"Number eight." He paused and then said, "That's it. There's no number eight."

"I know," she sighed. "I couldn't think of anything else." She lightly peppered the inside of the sandwich, then carefully wrapped it in Saran Wrap, put it on a plate, and stuck it in the refrigerator. "Unfortunately for you, Daddy, this means you're stuck eating a sandwich tonight."

"We got any chips?"

"Yes. We have some chips in the pantry. I fried them up a couple of days ago, so they still should be fresh. They're the ranch-flavored ones."

"Good! I love those."

"I know," Ainsley said with a smile.

The doorbell rang. Her father hopped up and soon was at the door greeting Garth. They exchanged their usual hearty handshake and bois-terous greeting, then her father led Garth into the kitchen.

Ainsley managed to act as if she were wiping the countertop when he rounded the corner. "Hi, Garth," she said, and though she tried des-perately to sound excited, she knew she sounded more like she were choking to death.

"You look nice." His eyes roamed from the top of her head to the bottom of her feet and back again. Ainsley suddenly felt a terrible headache coming on.

"Oh. And you look—" She examined the clip-on tie, the short-sleeved striped cotton shirt that needed a good dose of starch, and the light-colored khaki pants that belonged only in the spring/summer months. "You look so…doctorly." She knew that would appease him. "Well, no need for chitchat now or we might run out of things to say later." Ainsley gave him a tense smile. "Shall we?"

"Sure," Garth shrugged, patting Sheriff Parker on the back with a quick compliment on nabbing the two vandals. "I'm starving."

Ainsley pulled on her sweater without Garth's help and grabbed her purse, mentally assessing how much money she had. Garth was the type who would forget his wallet or not have enough for the bill. "Where are we going?" she asked as he escorted her outside to his old pickup truck.

"Pete's Steakhouse."

"Oh. Lovely." Ainsley hopped up into the truck, thankful that at least Garth was polite enough to open the door for her. Pete's Steakhouse was considered fine dining only to men who dreamed of beef. The atmosphere was smoky and gritty. A large sign out front offered a free steak to anyone who could eat the seventy-two-ounce steak without throwing it back up. The fine print also mentioned that you had to eat your side items and at least one bread roll. She was thankful, at least, that Pete had refused to rename the restaurant to fit the town's horror theme.

Garth hopped in and started up the truck with a roar. While still in park, he revved the engine and filled the air with exhaust. Then the truck sputtered a little and lurched forward. Ainsley quickly put on her seatbelt. "This little puppy can do zero to sixty in forty-five seconds." Garth winked.

"Ah. Good to know," Ainsley replied.

He patted her on the knee. "This is going to be a night you'll never forget."

Pete's Steakhouse was not crowded, but a two-foot-thick blanket of smoke hung from the ceiling. Garth had asked for a quiet table in the corner. They ended up at the last table before the kitchen, where the shouting cook gave distracting orders.

"You know, people come from miles around just to eat here," Garth boasted.

Ainsley tried to smile. What he really meant was that it was a nice place off the highway where truckers going from west to east liked to stop for a good meal. Their waiter, a college-aged kid, approached to take drink orders.

"What's your best wine?" Garth asked, his eyebrows arched with pretend maturity.

The kid thought for a second. "Well, we got red."

"That's terrific. Bring us out a bottle." Garth flashed a smile at the kid, then turned his attention to Ainsley. "This is the best beef around, darling. Now, I like mine bloody and mooing, but most little ladies can't handle it that rare. I'd suggest getting yours well done, almost crusty."

Ainsley looked down at her menu and said, "Actually, I think I'll have the pasta with blackened chicken."

"Chicken?"

"Yes."

Garth glanced down at his own menu. "I didn't even know they had chicken." Then he laughed. "Oh, of course they have chicken. Duh. Chicken fried steak. One of my favorites."

"That's actually beef."

"No, it's not."

"Yes, it is."

He crossed his arms. "Then why do they call it *chicken* fried steak?"

Ainsley pressed her lips together. "Because it's fried like chicken."

This took several seconds of massive brainpower for Garth to process. He shrugged and then said, "You like chicken over beef?"

Ainsley nodded, though what she really wanted to say was that she was not about to have Garth Twyne tell her what to eat and how to eat it. The waiter returned with a bottle of wine chilled in a plastic bucket. He pulled out his pad from the back pocket of his jeans. "All right. What can I get for you?"

"The little lady here's gonna have that pasta dish of yours with the black chicken. Does that mean the dark meat? At Thanksgiving, I don't want none of that dry white meat where you have to pour the whole bucket of gravy over it just to make it edible."

"Sir," the waiter said, "it's blackened chicken." The kid glanced at Ainsley and then said to Garth, "And what will you have?"

"The seventy-two-ouncer, rare, with Tommy Telly's steak sauce on the side. Now listen to me, kid. I want to see red, not pink, in the middle, okay? I want it mooing."

The kid smiled. "Gotcha."

"Just make sure my chicken's not clucking," Ainsley added with a short smile.

The kid was just about to ask about sides when Pete Manundra, the restaurant owner, sauntered over like the most important person in the world.

"Garth! Glad to see you! What are you doing sitting all the way over here in the corner?"

The waiter said, "That's what they wanted, sir."

Pete patted the kid on the back. "Is Jimmy here taking good care of you?"

"Yep," Garth said.

Pete glanced at the order on the kid's pad. "Oh no. Now Garth, don't tell me you're going to try to eat our seventy-two-ounce steak again."

"You betcha."

Pete's face turned worried. "Don't you remember what happened last time? You spewed like a geyser. It took two hours to clean up."

Garth glanced at Ainsley, his cheeks flushing with embarrassment. Garth pointed to Ainsley with a jab of his thumb. "Hey now, I got a little lady to impress here. By the way, this is Ainsley Parker, my *date*."

Pete glanced at Ainsley and smiled warmly. "Hi there. Welcome to Pete's. Ever been here before?"

"No, I haven't."

"Well, glad to have you. Hope you like the food." He cocked his head to the side. "You're Sheriff Parker's daughter, aren't you?"

"I am," Ainsley replied.

"Nice to know you. Irwin's a great customer." He looked back at Garth. "Now listen. I'm serious. You start feeling queasy and you stop eating. I don't think Miss Parker here's going to be too impressed with your guts all over the floor. Got it?" He winked at Ainsley, who could only stare blankly, trying to remember if this was reality or a nightmare.

"He exaggerates everything," Garth said to Ainsley after Pete left. "I mean, one time I ate two and a half of those steaks with no problem. I had the stomach flu that day, that's all."

Ainsley nodded and tried her best to smile, but she thought if her facial muscles moved at all she might just burst into tears. And it came to her that if she felt as if she was going to burst into tears, this probably wasn't what God had in mind for her. Garth was explaining how he'd neutered a dog that day, but all Ainsley could think about was the clock on the wall and how very slowly the seconds were ticking by. After dinner, she would insist he take her home, and then she would explain she'd made a mistake and that they weren't supposed to be anything more than friends. If that.

Their food arrived unexpectedly fast, and Ainsley wondered how they could blacken chicken in five minutes. Garth's steak hung over the sides of his plate, and there was barely room for the baked potato and green beans that came with it. Garth grinned and rubbed his hands together.

"Let's thank the Lord for our food," Ainsley reminded him quietly.

"Thank you Lord for this food!" Garth squealed and started sawing away, bright pink juices filling the platter in seconds.

Ainsley quietly checked her chicken to make sure it was not pink inside, then began to eat. The pasta dish wasn't bad, but she'd lost what little appetite she'd had to begin with. She watched Garth tackle his sirloin. They'd only been at Pete's Steakhouse for thirty minutes, but she felt as though half her life had wasted away.

As she cut her chicken into proper, bite-size pieces, she wondered if there was any way to get out of the rest of dinner. No sooner had the question crossed her mind than she saw her father making his way around the tables and toward them.

"Daddy!" she said with way too much delight. On any normal occasion, she'd wonder why he'd followed her to Pete's. But she stood, almost leaping over the table to greet him. "What are you doing here?"

Her father embraced her and then looked at Garth. "Garth."

"Hello, Sheriff Parker."

Ainsley looked at her father. "How did you know where to find me?"

"Well, where else would he take you?"

Of course. She noticed her father's solemn face and realized that he wasn't there to save her from this horrid date. His shoulders slumped with a heaviness she recognized from long ago. "Daddy?"

With his arm still around her shoulder, Sheriff Parker said, "Honey, I'm so sorry to have to ruin your evening like this, but I knew you'd want to know. Aunt Gert passed away. The hospital just called."

Ainsley buried her face in her father's chest. Garth stood with a mouth full of food and said, "Sowwy, Ainsley."

"Come on, sweetheart. Let me take you home."

Ainsley nodded and let her father guide her out of the restaurant. She managed a short wave to Garth, who stood at the table helplessly. She cried all the way home. She had thought the night couldn't get worse. But she had been so wrong.

CHAPTER 9

THEY BURIED AUNT Gert three days later, on Monday. She'd made all her funeral arrangements ahead of time, so there was nothing to do but say good-bye. Ainsley's father had tried to console her, but nothing could fill the void Aunt Gert's death left behind. In a way, Ainsley experienced the death of her mother all over again.

Aunt Gert had left a note for her, bringing a little comfort. She'd expressed all her love for Ainsley but tried to assure her she was in a better place. Ainsley had no doubt of that. She was mostly just feeling sorry for herself, because *she* was indeed *not* in a better place.

Garth had stopped by. Ainsley didn't want to see anyone, so her father handled him. He was kind enough to bring some flowers and a doggy bag full of the dinner Ainsley had left behind. It was a good attempt on his behalf, and even though she chucked the food, she put the flowers in a nice vase.

By Monday evening, Ainsley found the house suffocating. She didn't feel like cooking, and her father decided he'd go out to Pete's. She thought about taking a walk, but this fall felt more like winter, and the iciness in the air was the last thing she needed. The world was already a cold place.

She paced the halls for a while, thinking of her mother, praying, smiling at a few warm thoughts of Aunt Gert that managed to rise above the grief. And then it occurred to her: She had someone to thank. She grabbed her coat and scarf out of the closet, turned off all the lights in the house, and warmed up her car. As it idled in her driveway, she couldn't help but acknowledge the strange eagerness in her heart to go make this visit. Maybe she should have listened to her heart in the first place.

"Ms. Peeple?"

"*Miss* Peeple."

"Isn't that what I said?"

"No. You said Ms. I'm *Miss.*"

The poor guy stood awkwardly on the porch of her home, shivering in his expensive coat.

"I've never been married, and Ms. is reserved for someone who has and is widowed, or who hasn't but doesn't want people to know. Or the divorced. I'm quite proud to be none of the above, but to make it easier, you can call me Missy."

"I'm sorry, I'm—"

"For crying out loud, do I have to spell it out for you, Alfred?"

His eyes widened as he looked at her. "How did you know my name?"

"I know everything that goes on in this town, lad. For example, I know you went to see Wolfe three days ago. And I know you spent the night at the bed-and-breakfast here in Skary. And," she said with an eager grin, "I know why you've come to see me tonight." She sized him up and said, "They don't have winter in New York? You're acting as if you've never been exposed to the elements before, sir. Come inside before you catch pneumonia."

He slowly stepped inside, looking around apprehensively. Missy caned her way over to her rocking chair and offered Alfred a seat on her vinyl couch, recently covered in new plastic. He kept his hands in the pockets of his coat. With his slicked-back hair and his expensive shoes, Missy thought the man must think he was something awfully important, which made a sense of pride surge through her weary veins. He needed her help.

"It's quite unfair, don't you think?"

"What?" he asked, finally sitting down.

"Well, a man will always be a Mister, no matter what happens to him. How am I to know your marital status? Are you single, married, divorced, widowed, fornicating, what?"

Missy imagined that Mr. Tennison for the most part was a man with a lot of confidence, but she knew by the way his eyes shifted and startled at her words that, no matter who he was in New York, he was nothing more than putty in her hands here.

"I'm sorry your talk with Wolfe didn't go well."

"I don't suppose you're going to tell me how you know that."

"Knowing the business of this town is my business. How do you think I knew to call you?"

Alfred stared at his shoes for a moment and then said, "I'm at a loss as to what to do. He's made up his mind. He's not changing."

"Oh you of little faith." She met his eyes. "Let me tell you something, Mr. Tennison. I've only known you for a couple of minutes, but I can tell that you are a man who appreciates a good deal." She glanced at his shoes and Rolex watch. "And you are a man who appreciates money. So I'm going to tell you what you're going to do."

His eyes narrowed. "I'm not accustomed to people telling me what to do."

"From what I can tell, you're not accustomed to Timex or Hush Puppies either, sir."

"I'm listening."

The house looked old and creepy at night. It always had. It loomed over the little town and even had two windows that, when lit, resembled two large eyes.

An old gravel road led up to a small grassy knoll and a few cement steps, which led to a short path and the wooden porch steps. The porch light was dim, and Ainsley had trouble finding her way through the darkness.

The porch steps creaked, causing Ainsley to stop in her tracks and second-guess her decision to come and visit Wolfe Boone. Why was she here? She could've just as easily written a kind note and stuck it in the mail. Staring up at the old house, she felt her heart beat wildly. Was it the creepiness of this old house, or the anticipation of something else? How she wished she could read the signs of her own heart.

She made her way up two more steps and then to the front door. A heavy brass knocker reflected the porch light and her own small and timid looking self. She stood up straighter, took in a breath of courage, and knocked.

She heard footfalls on what sounded like a hardwood floor, and then the door opened. Wolfe Boone stood, backlit from the inside lights, staring down at her in astonishment. All she could do was stare back.

"Hi," he managed with a smile.

"How are you?"

"Fine," he replied. "Can I, uh, help you?"

She tried to peek around him, to get a glimpse of what this haunted mansion might look like on the inside. She figured a few axes would be hanging from the ceiling, but his big frame wouldn't allow even a tiny look.

"I'm here to…to…to thank you."

"Thank me?"

"Yes. For the book. That was so incredibly kind of you." Ainsley tried to suppress her emotions. "My aunt died Friday. I had a chance to read it to her before she died, and it meant the world to her. And to me."

Even backlit, Ainsley could see Wolfe's features soften. "You're very welcome. I'm so sorry she died."

"It was expected," Ainsley said. "But not easy."

Wolfe shuffled his feet and then said, "Would you like to come in?"

Ainsley hesitated. Would she like to come in? *Would she?* It wouldn't have been a difficult question coming from anyone but Wolfe Boone. "Umm…"

"It's kind of cold out there."

"Yeah."

"Yeah, you want to come in?"

"No."

"No, you don't want to come in?"

"No, I mean, yeah, it's cold out here." She tried to smile. "I'm sorry.

That was a simple question." She held her breath for a moment. "Sure. I'll come in. But just for a minute."

"Great," he said. "Do you mind taking your shoes off?"

"My shoes?" Her mind reeled with thoughts of why she should take her shoes off. Maybe he practiced some strange demonic ritual. Or maybe he thought the ground she stood on was sacred in some way. Was the house built on top of a cemetery? Why in the world would she need to take her shoes off? She felt her neck dampen.

"I've got two dogs. At night it's hard to see where they take their bathroom breaks in the yard. Plus all those crazy cats don't help."

"Oh." Ainsley slipped off each shoe. "Sure."

"Come on in." He opened the door wider. A few feet away, two noble-looking German shepherds sat near the living room, wagging their tails. "This is Goose and Bunny."

She smiled at the dogs and they seemed to smile back, as if they recognized her. She looked at Wolfe and pointed to the dogs. "I'm surprised they're not barking."

Wolfe was taking her coat. "Well, they're very smart dogs. They only bark when they sense evil. That's something unique about shepherds. Some of them can sense evil."

"Oh." Ainsley watched as Wolfe took her coat and scarf and hung them up in the coat closet. She'd never once seen a man do that. She looked around the house. It was decorated with warm, strong colors, but it wasn't in-your-face masculine. The furniture looked expensive, as did the tile and the rugs. She was amazed. On the inside it looked like a house out of *Architectural Digest.* She sauntered into the living room, grazing her hand against a vase with flowers. *Fresh* flowers!

His artwork was hung carefully, and he had just enough knick-knacks to make the room comfortable but not junky. A bookshelf cram-packed with hundreds of books lined one wall. A fire crackled in the fireplace, and the whole house smelled of pine.

Ainsley was speechless. Even in her wildest imagination, she had never thought this house would look...*normal.*

"Please, sit down," he said, and she sat on the couch while he sat in an overstuffed leather chair with an ottoman, one that looked to be his favorite by the way it was slightly worn.

"Your house is nice," she said simply, hoping not to sound shocked.

"Thanks," he shrugged. "I spend a lot of time here."

"You could use a few fall flowers out front." She shrugged and grinned. "Or maybe a couple of potted plants."

"Thanks. I'll try to remember that," he said lightheartedly. The kind of silence that fills the room when there's so much to say and not enough guts to say it rang in Ainsley's ears like chimes in the wind. She had just decided to compliment the fact that he liked to use his coat closet *and* had fresh flowers when a loud siren shattered the peace.

"What is that?" Ainsley shouted over the noise.

The dogs started howling, but Wolfe almost sat motionless, as if he didn't hear the sound at all. Then she noticed the small bead of sweat dripping down his temple, which led her to the tense look on his face.

"What is it?" she shouted again.

"It's the smoke alarm." He jumped up. "I think we have a fire."

Very few things frightened Missy Peeple, but one of them was how quickly she could devise a plan. As she sat there in her rocker, entertaining the suave but greedy Mr. Alfred Tennison, her entire plan came together so brilliantly, so perfectly, that she could do nothing but stand there in awe of herself for a moment.

But she didn't let the admiration last long. She hated to keep Mr. Tennison waiting.

"A book, you say?"

She could see his mind churning the idea as if it were sweet butter. She said, "Why certainly. A biography of the town made famous by a famous writer. The ins and outs of how a man like Wolfe Boone relates to the people of a small town. And how they relate to him. The history of how a nothing town became a famous tourist stop. And then there are the strange, unexplainable things that make this town even more mysterious."

"What do you mean?"

"The cats."

"The cats?"

"Sir, haven't you noticed all the cats running around this town?"

Mr. Tennison nodded. "Yes, as a matter of fact I did notice. They seem to be everywhere."

"Well, perhaps Mr. Boone made Skary famous, but Skary has given Mr. Boone a few story ideas too."

His eyes widened. *"Black Cats?"*

"Well, isn't it obvious?"

Mr. Tennison smiled a little. "I've never asked Wolfe where he got that idea." He pulled out a pad and very expensive looking pen and began jotting notes.

"So you see how brilliant this is? You write a book that makes you famous, about a man you made famous." Missy smiled studiously at him. "And you get really rich."

"I like how you think."

"That's just the icing on the cake."

"Oh?"

"It'll give you an excuse."

"An excuse?"

"Mr. Tennison, as much as you may think this plan is about you, it isn't. It's about the town of Skary and how to save it from utter destruction. You see, like you, we're doomed if Mr. Boone stops writing his books. What is Skary without a horror novelist? Just another dumb town with a dumb spelling of a name."

"I don't understand."

Missy Peeple moved to a spot next to him on the sofa. She sat down and scooted toward him, which for some reason seemed to unnerve him.

"It will give you an excuse to stick around Skary. And convince your most famous author that he has no choice but to continue to write. I don't care whether you write that book or not, you see. I'm concerned with one thing and one thing only."

Mr. Tennison eased away from her, then stood. "All right."

"I'm glad you agree, because, you see, you have no choice."

"Oh?"

"I'm the one that knows everything about everyone in this town. Your book would be nothing without the juice I have. You need me and I need you. You see how conveniently this works out."

"Yes."

"But let's get one thing straight. You need me *more* than I need you."

Mr. Tennison shook his head and laughed a bit. "You are quite the bully, aren't you?"

"I will give you information as it fits into my plan. And you will use it according to my purpose. When I'm done with you, then you can write your silly little book and make yourself a lot of money. But first things first. We get Wolfe back."

"No arguments from me."

She smiled graciously and said, "Good then. Let me begin by telling you about our mayor. Wullisworth is his name. A good mayor. Quite handsome, too. And like you, Mr. Tennison, he is quite fond of money."

They managed to put out the fire without an extinguisher, but by then choking smoke had filled the entire kitchen. Ainsley waved a dishtowel in the air and opened kitchen windows as fast as she could. Wolfe tried to look busy doing *something,* but he was clueless. And now he had an even bigger problem.

The smoke cleared enough for them to see each other and the black and crispy items that lay in the skillet in the sink.

Still waving the dish towel in the air, Ainsley said, "Hmmm. What was to be for dinner?"

"Pork chops," Wolfe sighed, joining her at the sink to look at the mishap.

"Two pork chops," she said. "Were you expecting someone?"

He smiled down at her. "Well, certainly not you, but I wish I could have made a better impression of my cooking skills."

She grinned, then suddenly her face turned solemn and worried. "Um…were you cooking for a…a…date?"

He laughed. "A date? No. For heaven's sake, no. I haven't had a date in…" He stopped himself. He was already looking foolish. No need to look desperate, too. He jabbed the pork chops with a fork sitting nearby. "No, this was for Reverend Peck. I was having him over for dinner tonight." He glanced up at the clock near the stove. "And it looks like we're going to have to do takeout." Staring down at the two black pieces of meat he said, "There's not a chance these can be saved, is there?"

Ainsley laughed. "I don't think so, unless you were planning on serving something close to pork jerky."

"Well, I hope the reverend likes pizza."

Ainsley looked around the kitchen. "We can pull something together."

A grin spread across his lips. *We.* He liked the sound of that. "I don't know. I mean, fried pork chops was a big attempt for me. Serves me right for trying to get fancy." He shrugged. "I don't have too much to work with here. I definitely don't have two more pork chops."

She went to the refrigerator, peeked inside, said, "Hmm," and then went to the pantry, stuck her head in, said another "hmm" and then turned to him. "No problem."

"Really?"

"How much time do we have?"

Wolfe glanced at the clock. "Fifteen minutes."

"Perfect." She started toward the refrigerator, then stopped and turned back toward him. "I'm sorry. I'm totally taking over. I do this in a kitchen. I think I own every stove within twenty miles of myself."

"Are you kidding? My other choice is to order pizza and look like the worst host ever."

She smiled and then gathered a few ingredients from the refrigerator. Wolfe stood back and watched in awe as she began to prepare the food.

"I do have one demand."

"Demand?" she asked, chopping the tomato without even looking.

"Yes. That you stay for dinner. That's the only way I'll let you save my behind."

She laughed, then moved her knife to the mushrooms. But she didn't answer. She glanced over her shoulder though and smiled.

Wolfe smiled too, then leaned against the counter and watched the chef in action. He'd never seen anyone make food look more appealing in his life.

"Now, I'm adding a dash of red wine vinegar here. When in doubt, add red wine vinegar to sautéed vegetables." She glanced over her shoulder to see if he was listening.

He was. Intently. He never knew cooking could be so interesting. But part of him knew it wasn't the cooking he was so interested in.

"I'm going to add the garlic now. You don't want to add garlic too early, but if you add it too late, you're not going to get the flavor you want." She looked over at the large pot of spaghetti boiling in water. "Looks like the pasta is cooking up nicely. We'll watch it closely. There's nothing worse than overcooked pasta. Except undercooked chicken."

He stepped next to her and watched her as she threw the garlic into the skillet. "You're very good at this. I could never take a look in the refrigerator and pantry and come up with something to cook."

She shrugged lightly. "Years of practice, I guess. And an insatiable appetite for Martha."

"Martha?"

"Stewart. She's pretty much my hero of all that is domestic and homey."

"Ah. Well, she should watch out. Her protégée seems hot on her trail."

Ainsley obviously relished that compliment. She added a little more olive oil and stirred the vegetables, causing them to sizzle. Setting the spoon down, she turned to him. "I have to confess something."

Her jubilant demeanor had vanished. Her face was serious. "Okay."

He swallowed hard. What was she going to confess? If she was going to confess what he hoped she was going to confess, then he should confess his feelings for her too. It was only fair, and he suddenly drew great boldness from her. By the look on her face, this was no small thing she was about to say. "I've got something to confess too."

Her neatly arched eyebrows rose with interest. "Is that so?"

"Yes."

"Well, okay. But I bet it isn't as embarrassing as what I'm about to confess."

His hands found his pockets, and he felt heat creep up his neck. "Oh, I wouldn't be so sure about that."

She smiled slightly, but her face was still serious. "Well, okay." She gripped the counter and took in a deep breath, hardly able to look him in the eye.

"Go ahead. Please."

She straightened her shoulders and engaged his eyes. "All right. Here it is. I butter my spaghetti." She threw up her arms and hung her head as if she'd just confessed to grand larceny.

Wolfe blinked and wondered if he'd heard right. "I'm sorry. You…you butter your…your what?"

"My spaghetti. It's not something I tell a lot of people. If Martha were dead, she'd roll over in her grave. I'm not proud of it, but I tell you this. If Martha came over to my house, and I was cooking spaghetti, I'd butter it. We'd have a grand debate, and I'm sure she'd win in the end, but I like my spaghetti buttered, and doggone it, I'm not going to apologize for it!" Her delicate features were intense with opinion, and Wolfe found himself utterly speechless. "You're looking at me weird. Have I forever marred your image of me?"

Wolfe tried to recover. "No. No…of course not. I mean, I think buttering is…um…why is buttering bad again?"

"Because," she said intently, "then the pasta won't stick together. That's the whole magic of pasta. That's how you can eat it with some kind of grace. When it's buttered, it slips and slides right off your fork. It takes much more effort to get it into your mouth, that's for sure."

"I see."

"But it tastes so good that way. And sometimes I think Martha over-looks simple things like what spaghetti *tastes* like with butter. She stares into that television screen as she's draining the water from her spaghetti and says in that deep voice of hers, 'Never, ever butter your pasta.' It makes me cringe." She salted and peppered the vegetables with author-ity, then turned her attention back to Wolfe, who was still trying to fig-ure out where he'd missed it. "Now, yours can't be that embarrassing."

"Mine?"

"Your confession."

Dread pinched the corners of his heart. Oh yeah. His confession. What in the world was he going to say now?

"Well, c'mon. I told you my deep, dark secret. Now it's your turn." She smiled sweetly at him, and for a moment he thought he might actu-ally confess all his feelings for her. Then he scolded himself for being so stupid as to think that she might confess feelings for him. They barely knew each other, for heaven's sake.

"I don't even know how to cook spaghetti."

She laughed. "You don't?"

He shook his head, wondering if that confession, which was a lie, was a worse proclamation than the fact that he'd been in love with her for years. "I, uh, thought you nuked it in the microwave."

She laughed heartily and shook her own head. "Well, that is quite a confession. How long has this package of spaghetti been in your pantry?"

Three days. "Three years." He smiled sheepishly, and she patted him on the back.

"I hope you've been paying attention, then." She pointed to the pot. "Boil the water, add a little salt, add the spaghetti, then boil uncovered for seven to nine minutes until it's al dente…that's slightly firm."

"Got it. I'm happy to know now."

"Good! Glad I could help." She took a fork and snatched a piece of spaghetti out of the pot. She handled the steaming string delicately, and then threw it in the air. It hit the ceiling and stuck. "Perfect!"

He stared up at it. "What'd you do that for?"

"That's how you can tell if your spaghetti is ready. If it sticks, it's done." She took the pot and poured the water out into the sink. Wolfe turned off the fire on the stove. She returned the pot to the stove and took a stick of butter out of the refrigerator. "Here it goes." She cut several pieces off the butter and put it on the spaghetti. She finished and looked at Wolfe, who was staring at the ceiling. "It'll fall in about three minutes."

"Oh. Good."

The doorbell rang, and suddenly Wolfe remembered he was expecting company other than Ainsley.

"That must be the reverend. I'll get the door." Wolfe left the kitchen. He opened the front door and found the reverend standing on his porch, right on time.

"Wolfe! Hello! Thank you so much for inviting me to dinner."

Wolfe smiled and shook his hand. "Thank you for coming. Come on inside." Wolfe took the reverend's coat and hat and hung it in the coat closet.

"Smells wonderful," the reverend said with a smile.

"Well," Wolfe said in a hushed voice, "we're lucky enough to have a special cook this evening."

"No kidding?"

Wolfe gestured toward the kitchen. The reverend peeked around the corner and saw Ainsley, who smiled and waved. The reverend waved back and turned to Wolfe. "My, the Lord can work quickly sometimes, can't He?"

Wolfe laughed, then cleared his throat as Ainsley moved to the entryway to greet Reverend Peck. "Hi there," she said and hugged him tightly.

"What a delight!" the reverend said. "Two of my favorite people here. Dinner will be marvelous."

"Let me get you some coffee, Reverend," Wolfe offered. He went back into the kitchen while Ainsley and the reverend made their way into the living room. He took a mug and poured the coffee, but his mind was still numb from what had just taken place in the kitchen.

What kind of idiot was he to think Ainsley Parker was going to stand in his kitchen and wear her heart on her sleeve? He shook his head and wondered if love had made him crazy.

He stood at the counter and resolved to be at his best tonight. He had to be charming, witty, smooth, and debonair. Everything he did tonight was going to be important. If he didn't win her tonight, he might not get another chance. He stood up straight and adjusted his shirt, making sure all corners were tucked in.

He walked into the living room and smiled engagingly as Ainsley and the reverend were speaking.

But she stood suddenly, her bright face dulling ever so slowly. "I'm sorry, Wolfe. I can't stay."

"You can't? But…but you cooked the whole meal."

"I ruined your first meal," she said with a small smile. "Besides, you and the reverend will have a lovely time together."

Wolfe's enthusiasm deflated. "Okay."

Then she laughed. Wolfe tried to laugh but had no idea what they were laughing at, and could only imagine that it was something he said.

Ainsley finally controlled herself enough to wink at him, point to his hair, and say, "I guess that spaghetti finally fell off the ceiling."

CHAPTER 10

MARTIN BLARTY, the town treasurer and a lifelong Skary resident, blinked as if he had something in his eye, but Missy knew it was just shock registering. She sat there quietly across the booth from him, sipping her beverage as if they'd just been discussing the weather.

"Marty, dear, take a drink." She pointed to his water.

His startled eyes complemented his scowling face nicely. "You know how I hate to be called Marty."

She played dumb. "Oh? Why's that—oh my, yes. I see. Then it would be Marty Blarty. I'm old, dear. Forgetful." How easily she could play that card!

Martin had small eyes, a small mouth, and a big face, and as Missy studied his features she realized what a nightmare it must be for him to find decent looking glasses. Perhaps that's why he always squinted so much. He could never find the right kind of glasses.

He looked over his shoulder and all around the restaurant before saying, "I don't know how you found this out, but it's none of your business."

"Marty, I'm not judging. Listen, it's a nice Chevrolet. If Oliver didn't have the right kind of car at his car lot, then why not go somewhere else?" Everyone knew how very upset Oliver could get when he learned an acquaintance had bought a car elsewhere.

Martin's eyes shifted back and forth. "Look, he's my friend. We've been friends for years. But Gordon MacNamera next county over had the same car for two thousand dollars less, *with* power windows."

"You don't have to explain, dear."

"I've had the car for twenty-four hours, kept it in my garage mostly. How did you know this?"

"That's not why I'm here anyway."

Martin blinked hastily again. He looked down at his untouched food. "Then why are you here? I don't recall seeing you much at this restaurant."

"No, dear. I hate the food. Who in their right mind could eat something called Swamp Mud?"

"Why are you here?"

"To warn you."

"Warn me?"

"Yes. You see, there's a man in town. And he's here to write a book about Skary."

"Oh?"

"Well, we are quite famous."

"True." Martin looked apprehensively at Missy. "What exactly are you warning me about?"

"Well, no doubt he's digging for dirt. Sells better, you know. I just wanted you to know your secret is safe with me."

Just the word *secret* caused his eyes to blink even faster.

"What secret?"

"Oh, you know, that little thing that happened between you and the mayor."

The blood drained from his face. "What…um, what thing?"

Missy was amused. She never knew this little tidbit of information would come in quite so handy. "Oh, you know," she said in a loud voice, "when you covered up his embezzling—"

"*Ssshhhhhh!*" Martin practically screamed.

"What, dear? I'm half deaf."

"Well, I'm not! Lower your voice!"

"Oh. Sorry. Yes. I do sometimes speak a little too loudly."

Martin blotted sweat off his brow. "How'd you know about that?"

"Oh, honey, it's not important. I mean, who cares what a little old lady like me knows, right?"

Martin grumbled. "Yeah, right."

"I'm just saying that this fellow might be poking his nose where it doesn't belong, you see. Wanting information. And I just want you to know that your secret is safe with me." She winked. "Along with where you bought your car. Though you'd better come up with some explanation for that. You know Oliver. He'll ask questions."

Martin breathed heavily and stared at the table. "The mayor is a friend. He had a moment of weakness. He's nearly paid it all back." He glanced up at Missy.

She grinned empathetically. "You don't have to tell me, Marty. I'm the mayor's biggest fan."

Though shaken, Martin seemed to be easing off the ulcer a bit and took a bite of his food.

"Listen," Missy said, "I'll let you get back to your lunch."

"Fine."

Missy smiled down at him as she stood. Yes, Marty Blarty would come in very handy, very soon. But first, while she was here, she had to take care of one little detail.

Marlee's jaw dropped, and she covered her mouth and squealed as if they were sixteen again. "Get outta town!"

Ainsley rolled her eyes a little, glancing up to make sure the customers were all engaged in their food and *not* in her conversation with Marlee. "I can't believe I'm saying it, to tell you the truth."

"Well, he's drop-dead gorgeous."

Ainsley smiled. "You think so?"

"Well, yeah! I mean truthfully, I'd never really noticed before, and that's saying a lot because as you know I'm quite fond of men."

"I was kind of mean to him, though. I was so shocked that he asked me out, I just sort of cut him to the quick."

"But you said you had a nice time over at his house."

"Well, yeah, I mean, I made him burn his dinner. It was the least I could do."

"He obviously still likes you."

Ainsley smiled a little. "Yeah. I'm just not sure how to go about asking him."

"Asking him out?"

"*No.* Asking him to ask me out again."

"Why don't you just ask him out?"

"Marlee, women aren't supposed to ask men out."

"Why?"

"Because...well, they're just not."

"I don't understand."

"It's not proper."

"Well, it works great for me."

"*Anyway,* I don't know what to do."

"Just go over there. Talk to him."

"You make it sound so easy."

"It *is* easy." Marlee looked Ainsley in the eye. "Swallow your pride."

"I'll go visit him tonight. Just to say hello. It can't hurt."

Marlee leaned on the counter. "*Maybe* you could be a little more forthright about your intentions in being there. After all, it took a lot of guts for this guy to ask you out. The least you could do is help him out."

Ainsley hugged her friend. "You're right. Thank you."

She sensed someone behind her and turned. "Oh, hello, Miss Peeple. I didn't see you standing there."

The old woman grinned at her. Her beady, cataract-ridden eyes, a misty and melting blue, seemed bright with mischief. "That's okay, dear. I just need change for a dollar."

"Sure." Ainsley fumbled in her pockets for four quarters. "What brings you by The Haunted Mansion? Don't see you here often."

Missy held out her hand for the quarters. "Well, honey, sometimes even when you're my age you have to venture out and do some things you're not comfortable doing." She gave Ainsley a little wink and hobbled out of the restaurant.

Marlee turned to her and grinned. "Good advice."

She had sat in the car for forty minutes trying to get enough nerve to go up to his house. He was home. She could see him through the windows. Eating dinner. Playing with his dogs. Starting a fire. He seemed comfortable being by himself. Being alone gave her a complex. But he was graceful at it, absurd as that sounded.

By the time she finally decided to get out of her car, night had fallen.

She walked up the hill and knocked. She could hear the dogs scurry to the door, but they didn't bark. The door opened, and he smiled as soon as he saw her.

"Hi."

"Hi," she replied.

"Come in."

"I can't."

He seemed a little amused and crossed his arms. "Oh? Well, if I'm lucky maybe my food will catch on fire, and you'll have to come in and cook me dinner again."

"You've already eaten." He raised his eyebrows and she cleared her throat. "I mean, haven't you?"

"Ainsley, it's freezing. Either come in, or tell me to get my coat and let's go somewhere."

Ainsley smiled. "First of all, I wanted to apologize for what happened to your dinner the other night. If I hadn't shown up on your doorstep unannounced, you wouldn't have burned those pork chops."

"True. It's all your fault. But once again you've shown up unannounced, and I still don't know why." He smiled warmly at her.

"Okay, I wanted to… I just needed to tell you that…or ask you… I mean say that…" She shook her head. "I seem to lose my vocabulary when I'm around you. Maybe because you're a writer."

"It's okay. I seem to speak the same language of incoherence when I'm around you."

She laughed at that. "Wolfe…"

"Yes?"

"The other day, when you came to my doorstep and you asked, well, you asked me...you asked me that question. You know the one." He shook his head. "Okay, I guess I deserve to have to say it out loud." She sighed heavily. "What I'm trying to say, and doing a poor job at it, is that maybe I was too hasty in declining your offer. Your offer to...to...do the date thing."

"Do the date thing?" He chuckled.

"Yes, and maybe I was a little harsh in my decline as well. It's hard enough to get rejected, but to get rejected with a good, old-fashioned scorning is twice as bad. I apologize."

He smiled. "Apology accepted."

"Thank you. And I would also like to say that, well, I'd like to... to...go...on a date with you." A few yards away, the bushes rattled. Ainsley startled. "Raccoons?"

"Probably."

"Yes, well, anyway, I don't think it's right for me to have you ask again. But I'm a lady, and I refuse to ask a man out. So you see, I have a dilemma."

She imagined in the dark that his face was bright with amusement. "I see that you do."

"And I don't exactly know how to rectify it."

Wolfe scratched his forehead. "Well, maybe we should just meet for lunch. Just as friends. Then your problem would be solved, wouldn't it?"

Indeed, it would. "That would be wonderful."

"How is Saturday? I'll pick you up...just to save gas, of course."

"Of course. Sounds nice."

"All right."

"All right." Ainsley held out her hand, and he shook it gently.

"You're freezing. Young woman, you need to warm up." She caught a gleeful twinkle in his eye. "I must insist you come in and sit by the fire, just for a little bit. Let me fix you some hot cocoa."

She gazed into his eyes. They were approachable and sensitive. She looked away but agreed, and he guided her into his house.

In spite of the three scarves, two coats, and two pairs of mittens she wore, Missy Peeple shivered, causing the bushes she sat by to rustle. Thankfully, only a couple of squirrels had noticed. She put the binoculars up to her face again. From her vantage point she could see Miss Parker in the kitchen watching him do something at the stove. They were chatting like old friends.

She'd learned to read lips years ago when she thought she was going deaf (only to find out it was a buildup of wax in her ears), but the distance was too great for her to pick up on any of this conversation. She guessed from the body language, though, that there was more chemistry in that kitchen than in a tenth-grade science lab. The thought irritated her so much she ground her teeth together. At least that stopped the chattering. Her instincts were right. Miss Parker was officially the very first kink in her plan.

A couple small pine trees stood twenty or so yards nearer to the house, and she wondered if she could make it to them without being seen. It was a risky move, but there was, after all, a lot at stake.

She seethed at the thought of how Mr. Tennison had failed to do anything more than make Boo more resolute. She could tell by the way the gentleman left with his coat buttoned tighter than a straitjacket, his head hung lower than his stooping shoulders, that the meeting had been a disaster. What would anybody do without her? At least she'd put Tennison on the right track, but now Wolfe was falling in love with the town saint. This was not good.

Missy knew there was dirty work to be done, and she was going to have to be the one to do it…with the help of a few unsuspecting friends. She rubbed her mitten-clad hands together in the chilly air.

Hunkering down in the bushes, she held her breath and tried to anticipate how much time it would take her to cane her way up the small hill to those two pine trees. Enough loose gravel covered the hill to lead to her everlasting demise. Still, if she could only read those lips…maybe she could rest assured. Maybe Boo was having doubts about the faith. Maybe that's why he'd asked her inside.

She stood up as straight as an old woman with a hunched back could stand, steadied herself with her cane, and let the binoculars rest around her neck. Drawing in a deep breath, she took one step forward.

She froze at the cracking of a limb, and then heard a voice say, "What are you doing?"

Garth Twyne swatted at the sharp twig that was poking the side of his head and kept his eye on Miss Missy Peeple, whose own eyes were wide as a raccoon's. A warm sensation of satisfaction flowed through his body at the thought of what he'd just witnessed.

Her face was powder white, and her mouth was hanging open. Garth finally broke the twig off the tree, threw it to the ground, and crossed his arms authoritatively.

"I asked you a question," he said.

Suddenly he heard Miss Peeple gasp for breath. Her mouth widened, and she clutched her heart. Her eyes were wide with terror and she looked straight at Garth. "No. Don't. Please. Please don't do this to me!"

Garth tried to back up, but there was no place to go. The brush was too thick. "Do what to you?"

"No. No! Stop! Please. Please, have mercy! Don't hurt me!"

Garth shook his head, hushing her with his fingers. "I'm not hurting you. What are you talking about! Hush! Be quiet!"

"Oh! The agony! Oh, please. Please don't kill me! Please!" She lunged forward and grabbed the side of his head. He shoved her backwards.

Garth felt himself grow angry and despondent all at once. Was he dreaming this? What was going on? "I'm not hurting you! What's happening here? Are you having a heart attack or something?"

Suddenly, with one big gasp of air, Missy Peeple tumbled to the ground and rolled on her side. She coughed twice and twitched a little before becoming perfectly still. Garth was paralyzed with fear. What had just happened? Was she dead? Had she just died in front of him?

He glanced around and then leaned over her, trying to feel for a pulse. The old woman was so bundled up he couldn't even find her neck. And what in the world was he supposed to do if he didn't find a pulse? *Revive her?* He knew CPR but had never actually used it, on a human anyway. He'd given mouth-to-mouth to a horse and a dog once, but he gagged at the thought of putting his lips on her old and crusty ones.

Carefully rolling her over onto her back, he tried to see if her chest was moving up and down. He could tell nothing. He knew as time passed, his chances of reviving her dimmed. With an unsteady stomach, he swallowed back the threatening bile and decided he'd better at least give it a try.

He started to bring his mouth to hers when suddenly her eyes flew open and she said, "What? You're going to kiss me now?"

Garth stumbled backward and yelped in fright, shivering next to the small tree. Missy Peeple managed, with great effort, to sit up and dust herself off. Garth felt as if he'd just seen someone rise from the dead.

"Are you crazy?"

She smiled deviously. "A little, dear. Does that scare you?"

"What was that stunt? Faking a heart attack?"

"That wasn't a heart attack. That was you attempting to murder me." With a fat mittened hand, she brushed her strawlike hair out of the way. "I just wanted to make sure we were on the same page."

"What in the world are you talking about?"

"Isn't it clear, young lad? You're out here. I'm out here. We're both hiding in the bushes, and it's not because we're nature lovers." She glanced toward Wolfe Boone's house. "Is it?"

Garth swallowed. "Look, I was just on the way up to see if Ainsley was okay. She's somehow got herself tangled up with that creep, and someone's gotta watch out after her."

Missy Peeple's eyes narrowed. "You expect anyone to believe that?"

Garth frowned and pulled the collar of his coat up, instinctively looking around. "Look, I don't know what you're up to, but—"

"It doesn't matter what I'm up to. What matters is that we have one thing clear here."

"What's that?"

"You never saw me. I never saw you."

Garth scratched his chin. "Okay. Fine."

"And if you decide it might be fun to tell someone you saw me out here, what you saw back there will pale in comparison to what I can come up with. Don't you see? Everyone always believes the little old woman. If I say you tried to harm me, they'll believe *me*. If I say you tried to rob me, they'll believe *me*. And honey, if I can fake death good enough to trick a man who clones pigs, then by golly, you better believe everyone else is going to fall for it."

"Wait a minute," Garth said, his fists in tight balls. "If I supposedly *murdered* you, then you'd be dead. How is a dead woman supposed to tell everyone who her murderer is?"

Miss Peeple smiled and cackled, then slowly opened her mitten. "Like this."

Garth looked at her hand. "Like what?"

"Look harder, dear. Don't you see it?"

"See what?" Garth asked with irritation. He leaned forward to take a closer look. Then he saw it. A few strands of his blond hair.

Her mitten clamped shut and she stuck her hand into the pocket of her coat. "DNA evidence. You should know about DNA, with your pig fiasco and all."

Garth shook his head. "This is absurd. And I didn't clone any pigs." He took a look around again. All was calm and silent. "Besides, I have a logical reason for being here. What I can't imagine is why *you're* here."

"You're so naive," Miss Peeple sneered. "You're here for selfish reasons. I'm here for the good of the—"

The front door opened, and the sound of voices poured over the hill. Before Garth knew what was happening, the feeble old woman in front of him had yanked him to the ground with the strength of a gorilla. After lifting his face out of the dirt, he managed to crawl between two bushes to get a better view. He gasped.

A stinky mitten slapped him in the mouth. "Shush!"

Garth batted her away and hunkered down. There she was, standing next to Boo, both of them laughing like the best of friends. Garth watched carefully as Ainsley hugged Wolfe, then walked down the sidewalk to her car. Garth remained motionless in the shadows, as did Miss Peeple. Ainsley drove away, and then the porch was silent again.

He glanced at Miss Peeple, who was looking at him.

"What?" Garth asked in a harsh whisper.

Her eyes narrowed in quiet satisfaction. In a very light tone she said, "You might come in quite handy after all."

CHAPTER 11

IN A DARK, dusty old room of the community center, long forgotten by everyone but Missy, she sat quietly in a chair, tapping her cane against the creaky wood floors. Alfred Tennison had just left, and she knew she had him on the right track. Driven by greed to write a best-selling book about her little town, he was nearly the perfect tool for all she had in mind to save it. She'd fed him more information, just enough to whet his appetite. Just enough to drive the plan further along. But not enough to give him more power than he should have.

Something continued to bother her though, and as she thumped her cane she tried her best to reason her way through various scenarios. But no amount of brain power could give her the answer she needed to one very simple question:

Who had witnessed to Boo?

Perhaps in the scheme of things it was not all that important, yet it nagged at her in a way that even disturbed her sleep at night. And she was not accustomed to missing her beauty sleep. She raised her fingers to her face and gingerly applied pressure to the bags under her eyes, all the while thinking about who could've done this thing. Who in their right mind would tell the good news to the one person single-handedly responsible for putting Skary, Indiana on the map?

It baffled her further because she knew the townsfolk well, knew what they were and were not capable of. She would have suspected the reverend if she hadn't heard enough of the conversation to know he was as surprised as anyone when Wolfe Boone arrived at his church. And it certainly wasn't Ainsley. She wasn't in the business of even speaking to him prior to his change of heart.

Then *who?*

Her mind shifted back to Ainsley. The town's dear heart was becoming more and more of a liability. What was the girl thinking spending time with this man? Missy knew good and well that if Ainsley Parker was involved, Wolfe Boone would be sure to hear more of the gospel in some form or fashion. She could think of no one in the town who hated what he had done to it more than Ainsley. In fact, she had seemed to be the *only* one who couldn't appreciate what he *had* done for Skary.

And now she was falling for him. This wasn't good. Not at all.

The door creaked, and Missy jumped. She squinted through the dark haze and recognized Oliver Stepaphanolopolis.

"Deary?"

Now Oliver jumped. "Miss Peeple! What are you doing in here?"

"What are you doing?"

"I'm trying to find a mop. Mr. Tetherbaum spilled his coffee again. I thought this was a storage closet." Oliver stepped further in and looked around. "I didn't even know this room was here."

"It's quite old. Nobody uses it anymore. Except me. When I'm… um…meditating."

"I'm sorry to disturb you. I'll get out of your hair."

"Wait a minute," Missy said and beckoned Oliver to come sit by her. He approached with great timidity, as if the room might be haunted.

"It's a little dusty, dear. That's all."

Oliver eyed her. "Don't you live alone? Can't you get this kind of quiet at home?"

"Well, sometimes you just have to get out of the house, if you're an old woman like me, spending so much time there."

Oliver swiped a hand across the seat of the chair across from Missy and then sat.

"Oliver, I suppose you've heard the news. About Boo. That he's, well, converted to the faith."

"Sure. It's going around. I don't know how many people believe it though."

"You know, I wonder who it was who told him."

"Told him what?"

"Told him the good news. Shared the faith. Preached the gospel."

Oliver shrugged. "I dunno." He glanced at Missy, and his eyes widened. "What? It wasn't me!"

"I never thought it was, Oliver. Relax. I'm simply saying that it might be wise of us to find out, don't you think?"

"Why?"

"Oliver, how's your car business?"

"It's doing really well."

"Is that so?"

"Yes. In fact, last year was the best year yet."

"Good for you."

"Do you need a new car?"

"Dear, I haven't driven a car since I reversed mine right into the front porch of Sam Brady's house." The truth was, she'd done it on purpose because Sam had tried to discredit her on a certain little scandalous story about the county commissioner. But when you're seventy-eight, everyone just assumes you're old and don't know what you're doing. She hadn't even gotten a ticket. "No, I don't need a car. I'm just worried."

"About what?"

"Well, about your little business and all. I mean, if Mr. Boone stops writing, and this town becomes nothing more than just a town, I suspect that people won't be buying—well." She looked at Oliver, whose eyes lit slightly with concern. "Anyhow, no use worrying about something that hasn't happened yet. But I am curious, aren't you?"

"About what?"

"Well, if it's a real conversion."

"Oh."

"I mean, if it's not, then he'll keep writing his books and this town will keep flourishing. But if it's real, well, better days may be over." She patted Oliver on the knee. "But no need to worry about that now."

Oliver blinked, as if ridding his eye of some horrible image before him. "I guess if we found the person who witnessed to him, we'd know it was for real. Wouldn't we?"

Missy feigned surprise. "Oh. Well. I guess you're right. You always have been so smart, Oliver. It takes a smart person to sell cars like you do."

He smiled a little. "Thank you. I can go ask Wolfe myself if you want."

"No!"

Oliver jumped. "No? Why?"

"Because dear," she said, "if it's not for real, then he might make something up. We want the truth, don't we?"

"I suppose you are right. Then we'd know for sure."

She glanced at him. "And knowing things can sometimes put a person's heart at ease."

"I could ask around."

"Sure. With subtlety, of course."

"Yeah."

"I mean, we'd hate to start a vicious rumor that it was, indeed, a *hoax*."

"A hoax? You think this is a hoax?"

"Well, isn't that what you're going to find out?"

"Yeah. Right."

She twirled her cane in her hand. "There are a few people in this town who might've done it. Make a list. Check it twice. Let's find out who's been naughty or nice, shall we?"

Oliver swallowed. "And, um, *nice* is what we're looking for, right?"

"Of course," Missy grinned.

He nodded nervously and said, "Okay, well, I guess I'll get going. See if I can find the...the great human being who did this."

Missy touched his arm as he stood to leave and with a gentle wink she said, "And honey, not a word of this leaves this room, you understand. I mean, we'd hate for this poor lad's religion to become a sideshow of some sort. Not everyone has the kind of integrity that we have."

Oliver nodded and then left quickly, and Missy starting tapping her cane nervously again. Oliver was gullible, which was a good thing, but he had a little bit too much of a conscience for Missy's comfort, even if he did sell used cars for a living. Surely he could sell the idea that he was just asking out of gratitude or curiosity.

At any rate, she'd planted a few seeds. She knew by the way Oliver drove around town proudly in his BMW that his business was his life. She just hoped he didn't end up becoming a regret of hers.

Missy clutched her cane and stood to her feet, wobbly for a few long seconds. As she gathered her things, she heard the creaking of the door again. She looked up, but the door to the small conference room in which she was standing had not moved. She heard the creak again, and shivered. Looking around the musty room, she squinted, trying to find something that would make that noise. Then, near the east corner, she found it.

Garth.

There he stood, in the doorway of an old closet, with a huge smile on his face. His hand was raised above his head, and in his hand was something small and shiny. He walked three paces toward her, his hand dropping to his side, and then stopped, only four feet away.

"Hello, Miss Peeple."

Missy tried to sound pleasant. "Why, Garth. What a surprise."

"I bet," he chided. He sounded very amused with himself. "Wondering what I was doing in the closet?"

"No doubt cloning rats."

He narrowed his eyes but still kept his smile. "No. Actually, I was, well…let me just show you." He opened his hand, and there sat a small voice recorder. "So, you see, two can play at this game."

Missy swallowed hard but did not lose her composure. She scratched her nose with one hand and tightened her grip around her cane with the other. "Well, well. What do we have here?"

"I'd venture to say it wasn't an innocent little conversation between two upstanding citizens of Skary. We could listen to the conversation again and decide, if you want."

She glared up at him, baring her yellow, coffee-stained teeth like a dog trying to protect its territory. "What do you want, Garth?"

"The same thing you want, except I'm going to be in charge from here on out. I'm not comfortable with little old ladies bossing me around and accusing me of murder. You can understand."

"I still have a sample of your hair."

"I have a recording that could set off more fireworks than the fourth of July." He patted his recorder. "So I guess we have a problem."

"Don't you think we can work *together* to achieve the same goal, young Garth? I mean, *we're* not the enemy…are we?"

Garth's hardened expression softened as he thought. "I want one thing out of this deal: Ainsley Parker."

Missy Peeple scooted forward and, in a wise elderly way, patted Garth on the sleeve of his coat and said, "Oh, honey, just stick with me, and she's all yours."

Garth tapped his fingers on the recorder as a reminder, then slipped out of the room. Missy let out a breath of frustration. That Garth Twyne. If ever there was a liability. She took a moment to gather herself, then got her mind back on track. The week was still young, and she had much to do, not the least of which was plan a way to let a certain somebody know his daughter was preparing for a forbidden date.

CHAPTER 12

AINSLEY DIDN'T BOTHER to find her slippers as she traipsed across the chilly, creaky wood floor to the bathroom. On cold mornings, the house always seemed even emptier than it was. A few years after her mother died, Ainsley and her father had discussed selling the house and moving into something smaller. Butch, her brother, had already moved away, and Ainsley had hoped to marry soon. Fifteen years later, still unmarried and still at home, she was glad they hadn't decided to sell the house. On cold, empty mornings, she had warm memories of her mother in every corridor of the house. Aunt Gert, in her more vibrant days, had practically lived here too.

Ainsley brushed her teeth and played with her hair, trying to decide exactly how she was going to fix it for her lunch appointment with Wolfe. She didn't want to appear flirty, but she did want to do something special. She spent ten minutes in front of the mirror before she decided to go downstairs and fix her father breakfast.

She hadn't seen him last night—she'd gone to bed early, and he'd apparently come home late—which was probably for the best. She wasn't quite ready to tell her father whom she was having lunch with. She just didn't know exactly how to put it. Her father had managed to run off every guy she'd ever dated, with the exception of the *one* that she wished he would run off. She sighed as she swung her robe over her shoulders and punched her arms through its sleeves.

How exactly was she going to explain that Wolfe wasn't a romantic interest, but that he *could be?* Her father would never understand such an idea, though she might get further with him if she could convince him that they were just friends. However, her father had a very stubborn notion that men and women couldn't possibly be just friends, so she knew that idea would fizzle as soon as it spilled from her mouth.

Perhaps she could express herself with boldness, maturity, and clarity. Her father couldn't run her life forever, after all, and it was high time she stood up for herself and told him how it was going to be. If he didn't like it, too bad!

Of course, she'd tried that approach before, and her sense of obligation always got the best of her. She melted under his demands and caved to his insistence. She stood in her bedroom doorway and felt her head throb. She looked at her watch. Wolfe would be here in four hours, and she was going to have to resolve this long before then.

It had taken her several days to get something else resolved as well. She'd been so angry with Wolfe Boone for so many years that her animosity had become part of her daily routine. Every morning she'd get up, make breakfast, sip her coffee, and dwell on what he'd done to her town. Certainly, a part of her was still unsure who he was. But as much as she hated to admit it, her anger toward him had been something of a twisted comfort. She was definitely out of her comfort zone now.

Ainsley knew one thing for sure: She had to forgive him. She'd been wrong to hold this kind of grudge for so long. God had forced her hand. Either forgive him and go to lunch, or refuse and let him pass on by.

It did help, she had to admit, that he had apparently turned from the dark and seen the light. Only time would tell if it was genuine or not. But in the course of only a few short days, she'd realized just what all that anger had done to her. It had made her cold. Indifferent. Bitter, certainly. And focused on the wrong things.

Friday night, quietly in her bedroom, she had finally knelt and asked God's forgiveness for her grudge. Then with all the might she had in her, she forgave Wolfe for what Skary had become.

She'd slept great.

Ainsley quietly made her way downstairs, hoping her father was still asleep. Maybe he'd sleep past noon, and she could sneak out without him knowing. She tiptoed across the living room toward the kitchen and

glanced backward at the stairs, relief filling her at the idea that she might
have another hour or so alone.

"Sneaking around for a reason?"

Ainsley whirled to the voice. Her father sat at the table, reading his
newspaper and sipping the orange juice she'd squeezed last night while
mulling over the forgiveness issue. She'd squeezed nearly a gallon!

"Daddy! You scared me to death."

His right eyebrow cocked. "Why is that?"

She tightened her robe and swept past him at the table and into the
kitchen. "I was thinking of French toast this morning," she said with a
ring of lightness in her voice. "Is that okay?"

"Fine," he said, but his voice wasn't as light or cheery. He stuck his
nose back in his paper and rattled it around. Ainsley quietly prepared the
eggs and turned on the gas flame underneath a skillet. She wondered if
her father was just tired. He had always been a morning person, and
cheery for the most part. She stole glances at him as she dipped the bread
into the egg batter, trying to decipher his real mood.

"Two or three?"

"Two."

"Blueberry sauce?"

"Yes."

"More orange juice?"

"No."

Ainsley sighed and flipped the first batch of toast in the skillet, careful to make sure the edges were crispy but not burned. When she had
two ready, she put them on the plate, drizzled the sauce over them, and
took them to the table.

"You were out late last night," she said as he folded his newspaper
and found his silverware.

He unfolded his cloth napkin and stared into her eyes. Something
was wrong. He was angry, but she didn't know why.

"Dad?"

He regarded his French toast, but then set his silverware down and threw his napkin onto the table. "Isn't there something you want to tell me?"

This doesn't seem like the right time. "Like what?"

His jaw protruded. "Did you think you could keep something like this from me?"

"Something like *what,* Daddy? I don't know what you're talking about."

"So you're sitting across from me acting as if you have no idea, *lying* to me."

Ainsley felt herself growing angry. "I'm not lying to you about anything! Why don't you just tell me what's got you so upset!"

"All right!" his voice boomed. "You're having an affair with Wolfe Boone!"

Her mouth fell open in disbelief. "How did you—"

"So it *is* true!" he cried in anguish. "How could you do this to me? How could you sit across the table and tell me you have no idea what I'm talking about?"

Ainsley held up her hands. "Wait just a minute. First of all," she said, her heart pounding with so much anxiety she could barely get her words out, "I am *not* having an affair with Wolfe Boone."

Her father eyed her skeptically. "Well, the look I just saw on your face was nothing short of guilt, young lady."

"No, that was not guilt. It was surprise."

"So you're telling me you're not having an affair with Wolfe Boone?"

"Yes. No. I mean…" Ainsley shook her head and tried to figure out what to say. Her father waited impatiently. "I am *not* having an affair with him, Daddy."

Sheriff Parker's chest heaved with relief, and he almost smiled. "I knew it. I knew you weren't." He looked her in the eye. "How could I have believed it? I know my little girl." He winked at her and cut into his French toast.

"But I am having lunch with him in three-and-a-half hours."

His fork rattled against the plate and fell to the floor. He stared at her, his cheek bulging with a wad of toast.

"It's *lunch*," she said. "It's civilized, proper, and perfectly normal. Just a lunch. That's it. Nothing more. Nothing less. Just lunch. Lunch, lunch, lunch." Her rambling belied her air of confidence, and her gaze fell to the table.

Sheriff Parker's hands were flat against the table and he leaned forward, making her look up into his gaze. "Okay, Ainsley. Let's say it is just an innocent lunch. I want to ask you a question. And I want you to answer me honestly."

"I always answer you honestly, Daddy."

"Fine. Did you, or did you not, ask *him* to lunch?"

Ainsley's eyes widened as she tried to remember. Had she asked him? Hadn't she insinuated that *he* ask her out? He asked her out first, but that was on a date, and then she declined, and then changed her mind, and so…so…what was the answer?

"By your inability to speak, I think I have my answer." Sheriff Parker pushed his plate away and stood up, ready to exit to the kitchen. But Ainsley stood too.

"Wait! Don't you move!"

Her father looked surprised. "Why not?"

"Because," she said, "this conversation is *not* finished."

"What more is there to say? First, you lie to me. And now I find out you're asking men out? And not just any man. Wolfe Boone, for Pete's sake!"

"There's nothing wrong with having lunch with someone. And Wolfe is a perfect gentleman, more so than any other man that I've been around."

"How would you know? You're naive, Ainsley! You wouldn't know a criminal if he asked to pick your pockets!"

"Well, whose fault is that? You're the one who has kept me sheltered all these years. You think if you keep scaring them off I'll die an old maid, here to serve you until *your* dying day!"

"That's not true. I was perfectly supportive of your date with Garth. What's wrong with Garth? He's nice, responsible, has a good and decent job—"

"What's *not* wrong with Garth?" Ainsley moaned. "He's nothing I want, Daddy. Why can't you see that?"

Silence covered their exhaustion as they stared at the floor. Finally Ainsley said, "I'm a grown woman. Why can't you accept that? I want to date. I want to get married and have children. But all you want from me is to stay around here and keep you company. I love you, Daddy, but it's not my fault Mom died, and I shouldn't be punished for it."

His eyes filled with sadness as he looked at her. "Is that what you think? I'm punishing you?"

Ainsley's shoulders slumped with fatigue. "It's what it feels like sometimes. I'm suffocating here."

"Then leave," he said, flicking his hand at her, his voice full of hurt. "If you hate it here so much, leave." He turned and walked to the stairs.

"I don't hate it here!" she cried after him. "I love you. I just need space. I need to be able to make my own life."

But he continued to climb the stairs without looking back. After a few seconds, she heard his bedroom door close. Tears streamed down her face, and she kicked herself for her insensitivity. As much as she wanted to express her feelings, she didn't want to hurt her dad in the process.

She cleared the breakfast dishes. "Just leave." She hoped he didn't mean it. Or did she? How could she make him understand that she needed a life? A love of her life? *Just leave.* She intended to do just that. But those words hovered in her mind as if begging to be reexamined.

As she scrubbed the skillet under hot water, she wondered how in the world her father had found out about her lunch with Wolfe. And how did he know that she asked him to ask her? Had he been following her? He wouldn't do such a thing.

She dried the skillet and put it away. Pouring herself a glass of orange juice, she sat at the breakfast table and rummaged through the basket of emotions inside her. She was still excited to see Wolfe, to have lunch with him. But a cloud hung over the day and would follow her every moment.

She prayed for a way to make this better, make it right. But there was no answer back, only the occasional thump of her father's footsteps, minding his business upstairs.

CHAPTER 13

WOLFE HAD CERTAINLY not been on many dates in his lifetime, and he'd only been in love vicariously through one of the characters in his novels. Even so, he admitted to himself that it was a bit strange to go looking for the reverend thirty minutes before his lunch with Ainsley.

As Wolfe made his way around the small church, he found the doors locked. The church appeared to be empty. He sighed and leaned against one of its stone walls. His knees wobbled at the thought of seeing Ainsley again. The more he knew her, the more he liked her. He'd written a lot of scary things in his life, but love scared him the most.

"Wolfe?"

The reverend stood at the corner of the church, with what looked like a litter scoop in his hand. "Reverend!"

"My goodness, what a pleasant surprise!"

"What are you doing?"

The reverend stooped next to a small fountain by the wall of the church. "Scooping up cat droppings."

"Oh. I like the fountain," Wolfe said, having never noticed it before.

"That silly thing? What a mess that was. We spent a lot of money on it a few years back. Thought it would add to the serenity of the sanctuary. Unfortunately, all it did was make people need to pee during the service. I'd never seen so many people come and go during my sermons. By the grace of God I finally figured out what the problem was, and so we moved it outside. Now it seems to be a nice bathroom stop for all these cats."

Wolfe laughed. "Well, that's certainly a story."

"What brings you by, young man?"

"Not much. Just…uh…" He avoided the reverend's quizzical look. "I'm going to lunch."

"Really? Well, I'm starving. Let's go eat! Haunted Mansion okay?"

Wolfe shuffled his feet in the dirt. "I meant that…well…"

"Good heavens, silly me!" the reverend said with a wave of his hand. "I'm sorry. I'm sitting here assuming you want to go to The Haunted Mansion, and here you are trying to leave that world behind. I'm sure the last place you want to go is a restaurant that likes to pretend ketchup is blood." The reverend chuckled. "You know, I've lived here so long, I just go down there and don't think much about what I'm eating. I guess you can't if you're going to eat something called Road Kill." He shook his head. "I'm convinced an eight-year-old boy came up with that menu! Well, how about the onion burger joint by the post office?"

Wolfe smiled and thought about what a gentle heart this man had. If only his could be as humble and good. "Reverend, I can't go to lunch with you."

"Oh?"

"I'm going to lunch with Ainsley."

"You are?" the reverend asked with excitement. "My goodness, that's wonderful news!" He then frowned. "So why are you here?"

Wolfe laughed. "I'm not exactly sure. I just needed some…encouragement, I guess. Some guidance. It's been awhile since I've, well, you know…"

The reverend winked. "Me too, son. Me too. Do you have it all planned out?"

"Yes," he smiled. "Down to every last detail."

"Well, throw that out the window because women have a way of messing things like that up." He grinned. "Just as long as you're flexible, that's all I'm saying. They like to be treated like queens, pampered, made a fuss over, but on their own terms and by their own book."

"Okay."

"Be yourself. We men think we know what women want us to act like, but in the end, it's just plain old us that they fall in love with, as scary as that sounds." The reverend stared into the sky as if collecting the thoughts he had placed there. "And just relax. Have fun. Enjoy her company."

Wolfe's cheeks flushed at the thought of spending time alone with her. "I can do that."

"Good. Is that what you're wearing?"

Wolfe glanced down at his flannel shirt, faded jeans, and leather boots. "Uh...yeah."

The reverend slapped him on the back. "Good. It's perfect."

The morning hours passed slowly for Ainsley. She and her father avoided each other as if they each carried the flu bug. It hurt Ainsley to be in this turmoil with her father, yet she had to stand her ground. It was time she lived her own life. Her aunt would want this, and so would her mother.

She knew where her father's protectiveness came from, and respected him for it...loved him for it. For most of her life he'd been her father *and* mother, a protector yet a surrogate. And though now it suffocated her to no end, she had to admit that she depended on a certain part of it to make her life safe. She shook her head at the thought of her lunch with Wolfe. This was definitely not "safe." Her emotions, heart, and mind all seemed to be speaking a different language.

After thirty minutes inside her closet, she emerged with a long silk skirt with muted florals that matched a wonderfully soft cotton turtleneck. She chose her dark leather boots and decided to pull her hair back away from her face, but not put it on top of her head. She clipped it back and let a few loose locks hang around her cheeks.

Glancing in her vanity mirror, she noticed Thief had come in through the cat door her father had insisted on. He felt like such an intrusion, and she frowned at him as he hopped onto her bed and observed.

She turned her attention back to her tasks, waffling over whether to wear makeup. She finally chose a soft blush, a neutral eye shadow, and clear lip gloss. She stared at herself when she was finished. She actually looked like a sophisticated woman.

Her eyes lingered on her perfume bottle. It was actually her mother's, a rare scent from Asia that her father had brought home after the war, years before Ainsley was born. Her mother only wore it on special occasions, and after all these years half the bottle remained. She clicked her tongue, trying to decide. Maybe just a little on her wrists. Or perhaps at the nape of her neck, too.

She folded her arms and sat down heavily on the stool in front of her vanity, blowing out air as she thought this through. She imagined Marlee laughing at her, and she scolded herself for being so conflicted over a little perfume. Still, was this an appropriate time to wear it? She'd never worn it in public, though occasionally after her evening shower she would put a little on, mostly because it reminded her of her mother.

"Forget it," she mumbled, discouraged by the thought of how long it took her to decide *not* to wear any. Taking in a view of herself from all angles, she decided there was nothing more she could do but go downstairs to wait.

She passed the time by making her list of people to invite for Thanksgiving, but after that, it still left her with fifteen minutes to wait. To her relief, her father had left the house an hour earlier. She'd had visions of him sitting on the front porch cleaning his shotgun when Wolfe pulled up to get her.

She was cleaning the kitchen counters when she heard a car door shut. Her heart stopped. It was time. He was here! A little early, but better early than late. She checked her hair in the oven door, smoothed her skirt, and fanned herself to try to keep the perspiration from dampening her freshly powdered skin.

Her heart started beating a little more normally, and she stood in the kitchen, gripping the edge of the counter. She closed her eyes, smiled, and waited for the knock. A few seconds later it came, and Ainsley turned to the front door, said a prayer for peace, and then went to answer it, as excited as she had ever been.

Wolfe stood, slightly amused and slightly bewildered, as the reverend rambled on about how to treat a woman. He'd assumed the man was an expert on all things spiritual, but the reverend's godly passion for women came as a surprise.

In the minutes that passed, Wolfe learned about the reverend's wife, who had died many years earlier. But the reverend still glowed in the face when he talked about her and told in great detail of how he had won over her heart.

Wolfe glanced at his watch, trying not to be too obvious. He wanted neither to make a bad first impression on Ainsley nor to be rude to Reverend Peck. The advice was good, the timing...bad.

"And you see," the reverend was saying, "it's hard to understand a woman. They seem fickle, and yet they are such deep, feeling creatures, moved by things men are hardly aware of. They're notorious for being chatterboxes and jumping from one topic to another, but in their minds it all makes sense, and if you concentrate hard enough, it will make sense to you too. It's because they're emotional, and—"

"Um, Reverend?"

"Yes?"

"Sorry to interrupt, but it's time."

"For...?"

"To go get Ainsley."

"Oh!" He grabbed Wolfe's shoulder. "And they hate it when we're late!"

Wolfe glanced at his watch again, gulping back the realization that he didn't have quite as much time as he thought. "I better get going."

The reverend looked him in the eyes. "She's a lucky girl to have a man like you taking her out."

Wolfe's anxiety morphed into surprise. He hadn't ever thought of it that way, but it sure felt good to hear.

"Good luck," the reverend said, waving him off. Wolfe walked around the corner of the church, where the wind picked up, its chill flushing his cheeks. Thank goodness it was cold. He needed something to explain the flush that would be there in spite of the wind.

"Red roses. Your favorite."

Ainsley's jaw dropped five inches as she stared at the caller on her doorstep. "What are you *doing* here?"

"What does it look like?" Garth asked, shaking the flowers as if she hadn't noticed them. "There's a dozen here, all freshly cut, wrapped in a bouquet, just the way you like 'em. And I don't have to tell you, a dozen red roses ain't cheap."

Ainsley closed her eyes and shook her head, hoping she was just imagining this. But he was still there when she opened her eyes, grinning and gawking like the buffoon he was. "Why are you bringing me flowers?"

Garth stepped inside uninvited, and he quickly scoped the rooms as if looking for something. He followed Ainsley to the kitchen. "Well, if I remember correctly, my pumpkin, we didn't get a chance to finish our date the other night, with your aunt's untimely death and all, so I figured it's a nice day, a little cold, but a nice day, and I can keep you warm in a blizzard, honey, so we don't have to worry about that."

Ainsley's eyes darted to the clock in the kitchen. *Please, Wolfe, be late!* She turned to Garth, trying to play it cool. The last thing she wanted was for Garth to suspect anything. He had a horrible way of sticking his nose in where it didn't belong.

"The flowers are nice," she said, reaching under the cabinet for a vase. She filled it with water and took the flowers from him, tore off the paper, and dunked the stems into the vase with little care. "But I can't do anything today, Garth. You really should call first, you know."

"What could you be doing on a Saturday afternoon?" he said, leaning against the counter and grinning at her as though his smile just might change her life.

She stared hard at him. "Garth, it's none of your business what I do." She tried to soften her expression as best she could. "The flowers are lovely. You're right, I love roses. But I'm just going to have to ask you to leave now."

His expression turned awkwardly concerned, and Ainsley sensed there was something more going on behind those innocent-looking eyes than she realized. "Is that any way to treat a man who just spent forty bucks on roses for you?"

"First of all," Ainsley retorted, "everyone knows your cousin works for the flower shop and you get all your roses half off." Garth's expression proved the accusation true. "Second of all, Garth, you must know that a lady likes time to prepare for such things, and that your just coming over unannounced isn't proper."

Garth shifted to lean against the wall opposite the kitchen counter, with his arms crossed against his chest and his legs crossed at the ankle. "You look ready to me. In fact, is that lipstick you're wearing, Ainsley Parker?"

"Lip gloss," Ainsley said defensively.

"Does your father know about that?"

"Garth!" Just saying his name with such sharpness took her breath away. "I am a grown woman, if you haven't noticed, and I'm perfectly capable of making decisions on my own. Sometimes I am *sure* the two of you came from the same gene!"

Garth smirked, which made Ainsley even angrier. He had something up his sleeve, and it was eating at her that she couldn't figure it out. Usually he was so transparent.

Knock, knock.

Ainsley whirled to the door, irritated to notice Garth still staring at her, his smirk even more prominent. "Expecting someone?" he asked.

Ainsley took a deep breath. How was she going to handle *this?* All her daydreaming about going to the door when Wolfe arrived had been shattered by Garth. She glared at him, though now he was looking toward the door.

Knock, knock.

"Want me to get it?" he asked, pitching a thumb toward the direction of the door.

"No, Garth, I don't," she snapped, marching past him. She glanced back once, hoping he'd disappear into the floral wallpaper, a literal wallflower, but he was still there, eyes wide with anticipation.

She opened the door.

"Hi," Wolfe said, smiling. For the first time she noticed he had dimples. They were long and lean, reaching from the middle of his cheek to below his chin.

"Hi there," she said, managing the most relaxed smile she could. But she realized she wasn't doing very well when his expression turned to worry.

"Is everything okay? Am I late?"

"You're right on time." Ainsley realized she had no choice but to invite him in and hope Garth got a clue and left. "Come on in."

She escorted him through the door and down the small hallway that led right to the kitchen, where Garth was now standing by the vase of flowers he'd brought in. She watched as Wolfe regarded him with surprise.

"Hi," Wolfe said, glancing at Ainsley.

"Wolfe, this is Garth Twyne. Garth, Wolfe Boone."

"Well, if it ain't the town celebrity!" Garth drawled, holding out a hand for Wolfe to shake. "And I don't mean the whole Thief incident."

"Nice to meet you," Wolfe replied, shaking his hand but still looking perplexed. Ainsley cleared her throat.

"Garth stopped by for a moment and was just leaving," Ainsley said.

"To bring her flowers," Garth added, pointing to the obvious bouquet sitting on the counter. "She likes roses—long-stemmed."

Wolfe smiled pleasantly but began to look very uncomfortable. Ainsley's own blood pressure rose, and she felt her ears burn.

"Garth, thanks again for the flowers. It was nice to see you."

"Oh. I guess that means you two want to be alone."

Ainsley thought she might have the strength to sling the jerk over her shoulder and carry him out herself. "Garth..."

He shrugged and grinned. "So this is a…date?"

"We're going to lunch," Ainsley said.

"A lunch date?"

"Garth, I just wish you would—"

"You see, Garth," Wolfe interrupted, "it's actually like this: We've been seeing each other for a long, long time, and we knew sooner or later we'd get caught, didn't we, snookems?" He wrapped his arm around Ainsley's shoulder. "And it's really better this way, because now we can be out in the open and tell everyone of our glorious love for each other. We've actually been married for three years now, and I'm just here to celebrate our anniversary, so yes, I guess you could call this a lunch date, but it's so…so…so much more than that." He winked at Ainsley, who found herself blushing and smiling. Wolfe turned back to Garth and smiled pleasantly.

Garth's eyebrows were straight across his face. "You're joking."

Wolfe shrugged. "Well, I do make my living in fiction, but you never know, do you?"

Garth scratched his head and glanced at Ainsley, who realized she was beaming.

"I better get going," Garth said heavily.

"So soon?" Ainsley said lightly, trying to suppress a laugh.

"Enjoy the flowers." He walked out the front door and slammed it behind him.

Ainsley burst out laughing, and Wolfe looked very amused himself. "That was fabulous!" Ainsley wailed. She couldn't remember the last time she'd laughed so hard. Wolfe was laughing too.

"Who was that guy?" he asked.

Ainsley gathered herself enough to answer. "He's the town vet. You don't take your dogs to him?"

"Oh…" Wolfe said. He shook his head. "No, I use a guy named Dr. Pratt over in Manchester. I adopted the dogs from him."

"Well, that's probably wise. As you can see," she said with a sigh.

Wolfe glanced at the flowers. "He seems to like you a lot."

"He's been in love with me since junior high and can't seem to take a hint." She looked Wolfe in the eyes. "I'm sorry he was here. He just dropped in. I was horrified. It must've looked really bad."

"No," he said gently. "*He* looked really bad. It was obvious what he was up to." He shifted his feet. "I hope I didn't step over the line with what I said. I just couldn't stand that guy treating you like that."

Ainsley shook her head and laughed. "It was great. It might start a rumor or two, but I'm up for a little adventure right now." She took in a deep breath, reassuring herself of that statement. "Let me get my coat and we can go."

She went to the coat closet and picked out her winter wool, but her mind was on Wolfe and the way he had taken up for her. His sense of humor only added to his allure.

He helped her with her coat and said, "Ready to go?"

She smiled and said, "Yes. But just give me one more second." She trotted up the stairs, went hastily to her room, and without a moment's hesitation, dabbed perfume on her wrists *and* the nape of her neck.

CHAPTER 14

INGRID'S, AN AUTHENTIC German restaurant thirty miles south of Skary, was well known in these parts, though Ainsley had never visited it before. She had no reason to travel thirty miles by herself to go eat German food, although she'd wanted to many times.

"This is great," Ainsley said as their waitress, a plump, older woman, seated them in a booth near the corner. "I've heard so much about this place."

Wolfe looked up at the waitress. "Frida, this is my friend, Ainsley Parker."

Frida gushed with joy. "Oh! My! What a lovely face! Such lovely hair!" She winked at Wolfe. "Quite a good pick, my dear boy." She pinched him on the cheek and Wolfe laughed, but didn't seem to be as embarrassed as Ainsley, who felt her "lovely face" burn with heat.

"Is Kaiser here today?" Wolfe asked.

"Dear heavens, yes, my son! When is he *not* here?" She fanned herself with her order pad and placed a chubby hand on one round hip. Ainsley loved her accent. She suspected Frida had lived in America awhile, but she still held on to that deep, guttural German accent. "He cooks and cooks as if this were his only life. Does he remember he has a wife? Two children? No! As long as the jägerbraten is perfect," she said, kissing her fingertips, "then all is well, eh?"

Wolfe smiled at Ainsley. "That's the house specialty. Prime rib topped with peppers, mushrooms, and tomatoes."

"Ah," Ainsley mused.

"So I bring you both a drink of water?"

Wolfe looked at Ainsley, who nodded. "Yes, thank you."

Frida thumped her heavy fingers against a menu on the table. "You take your time, order what you like." She looked at Ainsley. "Trust him. He knows what is good here." She laughed and went to get the drinks.

"You come here a lot, I gather," Ainsley said.

"Yeah. One of my favorites. It's because of restaurants like these that I've never learned to cook!"

They laughed. "German food can be hard to cook. It takes a lot of time and patience."

His eyebrows rose with curiosity. "Really? You've cooked German food before?"

Ainsley shrugged unassumingly. "I've been known to cook a Wiener-schnitzel or two in my time."

He smiled warmly at her, and Ainsley found herself needing that water to have something to do with her hands. Frida arrived as if on cue. "Here you go. Now, have we decided what we will eat today?"

"We haven't even looked at the menu yet, Frida," Wolfe admitted.

Frida's eyes glowed with some mysterious joy. "Oh! That's a good sign!"

Ainsley opened her menu to hide her flushed cheeks and stared at the extensive list as Frida walked away.

"Wow. This is wonderful," she said. "What's good here?"

"Everything. And I mean it. I haven't tasted a thing yet that I didn't like."

Ainsley glanced up at him. "Well, you're not making this any easier."

They were quiet for a moment as each looked over the selections. Ainsley tried to concentrate on the menu, but she could hardly stop thinking about Wolfe. She peeked over the top of the menu to study his features. He had smooth, light olive skin, deep-set brown eyes, and bone structure that begged to be admired. Ainsley sensed he was a little self-conscious of his great smile. He tended to close his mouth more than laugh openly, as if he didn't want to draw attention to the deep dimples carved into his cheeks.

She gasped a little as he looked up, and she realized she'd been staring at him as though he were dessert. She cleared her throat and sipped her water.

"Have you decided?" he asked.

She'd decided he was amazingly good looking, but hadn't gotten too much further. "Would you order for me?"

He laughed a little. "Really?"

"Sure," she shrugged.

"You just don't seem to be the type of woman who likes men to order for her."

"I don't?" *He's good.*

He tilted his head, studying her. "You're an amazing cook, and I can't imagine anyone knowing more about food than you do."

"I trust you. At least at Ingrid's. In your own kitchen, now that's another story."

He laughed, and his dimples showed. She liked that she made him laugh. He nodded and said, "Okay. I'll order."

Frida returned with a little twinkle in her eye and a self-satisfied smile on her face. "Well, dears, what have you decided?"

Wolfe closed his menu. "We'll start off with your gulaschsuppe."

Frida scribbled. "Fine choice."

"And two orders of bratwurst, with roasted potatoes and red cabbage."

"Very good." Frida left and Wolfe turned his attention to Ainsley.

"So," he said, "I guess this is where we find out a little more about each other."

Through the soup, Ainsley's whole perception of Wolfe Boone continued to change. He'd been merely a token presence in the town for so long, and an object of contempt for her. Sadly, she'd never much thought about him as even human, and as he told the tales of his life, she regretted these facts more and more.

She learned his mother was British (and that Wolfe was her maiden name) and his father half Scandinavian. This accounted for his slight accent, large frame, and chiseled features. Both had died ten years before in a plane crash, a devastating time for Wolfe. His mother especially had been such a source of encouragement during a painful childhood in which he sought to be included yet felt different from everyone else. He explained how his vivid imagination and deep sensitivities made for ridicule from some of his classmates. His mother had encouraged him to write his feelings, and with that came a new world of imagination that lifted him out of despair.

"So what made you decide to write horror?" Ainsley asked. She hated the way the question sounded, and there was no hiding her motives, but she had to know. At what point did all this fertile imagination turn dark?

He explained that he liked the element of surprise, and that at first he'd written mysteries, but then his boyishness got the best of him. As he grew into an adult, he explained, "The monsters came out of the closet and from under the bed and leapt into the corridors of my mind. Unspeakable fears lurk there for all of us." When he sought publication, the horror was what sold, and he banked on the fears of humanity, perhaps not consciously realizing the dangerous potential of making a monster of himself.

Ainsley listened with fascination, barely realizing the bratwurst had arrived. She thought back on her perceptions of him all these years, marveling at how much had changed—at least in her mind—in just a few short days.

"Try it before it gets cold," he said, pointing his fork in the direction of her dish.

"Oh." Ainsley looked down. She hardly had an appetite, but the food looked good. She took a bite. It was delicious. She smiled warmly. "Very good."

"That means a lot coming from you. Tell me, how did you get so interested in cooking?"

Ainsley cut her bratwurst into small, bite-size pieces. "Well, when my mom died, I learned to do a lot of the cooking and cleaning. And my dad wouldn't let me watch soap operas, so I started reading cookbooks, and then I got to know Martha Stewart."

"It's a good thing."

Ainsley gasped. "She says that!"

"I know. That's why I said it."

"Oh." She chuckled. "How do you know she says that?"

"Doesn't everyone know what Martha's catch phrase is?"

"You'd be surprised at what people *don't* know," Ainsley said somberly.

"Like what?"

"Well, for example, her maiden name is Kostyra, she grew up in Jersey City, and she started all this with a catering business, and that's what started the Stewart Empire, as some call it."

Wolfe laughed. "Well at least she still has a few of her fans left."

Ainsley didn't know what that meant. She probably sounded crazy for liking Martha so much. She shook her head. "I probably sound foolish."

Wolfe cleared his throat. "Hey, you're talking to a guy that makes his living off of trying to convince people there are ghosts in their closets."

She paused, then said, "I'm glad you brought me here. This is great food. And…great company."

"Well," he said with a twinkle in his eye, "the day's not over yet."

Directly across the street from Ingrid's, a lone car sat in an abandoned lot. And inside was a weeping woman.

"Why? Why must my heart break so?" she wailed. She clutched in her hands two books. One was a copy of *Black Cats.* She'd already read it five times. In the other was a copy of *Southern Desires,* the newest book by famed romance novelist Penelope Carrington.

Two figures came out of Ingrid's, and though she couldn't see them clearly, she knew who they were. Her chest heaved, but then she managed to gather herself a little. She wiped at the mascara beneath her eyes with a tissue and studied the picture of the voluptuous woman on the front cover of *Southern Desires.*

"If Lacey Steele can win back the love of her life, so can I," Melb Cornforth whispered.

Oliver had been mulling over all that Missy Peeple had told him to do when he decided to take a lunch break. The Haunted Mansion's special of the day was Grave Dirt—ground beef sautéed in onions, piled with marinated mushrooms, and topped off with a daisy.

He'd spent much of the week trying to find out who had witnessed to Boo. He'd made a list of suspects and began making inquiries. He had not gotten far. When he confronted Franny, the organist at church, she thought he was trying to sell her a car. When he talked to Dustin at the bookstore (a long shot, but worth a try), he left with three vampire novels and a book on the history of haunted houses. One by one his list was shrinking. But his stomach was not. So lunch it would be.

From his table Oliver studied Marlee Hampton and decided she might be someone who had witnessed to Boo. He'd seen her at church last Easter, and she *did* like to talk a lot. He would ask her about it when she returned with his Vampire Soda. Oliver looked around the room for other possibilities, and his eyes landed on Melb Cornforth, two tables over, eating Grave Dirt as well! She looked beautiful, though a little sad. He was trying to decide whether to go say hi when Marlee returned with his drink.

"Here you go," Marlee said.

Oliver scratched his chin. How should he approach it? He remembered his need to be subtle. Perhaps…yes…perhaps he should act as if *he* needed converting. Just to see what she'd do. Brilliant!

"Marlee, I'm…lost."

Marlee smacked her gum and regarded Oliver with concern. "You're at The Haunted Mansion restaurant, Oliver. You know, where you usually get the Bacon Booger with a side of Creepy Corn, except on Saturdays when you get either Grave Dirt or Road Kill." She chewed the tip of her pencil then said, "But hey, if you want to try something new, our other special today is the Ham from Hell."

Oliver blushed a little, shook his head, and said, "No. I'll take Grave Dirt. Extra 'shrooms."

She smiled and wrote it down.

"Marlee?"

"Yes?"

"I'm...when I said I was lost...I meant...searching."

"For what, your wallet? Do you, or don't you, have money to pay for the meal, Ollie?"

Oliver swallowed and tried to sip his soda casually. "No, what I mean is...I might be, um, you know..." He sucked in air, feeling a trickle of sweat at the edge of his hairline. "I'm unhappy in life. I need something more."

"Buy a car."

"I own a car lot, Marlee. Not *material* things."

"*Ohhhhh.*" Marlee's eyebrows rose, and she crossed her arms, eyeballing Oliver with great interest. "Oh. Oh. Oh. Oliver Stepaphanolopolis, you dog. I had no idea."

Oliver's expression grew sheepish. "Oh. Well, um...it's an easy thing to hide, I guess. I've been living a lie."

"I'll say," Marlee exclaimed. "You come in here at least three times a week and I never suspected a thing."

He smiled a little. "You have probably seen me pray over my food, haven't you? I was just faking it."

Marlee scooted into the booth across from Oliver. "So what you're saying is, when you bowed your head over your food, you were thinking of me?"

Oliver looked over at Melb, who *still* hadn't noticed he was sitting there. "Uh...I was thinking of how empty my life is. How much I need the truth. How much I'm missing in my life. How lonely I am."

Marlee's hand cupped her chest right over her heart, and her head tilted to the side with an expression of pity. "Oh, Ollie. I had no idea. I wish you would've said something sooner."

Oliver leaned across the table. "Marlee, tell me then, how? How do I go about...making my life complete?"

Marlee's eyes teared up. "Are you saying...I complete you?"

Oliver frowned. No, he wasn't saying *that.* "Can you help me?"

"Of course I can," Marlee said with great care in her eyes. "All you have to do is ask."

Oliver tried to suppress his anxiousness. Hadn't he *just* asked? What was it with this woman? Did he have to cuss like a sailor before she realized she might need to dig into some religious terms? "Okay, then I'm asking, Marlee. What must I do?"

"Just ask," she said again, her hand still across her heart.

His eyes narrowed, trying to find out exactly what she was missing. Maybe she hadn't heard him right. He tried again. "Marlee, what must I do?"

Her hand dropped from her heart and her shoulders slouched a little. "Ollie, are you deaf? Ask! Just ask!"

"I am asking!"

"You keep saying 'what must I do'?"

"And you keep saying, 'Just ask.'"

Silence hovered over the table for a moment as they both stared at each other. Finally Marlee said, "Oh my gosh! You've never... This is your first time to..." She gasped and blushed. "Oliver, I'm sorry. This must be humiliating."

Oliver bit his lip. Well, it was confusing at the very least. He shrugged. Marlee was still looking at him with empathetic eyes. "Marlee, I'll ask one more time...what must I do to be saved?"

She grinned and said, "Oh, that's so sweet. I've never heard it put like that, but if that's how you feel most comfortable saying it, then, okay, Oliver Stepaphanolopolis, I *will* go out with you."

"What?"

"Shocked that a girl of my beauty would say yes, Oliver? You should have more confidence in yourself, but frankly, most men don't put it quite as dramatically as being saved...they usually just say, 'Will you go out with me?'"

The palms of his hands dampened as if he'd just soaked them in a tub of water. He felt the blood drain from his face, and his toes started to tingle. "No...no, I meant...Marlee...I'm sorry, I meant..."

Her face bunched up with protest. "You meant *what?*"

"I was trying to…I mean…I wasn't—" Oliver's stomach lurched.

"Are you dumping me? You just asked me out!"

"But I—"

"What a freak!" She stood. Everyone turned to watch, including Melb. "What are you, some kind of freak? You freak! You *freak!*"

"Marlee…shush!" He waved his hands for her to sit down.

"Did you *not* just sit here and tell me you were lost…and that you were in need of someone to fulfill your life…and that you were searching for meaning…" She gestured toward the crowd. "That you were *lonely?*"

"Well, yes…" Oliver caught Melb's interested eyes. "No…"

"That you need a *savior?!*"

He glanced back at Marlee. "Yes, but—"

"What do I look like? Mad Cow Meatloaf?!"

A low murmur swept through the restaurant. Oliver looked up at Marlee, whose eyes were wide, and whose arm was still flung out into the air. She waited, as if she actually expected a reply.

Almost too afraid to answer, Oliver muttered, "No."

Her hands dropped, and she stared down at him with disgust. "I've got customers waiting." She stomped off, and Oliver slid down in his booth. He breathed a sigh of relief, at least thankful the dramatics were over. He glanced one more time over at Melb, who was trying unsuccessfully not to stare. Oh! He'd just ruined everything! How was he supposed to ask Melb out now that she'd seen him apparently ask Marlee out?

He pulled out the list from his breast pocket and a pen from his pants pocket, then drew a line through a name at the top. He knew one thing for sure. Marlee Hampton *was not* the culprit.

CHAPTER 15

THE MAYOR TREMBLED as he paced the slick wood floors of his mayor's mansion, which wasn't more than three thousand square feet but had a gaudy exterior to make it seem like something special. Missy studied him for a moment to determine his state of mind. She never minded gazing at the mayor. No one knew how long she'd loved this man. For years she had plotted and plodded her way closer to his heart. Now she had him right where she wanted him. Weak. Vulnerable. And needing a shoulder to cry on. Not to mention someone to save his bacon. Plus she was saving the town of Skary at the same time. Her brilliance was amazing.

As was her timing. Missy knew Alfred Tennison hadn't been gone from this house for more than thirty minutes when she dropped in for a chat. He'd spilled the beans to a woman he trusted, thanks to years of slightly questionable tactics.

"Mayor, you're distraught."

"Of course I'm distraught!" he said. "Who wouldn't be! " He sat on his leather couch and buried his face in his hands. "Who would've told that man of this? Who? I didn't think anyone knew!"

Missy joined him on the couch. "Do you really think the town will take it as hard as you imagine they will?"

He shook his head and stared at the carpet. "It will devastate them. And humiliate me. Not to mention put Martin in an awkward position. I'm ruined."

"Not so fast, deary. There is yet hope."

"Hope? What kind of hope? A man claiming to be Wolfe Boone's editor is here writing a story about Skary and digging up all its dirt. All its buried skeletons. Of which mine is the dirtiest skeleton of all. How can I stop him? He already knows."

Missy's voice was low and soothing. "Do you know *why* he's writing this book?"

"He said people would be interested in our little town."

"No."

"No?"

"No. Dear Mayor, he's writing this book because he's lost Wolfe Boone as a writer, and he needs the money."

"Lost Wolfe Boone?"

"Surely you've heard." Missy watched his eyes. It seemed to register, ever so slowly. "Yes, you see, Boo has found the faith and therefore, we presume, will stop writing horror novels."

"And?"

"Don't you see? If Wolfe were to return to writing horror novels, then Mr. Tennison wouldn't have to write a tell-all book about Skary. Life would be back the way it was...the way it should be. For him. For Skary."

She saw by the mayor's eyes that he was starting to catch on. "Why would he go back to writing horror novels?" he asked as he turned away, pretending to be interested in something on his bookshelf.

"Oh, dear, I don't know. There are many reasons people backslide."

"Backslide?"

"Why sure. It means—"

"I know what it means."

"Some enter into sin. Others grow bored. For some it's just a passing phase." She paused, letting these suggestions settle a bit before saying, "And for some, well, the burden becomes too difficult."

He turned back. "Burden."

"Why certainly. Thou shalt not covet. Cut off your hand if it makes you stumble. Forgive others a bazillion times. Things like that. You know, Mayor, the things *you and I* take seriously."

One of the mayor's eyebrows rose with steely determination. "Yes, I see what you mean."

She grinned at him while studying his picture-perfect features. "I thought you would."

CHAPTER 16

A FEW DAYS had passed since their lunch, but not one of them without a phone conversation with Wolfe. She felt as if she were in high school again. They'd had long conversations, sometimes about nothing in particular. She'd lie on her bed, feet in the air, her eyes closed, thinking of what he might be doing while talking to her.

They'd agreed by mid-week to go out again on Friday. They stopped for a quaint lunch at a small café just outside town that Ainsley adored. Wolfe said the rest of the date was a surprise. After lunch, she got into his car, and to her astonishment, they drove to a movie theater.

"A movie?"

"Yeah." He cut the Jeep's engine and quickly got out of the car, nearly hopping over the hood to open her door before she could. "Here you go."

"Thanks," Ainsley said, looking up at the kiosk. She hadn't been to a movie in ages. In fact, she never even knew anymore what movies were playing. She watched Wolfe close the car door, wondering if the movie would be a romance. Or maybe a historical drama. Her heart warmed at the idea of how much fun she was having. She couldn't remember the last time she felt this way. And she was glad she decided to wear the perfume again.

"It's turned out to be a beautiful day," he said. "Maybe going inside a dark movie theater isn't the best idea."

"It's perfect. What movie are we going to see?"

She noticed his Adam's apple bulge slightly. "It's called *Bloody Thursday*."

Ainsley's bright eyes dimmed a little. "Um. It sounds kind of familiar. Is it a war movie?"

"No," he admitted. He was second and third and fourth guessing himself, though something inside told him to stay on course. It was going to be painful, but it had to be done.

"Oh. Well, it sounds a little...bloody."

"Not so much. A little, perhaps."

"Wolfe, what's going on?"

He steered her toward the ticket booth. Only a few people mingled around. "It's the first movie they've ever made out of one of my books. I haven't seen it yet. I thought..." He glanced at her startled eyes. "I just want you to see what it is I do. You have an impression of me. I understand that. But aside from the horror and the ghosts and monsters, I love to tell a good story. My imagination is so much a part of who I am. And I want you to know every part of me. Even the darker sides."

Wolfe tried to read her, but it was hard. Her lips had frozen in a smile, and her eyes seemed to dance with indecision. He tried again.

"I understand this wouldn't be your first pick for a movie. But would you share it with me? This is a special time for me, and I didn't want to go alone."

Her eyes finally seemed to focus on him, and though there wasn't a trace of delight in them, they seemed to reflect trust. She nodded, and this time a genuine smile crossed her lips. "Okay. Sure. Why not?" She laughed a little. "As long as you're buying."

Wolfe grinned and stepped up to the ticket booth. "You'd think they'd send me a free pass or something." He paid for the tickets.

"Didn't you get to go to the premiere?"

"Oh, yeah, I was invited. But I've never much liked the Hollywood scene. Too many masks. You never really know who you're talking to, and why they're talking to you."

"So the mysterious writer becomes even more mysterious by not attending the premiere of his own movie."

Wolfe shrugged as he opened the theater door for her. "I guess that would be one spin."

They paused inside to adjust to the darkened room. Wolfe hoped he hadn't crossed the line with Ainsley, but she had to know who he was to understand who he had become.

It seemed that the closer she hovered next to him, the more relaxed she became. He tried to stand close to her. Looking up at him, she said, "Well, I can't guarantee I'm going to like the movie, but I'd be more than happy to try some popcorn and candy."

This was the weirdest thing that had ever happened to her. Here she was with the man she had once despised, on a date that up to this point had been magical, sitting in a dark theater waiting for his movie *Bloody Thursday* to start. What was he trying to prove? Why did she need to see this to understand him? His books were known for being dark and suspenseful. Is that who he was? Had she gotten the wrong impression of him? Her muscles ached at the idea of all this, and she found even light chitchat now painfully strained.

"Look," he finally said, after they'd made their third attempt at talking about the weather, "I know this is awkward."

"You're not kidding."

"And I'd hate to ruin our day. I'm not trying to ruin it. I'm just trying to show you every side of me. So you won't have any surprises."

Ainsley stared at the movie screen in front of her. She had to admit, the guy had a lot of guts. He had to know how she felt about him, about what he wrote. Why would he put himself in such a vulnerable position now? She was about to try to reassure both him and herself with a polite nod when the lights went down and the music began. *Dear Lord*...she prayed. But there were no other words to fill in the rest of the prayer.

An hour and a half into the movie, Ainsley's hand reached the bottom of the popcorn sack. She tossed it aside and stared at the screen. Elaina, the main character, was about to walk into a deadly trap. Where was Thomas? Where *was* he? Didn't he know how much danger she was in?

Ainsley sat back, trying to focus both on the movie and the irrational thoughts that were playing through her mind. She didn't realize there would be a love story in this...and such an intense one. She was captivated by Elaina, her passion, her vulnerability, her bravery. And Thomas was so complex, a hero in his own right, yet mysterious. His love for Elaina had spanned more than a decade, but until now she was unaware. If they could just get rid of that horrific ghost that haunted the mansion they both loved so much, their love could find each other! In the same thought, Ainsley marveled at how Wolfe's mind had come up with all these twists and turns. Her head throbbed as she was tossed between the thrills of the movie and the realities of her own thoughts.

"Don't open the door!" Ainsley whispered. "Don't do it!"

She could feel the tension of everyone in the theater as the door creaked open and Elaina found herself stepping into unknown places. "No! No! Don't you know what's there?" Ainsley's heart pounded with anticipation.

A man with a knife leapt from behind the shadows. Ainsley screamed, along with the rest of the audience. But Elaina was quick on her feet and grabbed a letter opener on the desk next to the door. In a violent struggle, Elaina managed to stab the man in the shoulder. He stumbled backward, wincing in pain, blood dripping down his arm. He hollered at the top of his lungs, and Ainsley screamed again, this time grabbing Wolfe's arm. But something felt weird. His muscles were completely relaxed. Ainsley could barely take her eye off the screen to glance over at Wolfe, but when she did, she gasped.

Wolfe was unconscious.

"Please, I'm fine," Wolfe said as two hefty men in theater uniforms helped him to a nearby bench in the theater hallway.

"I'll get you some water," one man said. The other had stepped away to find the manager. Wolfe had regained consciousness as soon as Ainsley returned with the men to help him, and at once he let them usher him out of the dark theater to try not to draw too much attention to himself. The movie, apparently, was much more interesting than Wolfe's plight, because not too many people took notice.

Wolfe leaned his head against the wall and stared at the ceiling. Ainsley sat next to him. "Are you okay?"

"Yes," he said with a short smile. "I promise."

"You scared me to death!"

"That was what *the movie* was supposed to do."

Ainsley couldn't help but smile. "Well, it was doing a fine job of it too."

The man returned with a cup of water and lingered for a moment until Wolfe indicated with a nod that he would be okay. The man stepped aside and tended to the trash.

"What happened?" Ainsley asked.

Wolfe grinned, then laughed out loud and could barely look at her. He shook his head, managed to glance at her for a second, and then said, "I pass out at the sight of blood."

"You *do?*"

He nodded. "It was really bad when I was young, and then I guess in the last few years I haven't seen much blood, and I don't really go to the movies that much. I thought I'd outgrown it. I guess not!"

Ainsley started laughing so hard the manager and the man with him turned to see if everything was okay. She gave them a quick wave of assurance but couldn't stop laughing. Wolfe joined in, and for a moment all they could do was laugh, look at each other, and laugh even more.

Finally Ainsley managed to say between breaths, "You're a horror novelist and you pass out at the sight of blood!"

He nodded and laughed again, finally able to speak himself. "I can write about it all day long, but if I see it, I drop. I even use an electric shaver, when I use one at all."

They laughed a few moments longer until Ainsley's sides hurt, and then they finally managed to gain their composure.

"That's the funniest thing I've ever heard."

Wolfe smiled and stared into his water cup. "Yeah, I guess it is pretty funny, isn't it?" Silence replaced the laughter for a moment. Then Wolfe said, "Ainsley, I know these movies and books aren't good. I'm not trying to say they are. I just wanted you to see. I'll never write anything like it again. I see how dark it is. I see what's wrong with it. But I'm not ashamed of it either. It's as much a part of my life as—well, as this moment is. That's all."

The doors to the movie theater swung open and the crowd dispersed, each one chatting as they went by. Suddenly Ainsley felt disappointed that she didn't know how the movie ended. She looked at Wolfe.

"What happens?"

"What happens?"

"At the end of the movie? Does Thomas save Elaina?"

He smiled. "What do you think?"

"I hope so." She looked at him. "Do horror stories have good endings?"

"Sometimes."

"So what happens?"

"The man at the graveyard—"

"Finds the box!"

"And puts it in the…"

"House?"

"No. The car. Because, remember—"

"Thomas can't drive a stick shift!"

"But Elaina can."

"And she finds the—?"

"Yes, and unlocks the secret to give to the—"

"So Thomas can save her!" Ainsley stared at the ceiling in amusement. "What a great ending!"

"Thank you."

She leaned against the wall next to him. "I have to say, I'm pretty astonished."

"Oh?"

"The characters—they were interesting. I was fascinated by them both."

"What fascinated you?"

"Elaina...so much has been expected of her all her life, yet underneath all those layers of expectations is a vulnerable woman. She's so together, but she doesn't have all the answers, and she needs a hero."

Wolfe was silent as he studied her. Ainsley continued. "And Thomas. An unlikely hero, I have to say. He's mysterious, he's got a past. But it seems in the end, Thomas has more of the answers, more stability, than she does." She shrugged. "I just thought horror novels were about seeing people's insides ripped out."

"Some are."

"So nobody's insides get ripped out at the end of the movie?"

Wolfe laughed. "Well, unfortunately the butler gets it."

"Oh. Well, he wasn't that fascinating of a character anyway." Ainsley watched as Wolfe sipped his water. "Can I ask you something?"

"Sure."

"There was one thing that didn't make sense to me in the movie."

"What's that?"

"It's about Thomas. And his love for Elaina. How could anyone be in love with someone for fourteen years and never say anything?"

Wolfe crunched his cup in his hand and tossed it in the wastebasket beside him. Then he looked at her and with a meager smile said, "Well, I guess that's why they call it fiction."

On the way back to her house, Ainsley learned Wolfe wore his hair long because his ears were crooked, and that for the first six months of Goose and Bunny's life he called them Dog and Girl because he couldn't come up with anything more creative. He finally got better names for them by watching Saturday morning cartoons.

Ainsley told Wolfe more about the death of her mother, the relationship she had with her father. She talked about how she'd gone to church her whole life and what it meant for her to be a Christian. Wolfe listened intently, and Ainsley wasn't sure she'd ever met anyone who seemed more interested in what she had to say. It thrilled her.

The drive back to her house seemed short, and Ainsley felt the heaviness of disappointment in her chest when Wolfe pulled his Jeep up to the curb outside her house. It was after five, and she knew she had to go inside and begin preparing dinner for her father. But so much of her wanted all this to last into the night.

"I had a nice time," he said.

"Me, too."

"Even with the movie?"

She smiled. "Yes, and you passing out."

"Good." He swallowed and said, "I was wondering…about church. I'm going Sunday. I just… Can I…sit by you?"

She patted his arm gently. "Of course you can. I would love it."

"I should've gone last Sunday. I sort of chickened out."

Ainsley had noticed his absence but thought it better not to mention it. "I can't wait for you to hear Reverend Peck preach. He's really good."

"Thanks."

"Thank you for a wonderful day. I had a lot of fun."

"Good." He grinned at her, and Ainsley felt her legs go numb. That grin was going to do her in.

She opened the car door and stepped out. "Wolfe?"

"Yeah?"

"I wanted to invite you to—" Ainsley paused, wondering if she should speak with her father about this first. She dismissed the thought quickly. Heavens, she'd worn perfume twice in one week. If that wasn't reckless abandon, what was? "To Thanksgiving dinner at my house."

"Really?"

"Yes. We always have a lot of guests over. I want you to come. You'll have a lot of fun, and I cook the whole meal, so that's reason enough, right?"

He laughed. "Sure. Thank you."

"Bye."

"Good-bye."

Ainsley closed the car door, walked up the sidewalk to her house, and turned to wave at him as he drove off. She stood on her porch until his car was gone, trying to relish every last second of their time together. She didn't know what their future held. But she knew she liked this man. She smiled at the thought of spending more time together and decided the chill in the air was telling her it was time to go inside.

She turned around to find her father standing inches from her in the doorway.

CHAPTER 17

MARTIN BLARTY STUDIED his friend's face as they sat across from each other at the Deli on the Dark Side, trying to determine if Oliver at all suspected that he'd bought a new car. Thankfully, Oliver seemed more interested in what Martin was saying than what he was driving.

Martin continued, trying to remember what exactly Missy had told him. Oh yes. Be sly as a serpent and interfere like a dove. It didn't sound right at the time, but he knew there was something in the Bible about serpents and doves.

She *had* made a lot of sense when she'd mentioned that it wasn't good for anyone involved if Wolfe Boone and Ainsley Parker hooked up. And since Oliver and Ainsley were longtime friends, surely he would be concerned enough to intervene in "a budding romance."

Then there was the whole argument about the "good of the town."

"I had no idea they were seeing each other," Oliver said. "I mean, I knew...at least I heard that someone had witnessed to Boo. But now Ainsley's interested in him?"

"I think it's more than interest, my friend. Much more."

Oliver studied the pickle next to his half-eaten sandwich. "I'd hate to see Ainsley hurt."

Martin shrugged. "One thing's for sure, Wolfe Boone can't be God's best for Ainsley."

Oliver nodded. "I agree."

"I always thought it'd be Garth, myself."

"I had my bets on Billy Hanover, but I guess he's not too fond of shotguns."

"So you gonna say something?"

Oliver threw some money on the table and stood, prompting Martin to do the same. "I don't know." They made their way outside, and Martin was just about to ask Oliver again when Oliver said, "New car?"

"What?"

Oliver pointed to Martin's Chevrolet, four cars down, which should have been hidden by a truck. The truck had left. Martin's knees grew weak. "Oh, um…"

"The Ford belongs to Sally Pratt. Bought it last fall. Traded in her four-door. The Nissan is Dave Bennett's. Still running after eight years. Sold it to him on his fiftieth birthday. And the white minivan is owned by Judy Johnson. Even though her husband wanted an SUV. So the only other car left is the Chevy. Yours?"

Martin swallowed hard. "My uncle's. Dead now. Left it to me."

Oliver smiled. "Oh, well good for you! Looks like an '87. That was a good year for that model."

"That's good to know," Martin said, with what little breath he had. "Well, good evening."

"See you soon, Martin."

Oliver turned and walked toward his BMW. A sigh of relief escaped Martin, who sure was glad he knew his Bible verses, because being sly as a serpent was coming in handy.

"I'm running a little late. I'll get dinner started," she said, walking briskly past her father and into the kitchen. She heard him follow her.

"Ainsley, please. Slow down."

"It's roasted chicken with rosemary, Dad. We're looking at over two hours to cook."

He grabbed her shoulders gently and turned her around. "It can wait. We need to talk."

Ainsley looked up at her father. His eyes were gentle and kind, as she knew them to be. She felt the knot in her stomach loosen. "Okay." Ainsley turned the oven on to preheat, then joined her father at the kitchen table.

"I'm sorry about how it's been between us, honey. I hate that I left the house when we were both so angry. And I'm sorry I haven't talked to you about it sooner. I overreacted. I'm sorry."

"Me too, Dad. I've felt horrible all week."

He smiled at her. "That was Wolfe? Driving the Cherokee?"

"Yes."

"Well, at least he has good taste in cars."

"And German food. He took me to Ingrid's last week."

"I've eaten there once. Several years ago. It *was* good. All right, good taste in food, too."

Ainsley leaned across the table. "He's great, Dad. I mean really great. I like him, and I haven't felt this way about a man before."

She could feel her father tense even though he tried to keep a smile on his face. "What about Garth? You two clicked, right?"

"Dad! Garth and I never clicked. Ever. He's nothing I want in a man or a vet. Don't you get that?"

Sheriff Parker held his hands up. "Okay, okay. I get it. Garth still needs to win you over."

"Why do *you* like Garth so much?"

He shrugged. "I know the guy. I've known him for years. You two practically grew up together. I know his family." His eyes met Ainsley's. "I don't know too much about Boo except that he writes horror novels."

Ainsley leaned back in her chair. "Okay, that's only fair. But will you give him a chance?"

Her father was silent.

"Please."

He nodded, his eyes shutting and his head bowing as if he'd just surrendered to something he'd long dreaded. But at least it was a start.

"Thank you, Daddy. You won't regret it. You'll love him."

"By the way," he said, "I have my Thanksgiving guest list made out for you. Worked on it yesterday at the donut shop."

"Good!" Ainsley said, relieved to be switching topics. "I have mine, too." Ainsley stood and retrieved hers from the kitchen. They exchanged lists. Ainsley scanned his quickly.

"You're inviting *Garth?*" Ainsley asked.

"And you're not," he said, eyeing the list in his hand. "You invite Garth every year."

"I didn't want to this year. Why did you?"

"Because I had a strange feeling you wouldn't."

Ainsley sighed and shook her head. Her stomach hurt at the thought of seeing Garth Twyne at all, let alone for an entire day at Thanksgiving.

"We've always said we can invite whomever we want, right? Anyone we think would be blessed by a huge Thanksgiving dinner. You're not changing the rules on me now, are you?" her dad asked.

Ainsley shook her head. "No, Dad. It's fine. Garth can come."

"Good," Sheriff Parker said with an obvious smile of satisfaction.

"But I have one more addition."

"Oh?"

"Wolfe."

Her father's cheery face fell into consternation. "You've got to be kidding me."

" 'Anyone we think would be blessed by a huge Thanksgiving dinner,' remember? Both his parents are dead, and I have a feeling he spends most Thanksgivings alone." She gave her father a pointed look.

He nodded and stared at the table. "How about putting that chicken on? We don't want to eat at midnight."

Ainsley stood and went to the kitchen. Her father would come around, once he met Wolfe. She'd had to overcome her first impressions of Wolfe too.

"What did you do on your date today?" her father suddenly asked, leaning over the kitchen bar on the other side of the kitchen.

Ainsley stuck her head in the refrigerator, squeezing her eyes shut. Did she *have* to tell every detail of the date? And what was she supposed to say about the movie? Her father would never understand. She took the chicken out and gently put it on the counter, trying to act nonchalant.

"We went to a movie."

"A movie?"

"Yeah, Dad, a movie. People go to movies, you know."

"You don't."

"I do. I just haven't been in a while."

Her father snorted disapprovingly. "What movie did you go see?"

Ainsley salted and peppered the chicken furiously, hoping to come up with something creative to say. "Um…it was a love story."

"A love story?"

"Are you going to repeat everything I say?"

Her father frowned. "A love story on the second date?"

"It was good. It was about a woman everyone expected to be strong and perfect her whole life, and the imperfect man who came and saved her from a destiny of hardship."

Her father scratched his balding head. "I hope there wasn't a sex scene."

Ainsley couldn't help but smile. No sex scene. There was an axe scene, however. Luckily she didn't have to see that. "No, Daddy."

"Good. There can be such trash in those movies." He smiled at her. "And my baby's always been pure and good. I don't want anything to change that."

Ainsley smiled back, then turned to put the chicken in the oven.

It was after eleven o'clock on Saturday evening, two hours later than Reverend Peck normally went to bed. His eyelids drooped with exhaustion, and though he hated the sound of his pencil tapping against the wooden desk at which he sat, it managed to keep him awake. The words of his sermon blurred in front of him, and for the life of him, he couldn't even remember what he'd written only moments before. Nothing was flowing. It hadn't all week. Usually sermon ideas were no trouble. But this week, his heart had been unusually heavy, and only in the last couple of days had he begun to realize why.

Reverend Peck dropped his pencil, pushed his pad of paper back, stood, and began to pace the cold floor of his bedroom. The despair he felt amazed him; he was quite sure he hadn't felt this way since his beautiful wife had died nearly twenty years before. His throat ached with emotion as he realized with great pain what all this meant.

He had failed.

And he was going to fail again, by not having a sermon ready for tomorrow morning. How could he possibly stand in front of his flock with nothing at all to say? And with disappointment lingering in the back of his mind as well?

He sat on the edge of his bed, clasping his hands together as if to pray, though no prayer came to mind. But in a brief moment of clarity, he realized that his mental block must mean *something*. The fact that he couldn't put words to paper and come up with a sermon must mean God was trying to tell him something. But what?

For a long time he just sat on the edge of his bed, staring at the floor, trying to make sense of a long and draining week. And then, without warning, he realized with excitement there was a *test*. He sat up straight and lifted his eyes toward the ceiling. Yes, a test! Something he could do to see if his little flock had indeed been listening all these years. He stood and laughed out loud.

Yes! With one simple test he would know. Surely they would pass. It wasn't *hard*, after all. But he knew one thing for sure: The test would tell him if his church had put his words in their hearts.

He went to his living room as fast as he could, pulled on his warmest winter coat, and while still in his slippers and pajamas, went outside and scooted along the little pebble path that led from his humble cottage right up to the back steps of the church. His heart pounded with anticipation, for tomorrow would be perhaps the most extraordinary day of his ministry.

Wolfe rose early Sunday morning, earlier than normal. He wanted to beat the sun and watch it rise through the east window of his home. There was something spiritual about watching the sun rise while he held warm coffee in his favorite mug, and because he didn't yet have a good sense of how to talk to God, he figured starting the day out by watching the sun illuminate all of His creation would prepare him for his first day of church.

The early rays of light spread over the distant Indiana hills while Bunny and Goose, frisky in the cold morning air, trotted playfully in the nascent haze. Wolfe sipped his coffee and thought about how in all his years of writing, he'd never been able to capture the glory of creation. One could nitpick a descriptive paragraph to death and still not reflect what he could see with his own eyes. The glow of the earth in the early morning seemed like the perfect introduction to God.

Goose and Bunny scratched at the back door. Wolfe finished off his coffee, then went to let them in. They shook the morning dew off their coats before going to look for breakfast. Wolfe wasn't interested in breakfast, and as he headed upstairs to his bedroom, his mind turned to Ainsley. He'd slept decently last night, but his unconscious thoughts had been filled with her face, and even this morning her beautiful voice seemed to fill his head. It was hard to believe that after all these years his dream had become a reality, yet that reality was still fragile. He swallowed the fear away and went to his closet to try to pick out something to wear.

He didn't own a tie, and the best he could hope for was a nicely pressed cotton dress shirt. He found one near the back and shook it while still on the hanger to loosen the dust. He hadn't used an iron in years, and it took him twenty-five minutes to find the one he owned. When he finally did, he still couldn't locate the board, so he used the kitchen counter.

Goose and Bunny whined about their empty food dishes, but Wolfe didn't pay much attention. He tried as carefully as he could to remember how his mother had taught him to iron, and though he missed some creases and the collar ended up a little crooked, he thought overall it didn't look bad. There weren't any noticeable wrinkles anyway.

Back upstairs, he found a pair of dark trousers, slipped them on, and decided he'd better run a comb through his hair. He ran it through twice, once more than normal, and splashed a little cologne on, the same cologne his father used to wear. It always brought back good memories.

He picked up his shoes and sighed at the thought of how many times he'd told himself he needed to go get new ones. He stared down at the tattered leather and scuffed heel of his left shoe, shook his head, and decided there wasn't too much he could do about it today.

Bunny and Goose eagerly circled him when he landed on the last stair step. In the kitchen, he lifted the heavy bag of dog food out of the pantry and poured it. They wagged their tails in thanks and began to eat.

Wolfe still wasn't hungry but decided to scramble himself a couple of eggs, just for something to do. He glanced at the kitchen clock. Only one and a half more hours before church started. Time was flying by.

Wolfe dusted off his grandfather's Bible, the one he had given to twelve-year-old Wolfe just before passing away. Wolfe used it now and then, mostly when he needed a reference for one of his books. Even before his "conversion" he had understood it to be a book full of wisdom. Now he knew the words were alive. How alive he wasn't sure. But when he picked the heavy book off the table, he held it with a certain reverence that just seemed to come naturally.

The clock told him it was time to leave. He allowed himself a couple of minutes to walk down the hill, five minutes to find Ainsley and get settled, and three to four minutes of buffer time, just in case one or the other took longer. He settled Goose and Bunny, who couldn't imagine where he might be going this time of morning. Noses down, they approached with worried brows and soft whines.

"It's okay, guys," he said to them, patting their heads and rubbing their necks. "I'm going to church. Get used to this." Goose's ears perked up as he looked curiously at his master. "It's a good thing," Wolfe said in honor of his new friend. He stood and took his jacket out of the coat closet. It would be chilly this morning, but he wouldn't be outside long. No use getting out his wool coat. It was itchy and looked worse than his shoes.

Wolfe opened the front door, filled his lungs with the crisp fall air, and looked at the little church's steeple, steady and tall as it had been every day. This day, though, it symbolized something more than a quaint romantic notion.

He walked down the gravel path with his Bible under one arm, hands deep in his pockets, finding himself whistling an unknown tune, observing the birds, and thinking how wonderful Thanksgiving was going to be. The chill in the air couldn't penetrate the warmth he felt inside. For the first time in his life, he felt he was on track. Even with all the success he'd had as a novelist, the solitary life he led as a writer only exacerbated his inner void, and he had experienced days when he thought life was most definitely not worth living. Only his poetry, his dogs, and perhaps even God Himself, though unknown to Wolfe at the time, had retained some significance in his life.

A swarm of people mingled outside the front doors, and at first Wolfe thought that was where they gathered before church started. But it was awfully cold for that. No one seemed to notice his approach, and by the low murmur of the crowd, it dawned on him that something unusual was happening.

He looked around for Ainsley, but couldn't see her. His eyes darted through the crowd for Reverend Peck. He wasn't around either. What was going on? Wolfe felt he might just turn around and leave, when a hand touched his shoulder.

"Garth," Wolfe said.

Garth was smiling at him. "You're at church."

"Yes."

"Well, that's one way to get the girl." Wolfe was about to protest when Garth continued. "So I heard about your incident Friday."

"Incident?"

"Passing out. At the theater." Garth chuckled. "What happened?"

Wolfe was about to tell Garth to mind his own business, when Ainsley appeared.

"Ainsley!"

"Hi." She smiled. "I'm so glad you came." She eyed Garth, who managed to get the hint and walk off.

"What's going on?" Wolfe asked.

Ainsley took him by the arm and led him to the front of the church steps. "That's what's going on."

A heavy chain encircled the handles of the front door, and over the chain was a sign taped to the door. It read: GO AND DO WHAT I'VE TAUGHT YOU TO DO.

"Where's the reverend?"

Ainsley shrugged. "No idea. He's not at his house either. We already checked." She glanced at the sign. "Kind of weird, huh?"

"Your attention *please!*" a loud, scratchy voice rang out. Ainsley and Wolfe turned to see a woman standing on the sidewalk, waving her cane at the crowd.

"That's Missy Peeple," Ainsley said. They went to join the crowd.

"Your attention PLEASE!"

The lady stood there with an aggravated expression that begged attention, and the crowd hushed. Wolfe wondered why everyone was so quick to listen. Perhaps she had some high position in the church.

"Now," she said, her voice carried by the morning breeze, "in all my years of going to church—and that, mind you, has been since I was birthed on the fifth pew in the middle section—I have never come on a Sunday morning to see the doors locked, the lights off, and the church closed. Never!"

The crowd mumbled agreement.

"The sign and what it says," she said, pointing dramatically behind her at the church doors, "indicate one thing, and one thing only!"

Suggestions followed without pause.

"We need to pray for the reverend!"

"We need to *find* the reverend!"

"I say we stand out here and wait for him to come back!"

"Let's go have breakfast!"

"I think we oughta march around the building seven times!"

"No, no, no. *No,* NO!" Missy Peeple waved her hands wildly, a painful wince pinching her face as if each suggestion was more insulting than the first. "No! You people, you must listen. Be attentive! Think it through!"

The crowd hushed again, and from the back someone shouted, "What *are* we supposed to do then?"

Missy Peeple's sagging skin tightened into what Wolfe thought was a smile, but he wasn't sure. The lips were turned up, but she didn't look happy. She leaned on her cane and eyed the crowd.

"Well, isn't it obvious? We will hold a *meeting!*"

CHAPTER 18

IT TOOK ONLY fifteen minutes for the entire church crowd to move to the community center for the meeting. Wolfe and Ainsley stood at the back of the auditorium, watching the crowd speculate.

"I can't imagine why Reverend Peck wouldn't be at church," Ainsley said. "It's not like him at all. He never misses church. I can't even remember the last time he took a vacation."

She felt Wolfe's strong hand on her shoulder, and her anxiety melted beneath it. It felt good to lean on someone. She'd been the one people leaned on for so long. Now maybe it was time to give up control. The concept was good. Doing it was going to be a whole other story, though.

She was about to look up and smile at him when she caught her father staring at them from across the room. She gave him a quick wave, but he only looked away. She glanced up at Wolfe, but fortunately he hadn't seen the exchange. He was busy watching Missy Peeple.

"She's an odd one," Wolfe said, still watching up front.

"Miss Peeple?"

"I haven't figured her out yet."

Ainsley smiled, glad his hand was still on her shoulder. "Well, don't try too hard. She's not easy. She's been around for ages, and when her sister was alive, they were quite the pair. These days she spends her time meddling in other people's business. She's a good source of information for my dad and his job, but I'd steer clear if I were you."

"Thanks for the advice," he said with a wink. A look of concern suddenly replaced his curiosity. "What in the world…?"

Ainsley followed his glance to a man she didn't recognize. In his expensive coat and shoes, the man seemed out of place in her small town.

"Wolfe, what is it?"

He glanced down at her. "Nothing."

The microphone screeched, and Missy Peeple raised her hands for silence from behind the podium, where she stood barely visible behind its dark wood. She was talking, but you couldn't even see her mouth move. Her eyes, lacking expression and brightness, stared down the crowd.

"...and I don't think I have to say that we've got a problem on our hands. Now folks, as long as I've been a Christian, I have *never,* and I mean not once, missed a Sunday service. When I was nearly on my deathbed with some crazy strain of botulism, I *still* made it to church. Now look, I'm not accusing here, and I'm the first one to stand here and say we must get to the bottom of this, but I think it's awfully strange that our dear and beloved pastor would just not show up on a Sunday morning..."

Missy Peeple droned on, and Ainsley found herself becoming more and more worried about what might have happened to Reverend Peck. Part of her wanted to run up to the podium and tell everyone she was *sure* the reverend had his reasons. The other part wanted to grab her father and go look for him. Had something dreadful happened? Just as she was about to decide to do something, she felt a tug on her elbow.

"Ainsley," Wolfe whispered. "Come with me."

Ainsley followed Wolfe out of the auditorium and then to the sidewalk on the north side of the building, away from the wind.

"What is it?" she asked.

Wolfe looked around and then said, "I think we should do what the reverend said."

"What?"

"The sign. On the church."

Ainsley thought for a moment. What exactly did it say? To go and do what he'd taught them. She looked at Wolfe.

"What does it mean?" he asked.

Ainsley leaned against the brick of the building, staring at concrete below her feet. She thought of all the possibilities, shaking her head at the absurdity of it all.

Finally she took a deep breath and said with a small smile, "Come on. I know what to do."

⁓

"Mrs. Owen? Hello? Mrs. Owen?"

"Ainsley? Is that you?"

"Yes, ma'am."

"Well my goodness! What a surprise! Come in!"

Wolfe followed Ainsley through the entryway of the humble house to the living room, where an elderly woman with bright blue eyes sat in a matching blue recliner. A multicolored quilt covered her legs. She leaned forward and squinted.

"Dear, who is that with you?"

"This is a friend. His name's Wolfe."

"Oh my. Well, glad to have all the company I can. Please, come in. Sit down. Isn't this Sunday? Why aren't you at church?"

"Long story," Ainsley told her, patting her on the knee before sitting on the couch next to her. Wolfe sat next to Ainsley, wondering what in the world they were doing.

"Well, honey, how are you?"

"I'm fine," Ainsley said. "I'm just getting ready for Thanksgiving dinner."

Mrs. Owen's eyes turned sad. "Yes, I'm hoping my son can come home. He's awfully busy, you know." She glanced at Wolfe. "He's a very successful businessman. He was home five years ago for Thanksgiving, and ever since last Christmas when he had to cancel at the last moment, he promised me he'd be home for Thanksgiving." She smiled at the thought. "I can't wait to see him. He's such a handsome young fellow. And sharp as a tack." Her eyes brightened. "And single, Ainsley. Still single."

Ainsley blushed and glanced at Wolfe. Mrs. Owen seemed to pick up on the subtlety because she covered her mouth and then said, "Oh my! Are you two…?"

"Um…" Ainsley managed. Wolfe knew she was dying inside.

"I'm hoping so," Wolfe said, grinning at Ainsley.

Mrs. Owen leaned forward. "Aren't you a handsome young man? Could use a haircut. What is it that you do for a living?"

"Well, that's a tough question. I'm a writer, but I'm currently looking for a new topic on which to write." He glanced at Ainsley, whose smile was delightfully iridescent.

"Hmm. That's a tough occupation, young man. Many people say they want to be writers, but very few have the resolve to stick with it, keep going in the face of all those rejections."

"Yes ma'am."

"I like poetry myself. It's old-fashioned, I know. But poets have a depth to them that I think most writers just don't have. Poets must have command of the language. They must know more than the meaning of a word; they must know its influence. Paul Engle said, 'Poetry is boned with ideas, nerved and blooded with emotions, all held together by the delicate, tough skin of words.' He said that in '57, I believe. Was it the *New York Times?* I can't remember. In my brain there floats this uncanny fog." She shrugged. "Anyhow, it *was* Paul Engle who said it." She smiled away the thought and looked at Wolfe. "What do you write, dear?"

Ainsley piped in, "Uh, definitely not poetry." She glanced worriedly at Wolfe.

But Wolfe smiled back at Mrs. Owen. "Hopefully things that are meaningful."

"Good for you, good for you. Keep your head up. Don't let those rejections get to you." She then turned her focus to Ainsley. "And how's your father?"

As Ainsley and Mrs. Owen spoke, Wolfe had no doubt why they were here. And he knew they were doing what the reverend would want them to.

With the meeting adjourned and parishioners busy disseminating information in huddled groups around the community center, Missy Peeple felt it safe to talk openly with Oliver Stepaphanolopolis, Mayor Wullisworth, and Marty Blarty. And *Garth,* the scoundrel. All separately of course. Dressed in her Sunday best, she made her way around the room like a young and dazzling socialite.

"I don't know what's going on," Martin Blarty said. "But this whole town is freaking out. First Boo decides to get saved—did you see him here with Ainsley?—then the reverend decides not to do church. What's next? I shudder to think!"

"So you see why we must do the grave thing of interfering, don't you, Marty?"

"Martin. And I already have. I talked to Oliver. He's going to talk to Ainsley." Martin glanced over his shoulder. "They looked rather chummy this morning. And I'm gathering the well-dressed, hoity-toity man was the fellow writing the book?"

"You don't worry about Alfred. Now, Marty, let me be clear. If Oliver is unable to get through to Ainsley, the task is up to you."

"I don't know her very well. I'm more familiar with her father."

"Exactly." Missy smiled and moved on, finding the mayor hiding out near the water fountains.

"Take a deep breath, Mayor," Missy said, sensing that all this was just about to give the poor, handsome man a breakdown. "Everything is under control. I'm going to see Mr. Boone today. Straighten this whole thing out."

"How?" Mayor Wullisworth's voice boomed.

"Mayor Wullisworth," Missy Peeple said, "do not presume to understand the ways of a spiritual woman."

Mayor Wullisworth scowled and then dropped his head as if he might be dodging bullets. "But things are going south. People are starting to wonder whether Boo's new novel is his last one. We've got businesses around here starting to think about changing their names. I mean, what is Tombstone Used Cars without Boo? Huh? Or The Haunted Mansion? Or Arsenic and Old Lace?" His voice rose with panic. But Missy knew his real concern was that his secrets might be found out.

"Shush. You're acting faithlessly." She leaned on her cane toward his face. A Stetson man. She liked that. "Trust me."

The mayor swallowed and sweated and sucked air through his teeth, but finally nodded and sauntered on into a small crowd.

Missy spotted Oliver looking around, no doubt trying to find Melb Cornforth. Out of all the people she had assigned tasks to, Oliver seemed the most…unpredictable. She had to find a way to make him more stable. This would take some thought first. So with one more scan of the crowd, she decided her work here was done. She buttoned up her coat, threw her scarf around her neck, and made her way to the door. But before she could reach it, a hand grabbed her shoulder. *Ah, Mr. Mayor, still needing comfort?* She turned around with the most endearing expression she could muster and found herself face to face with an unhappy Oliver.

"I'm not doing this anymore."

"Doing what, Oliver?"

He lowered his voice. "I didn't find anybody that witnessed to Boo, and I'm not looking anymore."

"So it could be a hoax then?"

Oliver studied her. "I don't know. But I feel a little, well, it just feels a little…a little…"

"Spit it out."

"Wrong. Okay? Wrong. It's no one's business who did this. If it's a hoax, then it's a hoax, but I'm not comfortable going around, *snooping* around, for this information."

Missy smiled graciously. "Oliver, you always were such a fine, upright man. Honest. Even for a used car salesman. I like that about you."

Oliver let his guard down a bit. "So you understand."

"Sure. You know, you remind me a lot of Ainsley Parker." Oliver frowned, not following. "You know her, don't you?"

"Of course. We've been friends for years."

"I thought so. She's a fine young lady. I hope she knows what she's doing…I mean, with Mr. Boone and everything."

She watched with great delight as Oliver's expression exposed his vulnerability. "Me too," he said softly.

Missy needed Oliver. Badly. His task was perhaps most important of all. If no one witnessed to Boo, then he was for sure not converted, and therefore could still be saved back to his old self. But Oliver had more conscience than she'd counted on, so she would have to handle him carefully and with much cleverness. She would have to find one more angle to help the poor soul along.

She always did love a challenge.

Melb Cornforth's fantasy about riding a horse at sunset ended abruptly when she saw Missy Peeple leave the community center. She rushed her like a strong south wind.

"Miss Peeple!"

"Good heavens, child! I'm not deaf!"

"I'm sorry. I get a little overanxious, and I haven't eaten lunch, so that makes my blood sugar drop, and then I get fidgety, and I start biting things." She glanced at Miss Peeple. "Mostly just fingernails."

"What do you want, dear? I'm in a hurry."

"I've been reading those novels."

"What novels?"

"You know," she whispered. "Those romances. The ones you told me to."

"Oh yes."

"Yes, well, they're quite, um, descriptive as you might imagine. But they have depth, just like Boo's novels! The characters, they're so real. The plots, so complex! I've read five in five days. And I've come to a conclusion."

"What is it, Melb? I'm quite busy, and though I'm sure your reviews of that smut are insightful, I—"

"I'm in love with him."

"They're characters, Melb. Tall, strong, muscular men with long, flowing blond hair don't exist. At least not with that kind of tan."

"No. Not with a character. With"—she leaned forward—"with *Boo*."

Missy did not seem to have anything to say, though Melb thought she saw her eyebrows lift ever so slightly.

"It's taken these novels to make me realize what I'm missing in life. It's him. He's the one for me. I just know it. I didn't realize it before. I thought I was just a fan of his work. But…I'm a fan of *him*."

She watched Miss Peeple's face soften into something thoughtful. "Is that so?"

"Why yes. Don't you think we'd make a perfect couple? I've met him in person, you know, and he took quite a liking to me. There was this chemistry that I can't explain. Like in those books. Love at first sight. It *does* exist."

The old woman stared at Melb. "Deary, I think you're going to come in handy. Yes. Handy indeed."

"Handy? What do you mean?"

A tall, lanky man walked up to Miss Peeple as if Melb were invisible and said, "We need to talk. And I mean now. I'm sure you noticed the two of them at church, or lack-thereof church. Things are happening. Bad, bad things."

His eyes took notice of Melb. She tried to smile politely. She knew him to be the town vet, Garth Twyne. She didn't know him well. He was an intense sort of man. Sort of like Brandt, Belle's love interest in *Summer's Eternal Flame*. But he certainly didn't have Brandt's build…or Boo's, for that matter. She turned to Missy Peeple, who was grinning from ear to ear.

"Garth Twyne, this is Melb Cornforth. Have you two met?"

Four hours later, after a long visit with Mrs. Owen and a shorter visit with Mr. Laraby, who had offered them coffee and a long conversation about nothing in particular, they found themselves at Deli on the Dark Side eating a late lunch. Ainsley tried not to worry about the reverend.

Wolfe spoke about his life as a famous novelist, and for the first time Ainsley thought she really understood him. He preferred obscurity to fame, which was why he chose to sink his roots in a small Indiana town. He despised the image that people created for him. For one, he could never live up to it, and two, he thought it was hokey. She laughed when he told her about some of the crazy fan mail he'd received over the years.

"So what about you?"

"Me?" Ainsley asked.

"Yeah. I've told you why I'm in Skary. Why are you in Skary?"

"I don't know what you mean. I was born here."

"I know. But I have this feeling that all you want to do is leave."

She smiled a little. Read like a book. "It's complicated."

He narrowed his eyes, studying her. "I see a woman who's carried a tremendous burden on her shoulders her whole life. She's taken care of her father since she was little. And even though she's grown and he's been widowed many years, she still can't let go of that sense of duty."

"It's not a duty. I love my dad."

"Your father's able to take care of himself." Wolfe leaned forward, as if to make sure she heard it.

Ainsley looked away. She heard the words, but it was hard for her to understand them. Just listening to them felt like a betrayal. "It must seem so simple to you," she said. She tried not to sound resentful, but she knew she did. "As if I could just walk out the front door and go do my own thing."

"You could."

"Black and white. Easy for you to say."

"Hard for you to say, I know," Wolfe said. "I know, Ainsley. I see your struggle. I see sadness in your eyes. I hear bitterness in your voice. You're the darling of the town, the person that everyone has such high expectations and hopes for. You're the girl every father wants his son to marry. You're a rock. But you never wanted this. Just like me. You were labeled, given an identity that others thought you should have."

"You should've known my mother. She *was* the darling of the town. Perfect in every way. She was a friend to everyone. A saint. An amazing cook. Seamstress. Gardener. Wife. Mom. Whatever. Her death left this huge hole in the town."

"You've been trying to fill that hole ever since." Wolfe grabbed her hands. "You're like my Elaina."

"Who?"

"Elaina and Thomas. Don't you remember? You said that underneath all of Elaina's layers was a vulnerable woman, without all the answers, in need of a hero."

Wolfe was indeed peeling away her layers, and it was making her uncomfortable. Everyone else had always let her be her way. But now she was being questioned. Sure she was miserable, but there was a certain comfort in being the same way for so long. Didn't he understand that in a town this size nobody rocked the boat? Nobody came out of his shell? No one broke free?

"I have to go home and let my dogs out," Wolfe said. He winked. "They're used to me being home a lot more than I have been."

"I understand." She tried to smile back at him, but the lump in her throat made it hard. "I'll just finish up my coffee here. I'll walk home. It's just a few blocks."

He stood and put his coat on, studying her. "I hope I haven't upset you."

"Not at all," she lied.

"It's the affliction of a novelist," he said as he buttoned up his coat. "We can see things about people. Their mannerisms. Their expressions. All tell a story. We've studied these our whole lives in order to write them into our stories. We're observers of human nature, and sometimes knowing us can be a curse." He shrugged and laughed at himself. "You can probably see why I haven't had a date in some time. That's not exactly the way to endear yourself to a person."

They exchanged pleasantries, and then she waved at him as he left. Her coffee was cold, but she didn't want to bother trying to flag a waiter for a warmup, so she sipped on it absent-mindedly, trying to understand why Wolfe seemed to think he had her all figured out. *Did* he have her all figured out?

"Bitter's an awfully harsh word," she mumbled, just in time to notice someone standing across the table from her. She looked up.

"Martin?"

"Hi, Ainsley. I'm, um…I'm sorry to disturb you. I was just leaving, and I wanted to see if I could, uh, talk to you."

"Sure. You look like something's troubling you."

"Well," he said, taking a seat across from her, "I have to be honest. There is."

"What is it?"

"A woman."

"A woman?" Ainsley smiled. "We do have tendencies to cause trouble."

"Yes, well, I don't know what to do. I'm quite smitten with her."

"Who is it?" Ainsley asked, leaning forward.

"You wouldn't know her. She's from, uh, Giford."

"Really? That's kind of far away. Where did you meet her?"

"Not important," Martin said, with a wave of his hand. "What's important is whether I should date her." He looked her in the eyes. "And I thought I'd ask you, since you are, well, you're just so upright, and good, and you've been to church your whole life. I mean, I figure you should know about such things."

Ainsley frowned. "Martin, I'm sorry, I'm not following. How does me going to church help you with this woman?"

"You see, she's…*unchurched*."

"Oh."

"Really unchurched. Not a clue."

"Oh."

"Doesn't even own a Bible." Martin shook his head. "I just thought maybe you could help me decide. Since you're such a righteous person, Ainsley. And you love God so much. I mean, would I be *betraying* God? Am I um…what's the word…*compromising?* Just because she's cute?"

Ainsley stared at Martin and disappeared into her own thoughts. Her head pounded with indecision. Martin's eyes followed hers as she searched for an answer for him.

"Look, I've probably put you on the spot here, and I'm sorry," Martin said. "I just don't know too many people who take God as seriously as you do. And I just wanted to know I wasn't making a mistake. A life-altering mistake. One huge, gigantic mistake."

"Martin, you're being a little overdramatic, aren't you?"

"Sorry," he said. "It's just that"—he paused dramatically—"what if she *changes* me?"

Ainsley swallowed, and to her horror all she could hear was Wolfe's voice in her head, his *suggestions* on how to set herself free. She became aware of Martin's quizzical eyes.

"Look, Martin, I appreciate you thinking of me. And I wish I could help. But I'm not…I'm not all that you think I am."

"Sure you are. You're the most righteous person I know."

"Then you don't know too many people."

"Listen to you. Humble."

Ainsley shook her head. She had no idea what to say.

"I'm just thinking that even though she's cute, and she likes me, and she makes me feel a way I haven't felt in years, it might not be in my best interest to continue to see her." Martin leaned forward. "Don't you agree? She might, in the end, be bad for me?"

Ainsley stood and zipped her coat, looking down at Martin but not really seeing him. "Martin, it doesn't sound like you need me to figure this out."

"You have to go?"

"I'm sorry. I've got to get home to my dad." She closed her eyes and sighed. "I've got things to do."

Martin stood too. "So I should just follow my heart?"

Ainsley bit her lip and sighed heavily. "I don't know. I guess the heart isn't always the most reliable ally on the narrow road."

Martin held the door open for her, and they both walked outside. "Well, thanks for the advice, Ainsley. I really appreciate you listening to me. See you later."

Ainsley waved and watched Martin walk to his car. Oh, how she wished Aunt Gert were still here. She slowly made her way down the sidewalk in the direction of the park, dragging her feet, wondering how so much that was right just a day before seemed wrong now. She needed to sit and think awhile.

She saw him at the first park bench in sight. "Reverend!" She rushed to him. He looked up and offered a mild smile. "Reverend, are you okay?"

Without lifting his eyes he said, "Is the meeting over?"

"What meeting?" Ainsley asked.

"The meeting everyone had instead of church."

"I don't know," Ainsley replied. "We didn't really go. Me and Wolfe."

The reverend looked up. "Oh? What did you do?"

"We went to visit Mrs. Owen and Mr. Laraby. They're always fond of people coming by, even on a Sunday."

"That's my girl. I knew it. I knew *someone* must've been listening all these years."

"Listening to what?"

He shook his head. "It doesn't matter."

"It matters to me," Ainsley said softly.

The reverend focused on an empty flower bed in the middle of the small park. "Do you know how often I've thought of being somewhere else? Don't think I haven't thought about that big church in the suburbs. Nice office, plenty of bookshelves. A large crowd hanging on my every word. I've thought about it all my life. I think about it more and more every day. But for all the wrong reasons, if there is a right reason at all."

"What are you talking about?"

"I'm talking about the fact that I've been here nearly my whole ministry, and life goes on every day as if I haven't uttered a single word. Ainsley," he said, turning toward her, "don't you understand? I've failed."

"Failed?" Ainsley took his hands. "How can you say that?"

"Look at the people in this town. Look at their lives. No one seems to be paying attention to what I'm saying. I stand up there and talk, and everyone feels good about hearing me talk, but that's where it ends. It all ends the second everyone leaves church." He patted her on the knee. "At least for almost everyone."

"Reverend," Ainsley said intently, "you can't really believe that all you've done over the years has been in vain."

The reverend only stared at his shoes. They sat in silence awhile, each watching something different in the park.

"See that man over there? The gardener?" Ainsley pointed to the man working on the hill in a flower bed. "What is he doing?"

"I don't know."

"He's planting bulbs." Ainsley put her hand gently on his shoulder. "He's putting the bulb deep into the earth, and with a lot of watering and care, eventually that bulb will grow into what I suspect will be a tulip. Which," she said, turning to him, "is exactly what you do. Don't you know that? You're planting the seed of God's Word in our hearts. When it blooms is up to God."

The reverend smiled at the thought. "Ainsley, you've always been so wise."

"Because you've been my pastor since the day I was born."

"I hate for you to see me like this."

"To see you like this gives me hope that God loves the deepest part of our humanity."

"Well," the reverend said, "I suppose I should go. Spend some time in prayer." He stood and smiled at Ainsley. "Have a good day."

She watched him walk down the sidewalk and out of sight.

CHAPTER 19

WOLFE HAD BEEN whistling for nearly an hour. It was driving Goose and Bunny nuts. Their ears would perk; they were just sure they were supposed to run somewhere, fetch *something*. But there was no further command…just whistling. And Wolfe couldn't stop, despite the fact his two dogs were walking in circles of confusion. He certainly hadn't expected this day to turn out so wonderfully, but it had. And as dusk began to settle over the small town of Skary, Wolfe's wild imagination, which had always been reserved for his books, now wandered to Thanksgiving, to Christmas, to spring…to a wedding, to a honeymoon, to children…to life. Real life. With Ainsley.

His daydreaming was intruded upon by only one thing, and that was Alfred Tennison and why in the world he was still hanging around Skary. Wolfe thought he probably had something up his sleeve, some scheme to get him to start writing again.

His lips finally tired, and his whistle turned to a hum, something he thought might have been a hymn he'd heard long ago. He didn't know, but he liked the melody. He was just about to fix himself a light dinner when a knock came at the door.

But what startled him more was Goose and Bunny's reaction. Instead of hopping up and wagging their tails in excitement of company, they hunkered down, both with a low, guttural growl that chilled his spine.

"Hey," he said, taking them both by the collar. "What's wrong?"

They continued to growl and slowly approached the door, their ears standing straight with the second knock. Wolfe commanded them to stay back and went to look through the peephole.

Unfortunately, the figure was backlit by the setting sun, and he couldn't see who it was. But the body was small, frail, a bit hunched over. Hardly someone threatening.

"Stay," he told his dogs again, then opened the door, and to his surprise the woman who had organized the morning meeting, Miss Peeple, stood there on his porch. "Oh, uh…hello."

"Hello, Mr. Boone," she said, a crooked grin forming on her lips. "How are you this evening?"

"I'm fine. What can I do for you? Miss Peeple, right?"

She straightened on her cane a bit. "May I come in, dear? I don't stand well, and it's chilly, you know."

"Sure. I'm sorry. Please."

She stepped in, and Goose and Bunny barked wildly, scaring them both half to death. Wolfe grabbed Miss Peeple by the elbow to make sure she didn't tip backward.

"Goose! Bunny! Stop it!" He thought all that whistling must've put them on edge.

They kept barking and growling, and Wolfe thought Miss Peeple just might pass out in fright.

"I'm sorry," he said over the barking and chaos. "I'm not sure what's gotten into them. Just a second." He gently pushed her back onto the front porch and shut the door.

He grabbed both dogs by the collar and dragged their unwilling bodies across the wooden floor to the back door of the house. He pushed them outside, then hurried to the front door to let Miss Peeple in before they could get around the house. Grabbing her by the arm, he nearly lifted her through the door and quickly shut it. Only seconds later he could hear the dogs scratching and barking. Miss Peeple was shaking.

"They're harmless, I promise," Wolfe said, taking Miss Peeple's coat. "A little rambunctious, but harmless. They've been in the house most of the day." That was hardly an explanation, but Wolfe didn't know what else to say. "Please, have a seat."

"Your house," Miss Peeple said, looking around. "Extraordinary. What fine taste you have."

"Thank you. Can I get you some coffee?"

"No, dear. You might as well offer me liquor."

"What?"

She turned to him, wobbling on her cane. "I was addicted to the stuff for years. Had to have three cups in the morning, one by noon, and I gargled with it at night. It was practically an idol in my life, I worshiped it as if it were. Do you know what I mean?" Her small eyes narrowed as she looked at him.

"Not really."

"Oh yes," she said, in a lighter tone. "I'm sorry. You're new to this."

"To what?"

"Religion."

Wolfe swallowed. She was here to talk about religion? He suddenly felt uncomfortable. She was, after all, just a little old lady. But Ainsley had warned him to stay away from her.

She made her way over to his chair near the fireplace, propped her cane against the wall, and sat down. "But I will take a glass of water."

"Oh. Okay. Sure." After getting her the water, he took a seat across the room. He almost wanted to start a fire, too. There seemed to be a chill in the air. "So, Miss Peeple, what brings you by?"

She looked at him as if surprised by the question, then smiled slightly. It turned into a grin, and before he knew it, she was baring a full set of yellow crooked teeth. He bit his lip in anticipation of what she might say.

"Why deary, I just came by to chat, that's all."

Ainsley spent the rest of the afternoon alone, thinking. She'd taken a long walk, window shopped, and then found herself at Sbooky's. Whereas once she would pass the aisle that held his books feeling only contempt and anger, now she was curious. She walked the aisle, looking at each book, daring herself not to pick one up. She came to the end-cap, where a life-size cutout of him stood, promoting *Black Cats*. The image, shot at a creepy angle, didn't look a thing like him. She tried to imagine him sitting in that old house of his writing these novels. She couldn't. She supposed it was because she knew a different man. A changed man. A man whose feelings ran deep and wide.

"Grab one while you can," the clerk named Dustin said from behind her.

"No thanks," Ainsley said. "I'm just looking."

"That's our second shipment in two weeks. We can hardly keep them in stock. Tourists coming through for the holidays and all."

The boy went back to doing his work. Ainsley stared into the eyes of the poster. This man she had hated for so long. This same man she could now hardly keep her mind off of. Could she really be falling in love? After all her prayers to be married, *this* was who God had for her? The mysterious ways of the Lord never ceased to amaze her.

Her conversation with Martin Blarty interrupted her reverie. She had new reservations today. Was Wolfe tainting her? Was he pulling her away from what she knew to be good and right? She'd gone to see a horror movie with him!

She decided to return home. Her father would be wanting dinner, and they had a lot to discuss about the day's events. Her father had always been very fond of Reverend Peck, and she knew he would be worried sick.

Opening the front door revealed voices coming from the living room. Not aware they were expecting company, she hung up her coat, tucked her windblown hair behind her ears, and walked in. Garth and her father sat on the couch, Thief the cat between them, watching football.

"Ainsley, how are ya?" Garth said, a twisted smile on his narrow face.

Ainsley folded her arms, glancing at her father, who was more into the football game than their exchange. "Garth, what are you doing here?"

"What does it look like I'm doing?"

"I couldn't imagine."

"Watching the game with your dad, of course. And"—he held up a can of Coke—"enjoying a cold one."

Ainsley rubbed her temples and shook her head. "Right. Well, I'm going upstairs to lie down. I'm tired."

Garth hopped up off the couch. "Quite a day at church, wasn't it?"

"Quite a day."

"Wonder what's gotten into the reverend?"

"Are you asking out of concern, Garth, or just because it's something to talk about?"

Garth scowled. "Why don't you take a couple of aspirin? Headaches make you a little grouchy."

"And what do they do for you, Garth? Make you do a song and dance?"

"Quiet, you two," her father said. "I'm trying to watch the game."

Garth moved out of the living room, closer to Ainsley. "Actually, I came by to talk to you and your father about Thanksgiving."

"Oh, you're busy. Too bad. Maybe next year."

"Noooo," Garth said with a frown. "I came to see if I could bring a guest."

"A guest?"

"Yes, a guest. You know, it means an invited—"

"Garth!" Ainsley snapped.

"I said it'd be okay," her dad said from the living room, his eyes glued to the television. "Figured we'd have enough room."

Ainsley looked back at Garth. "Fine, bring a guest."

"Don't you want to know who it is?"

"No."

"Are you sure?"

"I bet you're going to tell me anyway."

"We've been seeing each other for a while now. I wasn't sure how to break it to you."

Ainsley suppressed a laugh. Garth was *seeing* someone? "Who?"

"I bet you're dying to know now, aren't ya?"

"Garth, for crying out loud. Who is she?"

"Melb. Melb Cornforth."

"From church?"

"Yes, from church."

"Oh…um…" Ainsley had to try harder not to laugh. "Isn't she in her…late forties?"

"So?"

"I didn't realize you liked older women."

"They have a maturity that other women I know don't have," Garth said. His nose tipped upward into the air.

Ainsley's laugh slipped out as a violent burst. Her father even turned around momentarily.

"Something funny?" Garth asked.

"No, no," Ainsley said, covering her mouth and shaking her head. "I'm sorry. I just…never pictured you two together."

"Opposites attract. And there's a *major* attraction there. We can hardly keep our eyes off each other."

Ainsley's eyes teared up with each word Garth spoke. She finally gained control of herself and managed to smile.

"So," Garth continued, "I wanted to bring her to Thanksgiving dinner."

"Of course," Ainsley said. "She's welcome."

"I *hope* we can stay long enough for turkey. We like to spend a lot of time alone, you know. People in love often do."

"No! Oh, you moron!" her father shouted at the television. "Blakely just threw an interception!"

Garth winked at Ainsley before returning to the living room. "I thought the day they drafted that guy they made a huge mistake," Garth said. "Well, I've got to get going." He strutted past Ainsley and out the door with a charmed look on his face.

Ainsley went to the kitchen, leaned on the counter, and laughed some more. Garth and Melb Cornforth? Was this a joke? She squeezed her eyes shut and tried to imagine those two together. Remarkably, it wasn't hard, and Ainsley hoped that maybe, for once in his life, Garth might leave her alone and find true happiness with someone else.

It seemed, frankly, like a pipe dream.

"To chat?"

"Why yes. And to welcome you to the church, of course."

"Oh. Thanks."

"Tell me a little about your religious background, dear."

Wolfe stared at the woman, trying to understand what she really wanted to talk about. He watched her gulp her water as if it were something special. Surely she was just a nice, elderly woman with good intentions. Lonely, maybe. Hadn't Ainsley shown him how to behave just this afternoon? He thought about how she'd treated those two people with such respect, compassion, and grace.

"Well," Wolfe said, "I don't really have a religious background."

"None at all?"

"No."

"Dear heavens, child. At least tell me a Mormon has come and knocked on your door."

"Not that I recall."

This seemed to disturb her deeply.

"My parents raised me to appreciate God and respect others, but I suppose I've let even that slip away over the years. I've never prayed or gone to church. But I've always felt Him near. When I walk in the early morning, or watch the sun set, or—"

"Yes, yes, dear, that's nice and all. But we don't worship the sun, you know. And besides, the question here is, do you fornicate?"

"Excuse me?"

"Or drink? Or smoke? Or curse?"

"I'm…um…?"

"Or fornicate?"

"You already said that."

"Did I? Well sometimes that particular sin is worth mentioning twice. Although it almost feels like a sin just to say it." Her eyes seemed to suck all the light out of the room. She leaned forward in her seat a little. "Oh, honey, don't look so concerned. I'm sure you're not wrapped up in any of those things."

"No, I—"

"But don't think the devil won't come in and tempt you. You're an enemy now, son. And before you know it, the smell of alcohol will entice you, and women will start looking good to you."

"Women never looked bad to me."

"Yes, but the draw will be such that you won't be able to resist. Even an old lady like me might look inviting." She winked, and Wolfe felt his stomach turn. "The devil has a way of laying traps, traps that will trip you up, make you fall. Or, as we're fond of saying, *backslide.*"

"Miss Peeple, with all due respect, I'm not exactly sure what your point is. I thought that now I would be able to resist temptation."

Miss Peeple blinked precisely twice. "I just don't want you to get the wrong idea."

"About what?"

"Love, peace, joy, faith, grace, et cetera, et cetera. All those fun little phrases Christians like to throw around like chicken feed. The Christian life is about *righteousness. Holiness.* People don't like to use those words much. They like those mushy, feel-good words. But if the Christian life were *that* easy, everyone would embrace it, wouldn't you say?" A strange twinkle glinted off her eyes.

"So what's the good news then?"

"Excuse me?"

"I always thought that *gospel* meant 'good news.'"

"Oh it does, dear. The good news is that you have me." She lowered her voice, as if someone might be listening. "There aren't too many people who'd come up here, tell it like it is. I'm here because I don't want you to be *deceived.* Incidentally, another word Christians are fond of pretending doesn't exist. *Deceeeeiiiived.* You should be comfortable with saying that word." She said it again, like a snake hissing.

Wolfe leaned back against the couch, thinking this woman was nothing like Ainsley *or* Reverend Peck. Their lives seemed simple. Good. Pure. Happy. This woman seemed…complicated. But then, she'd lived a long time. Elderly people, he'd always presumed, possessed a wisdom that was hard to find among the general population.

"Son, what I'm trying to tell you," she said, interrupting his thoughts, "is that being a Christian is *hard*. I don't want you to come in with the wrong idea. You have to work at being good, work at defeating the devil, work at doing good works. Do you understand? Many are called, but few are chosen. There's a reason that scripture is in the Bible. Not *everyone* is good enough."

Wolfe stared at her, but he couldn't see her. All he could see was his past and everything he'd done. His thoughts quickly turned to Ainsley, and what a wonderful human being she was, how *good* she was. His head throbbed suddenly with the realization of who *he* really was. He hadn't thought about it once in the last week. But now it consumed him. Was he truly deceived into thinking that he could ever be like Ainsley? What was it, exactly, that Reverend Peck had said about being a new creation?

"May I have another glass of water?"

"I'm sorry?"

"Water?" She held up the empty glass. "The air's a little dry. I'm parched."

"Sure. Water."

He hardly took notice of her as he grabbed the glass and went to the kitchen. His heart felt heavy. How could he have imagined that this new life would be easy? Uncomplicated? And *right* for him? He rubbed his forehead. Something wasn't right, but all he felt was confusion. And dread...at trying to live up to standards he barely knew anything about.

He realized water was spilling over the side of the glass and onto his hand. He quickly shut off the faucet, poured a little more out of it, dried the outside of the glass, and took it back into the living room.

To his surprise, Miss Peeple wasn't sitting in her chair. Her cane, however still leaned against the wall next to it. Where in the world could she be?

His heart seemed to stop.

She was on the floor, flat on her back, unconscious, and looking very, very stiff. And then he noticed something even more frightening...blood trickling from her head.

He tried to look away, but it was too late.

CHAPTER 20

OLIVER SAT AT the breakfast table in the Parker home, watching Ainsley prepare hot chocolate. He loved her hot chocolate. Always topped off with real whipped cream and chocolate slivers.

"I'm so glad you dropped by, Ollie," Ainsley said, joining him at the table. "How's the business?"

"Fine. Your car still running good?"

"Of course." She smiled.

"Good, good."

"You okay?" Ainsley said, peering at him. "You look like something's bothering you."

Oliver swallowed. A transparent fellow he'd always been. He was being pulled in one direction by his heart and in another by his conscience. Part of him thought he shouldn't interfere with Ainsley and Wolfe. Yet with the news that Missy had just told him—how Melb had hooked up with Garth—things were different now. More was at stake. How would he ever get to Melb with Garth in the picture? And the only way to get Garth out of the picture was to get Ainsley into the picture. According to Missy, the only person Garth was more smitten with than Melb was Ainsley. If Ainsley and Garth were together, then...

"Oliver?"

"I'm sorry. I just faded out, didn't I?"

"Yes." She chuckled, then her face turned concerned. "Are you okay?" He glanced to the living room, where the sheriff was watching football. She smiled. "It's okay. If there's a game on, he tunes out *everything* else. He wouldn't hear me if I told him the house was on fire."

"It's about Boo."

"What about him?"

"I know you're seeing him."

She patted Oliver on the hand. "Oliver, it's okay. He's a nice guy. Genuine. Good heart. You have no reason to worry."

Oliver swallowed. Okay. Well, that went poorly. What was he supposed to say now? Ah yes, a couple of good words came to mind. Not his. Missy's, actually. But it would seem they might come in handy now.

"Aren't you unequally yoked?"

Ainsley's bright green eyes studied Oliver intently. "I don't know."

"Especially if you're not sure he's really, you know...saved," he said in a whisper, as if the very mentioning of it might cause the walls to fall.

Oliver watched her stare down her drink. Then she looked up at Oliver. "I know your heart's right, but you have no reason to worry."

"Oh. Good." Oliver smiled and licked the cream off his hot chocolate. He tried to seem casual and high-spirited, but the only thing he was thinking was what a disaster this was, and that if she were a Chevy he'd have her sold. But she wasn't. She was a woman with an enamored heart. As disastrous as this was, he still had one more angle to try.

"Did Boo ever mention how he got saved? I mean, who it was that shared the...that witnessed...that, you know, got him saved?"

Ainsley's forehead wrinkled. She was just about to say something when the shrill sound of the phone interrupted their conversation. The sheriff stood. "Who is calling me during the *game?*"

"As if the world revolves around football," Ainsley said with a laugh. She sipped her hot chocolate while they both watched the sheriff make his way to the phone.

"I have *two* days off, I want to watch the game, and someone feels they have to *call me?*" He grabbed the receiver. "Hello?" A pause. "What? When? Are you sure? Yes, I'll be right there." He hung up the phone quickly and went to get his coat.

"What's wrong, Dad?"

Without turning around he said, "That was Garth. Missy Peeple is unconscious on the floor of Wolfe Boone's house. And Wolfe Boone is out cold too. Rescue units are on the way."

Three police cars, an ambulance, and a fire truck surrounded Wolfe's house. Ainsley and Oliver followed her father up the steps. Her heart pounded with anxiety, her head with a thousand questions. *What happened? Why was Missy, of all people, at Wolfe's house? And how did Garth find them?*

She walked through the front door just in time to be in the way of two EMTs pushing Miss Peeple on a gurney. "Excuse me, Ainsley," one of them said.

"Sorry," Ainsley breathed, stepping aside. By the looks of things, Miss Peeple still appeared to be alive, but barely. Ainsley spotted Wolfe on his couch, his head in his hands.

"Wolfe," she said, rushing over to him.

He looked up with tired eyes. "Ainsley."

"Are you okay? What happened?"

He shook his head, staring at the carpet. "I don't know."

A shadow fell over Wolfe's body. Ainsley looked up to find her father hovering. Wolfe's eyes opened attentively.

"Wolfe Boone, I'm Sheriff Parker," he said, his voice low and authoritative, the way he spoke on the job. Dread filled Wolfe's expression, then overflowed into her own heart.

"Hello, sir," Wolfe said, standing and shaking hands with him.

"I'd like to ask you a few questions."

"Okay." Wolfe sat back down, but her father remained standing.

"What exactly happened here?"

"I'm not sure," Wolfe said. "I went to get Miss Peeple a glass of water, and when I came back, she was on the floor."

"And how'd you get on the floor?"

"I just passed out, I guess. The blood. On her head."

"Why was she in your house?"

"She said she came by to welcome me to the church and just talk. I'd never met her before. I didn't even know who she was until I saw her at church this morning."

"So she just came knocking on your door? Unexpectedly?"

"Yes."

"And how long was she here before this incident happened?"

"A few minutes, I guess. Fifteen."

"What did you talk about?"

Wolfe glanced at Ainsley, then back at her dad. "Well, she was here explaining the Christian faith to me."

Her father frowned as he jotted some notes down. "I see. And then you went to get her some water?"

"Well, she asked for a glass right when she came in. So I gave her some. She drank that quickly, talked a little more, then asked for a second glass. That's what I was doing, getting her another glass of water, when I came back in and found her on the floor."

Sheriff Parker stepped back a little and looked at the wood floor near the couch. "And why, exactly, is there shattered glass here on the floor, son?"

"I must have dropped the glass when I passed out."

"I see." Her father took more notes. Ainsley hated the tone in his voice. It was accusatory and unnecessary. She tried to catch her father's eyes, but he was avoiding her. Ainsley couldn't stand the tension anymore. Taking her father by the elbow, she steered him to a corner.

"Surely it's pretty clear what happened here," she said.

Her father didn't look up from his notepad, as if he had expected her at some point to speak. "Is it? What exactly did happen, then?"

Ainsley sighed. "We don't know why Miss Peeple passed out, but Wolfe obviously didn't do anything wrong."

Her father stuck his notepad in his pocket. "His passing out seems pretty suspicious to me. He can't explain it."

Ainsley sighed again. "Dad, he doesn't want to explain it. He's... embarrassed."

"About what?"

"He passes out at the sight of blood, okay? Satisfied?"

She watched this register in her father's face, and then he looked at her. "How do you know?"

She swallowed. How did she know? The movie. Oh no. She'd have to—

"Well?"

She knew this would help Wolfe. She took a deep breath. "Because he took me to the movie *Bloody Thursday,* the one based on his book. And there was blood and he passed out."

Her father's eyes narrowed ever so slightly, and Ainsley could see the disappointment.

"Thief. Thief? Come on. Let's go." Her father looked around the house for his cat. "Thief? *Thief? Thief?!*"

The cat bounded in from the outside porch, and her father sighed with relief. He picked the cat up and said, "Be careful around here. This isn't a safe place." And then he left. Ainsley shook her head and went back to Wolfe.

She took his hand. "I'm sorry. My dad can be that way sometimes."

"He's just doing his job."

"Well, don't you worry about a thing." Ainsley could tell that nothing she was saying was making Wolfe feel better, so she decided it might be best not to say anything for a moment. She saw Garth pacing nearly in circles near the staircase, his hands clasped behind him. She excused herself and walked over to him.

"Garth," she said in a severe tone, "what is going on?"

"How should I know?"

"Why did you come here?"

"Shouldn't you be thanking me for saving your boyfriend?"

"You were up to something."

Garth sighed and stopped pacing. "I just wanted to make sure his intentions were right with you."

"You have got to be kidding me! You came over here to give Wolfe a *lecture?*"

"I was looking out for you. That's all. Couldn't you be a little more appreciative? I mean, who knows what would've happened to these two had I not shown up in the nick of time?" Garth glanced over at Wolfe. "So what's the deal with him, anyway?"

"What do you mean?"

"The passing out. Twice now."

"How do you know about the first time?"

"I know people at the theater."

Ainsley sighed. "It's none of your business. What's wrong with you? You're pacing over here like an expectant father. What's the matter?"

"I don't know what you mean."

"You're not well acquainted with Miss Peeple."

"Well enough to be concerned," he said, though his eyes darted away. Ainsley sensed there was something more going on.

"I'm sure she'll be fine."

He stared out the window. "Yeah. Old people tend to want a lot of attention. Sometimes they become hypochondriacs later in life."

Ainsley frowned. "Excuse me?"

Garth seemed to snap back into reality. "What? Oh…I mean… nothing. Who knows what's going on?" He stood straighter and put on a more serious expression. "I hope she'll be okay."

"Let's go to the hospital. She doesn't have any family. She needs support."

"I'm not sure I should leave the crime scene."

Ainsley nearly shouted. *"Crime scene?!"* A few people turned around. Ainsley lowered her voice. "This isn't a crime scene, Garth."

"Not yet," he said.

Ainsley was just about to say something she was probably going to regret when Wolfe stood and said, "I can take you to the hospital."

"Really?" Ainsley asked.

"Sure. I'm as concerned as anyone. I want to know that she's going to be okay."

Ainsley walked back to Wolfe. "Everything's going to be okay."

She wasn't sure who she was trying to reassure.

The news had apparently traveled fast, because when they arrived at the hospital, a small crowd had stationed itself in Missy Peeple's room. Oliver Stepaphanolopolis, Martin Blarty, Mayor Wullisworth, and Melb Cornforth all gathered around her bed. Ainsley walked in the room first, followed by Wolfe and then Garth.

"How is she?"

"We don't know," Oliver said. "We're waiting for the doctor."

Garth pushed his way through the crowd and to her bedside, staring at her in the most uncanny way. "Miss Peeple?" he said loudly. Very loudly. So loudly everyone in the room gasped. "Miss Peeple?"

"Garth," Ainsley said, making her way to the opposite side of the bed, "what are you doing?"

"She's unconscious, you moron," Mayor Wullisworth said in his deep, booming voice. "Shouting at her is hardly helpful."

"Are you a doctor?" Garth snapped.

"She needs her rest," Oliver said timidly from somewhere in the corner of the small room.

"Nobody in this room knows what she needs!" Garth said, and his fury made everyone take a small step back. "And I don't think we've gotten a diagnosis yet."

"What is wrong with you?" Ainsley said to him from across the bed.

"Nothing. I'm merely pointing out that nobody knows what's going on here, so why are we all pretending that we do?"

"Well, something is seriously wrong, I think we can be sure of that," Ainsley said.

Garth shrugged. "Maybe. Or maybe...she's...faking it." Another gasp from the crowd. Garth looked around the room with mustered confidence. "I see that may take some of you by surprise. But let me assure you, I don't come to my conclusion lightly."

"Garth," Ainsley said in a harsh whisper, "stop this! You're acting crazy!"

"Am I? Or is she? Maybe she's the crazy one!" Garth looked down at Miss Peeple. "Aren't you, you old hag!"

"*Garth!*"

"What? Listen, people, step back. I'm going to prove my point once and for all." He stooped down over Miss Peeple, and tapped her lightly on the cheek. "Come on, now. Game's over. Time to wake up." He tapped her cheek again. And again. And then harder. And harder. He had started to shake her shoulders, to everyone's horror, when an unfamiliar voice from the back of the room said, "Excuse me. Please step aside."

Garth let go of Miss Peeple, plopping her back onto her pillow. He stood back, befuddled.

"I'm Dr. Parsons. Who are all of you?"

Ainsley glanced coldly at Garth. "Concerned friends. She doesn't have any family."

"I see. Well, it's nice of all of you to come, but I'm afraid Miss Peeple is going to need her rest."

"What's wrong with her?"

"She's dehydrated," Dr. Parsons explained. "It happens frequently in elderly people, and though this was a pretty severe case, with a lot of rest and fluids she's going to be just fine." Ainsley noticed Melb Cornforth at the back of the room. The poor lady was just standing there, and Ainsley felt so sorry for her, having to watch her boyfriend do such a horrific, public thing. Then Ainsley realized Melb was staring at Wolfe. She couldn't take her eyes off him, and though it disturbed Ainsley for a moment, she thought Melb was probably so traumatized by the event that she was just in a zombielike state. Her mouth was even hanging open.

As the doctor ordered everyone out of the room, Ainsley quickly made her way around the small crowd and to Melb's side. "Hi, Melb."

Melb looked shaken as she acknowledged Ainsley. "Oh. Hi."

Ainsley tried to be friendly in hopes of calming this woman's nerves. She knew Melb well enough to say hi on a Sunday morning or to chitchat lightly at a potluck. But that was about it. "I just wanted to say that I'm looking forward to having you over for Thanksgiving dinner. I know Garth is really excited."

"Excuse me?"

"I'm sorry. He hasn't told you?"

"Told me what?"

Ainsley smiled, patted her lightly on the back, and winked. "Garth tells me you two are quite an item. He wanted you to join him at my house for Thanksgiving. I guess he hasn't told you yet, but you're of course very welcome."

Melb's confused expression was interrupted by Garth's sudden presence. He squeezed Melb by the shoulders. "What's going on here?"

"I was just telling Melb how glad I was that she's coming to Thanksgiving dinner and—"

"Yes, well, this is hardly the time or place to think about roasting a turkey, is it?" He looked down at Melb, gave her a quick, unaffectionate smile, and looked back at Ainsley. "I'll see you around." He pulled Melb with him toward the door.

"Wait!" Ainsley said, grabbing his arm. "What in the world was going on back there? How could you think—?" She glanced at Melb, whose eyes were wide as saucepans and whose breathing had suddenly accelerated. She'd already been humiliated enough. "Never mind. I'm just glad Miss Peeple is going to be okay."

Garth guided Melb down the hospital corridor and around a corner, out of sight. Ainsley shook her head. What had started out as a bizarre incident was becoming more bizarre by the minute. She turned to find Wolfe. She hoped he hadn't freaked out too.

Melb stared into Garth's wild eyes. He'd pushed her into a small supply closet and was now breathing hard as he stared at her. "If this is going to work, you're going to have to play the part."

"What part?"

"What do you mean 'what part?' The part of my girlfriend. My *lover*. Have you completely forgotten the plan?"

Melb stepped back, trying to breathe. "It all took me by surprise, that's all. If you're going to invite me to Thanksgiving dinner, you should probably let me know!"

Garth's lip curled into a snarl. "You have to think on your feet. Be aware at all times! We're madly in love," he barked. "Can't keep our eyes off each other. Thinking of each other 24/7. Is that so hard?"

She pointed a round finger at him. "Don't talk down to me. This wasn't my idea, and I'm only going along with this because—"

"—you're as desperate as the rest of us." Garth's eyes narrowed at her. "Aren't you?"

Melb stared at her shoes. "I don't like deceiving people. And besides, this isn't how it's supposed to be."

"How what's supposed to be?"

"*One* of us is supposed to be desperate. I'm not arguing about that. And there is definitely supposed to be another love interest in the way. Someone who looks totally right but is really all wrong." She glanced up at Garth. "But he should be pursuing me, not the other way around. And I'm certainly not supposed to be *lying*. I'm supposed to be the one with a pure heart who falls for the rebel who on the surface looks no good for me but in reality is what I needed my whole life."

"*What?*"

Melb managed to look him in the eye. "It's in the books."

"What books?"

She bit her lip. "Romance novels."

Garth clenched his jaw together as though trying to restrain himself from jumping forward and biting her. She clutched at her sweater. "That's *fiction,* Melb."

She blinked.

Garth continued. "It's *ludicrous* to think that a damsel in distress gets swept off her feet by the man of her dreams, a rebel on the surface but a good guy at heart, and chooses a better life with him as opposed to a solid and secure life with a man of stability. That's laughable! That doesn't happen! Ever!" Melb felt her lower lip quiver, and Garth visibly calmed himself. He tried to smile at her. "A much more *realistic* scenario would be that two people *pretend* they're in love in order to get the other two people, who incidentally *really are* in love, jealous so that they will come running back to us, the two people they *really should* be in love with, who, incidentally, are not rebels, but good and decent people, who, incidentally, have gone to church their whole lives."

"Oh."

"Now listen, Melb." He placed a heavy grip on her shoulder. Melb shuddered. "This isn't difficult. You look at me adoringly. I hold your hand protectively. We convince the world of our love. Boo and Ainsley won't be able to resist." He let go of her shoulder, his eyes growing a little distant. "Ainsley's always been afraid of stability. Of courage. Of true love. Of everything I have to offer her. I think it has something to do with her mother dying." He looked at Melb. "But I *am* the man for her. And you, obviously, have a thing for creep-o." Garth cleared his throat. "Sorry."

"He's a lovely man."

"I'm sure. So what we're really doing here is saving the ones we love from making a horrible mistake. And in doing that, gaining true love ourselves."

All Melb could see was Wolfe Boone's face. He was so handsome. So tall. So strong. And his hair, messy and wild. For a moment she saw them on the cover of a book, his arm around her, while she looked ready to faint, one hand over her brow, with the sun setting in the background, yet somehow radiant light reflecting off every inch of their exposed skin. Her chest heaved at the thought, and before she knew it, she'd decided to become a writer. Boo could teach her and write down their love story for all to share. She smiled, then looked at Garth. "Okay."

Garth sighed in relief. "Good. Now, let's get outta here before somebody finds us in the closet." Garth opened the door and walked out. Melb followed closely. But then Garth stopped, and Melb ran into him. She peeked around him to find Ainsley and Wolfe walking toward them down the hallway, both with amused looks on their faces.

"Breathe hard," Garth instructed her in a harsh whisper. He then grabbed her shoulder and did a little light panting himself. Melb had never been in shape her whole life, and though walking a flight of stairs had always caused her to breathe hard, actually doing it on purpose was harder than she ever imagined. She was beginning to feel lightheaded.

"Um, hi…" Ainsley said as they passed by.

Garth smiled and squeezed Melb harder, crushing her to where she thought she might not be able to breathe at all. He let go of her as soon as they rounded the corner. Melb almost fell to the floor. Garth crossed his arms and said, "Well, that was a start. Their imagination can fill in the rest."

Melb caught her breath, leaned against the wall, and wondered whether she, indeed, had enough energy to be in this kind of torrid love affair with a man she absolutely abhorred.

"For you, Wolfe, all for you," she mumbled as they walked off.

CHAPTER 21

"I CAN'T BELIEVE you cook all this for Thanksgiving!" Wolfe was sitting at the breakfast table watching Ainsley count ingredients and make lists. She smiled and turned to him. They'd spent every day together since Missy collapsed, and somehow the company made both of them feel better.

"It's my favorite day of cooking, even more than Christmas."

"Why?"

"Well, at Christmas there are the presents, you know. But at Thanksgiving, it's all about the food." She wiped her hands on a dishrag and jotted another thing down. "It usually takes me a week to put it all together, and two days before to prepare and start baking. But it's worth it. The more food, the more thankful people are!"

"It's nice that you and your father invite people over."

"It was my dad's idea, a few years after Mom passed away. He has a good heart." She looked up at Wolfe. "I know he seems a little intense right now. But the doctor confirmed Miss Peeple was dehydrated, so you're off the hook."

"At least as a suspect of a crime," Wolfe said, leaning back in his chair. "I think I have a lot more to prove before he'll like the idea of me dating you."

Ainsley laughed. "I suppose that's true. You'll win him over. You won me over."

Wolfe felt his heart skip a beat at those simple words. He'd never thought it possible.

"We have quite a guest list," Ainsley continued, "I think more people than we've had any other year."

"Do I know anyone who is coming?"

"You do now," Ainsley winked. "You, of course. Reverend Peck. Garth and Melb. Miss Peeple, if she's feeling up to it. Oliver Stepaphanolopolis. Mayor Wullisworth. Martin Blarty. My friend Marlee. Oh, and my brother."

"You have a brother?"

"Yes."

"You've never mentioned him before."

"Well, we don't see him much. He joined the army, and off he went. He comes home for the holidays when he can, and we stay in touch by phone, but he talks mostly to Dad. He's a really nice guy. A teddy bear."

"What's his name?"

"Butch."

Wolfe breathed his name. "Butch."

Ainsley looked up from her task. "What? You sound worried."

"A teddy bear of a guy named Butch? And in the army? I can't imagine that he's not going to be a little protective of his sister."

"He's actually in special forces now, and yes, he's a teddy bear. I know you'll love him." Thief hopped up onto the counter. "Thief! Down! You're not allowed up here!" She practically had to shove the black feline off the counter. He hissed disapprovingly but went on his way. "That cat has no manners," Ainsley said. "Dad treats him like a king instead of the furball he is. He thinks he owns this place!"

"Your dad doesn't seem like a cat person."

"I know," Ainsley said. "He found Thief a few years after Mom died and for some reason just grew completely attached. It's weird. If I had allergies, Dad would probably insist I find my own place. But Thief goes everywhere with Dad. They're partners, I guess you could say."

"So that accounts for all the cat doors around the house?" Wolfe had to chuckle. He'd noticed them before. Little cat doors everywhere.

Ainsley shook her head. "Weird, huh? I'm not kidding, there's a cat door on every single door in this house, except the one leading out to the garage. Dad installed them so Thief has complete access." She shook her head.

Wolfe's thoughts drifted back to Butch. "Do you really think it's a good idea I come to Thanksgiving dinner?"

"A good idea? Why wouldn't it be?"

"I don't think your father's too fond of me, and I'm sure your brother will pick up on some of the vibes."

Ainsley walked across the kitchen and leaned across the counter, her face near Wolfe's. "I don't care what either of them think, and I can invite anyone I want to Thanksgiving. So it's final. You're coming."

Wolfe pressed his lips together, not sharing her confidence. "If you say so."

She grinned. "Good. Besides, I wouldn't dare let you miss all this great food!" Ainsley continued talking, mentioning that the Weather Channel was predicting some big Thanksgiving storm-of-the-century. Wolfe tried to listen, but all he could think of was meeting yet another Parker family member.

Her doorbell rang. Then it rang again. And a third time. *"I'm coming, you moron!"* Missy Peeple shouted, wobbling her way out of her easy chair. Her nice Yankee quilt, three generations old, fell onto the ground at her feet. She grumbled and grabbed her cane, shuffling across her dirty floor. A fourth time. *"Settle down! I'm an old lady, you stupid—* Oh, hello."

A huge bouquet of flowers filled the doorway, and all Missy Peeple could see were two strong hands holding them in front of her. A head peeked around the side to reveal a young, handsome delivery boy. "Are you Miss Missy Peeple?"

"These are for me?"

"If you're Missy Peeple."

"I am."

"Then they're for you."

"Oh." Missy took the bouquet, and its vastness almost knocked her over. "How much do I owe you?"

The boy looked at her curiously. "Excuse me?"

"You're deaf, are you? How much do I owe you?"

"Uh…nothing. They were…uh…sent to you." He smiled sheepishly. "But you could give me a tip as a gesture of—"

She shut the door and stared at the flowers in her hands. She'd never been sent flowers in her whole life. What did it mean? She crossed to her small dining room table, where she carefully set the flowers.

There were at least a dozen roses, all red, and all alive and vibrant. She swallowed back an emotion…what emotion was that? It seemed vaguely familiar but she just couldn't put her finger on it. She'd been out of the hospital for a few days now and had received a couple of cards and a phone call or two, but nothing like *this*. No flowers. She gasped at the idea that they might be from the mayor. The mayor had sent her flowers!!

"You scoundrel," she mumbled, fingering her way through the bouquet to the card, "after all these years, you wait until I'm practically on my deathbed to come to terms with your feelings for me!"

Her hands shook as she grasped the card and pulled it out of its leafy surroundings. It took her several moments to get into the tiny, tightly sealed envelope. She pulled out the card, then went to find her reading glasses.

They were sitting by her chair on the table, on top of Wolfe Boone's book. She'd only read thirty pages so far, all of it disgustingly dark and gruesome, in hopes of finding something she could use to knock some sense into the boy. She had been on quite a roll when she'd passed out at his house. The timing was so unfortunate. But she sensed her opportunity was slipping away. He'd asked intelligent questions, and his eyes…they had that strange peace in them.

She placed her reading glasses on her nose, hardly able to contain the anticipation of reading Mayor Wullisworth's affections.

Dear Miss Peeple,
Was sorry to hear about your accident. Hope you are feeling better, because we need to talk. Soon.
    Regards, Alfred Tennison

Below his name was a phone number, and Missy Peeple had to sit down and process what she'd just read. A wide smile of satisfaction slipped onto her lips, and suddenly she was feeling better. Much better.

Dustin was just about to discover whether the vampire was going to get the unsuspecting chef when a strange noise in the bookstore interrupted his reading. He looked up to find a group of people huddled before him, all staring at him as if *he* were the vampire. He scratched his head, realized his boss wouldn't be back from lunch for another thirty minutes, and decided to ask, "May I help you?"

It was apparently the wrong question.

"Is it *true?*"

"We heard he was quitting!"

"Is this his last book?"

"What happened?"

"He lost his mind, didn't he?"

"He's gone crazy!"

The questions and comments came at him like machine-gun fire, and Dustin just stood there and listened. He wasn't sure what to say or how to say it because he didn't know what they were talking about, until someone from the back shouted, "Hey kid! Is Boo going to write another book or not?"

Dustin looked at the crowd, trying to pick out a pair of eyes that didn't seem threatening or angry. He didn't find one. He shut his book and said, "I...uh...don't know."

"We heard through the grapevine that he's hanging up his horror hat and turning to religion. That's not true, is it?"

Dustin scratched his head again. Was this what this chaos was about? He hadn't heard a thing, but then again he wasn't really up on the religious news of the day. He could tell you what city Anne Rice was signing in next weekend but had no idea what time the church down the street started.

All he could think to say was, "Well, I'm sure it's just a publicity stunt. Sometimes they release rumors to get buzz going, especially when a new book comes out."

The chill of the crowd seemed to thaw slightly, and Dustin realized he needed to take a breath as well. He smiled at the crowd and said, "Now, who would like a copy of *Black Cats* before we're sold out?"

In the solitude of his private study at the church, which measured six-by-eight feet and barely held a desk (which could only be assembled once all the pieces had been brought into the room), Reverend Peck bowed his head solemnly and prayed to God.

He couldn't use words. He was beyond words at this point. But he knew the Good Lord heard his heart, which held great sorrow for his community and its people. Yet Reverend Peck did not know what to do about it. He was completely at the mercy of God. He'd spent several sleepless nights going over all the possible ways that God might intervene in the crisis of this little town's soul. But the reverend knew that what he needed was a full-blown miracle.

After forty-five minutes of prayer, he felt only mildly better and still had not a single answer to his dilemma.

Missy brought Alfred a cup of tea, glancing at the flowers he'd sent as she passed the dining room table. So this was how "business" was done in New York, eh? She'd never wanted to leave Skary before, but things like this might make her give the city a try.

"What a nice thought, Mr. Tennison, to send me flowers."

"How are you feeling?" He took the tea.

"Do you really care?"

"No."

"I didn't think so. But I respect your honesty. Now, let's get to the bottom of why you are here."

"I think we both know why."

"You need my help."

"As far as this book idea of yours goes, it doesn't seem to be accomplishing a purpose, other than the fact that I've got some pretty good scoop on the residents here."

"You of all people should know how important information can be. And I doubt you got to be where you are in this business by being an impatient man." She actually suspected the opposite, but stroking a man's ego was never a tactic she underestimated.

"Miss Peeple, you understand how detrimental Mr. Boone's sudden decision to leave the writing world is. Not only to me but to the publishing house and fans worldwide. And of course your town has quite a stake in all of this."

"What is it that you want, Mr. Tennison? I'm old, and quite frankly I don't take my tomorrows for granted. Let's just get to the point."

"I don't have to tell you that this conversation never took place." He paused and then said, "I need you to do whatever it takes to get Wolfe Boone writing his novels again. And soon. It's of the utmost importance. He won't even return my phone calls anymore. I am relying on you."

Miss Peeple smiled. She was way ahead of him. Before visiting Boo on Sunday, she'd craftily decided that the whole town needed to be informed of what was going on, so she left a few messages scribbled on bathroom walls, dropped a few hints at the local beauty shop, and even appeared at the local bar to get some talk going around a pool table. She wondered if any of the rumors had taken root yet.

"Well, Mr. Tennison, it's going to take a lot more than flowers, but you've come to the right person."

"Oh? And what will it take?"

Missy Peeple could not help but smile. "Well, sir, love is in the air."

CHAPTER 22

AINSLEY PARKED HER car in front of the market and got out, pausing briefly to smell the early morning air. There was no doubt it was Thanksgiving. Out of every home that had a chimney, misty, swimming streams of smoke floated to the sky like featherweight ribbons. And the aroma in the air was sweet and warm, as if every oven in town was baking something special.

Ainsley made sure she had her list and went into the store. She grabbed a basket, not a cart, because she didn't have a long list: a few things she preferred to buy fresh Thanksgiving Day, and a couple items she'd forgotten on previous trips. She strolled the aisles as if in a department store looking for a gown to wear to a ball. Every spice, every cut of meat, every fresh-picked vegetable—they all interested her.

After crossing off everything on her list, she decided to pick up one more fresh bouquet of flowers. She was pretty sure there could never be enough flowers around. The more orange, red, and yellow she had around the house, the more festive it was sure to become. A nice fall arrangement sitting on the florist's counter caught her eye, and with a little maneuvering she managed to lift it and her basket and take it all to the front register.

Kay McCauley, the granddaughter of John C. McCauley, who had opened the store sixty years ago, was twice divorced, once a Jameson, and more recently a Cowen. Now she was back to McCauley, a very rich McCauley who got the house and his two sports cars. She stood behind the register, busy making a list of her own. Kay was now in her sixties, though she looked more like forty. She had youthful eyes and a pleasant smile that Ainsley was always glad to see. Although the McCauleys had had to hire outside the family over the years, they always made sure a family member worked the important holidays. Thanksgiving was no exception. They opened at 5:00 A.M. and closed at noon.

"Ainsley," Ms. McCauley said, setting down her pen, "happy Thanksgiving to you!"

"Thank you! To you, too."

"Picking up some last minute items? I love that bouquet! You know, Renata worked on that for hours yesterday. I'm glad someone bought it."

Ainsley studied the piece carefully. "It's gorgeous. I think it will be the perfect centerpiece for the dinner table."

Ms. McCauley began ringing up Ainsley's groceries. Gobblin's had never installed a scanner and still priced each item individually. Things like this made Ainsley feel her small town was still special. A new Wal-Mart had gone in twenty minutes away, but Ainsley refused to visit it. She liked the fact that someone knew her name at the store.

She noticed that Ms. McCauley was studying her. The kind woman finally said, "You have quite a special day planned, don't you?"

"Well, yes. Dad and I always do like to have a good group over, as you know. When did you come? Four or five years ago?"

"Yes, it was splendid. The best turkey I've ever had! I don't know how you do it without drying that bird out. It melted in my mouth! I still think you should start a catering business, Ainsley. You know how much this town loves your cooking."

Ainsley grinned. "Maybe someday."

Ms. McCauley was now bagging the groceries. "But this is an extra special Thanksgiving, isn't it?"

Ainsley cocked her head to the side. "Well, um…"

She shook her head. "I'm sorry. I'm being nosy." She stopped bagging groceries and lowered her voice, though there were only a few other people in the store this early. "I just heard that you and, um, Boo…"

Ainsley felt her whole face burn, and she had to look away. People knew. That was okay, right? But it was quite something to hear people speak of it. She wasn't ashamed, just still getting used to the reality of it. "It's true. Wolfe's a wonderful human being. We're having a lot of fun together. And he's coming over today."

"Oh, now that's quite a big step. Inviting him over to meet the family, eh?" She winked and finished bagging the groceries. "Well, I'm happy for you, Ainsley. I really am."

Ainsley grinned. Yes, she was happy too. Happy for herself. She held her head high with that idea.

"Twenty-three dollars and five cents," Ms. McCauley said. Ainsley handed her the money, and as soon as the register popped open, so did Ms. McCauley's mouth: "But is it true he's not going to be writing those books anymore?"

It occurred to Ainsley that Ms. McCauley looked more worried than pleasant now. Ainsley scratched her head, unable to decide what to say. Didn't anyone care that this man's whole life had changed? Who cared about those stupid books anymore? They were just trash! Didn't they see that?

Ms. McCauley leaned forward on the counter. "Then it *is* true."

Ainsley met her eyes. "Why does it matter? He's changed. He's devoted his life to God. Doesn't that mean something?"

"It's just…just…astonishing, that's all," Ms. McCauley said, avoiding Ainsley's eyes. "Our little town depends on him, you know. Ainsley, since Boo moved here, my little grocery store makes nearly three thousand dollars the week of Halloween on candy sales alone. That doubles our sales for October nearly every year. I've been able to do things I'd never dreamed of. Last year I took my first cruise. And next summer I'd like to go to Europe."

Ainsley sighed, sure Ms. McCauley's new lifestyle was due in part to Mr. Cowen's decision to ditch her for a twenty-five-year-old, but she kept her mouth quiet and took the sack of groceries. She tried to smile. "Have a nice Thanksgiving, Ms. McCauley."

"Thank you. You too."

Ainsley carefully put her groceries in her car, and then sat in the driver's seat while the heater warmed up. The disappointment she was feeling about Ms. McCauley's remarks faded as she thought more about her day. Who cared what people thought Wolfe should do? He'd made his decision. He'd left that world. And today was Thanksgiving. She had a lot to smile about.

By the time she arrived home, she was looking forward to getting things under way. It was almost seven and she had a lot to do before the crowd arrived.

She put her groceries away and checked the turkey cooking slowly in the oven.

"Smells wonderful, honey," Sheriff Parker said, squeezing Ainsley by the shoulders from behind. Ainsley turned and kissed him on the cheek.

"Good morning. You're up early."

Her dad opened the door of the second oven and inhaled deeply. "Pumpkin. My favorite."

"Mine too," Ainsley said. "And it was Mom's." She watched her dad smile at the thought, then gently close the oven door.

"Are you wearing perfume?"

Ainsley caught her breath as she answered. "As a matter of fact, I am. Smells good, doesn't it?" Ainsley concentrated her attention on rinsing her mixing spoons. "I think I've outdone myself this year. But I think I say that every year. It's going to be a great day."

"What time are our guests scheduled to arrive?" His voice was cheery again.

"Any time after eleven. We'll eat at two."

Sheriff Parker rubbed his hands together. "Good. I can at least watch some football in peace for a little while."

Ainsley laughed as she pulled banana-nut bread batter out of the refrigerator and poured it into her bread pans. "I'm so glad this day is here. The weather seems perfect. Cold enough to start a fire, but no snow."

"Forecast says there's a chance."

"Oh, what do they know?" Ainsley pushed the bread into the oven as she thought of snuggling with Wolfe on the couch in front of the fireplace. This was going to be a good day. Maybe this would be the day they would finally kiss. "I wonder what everyone's doing this morning?"

Her father sipped his coffee. "Well, probably thinking about how good they're going to eat today!"

And with that, Thief appeared at his empty food bowl, a pathetic meow reminding his owner that his feast should begin now.

"You are going to make me lose my appetite!"

"Well, stop being so pushy. It wouldn't be so hard to fall in love with you if you weren't so horribly unlikable!"

"I'm *trying* to help you! I'm *trying* to make you see the importance of all this. Have you always been such a slow learner?"

"With that kind of charm, how could I possibly not melt at your feet?"

"May I remind you that we're not really in love?"

"No reminder needed."

Garth groaned as he sat next to Melb on the couch. "I'm not trying to charm you. I'm trying to teach you how to be madly in love. We're supposed to be over there in three hours, and I can barely get you to look lovingly into my eyes."

"There's a reason for that," Melb quipped.

"Look," Garth said, "if you could just focus on the end result, everything would be fine."

"Everything is not fine!" Melb said. "First of all, I don't see how all this is going to work. If *they're* in love, why do they care if *we're* in love? And if we're in love, why would they want to break us up?"

"It's simple," Garth said, reclining against the back of the couch. "Wolfe and Ainsley aren't in love. They're in love with the idea of being in love." Garth reached across Melb and grabbed her book that was sitting on his coffee table. He turned the cover toward Melb. "This is what people think being in love is. A woman draped across the body of a man, looking faint and weak, while the man, with rock-hard muscles and a golden tan, holds her as if she were a feather, looking off into the distance as if there's something more important than what seems to be dying in his arms."

Melb blinked. "So?"

"*So* that is not love, Melb. Just once I'd like to see a man and a woman on the cover showing what real love is like."

"And you're experienced in this?"

"Sure. It's not hard to figure out. True love is a man and woman hooking up, saying the vows, being fruitful and multiplying, if you know what I mean, and then being pillars in the community."

"How utterly romantic."

"*This* is not romantic!" Garth pointed his long finger right in Bridgette's face. "Have you ever tried to hold another human being up like this? When their arms are dangling, they're dead weight! There's nothing romantic about it."

Melb shook her head and sat limply on the couch. She already dreaded having to see Ainsley and Wolfe together at Thanksgiving, but the idea of holding hands with Garth made it even worse. His perpetually sweaty palms made it nearly impossible to hang on anyway.

Garth threw the book down on the couch between them, and Melb continued to stare at the cover. She just couldn't shake the idea of Wolfe holding her in his strong arms as she stared into his dark eyes.

The thought of them together gave her strength to do the unthinkable.

"All right," Melb said, though rather solemnly, "I'll do it. I'll do whatever it takes."

"You'll hold my hand?"

Melb took his hand and tried not to think of the moisture.

"You'll look lovingly into my eyes?"

Melb gathered herself and focused her attention right between his eyes so she wouldn't have to concentrate on the tiny sty that had begun to erupt on his left tear duct.

"You'll say adoring things to me?"

"Oh Garth…oh Garth… Oh, oh Garth…"

Garth frowned. "Yes?"

Melb thought hard. "Is there anyone who can neuter a cat with as much skill as you?"

Garth smiled. "And you'll kiss me?"

Melb swallowed. Kiss him? On the lips? Those dry, flaky lips? Garth puckered. Melb could hardly breathe. She closed her eyes, leaned forward, kissed him briefly, and decided his lips were quite smooth after all, though his breath smelled like dog chow. She opened her eyes and smiled.

"Well," Garth said with a scowl, "I've never been kissed on the nose before, but if that's the best you can do, I guess I'll have to live with it."

"Sorry," Melb said, biting a fingernail.

"What's important," Garth said after a moment, "is that we come across as genuinely in love, and that we use this to our advantage. We must look for every opportunity and seize it. Do you understand?"

"Yes."

"Good. Now, why don't we try that kiss again?"

Melb cleared her throat. "Garth, I think the more spontaneous we are about this, the more genuine it will be. If the opportunity presents itself, we'll kiss. Okay?"

Garth didn't seem too excited about that approach, but he agreed with a nod. And Melb prayed that the opportunity wouldn't present itself under *any* circumstance.

Missy Peeple could hardly believe how intelligent she was for her age. Most of her friends were losing their minds, but not Missy Peeple. No. She would save her little town from certain destruction and fall in love—all at the same time. She'd spent the morning getting her hair done at the parlor, raising a few suspicions about why she wanted her makeup done as well. They could talk. Talk was good. It was only going to help her at this stage of the game.

She had taken all morning to pick out an outfit, but she'd finally decided on a nice orange polyester suit with a yellow scarf and her favorite brown shoes. She stood in front of the mirror without her cane, inspired by the beauty before her. How good she looked! How good she felt! Mayor Wullisworth would not be able to take his eyes off her. Not today. Not ever again. She found her cane and steadied herself for the walk over to the phone. She dialed the number.

"Hello?"

"Good morning, Garth. And happy Thanksgiving to you."

A pause was followed by, "Hello."

"Is Ms. Cornforth with you?"

"Yes."

"Then I'll make this brief. I'll be bringing someone with me today."

"Oh?"

"And I intend on using him to our advantage. Don't let his coming throw you off."

"I see."

"I realize you can't say much right now, and that is probably a good thing. Your mouth always did get you in trouble. Just stick with the plan. Our day has arrived. And Skary will be better for it. Good-bye."

Miss Peeple hung up just as the doorbell rang. She straightened her suit, patted her hair into place, and rubbed a finger across the front of her teeth. She went to the door slowly, opened it and said with a smile, "Hello, Alfred. You're right on time."

"Settle down, kids," Wolfe said as Goose and Bunny strained their leashes to find something fun and exciting on their morning walk. The cold air didn't seem to bother the dogs, who burst through each frozen breath with ease. Wolfe, on the other hand, found it a little hard to breathe and was panting by the time they reached the back steps of his house. He released them from their leashes, and they trotted around the house, not ready to come inside. Wolfe removed his shoes, took his stocking cap off, and unzipped his coat as he went through the door.

Upstairs, he showered, warming up in the hot water, and then came back down for a light breakfast. Nothing sounded good, though. In anticipation of this day, he'd lost his appetite. But it was a good thing, because he knew Ainsley's feast would be nothing short of grand, and he didn't want to spoil his appetite.

So instead of eating, he went to his study, found his keys, and unlocked the only drawer that was locked in his whole house. There was one thing in it…the only thing that had occupied it for more than ten years: a ring.

He carefully pulled the box out and opened it up. There in the middle was the dainty gold band holding up a diamond solitaire. He thought of his mother's hands running through his hair, and the ring that would sometimes catch on a tangle.

She hadn't been wearing it the day she died. She never wore her jewelry when she traveled. Wolfe had inherited it, along with everything else his parents owned, but this ring in particular meant so much to him. He could hardly hold it without a lump forming in his throat. Today was a little different, because with the lump also came a rare and unspeakable joy, and an anticipation and nervousness that he could hardly utter.

He held the small ring up in the light. It still gleamed beautifully. He knew she would like it. It wasn't fancy, but it had meaning and warmth attached to it that more gold and diamonds would obscure. He thought Thanksgiving might be a nice time to ask. He had so much to be thankful for. And all her friends would be there to witness it. His heart trembled, but whether from nervousness or excitement he couldn't say.

He realized it might seem rushed. They'd been dating for less than a month, but for Wolfe, the love affair had gone on for much longer. And now that his highest hopes had come true, what else could he want than to spend the rest of his life with her? He loved her, wanted to take care of her, wanted to make her happy. He held the ring tightly in his hand and thought of kissing her on their wedding day.

A dominating presence intruded on his blissful images of a life full of love…her father. He would have to ask permission. He knew Ainsley would want that. But only a few days ago her father thought him capable of murder. How would he ever convince him he was right for his daughter? The thought paralyzed any more daydreaming, and soon he returned the ring to its box and set it on the desk.

His thoughts turned to the last Thanksgiving he'd spent with his parents. It had been a quiet one, but with all the fixings. He hadn't spent a holiday with a turkey since. Today he was going to eat turkey and pumpkin pie and who knew what else. He was going to be around people, enjoy fellowship. And mostly he was going to spend time with the woman of his dreams. This day was setting up to be just about perfect, Sheriff Parker notwithstanding.

He sighed away his dreamy thoughts and put the ring back in the drawer. But he didn't lock it. His mind was not made up yet.

CHAPTER 23

THEIR ATTIRE CLASHED. She wore orange. He wore pink. She'd been around a lot of years, but she couldn't say she'd seen too many men in pink. The tie had pink in it too, but also some more masculine colors like blue and green. Thank goodness for that.

Alfred looked around her living room as if he hadn't been there before, his face registering no certain impression. She lived modestly, it was true, and there was probably a layer of dust on everything, but she reminded herself that he wasn't the one she was trying to impress anyway.

He glanced at his watch. "What time are we supposed to be there?"

"Any time after eleven."

He rolled his eyes and leaned back onto the couch, folding his arms against his chest, hardly looking her in the eye. "I can't say I'm comfortable with this arrangement."

"And what arrangement is that, Mr. Tennison?"

"Do I have to say it out loud?"

Miss Peeple smiled at him. "I'm afraid you'll have to be more specific. You're not comfortable with coming to Thanksgiving as my date unannounced, or you're not comfortable with scheming your way back into Wolfe Boone's life in a quite compromising way?"

He swallowed, his dark eyes seeming to sink into his bony skull. "Yes."

She laughed. "Well, you are quite desperate, Mr. Tennison, and desperate times call for desperate measures."

"I don't believe I'm the only one who's desperate," he said. "Let's not forget that."

"Oh, I could hardly forget that. A lot is at stake on this Thanksgiving Day."

He clicked his tongue precisely with the second hand of the nearby clock, his eyes fading with thought. "I'm not sure this is the right thing to do," he said suddenly.

Missy Peeple sat up straight in her chair and leaned forward on her cane. "Who said anything about *right*, Mr. Tennison?"

"It's a cutthroat business, sure. But I've never stooped this low." Miss Peeple hoped he wasn't referring to accompanying her to the Parkers'. "Wolfe is a good man. He always has been, despite the perception people might have of him. It's just an image."

"And your *point?*"

"I've always considered him a friend. I don't have many friends. This isn't a business about having friends. But Wolfe I guess I could call a friend."

"You could also call him your bankroll, Mr. Tennison. He's the reason you can wear those fancy shoes and that fancy watch and slick your hair back like you're someone special. Am I right? Without Wolfe Boone, you're merely another editor groveling at the feet of those more powerful than you."

Mr. Tennison's eyes reflected a distant bitterness. Then his face turned stern. "Wolfe owes me."

"Oh?"

"I'm the reason he is where he is today. Wolfe Boone's career would've had a three-month shelf life along with all the other writer wannabes if it hadn't been for me. You know, he's not that good a horror writer to begin with. His language—much too flowery. His characters always have too much depth. I've had to steer him along the way, show him what the world wanted from him. If it hadn't been for me, he'd be writing poetry in a coffee shop somewhere on the West Coast."

"He does owe you, then."

Mr. Tennison's reserved anger released in the form of a hot sigh. "Editors are endlessly underappreciated."

"I can imagine. So then you're not going to have a problem carrying out our plan?" Miss Peeple said. "Somewhere between stuffing your face with dressing and indulging in one of the fifteen desserts I'm sure Miss Parker has prepared, you're going to rise to the occasion, aren't you?"

Mr. Tennison settled into the couch and nodded. Then he said, "But I don't know how he's going to respond when I arrive, crashing Thanksgiving in the form of your arm piece."

Missy flashed a grin at him. "Don't underestimate the element of surprise. And believe me, this will be quite the surprise, sir. We'll just have to convince him of the chemistry between us, so as to distract him from the real reason you are there…"

Mr. Tennison stood and said, "I need to use your toilet."

"Are you about done in there?"

"I'm hurrying. What time is it?"

"Twenty till."

Despite the cold weather outside, Melb Cornforth was sweating up a storm in Garth Twyne's small, tiled bathroom. She managed to pull the T-shirt over her head, but that was all the progress she'd made.

It was Garth's lousy idea that they wear matching long-sleeved T-shirts. He happened to have two identical ones that he'd won at the fair three years ago while tossing beanbag frogs onto lily pads. "Couples in love wear matching T-shirts," he'd assured her. "Don't you see them on the streets? At the store? The carnivals? They hold hands and wear matching T-shirts."

Sure, they wore matching T-shirts. But the problem was, Garth Twyne was a skinny rail of a human being with hardly a patch of fat on him. Melb Cornforth, on the other hand, was what she liked to call… well…"voluptuous," though the scientific community insensitively referred to her frame as "overweight." She was big-boned and tall, that was all.

She tugged at the arm holes of the extra-small T-shirt, trying to get at least one arm in. She almost suffocated herself at one point when she managed to jab the first part of her arm through one hole but got stuck with the rest of the T-shirt snug against her face. After what seemed like an eternity, she found the other arm hole and got the other arm through, but now her arms were stuck straight up in the air and the rest of the T-shirt was wrung around her neck.

"What's going on in there?" Garth asked from the other side of the door. "How much primping can someone do with a T-shirt?"

With arms straight up in the air and the rest of the T-shirt choking her neck, she managed to say, *"Shut up!"*

She wriggled her body left and right and thought for a moment she'd created quite a dance move. But then her thoughts went back to the task at hand. The trick would be to pull it down without ripping a hole in the shirt. She'd seen the way teenagers dressed these days, with no regard for modesty, but she was no teenager, and she wasn't about to wear something with a gaping hole in it, no matter what people "in love" do.

"What man wears an extra-small T-shirt?" she growled with maddening restraint. Then, without warning, the T-shirt dropped two inches, releasing her arms to her sides. She laughed with relief and carefully rolled the rest of the material down, sucking in her rib cage and everything else that would constrict, until once and for all the T-shirt was in place. She could hardly breathe.

She turned to the mirror and bit her lip. Sweat had smeared her makeup, and her curls were now soggy and limp. She took a few pieces of toilet paper, blotted her skin, and tried to fluff her curls with her fingers, though now she was scarcely able to *raise* her hands above her chin without the shirt riding up on her belly. She decided maybe the crisp air outside would dry her off a bit, and she turned to the full-length mirror on the back of the bathroom door. She gasped.

She looked horrible, as if she'd shrunk her ten-year-old nephew's T-shirt in the dryer and then decided to put it on. Every curve, roll, and bump she had was not only noticeable but accentuated. How could she leave the house?

But the more she studied herself, the more she realized that the shirt wasn't a far cry from the tight bodices worn by all those women in all those romance novels. So there wasn't a stitch of lace to be found—it *did* make her look a bit skinnier. She'd always wanted to wear a bodice, and maybe this is what it *felt* like to wear a bodice. She turned to see herself at every angle, and just as she was about to toss her head back and strike a romantic cover pose, Garth shattered her fantasy. "*Helloooo?* You dead in there or something?"

"Give me a second, will you?"

"It's been fifteen minutes! We're going to be late!"

"We'll tell them we've been making out all morning, okay?"

"Ooo, good idea," she heard Garth say.

She looked in the mirror one more time, puckered her lips, and reminded herself that under *no* circumstances could she raise her arms above her head, and that at all times she was going to have to be sucking in. This did *not* make for a good Thanksgiving Day scenario, but she wasn't there to eat turkey anyway. She was there to win the man of her dreams. She opened the bathroom door.

Garth's eyes widened with astonishment. "Oh…my…"

"Don't say a word." She said this carefully, because with her organs sucked in she could only manage four or five words at a time. "This was your lousy idea. Besides, I think I look a little sexy."

The corner of Garth's lip twitched, but he managed to keep a straight face. What did he know about style, anyway? This was a guy who had to punch extra holes in his belt to get one to fit around his nearly non-existent waist, and who thought they sold Wranglers on Rodeo Drive.

"Well, I guess we should go," he said, then turned back to her and added, "my love."

"Yeah, yeah," Melb said, following him out the front door. She had little breath for conversation.

Oliver Stepaphanolopolis knotted his tie precisely, and for the first time since he was a teenager he put some gel in his hair. He only had a few wisps on top, but a little gel helped them stick up in a much hipper way. He put on some cologne and then went to his closet, trying to decide which pants to wear. His size 38s made him look fit, but on Thanksgiving Day, who wanted to wear pants one size too small? But for Melb…yes, the 38s.

His heart sank for a moment, remembering that Melb was spoken for. But not in a till-death-do-us-part sort of way. He had to do something. Find the courage somehow to express his feelings for Melb. He'd already waited too long.

He bit his lip and stared into the mirror. Of course, there was one sure way, according to Miss Peeple, to win Melb's heart: Break up Wolfe and Ainsley. Ainsley would reattach to Garth, and he would be there to sooth Melb's wounded heart. Ainsley's words of reassurance that Wolfe was the "one" echoed in his mind. If only he could prove somehow that no one had ever witnessed to Wolfe. Then he'd know for sure, and so would Ainsley.

He shook his head at how complicated things were getting. He just hoped no one got hurt.

Mayor Wullisworth hung up the phone, breathing hard. It was him again. Calling again. And again. Didn't he understand "no comment"? The mayor paced his kitchen. What exactly did he know? Perhaps nothing if he was still calling. But…but…maybe too much! Anxiously he picked every crumb off the counter.

And then he stopped. He stood up straight. He was no coward. He had not become mayor of Skary by bowing to every bully that came along. In fact, he did have some control over this situation. All he had to do was get Boo back to his old self. Writing those novels again. Knock some sense into the man. Get that pesky editor of his off this tangent. Yes. Easy.

And, as Missy had suggested, if Wolfe knew how *difficult* the

Christian faith was, perhaps…yes, just perhaps Boo would go back to being who he was supposed to be in the first place. And then things would be quiet again.

Quiet—oh how he liked quiet. His fingers moved to beneath the toaster, where many crumbs were to be found.

But how? How would he convince Wolfe Boone of the difficulties of the faith without giving himself away and at the same time sounding like a general twit?

It would have to be in casual conversation, sound genuine, something you'd talk about on Thanksgiving Day. Maybe they could talk about the Bible. Yes! Perfect! He would simply mention the passages that could make a grown man cry. What could a babe in the faith like Boo know about context?

Brushing off his hands, the mayor ran to his study, trying to find his Bible. But he couldn't. It had been years since he'd used it. Rubbing his temples, he tried to think of what to do. If he thought hard enough, perhaps he could remember enough to make him look good. He found a stack of three-by-five cards. As fast as he could, he began writing down everything he could remember. Who knew if he was getting them exactly right? It would be close enough.

"So? What do you think?"

Goose and Bunny thumped their tails against the hard wood, their eyes bright with doggy wisdom.

"Too soon? I'll look like a moron if I ask Ainsley to marry me today?"

"Woof!" Bunny said.

Wolfe stared at the ring in his hand. "But why wait? I love her."

"Woof!" Goose replied.

"You two are a lot of help." Wolfe sighed and put the ring back in the box. It was nearly noon. He didn't want to arrive too early but didn't want to be late either. He stood up from the bed, examining himself in the full-length mirror. He looked all right, he supposed. He turned back to his dogs.

"Okay, kids. You be good. I promise to bring some turkey back for you." Then, without further hesitation, he took the ring out of the box and stuffed it in the front pocket of his pants. "If it's supposed to be, it will happen," he breathed. It was time to go. But not without a prayer first.

CHAPTER 24

GUESTS WERE ARRIVING every two to three minutes, and Ainsley couldn't have been more pleased. She noticed the way they stopped and looked at the Thanksgiving wreath on the door and the way they raised their noses as they entered the house, each commenting on their favorite smell. The fire crackled in the corner of the living room where most of the guests were gathering, including Wolfe, whom Ainsley found remarkably handsome.

His tall figure towered above the rest, and every once in a while he'd look away from the conversation and smile at her. She melted every time. She'd decided early in the morning to try not to interfere with the day at hand. So much of her wanted to control every moment, to make sure her father behaved himself around Wolfe, to make sure the guests completely enjoyed themselves, to make sure Wolfe felt secure. But she knew she couldn't do all those things and would just have to enjoy the day and all that it offered…which was so much.

The doorbell rang, and Ainsley answered it. Standing there was Missy Peeple, her arm wrapped around a middle-aged man with dark hair and a dark coat to match. Miss Peeple smiled graciously. Her friend—a man she recognized as being at the church meeting—looked very uneasy.

"Miss Peeple, welcome," Ainsley said, stepping aside to usher them in. "You brought a guest! How lovely." She offered her hand. "I'm Ainsley Parker."

The man said, "Alfred Tennison."

"I hope it won't be a bother. This was a last-minute decision," Miss Peeple said.

"It's fine," Ainsley said. "We've got more food than we'll know what

to do with." She mentally juggled the seating arrangements and hoped
no one would mind scooting down on one side of the table. "Everyone's
in the living room. We have plenty of hors d'oeuvres and drinks. May I
take your coats?"

Ainsley couldn't help but notice how uncomfortable the poor fellow
was. Maybe it was because Missy Peeple was clutching his arm as if she
thought it might fall off. She took their coats, hung them in the closet,
and watched the odd pair join the crowd.

"Alfred?" The question came from Wolfe. Ainsley caught his surprised expression and stepped into the room to join him.

"Hi, Wolfe," Alfred extended his hand. "Happy Thanksgiving."

"What are you doing here?"

The chattering crowd hushed to eavesdrop.

"He's with me," Miss Peeple said. "We met when he was in town
last, and—well, let's just say we hit it off." She looked at Mr. Tennison
with adoring eyes. "I can see why you like him so much, Mr. Boone."

Wolfe's eyes went wide. "You two are dating?"

Missy Peeple was about to say something when Mr. Tennison said,
"Well, march us up to the altar already, would you? We're getting
acquainted, let's just say that."

Wolfe looked at Ainsley, who could only shrug with bewilderment.
Alfred offered a nervous laugh, which seemed enough to break the tension. Ainsley steered the two over to the drink table. After she got them
situated, she found Wolfe, who had abandoned the group for a quiet
corner of the kitchen.

"Alfred's my overly ambitious editor," Wolfe explained. "I can't
believe he's here. I knew he was in town. Did you know he was coming?
I thought he was just lingering, trying to get me to talk to him."

Ainsley shook her head. "He seems nice enough."

Wolfe bit his lip. "I guess so. I can't believe he and Miss Peeple are
an item, or whatever you want to call it. It just seems so weird."

"Well, something must be in the water, because the last two people
I would've hooked up would be Garth Twyne and Melb Cornforth."
The doorbell rang. "Speaking of, maybe that's them. Excuse me."

Ainsley went to the door and opened it. There they stood, Garth's arms wrapped around Melb's neck, Melb smiling as though she'd just won a million dollars. "Hi there, you two."

"Happy Thanksgiving," they both said.

"Come on in. Can I take your coats?"

Garth slipped his off, but Melb said, "No. Um, no. I'll keep mine." She wrapped her arms around herself as though Ainsley might take it anyway.

"Are you sure? It's plenty warm in here. I've got the fire going."

"I'm *very* cold natured. I wear sweaters in the summer. I sleep with four blankets. I have more wool socks than a sheep. No…um, thanks."

"Well, of course I want you to be comfortable. The crowd's in the living room."

She watched the two hug and kiss their way down the hallway and into the living area. She hoped she wasn't going to have to watch *that* all afternoon. She went back to find Wolfe, but he was gone. And, she noticed, so was Mr. Tennison.

❧

"She's a hundred years old, Alfred!" Wolfe said as they stood in Sheriff Parker's den. Alfred was swishing the ice in his drink, but Wolfe could only stand there and demand more of an explanation.

"Look, when have you been concerned about my love life?"

"I don't care about your love life. I care about your motives. It's a little hard for me to believe you came into town, met Missy Peeple, fell in love, and are now spending Thanksgiving with her. I just can't believe it…and you're talking to a fiction writer here."

Alfred smiled a little, still engaging his drink rather than Wolfe, but then he said, "You haven't been returning my phone calls."

"So that's what this is about!"

"No," Alfred said, finally making eye contact. "But I want to know why."

Wolfe leaned against the wall. "Because I know you, and I know why you're calling, and you can't take no for an answer. I've already told you that I'm not interested in writing any more horror novels."

"You said you were *thinking* about not writing any more. Your decision is final then?"

"Yes."

"Then I should tell you, and I almost decided not to, but…" Alfred's voice drowned in his drink.

"What?"

Alfred shook his head. "Nothing."

"Al, I'm running out of patience."

"You've never cared about reviews anyway. As long as I've known you, you've never read a single review of any of your books."

"What are you talking about?"

"Black Cats."

"What about it?"

"The reviews are…less than flattering."

"What's new? Ever since I hit the million dollar mark, the reviewers have always been rough on me."

"This time it's…bad."

"How bad?"

"They're saying you've lost your mind…in a literary sort of way."

"Lost my mind?"

"Things like…I'm sorry, this is just hard to say…that you're a joke of a writer. That *Black Cats* is one of the worst books of the decade. That you couldn't scare a reader in a dark room with a knife…that was Marge Pendleton from the *Times*."

"Marge never liked me."

"I'm sorry, Wolfe. It pains me to tell you these things. The list goes on. Geoffrey Myans from *Newsweek* called you a—"

"Enough." Wolfe held up his hands. "I don't need to hear any more. I just don't care."

Laughter erupted from the living room. Then Wolfe said, "This is so strange. It took me a year to write *Black Cats,* and as you know that's six months longer than it usually takes me to write a book. The characters were well developed. The plot was unique. And to say the book isn't scary is just flat-out absurd. Maybe this culture is getting too calloused against such things."

"Well, we both know the bump-in-the-night tale can't even scare a two-year-old anymore. But listen, I'm not buying into the idea that you're a has-been."

"A *has-been?*"

"Pat Parker, *P.W.* Listen, everyone knows you've always been a little old-fashioned, and that's what made you so endearing. You gave off this persona that you're as creepy as unidentifiable food in the back corner of the refrigerator, yet wholesome as apple pie on the fourth of July."

Wolfe glanced up at Alfred. "Where'd you come up with that?"

He shrugged. "I take some of the blame here, Wolfe. Maybe I should've seen this coming. I don't know." Alfred paused. "Look, you've tended, in the past, to be a little too sentimental for your own good."

"Sentimental? If you're referring to fully developed characters with motive and heart—"

"You write horror novels, Wolfe. No one cares about a developed character. They just want to pee their pants when the monster jumps out of the closet." Alfred set his drink on the desk. "That's where I've come in, all these years. I've helped direct you in your writing. I've shown you what the people want." Wolfe watched Alfred trace a pattern on the floor with the toe of his shoe. "And that's what I want to do for you again."

"What do you mean?"

"I mean, we can't just leave your career hanging like this, where the last word out of everybody's mouth is that you're a loser!"

"Loser?"

"Jim Mackey, the *Globe.*"

"I've never cared what the critics say. Why start now?"

"Because you're ending your career as a horror novelist, so you say. Is this really how you want it all to end? With people disrespecting you as a writer? Do you really want to give them a chance to speculate about you and say more terrible things about you?"

Wolfe realized he'd been holding his breath. He breathed deeply several times before answering. "If they hate the book, they hate the book." He noticed Alfred was beginning to wring his hands.

"But that's what everyone's going to remember you by! Not the ten brilliant best-selling books you've already written, but the eleventh book that was a bomb."

"I just can't believe it's getting such bad reviews. I really thought this was my best work to date. You said so yourself."

"You can redeem yourself, Wolfe. You can show them. Prove to them."

"Show them what? Prove what? They're going to say what they're going to say."

Alfred put a gentle hand on Wolfe's shoulder. "Show them what a good writer you are. Prove to them you're not all washed up...Betty Styler, the *Post*."

"In other words, write another book."

Alfred grinned. "Your words, not mine. But a brilliant idea, nevertheless."

"I told you I was finished writing horror."

Alfred's stress wrinkles seemed to sink deeper into his face. "Then you're finished as a respected writer. At least in the eyes of the world."

"That's your opinion."

"No, that's what's already being printed in millions of newspapers across the United States. Is that what you want?"

Suddenly Wolfe smiled, and an unfamiliar peace swept over his heart. He looked at Alfred. "No, but if that's what it takes to get what I want, then it's worth it."

"What *do* you want?!" Alfred squealed.

"*There* you are!"

Wolfe and Alfred turned to see Missy Peeple wobbling across the floor toward them.

"I've been looking everywhere for you."

"Oh, hi, um, Miss...uh, Missy." He glanced up at Wolfe's curious stare and then smiled down at the old lady next to him. "Sorry to be hiding from you. We were just talking."

"Am I interrupting?"

"Not at all," Wolfe said, glancing at Alfred. "I was just needing to go find Ainsley. I'll leave you two alone."

Wolfe walked out of the room, tempted to glance back at the two purported lovers. But the idea that he might see confirmation of a real relationship kept his eyes straight ahead.

⁂

"What are you doing?" Alfred said, pushing himself away from Miss Peeple. "I had him right where I wanted him."

Miss Peeple shook her head and adjusted her blouse. "Hardly. I've been around the corner listening for ten minutes, and I don't believe I'd agree with *that* assessment."

"Is that so?"

"First of all, the reviewers are calling this the best book he's ever written. What are you going to do when he finds that out?"

Alfred picked up his drink off the desk as he leaned against the back of the chair behind him. "Believe me, he won't. He's never read a review in his life, and I'm always the one that has to call him to tell him he's number one on the bestseller list. He's clueless about such things."

"Either way, I don't believe he's too convinced he should write another book. Are you?"

Alfred scowled. "What *is* it that he wants, anyway? He's willing to throw away his career for something. What is it?"

Miss Peeple took him by the shoulders and steered him to the doorway. "See that pretty little blond serving pastry bites over there? *That's* what he wants." Then Miss Peeple turned him a little more to the left. "And see the handsome fellow by the fire smoking his pipe? That's what *I* want. So what do you say we make an appearance nearby, and you can sing my praises next to him for a while."

"Well, *I* want Wolfe to write another book. Wasn't that the whole idea of my coming here in the first place?"

"The day is young, dear Alfred. But I am not. Now let's get over to the mayor before I keel over in my pumpkin pie."

CHAPTER 25

MELB CORNFORTH HATED being so deceptive, but Wolfe and Ainsley had hardly separated, and soon it would be time to eat. She hadn't even had a chance to talk to Wolfe yet! So it bothered her, though only mildly, that she'd approached Ainsley saying, "Hon, I think I smell something burning." Ainsley was gone in a heartbeat, and now she found herself—finally!—alone with the man of her dreams. She considered taking her coat off—she was sweating up a storm with it on—but standing next to Wolfe made her suddenly aware of exactly how tight her T-shirt was. The thought of prancing around as though she'd dressed in green Saran Wrap made her decide a little sweat might be more enchanting.

"Well, hello," she said to Wolfe, careful to regulate her breathing. She'd felt lightheaded only twice so far, but she managed to keep conversations to a minimum in order to save her oxygen supply.

"Melb," Wolfe said, looking up from the small plate of food he had on his lap. "Hi there."

"Hi," she said. "Mind if I join you?"

"Not at all," he said, moving his cup off the seat next to him. "You look a little warm. Can I take your coat for you?"

"No…I'm fine, um…it's hot flashes. It's not menopause," Melb added quickly, feeling herself sinking into the hole of humility, "because I'm nowhere near *that* stage in my life. I get cold, I get hot. You know that hormonal thing. Next thing you know I might burst into tears. But thanks for asking." Melb realized she'd said too many words in a row, depleting her brain of oxygen and causing the room to spin for a moment.

"Oh, okay. So is this your first time to come to Thanksgiving at the Parkers'?"

"Yes."

"It's a nice time. I can't wait to try all the food at dinner."

"Uh-huh." *More oxygen. Get more oxygen.*

"You and Garth seem very happy together."

"We are."

Wolfe nodded but then seemed to have nothing more to say. Melb tried to think quickly of what she might ask in order to keep the conversation going without having to do a lot of talking. *You come here often?* seemed a little generic, plus it would probably instigate talk of Ainsley, which was the last thing she needed. Then she had it! She'd talk about *Black Cats!* She'd just finished reading it a sixth time, and just this morning she saw a glowing review of it in the newspaper, not to mention it was already number five on the bestseller list! As she was thinking of how to get the conversation started in five words or less, she heard, "Hi, I'm Mayor Wullisworth. I don't believe we've ever met."

Mayor Wullisworth, of all people! That man could talk to a stump for hours! How was she going to get him to shoo?

"Hi, Wolfe Boone."

"Glad to meet you." The mayor sat down, and Melb noticed him stuff a stack of note cards into his jacket pocket. "I'd just like to say how thankful we all are here in Skary for the—how shall I put this?—economic advantage you've given us over the past few years. We wouldn't be where we are without you."

Wolfe nodded but was silent.

"I heard you were at church Sunday."

"I was."

"That's good. Blessed are the churchgoers, for they shall go to church and give lots of money."

Wolfe glanced at Melb, who couldn't recall ever hearing that beatitude.

"I'm just kidding," the mayor smiled. "Just testing your knowledge of Scripture."

"Do you attend Reverend Peck's church?" Wolfe asked.

"Well, Sunday is a very busy day for mayors. I work seven days a week, actually."

"Oh."

"And you know what the Bible says about laziness."

"Uh, no, not really."

The mayor cleared his throat. "Well, just that it's bad. I think it might actually call it a sin."

"But aren't we supposed to rest on the Sabbath?"

"Well not if we're going to be doing the Lord's work!"

Melb quickly understood that Wolfe's attention had completely shifted from her to the mayor, that the mayor's profound ignorance of the Bible was beginning to intrigue Wolfe, and that Wolfe was beginning to forget she was sitting there, so in a moment of complete desperation, Melb threw off her coat in order to be, at the least, shocking, and at the most, well, attractive. The air of the room offered relief to her very damp skin, and she closed her eyes, thankful to be cooling off just a little.

But even with this very, very, very tight T-shirt on, no one seemed to notice her. Not even Wolfe and the mayor, who were right next to her. How could this be? Didn't women in tight T-shirts *always* get noticed?

Perhaps the subtle clearing-of-the-throat tactic might work. But before she got a chance, Garth walked by, and Melb got a whiff of his cologne, which he always wore way too strong. And cheap. It gagged her and then made her sneeze with such force that if she'd been pointed toward the fireplace, she just might have blown out the fire.

"Bless you," she heard from several people, including Wolfe and the mayor.

The sneeze brought Melb a newfound sense of freedom that she couldn't immediately identify. She could breathe, for one thing. And had someone left the door open? There seemed to be a breeze in the house. Then with utter terror she realized she'd blown out her T-shirt's side seams and now wore what looked like a knit poncho, flapping in the breeze of the nearby conversation. She gasped, jumped up, threw her coat back on, and rushed down the hallway to the bathroom, tears of humiliation welling in her eyes.

She ran smack dab into Ainsley Parker, throwing her against the wall. "Oh…sorry! So sorry!"

Ainsley called out after Melb. "Are you okay? What's wrong?"

Melb could do nothing but burst into tears.

Ainsley shut the door to her bedroom and turned to Melb, who was sitting quietly on the end of her bed, sniffling.

"Melb, don't worry. We'll find you something to wear."

She saw Melb's eyes study her figure and then she shook her head. "I doubt that."

"Listen, it was probably a very poorly made T-shirt. These days they never double-stitch a seam, and it shows, I tell you. It could've happened to anybody."

Melb blotted her eyes with a tissue. "It was Garth's dumb idea to wear matching T-shirts."

Ainsley turned from sifting through the clothes in her closet. "Well, Garth can be demanding like that sometimes. You should stand your ground with him, don't let him push you around. He thinks he always knows best, but he doesn't."

"You've known Garth for a long time."

"Since we were children." Ainsley moved hangers down the rack, trying to find anything that might work for Melb. "I'm sorry, I shouldn't say those things about Garth. I'm not trying to be rude. I know you really like him. And he really likes you."

"Yeah, we're a dream come true," she heard Melb say, though her tone sounded flat.

"What made you two decide to date?"

She turned to find Melb chewing furiously at a fingernail. Melb glanced up, startled to find Ainsley looking at her. "Oh…well, there's always two versions to a story, I guess."

"But what made you fall for him?"

"I've always loved animals. So that was a start."

"Oh."

"How's it coming over there in the closet?"

Ainsley pulled out a green cardigan, big and boxy, that she wore mostly around the house. It was one of her favorite sweaters. She hoped with all her might that it would work for Melb. All the poor woman needed was more humiliation.

"Try this. It should work. And it's really warm, since I know you're cold-natured." She held it up for Melb to see.

"I was hoping for a tank top soaked in ice water, but this will do," Melb said, standing. She looked at Ainsley. "I'm not cold-natured. I was just embarrassed about the T-shirt. I think I about had a heat stroke."

Ainsley smiled and handed her the sweater. Melb closed the door to the bathroom, and when she came out, the sweater was on, fitting nicely.

"It looks great on you! Green is definitely your color."

Melb turned to the nearby mirror. "Well, it does flatter my figure, I have to say."

"Very much so."

Melb turned back to her. "Thank you. I'll get this back to you. And I'll try not to drip gravy all over it."

Ainsley reached for her shoulder. "Melb, are you sure everything's okay? I mean, are you and Garth doing okay?"

Melb sniffled and said, "Couldn't be happier." And then she walked out.

"Look, I don't know what to say. I did the best I could."

"Are you trying to tell me that you talked to Boo for twenty minutes and came up with nothing better than 'Thou shalt not steal' to steer him away from the faith?"

"First of all," said the mayor, "I was a little taken aback by how much Scripture he already knows."

"So he outdid you, did he? Knew more than you did? Threw you for a loop? Why weren't you prepared? You know how much is at stake here!" Missy Peeple leaned forward on her cane, staring at the mayor with harsh eyes.

"I was prepared!" The mayor removed a stack of note cards from his pocket. "See? All kinds of scriptures here. I've got envy. Judging others. Adultery. Murder. Just fitting them into a conversation was a little awkward, that's all. I mean, 'Thou shalt not murder' doesn't really fit in with, 'Have you tried the eggnog yet?'"

Missy shook her head. "In this life you will have trouble."

"What?"

"The Bible says that, you know. In fact, it's a *promise*."

"Well that's inspiring," the mayor said blandly.

Missy sighed. "Just go. Get back in the game. You're not doing any good standing over here with your note cards. Just remember, sir, that if you don't succeed, a certain somebody's going to be writing a certain book about a certain scandal that I'm certain you'd rather not see in print." The mayor was annoying in his ineptness, but he still had gorgeous eyes. She smiled. "But I trust you won't fail."

Missy Peeple met Garth's look from across the room. He was standing near the fireplace, staring at her.

"Excuse me for a moment, will you?" Miss Peeple said. But the mayor grabbed her arm.

"Not so fast, Missy," he said. "You're not going anywhere until I get a straight answer from you."

Missy stared into his glaring eyes. "An answer to what, Mayor?"

"Why are you here with this Tennison fellow? Like he's your date? What's going on?"

Miss Peeple smiled. "Does it concern you, my dear?"

He frowned. "Only in that I think it's a distraction to the task at hand." He lowered his voice. "Do *I* have to remind *you* what is at stake here? My reputation at the very least."

"I'm hardly distracted."

"Oh? Then are you trying to tell me while you're making ga-ga eyes over him, you're remembering that Skary is at stake?"

"Everything is under control. Don't you worry your pretty little self over that, sir."

Mayor Wullisworth's eyes showed surprise, and he stood up straighter, glancing around at the crowd. "I'm, um…I'm not worried. I just want to make sure you're not distracted."

She watched his gaze land on Alfred, who was standing next to the snack plates, dripping ranch dressing down the front of his shirt as he attempted to bite into a carrot. Missy cleared her throat. "He is quite a looker, wouldn't you say? But Mayor, I've always been able to do more than one thing at a time. And I assure you, though the attraction is quite intense between the two of us, Alfred is here for other reasons as well. Remember, he's got a stake in this too."

She carefully edged over to Garth.

"Garth," she said confidently, "if you stare at me with much more angst, you're liable to have that handsome fellow over there on to you."

"Don't give me that song and dance," Garth said with narrowed eyes. "I know what you're up to. I know Mr. Tennison is Wolfe's editor, and you two have as much chemistry between you as two pieces of white bread. Now I want to know what's going on. Have you made any progress?"

"Progress is hard to measure, lad," Miss Peeple said, "but if you must know, all is going as planned."

"What's up your sleeve? I want to know."

"You don't need details. It will just make you a liability. What you need to concentrate on is your assigned task. Have you or haven't you?"

Garth glanced around her to make sure they weren't in earshot of anyone. "Not yet. The timing hasn't been quite right."

"Well honey, the party's not going to last all day. Get your act together." She turned and saw Wolfe standing by himself near a shelf of books. He had been talking to Marlee Hampton, who was headed for the drink table for a refill. Ainsley was at the front door, greeting Oliver. "There's your chance. What are you waiting for?"

"Fine. I'll do it."

But before Garth could even get around Miss Peeple, Ainsley entered the room and said, "All right everyone! It's time to eat! Let's gather in the dining room!"

The crowd quickly filed out behind Ainsley, and Garth sighed in frustration.

"Are you up for this or not?" Miss Peeple scowled at him.

"I know what I'm doing."

"I hope so," Miss Peeple said as she shuffled toward the dining room, "because if you don't, Boo and Ainsley will most likely be sharing Thanksgiving dinner together again next year. And I feel certain you won't be invited."

CHAPTER 26

WOLFE FOLLOWED THE group into the lavishly decorated dining room. Ainsley had outdone herself. The long table had an exquisite runner down the middle with fall-colored leaves arrayed delicately around several votive candles. The dimly lit room glowed with a warmth that was both familiar and awe-inspiring.

"Everyone has an assigned seat, just find your name," Ainsley instructed, and so everyone obeyed, circling the table.

"It's snowing!" someone announced, and the crowd turned to look out the bay window. Sure enough, large white snowflakes poured to the ground en masse.

"Well, they finally got it right!" Sheriff Parker said.

"I heard it's only gonna be flurries," said Oliver.

Wolfe moved to the window. He loved snow. It seemed to bring a peace down to earth straight from the heavens. But as he gazed out, he knew these were no small flurries. Already the snow had begun to accumulate, and the large flakes were falling fast. The clouds were dark blue, their bosoms bursting with moisture. He turned to find his seat.

On the other side of the table, he found his name, surprised to be sitting next to Garth Twyne.

"Hey, looks like we're dinner partners," Garth said with a seedy grin.

"Garth, what are you doing there?" Ainsley said suddenly from behind Wolfe.

"Sitting."

"But I'm sure I didn't seat you there," she said, examining his name tag at the top of his plate. "I seated you by Melb."

Wolfe looked up to find Melb across the table, two people down, sitting between Mayor Wullisworth and Reverend Peck. She gave a polite wave.

"Well, listen, don't go to any trouble. I'll sit over here next to our resident celebrity. It'd be my pleasure."

"I know I sat Wolfe by Reverend Peck. And you should sit by Melb," Ainsley insisted.

"Trust me, we'll get to spend *plenty* of time together later, right, my flaky little pastry?"

Melb blushed, nodded, and glanced at Wolfe.

Ainsley apologized. "I must've accidentally switched them when I was making room for Mr. Tennison." She looked at Wolfe as she took her seat next to him on the other side. "Sorry," she whispered.

"It's fine," he assured her.

Wolfe noticed an empty chair at the end of the table. "Your brother. Isn't he coming?"

Ainsley laughed. "Don't worry. He's never early but rarely late."

Sheriff Parker clinked his fork against his water glass. "Good afternoon, everyone, and welcome to the Parker residence. Happy Thanksgiving!" The table erupted in quiet applause. "Some of you have been here before on Thanksgiving. Others are new. We welcome you all. First of all, as is tradition here every Thanksgiving, we go around the table before we eat and say something we're thankful for. Now—"

Just then, as if a light and a string quartet had announced him, a tall blond man in his thirties with tanned skin and dazzling eyes walked through the door. Everyone at the table sensed his presence before he walked in, and when he did appear, there were gasps and cheering and clapping as if a prince had entered.

"Butch!"

Some stood, others just smiled happily. Wolfe studied the man as he greeted everyone warmly. He resembled Ainsley in many ways, as he did Sheriff Parker. The name "Butch" did him some justice, as he had a very athletic build, but his features and expressions also reflected intelligence, and the obvious charisma he carried pretty much rounded him out to be the perfect male, not to mention he was about the best looking man

Wolfe had ever seen. Wolfe swallowed three sips of water and watched as Butch finally made his way around the table to his father, whom he hugged warmly, and then to Ainsley. He messed up her hair and then hugged her, too.

"Am I late?" he said.

"Just on time, as always," Sheriff Parker said proudly. "Good to see you, son. You're looking fit. How's the Delta Force?" Sheriff Parker glanced around the table, his face unashamedly preened.

"Dad, nobody wants to hear about that," Butch said, and everyone naturally protested. He smiled humbly and winked, for no apparent reason, at Marlee, who blushed and giggled like she was fourteen. Butch's attention suddenly shifted to Wolfe. "I thought I knew everyone here, but I don't believe we've met."

Wolfe stood, glad he was as tall as Butch. Butch flashed a killer grin and held out his hand. "I'm Butch Parker."

"This is Wolfe. Boone." Ainsley stood quickly, nervously.

Butch's eyebrows rose. "Oh? No kidding." The room quieted as the two shook hands. "Well, nice to meet you! And have you to our home for Thanksgiving!"

Wolfe relaxed. Butch's charisma was contagious, his smile genuine. Wolfe felt truly welcome. Butch slapped him on the back and went to the other end of the table to sit down. "Well? What are we waiting for? Let's eat! I wait all year for this kind of meal!"

"Huh-uh, not yet," Sheriff Parker said, standing again. "Not before we do my favorite tradition, which is to go around and tell what you're thankful for." Sheriff Parker looked to his left. "Miss Peeple, why don't you start?"

Miss Peeple nodded her head and said, "Of course. I'm thankful for"—she paused, as if thinking deeply—"Skary, Indiana. And all that it is." She smiled decisively and then looked toward Alfred Tennison on her left.

Alfred cleared his throat nervously and shrugged. "I, uh... I guess I'm thankful for the food. It's been a long time since I had a turkey for Thanksgiving."

Reverend Peck, a certain sadness still lingering in his eyes, said, "I'm thankful for Thanksgiving. It always reminds me of how much we have."

Melb was next, and she stared oddly across the table at Garth before saying, "I'm thankful for Garth Twyne." She punctuated this statement with a small smile. "The love of my life."

Garth grinned at her and then glanced, for no reason, at Ainsley, who just smiled back at him approvingly.

Mayor Wullisworth said, "I'm thankful that God hates tattletales but favors plagues for those who are so inclined." He glanced at Alfred Tennison and then gave a stiff chuckle. "Just being humorous. No, I'm glad to be the mayor of Skary, Indiana, the greatest place to live in the world."

The crowd offered an apprehensive laugh.

Marlee Hampton said, "I'm thankful for Mary Kay, the woman and the company, and especially their new line of eye shadows that are guaranteed to stay on through the longest of dates." She batted her eyes at Butch.

Butch was next and he said, "I'm thankful to be alive. I can't give you details, but I had some close calls this year."

The crowd gave a somber, collective moan and shook their heads.

"I'm thankful for…Oliver!" Martin Blarty said.

"Oliver?" a few said in astonishment.

"Why yes. A *great* friend and the *best* used car salesman this side of the, uh, the equator!"

Oliver smiled proudly. He said, "Why thank you, Martin. I'm thankful to own my own business, and to be able to sell cars at more than 20 percent less than my competition, plus offer my customer satisfaction guarantee and personal service you just can't get anywhere else."

Then it was Garth's turn, who said with a bit of a dramatic flare, "I'm thankful for the Parkers."

"Hear, hear!"

Garth smiled radiantly. "They're wonderful people to open their home to us, aren't they?"

Everyone agreed heartily, and Wolfe watched Melb melt into her chair with a strange, silent anger. But then it was his turn, and before he knew it, all eyes were on him, and enough time had passed to cause an awkward silence. Still, he didn't want to rush things. He had so much to be thankful for this holiday season, and to name just one seemed impossible. Yet as he thought about it, he knew he could sum it all up with one word. And he needed to quickly, he realized, because Ainsley was fidgeting next to him in the silence, worried, he was sure, that he had nothing to say.

"God."

The word seemed to reverberate off the walls, and by the way everyone glanced nervously at each other, Wolfe thought maybe he'd pronounced His name wrong.

"I'm thankful for God," he said again, and a peace poured through his body as he said it. He knew every good thing he had came from God, and though it was a simple thanksgiving, he meant it. He caught Reverend Peck smiling at him warmly.

He turned to Ainsley, indicating it was her turn. Ainsley paused, and then said, "Me too. I'm thankful for God too."

It was Sheriff Parker's turn, and he said with an exacting expression, "Well, who isn't thankful for God?"

Everyone nodded but said nothing.

"It's time to bless the food," Sheriff Parker said, and then he turned to Wolfe. "Wolfe, why don't you lead us in prayer?"

"What?" Ainsley said.

"I said, Wolfe, why don't you lead us in prayer?" Sheriff Parker said without taking his eyes off of Wolfe.

"Daddy," Ainsley said in a lowered tone, "you *always* pray at Thanksgiving. I can't think of a year that you haven't prayed. It's practically a tradition."

"Well, times change, honey," he said. "After all, it was Mr. Boone here that said he was thankful for God. What better way to show his gratitude than to lead us in prayer on Thanksgiving?"

Wolfe knew Ainsley's apprehension. He wasn't eloquent and had no practice praying in front of people. In fact, the prayers he had managed so far had been so deeply personal and private that he'd had trouble expressing them in words. They'd been uttered from the innermost part of his heart. He scratched his head, wondering how in the world he would pray on behalf of everyone at the table. How could he even try to sound articulate? His mouth went dry as he looked around the table at the many eyes staring at him.

"Well?" said the sheriff.

"Daddy…"

"Sure, of course," Wolfe said, standing. "I'd be honored."

The sheriff looked a bit surprised, as did everyone else except the reverend, who had already bowed his head. Wolfe cleared his throat, took quick note of the reverend's folded hands, and folded his own in front of him.

"God, today is Thanksgiving, and I thank you for it." He paused, trying to think of what else he could say. "We're thankful for the Parkers, as Garth mentioned, and for inviting us all here to eat. And for a nice warm house, a good shelter from the cold snow outside." He heard a few nervous throat clearings, but figured he'd better continue, because he was pretty sure he hadn't prayed long enough.

Then, suddenly, something exceptional happened. He felt everything around him fade and realized he was speaking directly to God—and that, remarkably, God was actually listening. And before he knew it, he was expressing all that he'd been feeling for God and everything he was thankful for, and to his astonishment he wasn't at all having a hard time finding the words, and in fact they were flowing out of him so fast that he could hardly even think. Yet inside, his spirit felt free and joyful and truly thankful. He spoke of the character of God, the very attributes to which Wolfe had been drawn at the beginning. He spoke of love and forgiveness and salvation. He thanked God for the church and the people in the church and for newfound friends and fellowship. On and on he went, until finally, with hardly enough breath for it, he said, "Amen."

He opened his eyes, but it seemed to him everyone else had already opened theirs long ago. Eyes gawked at him, and he wasn't quite sure why, but he tried to smile as he took his seat again. He looked at Sheriff Parker, whose mouth was hanging open just slightly.

"Well, wasn't that an interesting prayer. Um, thank you, Wolfe. You did, however, forget to bless the food."

"Daddy," Ainsley said, "I think God got the point." She glanced at Wolfe. "I thought it was a wonderful prayer, straight from the heart."

"Yes, well, what do you say we stop talking and start eating before this wonderful food gets cold!" the sheriff said, and everyone began digging in.

Wolfe felt Ainsley's hand on his shoulder. "That was a lovely Thanksgiving prayer, Wolfe."

"So," Garth Twyne said as they were all getting seconds, "how's the writing going these days?"

Though they'd been sitting next to each other for the entire meal, this was the first time they'd spoken. Ainsley was engaged in conversation with her father and Miss Peeple. Wolfe didn't want to be judgmental, but there did seem to be something a little off about Garth, and he never quite knew how to take the guy.

"The writing?"

"Yeah, like the next book. When's it coming? What's it about? You can discuss these types of things, can't you? I mean, it's not top secret or anything, is it?" Garth laughed—it was more like a snicker—and picked at a piece of turkey between his teeth.

"It's not top secret, but there's nothing to tell you. I'm not working on anything right now."

"You've got to be kidding. Aren't writers always working on something?"

"Usually. But I'm not right now."

"So any ideas? I mean, somewhere in that dark mind of yours has to be a story just waiting to jump out and scream bloody murder."

Wolfe tried not to seem impatient, but he didn't really want to talk about it. Apparently everyone was having a hard time dealing with the idea that there were going to be no more horror novels from Wolfe Boone.

"Listen," Garth said after a moment, "I heard a rumor, and listen, I'm not one for rumors. I mean, frankly, I think you should just come right out and ask someone about something if you're not for sure. So the rumor is that you're not going to be writing any more of those scary books. Is it true?"

Wolfe scooted his cranberry sauce around his plate. "It's true. I don't want to write those kinds of books anymore. There are plenty of stories to tell without deliberately creating fear in people."

"So this is all a result of your new conversion."

"I guess it is."

Suddenly something rubbed Wolfe's leg, and he jumped before realizing it was just Thief. Wolfe shooed him away.

"Thief thinks he's one of the family," Garth said.

"I'm not really a cat person. More fond of dogs."

"I know what you mean." There was a long pause before Garth said, "Look, I think it's the totally right thing to do. About the writing."

Wolfe set down his fork. "You do?"

"Sure. I mean, it's a conviction, right? It's what you feel you need to do. I respect that."

"Thanks."

"Yeah, I mean, it must be a hard thing to turn from a career that's brought you so much fame and money and stuff."

"Well, I never wrote because of that. I guess I got into horror because I liked to surprise the reader, and when I was a kid I loved ghost stories. But somewhere along the way, it turned into something a lot scarier, a lot worse than just a ghost story. I guess I caved to the will of the market, so to speak, and I feel that—"

"Uh-huh, well, I gotta tell you that you're a bigger man than I am. And that's saying a lot. But," Garth said, his voice suddenly hushing, "you're probably going to have to break the news to a certain somebody rather gently, if you know what I mean."

"No, I'm sorry. I don't know who you're talking about."

Garth's eyes averted to Ainsley, who was nodding politely to Miss Peeple.

"Ainsley?"

"Yeah. I mean, I think she'll eventually come around to the idea, but it won't be easy at first."

"What won't be easy?"

"About the books. That you're not writing them anymore." Garth stuffed a huge wad of dressing in his mouth.

Wolfe let him chew, trying to process what Garth was trying to tell him. "Are you saying… What exactly are you saying?"

Garth swallowed and looked concerned. "She hasn't told you?"

"Told me what?"

Wiping his mouth he said, "I'm sorry, I just assumed. It's just that…" Garth again looked around at Ainsley before he spoke. "She was really excited about being in a relationship with a novelist. She just keeps talking about it, like it's her dream come true. She even said she hoped you'd take her to New York sometime. I mean, who doesn't dream of being hooked up with a famous novelist?"

Wolfe stared at his plate. Could this be true? Ainsley had never given any indication that she liked him because he was a writer. And in fact, he was pretty sure she'd always been very turned off by what he wrote.

"Where did you hear this?"

Garth shrugged. "Bits and pieces here and there. Ainsley's a private person, but she's let it be known. Perhaps she's given you the opposite impression, but you know how women are. They say one thing but mean the other."

"To you? Did she say this to you?"

Garth's face seemed tight with apprehension. "Well, not to me directly, I guess, though I've picked up on it on my own—"

"So it's a rumor."

"A rumor. Yeah, I guess, it's a rumor. But rumors tend to be awfully reliable in small towns."

Wolfe reached over and tapped Ainsley on the shoulder. She turned to him with a smile. "Hi."

"Hi. Sorry to interrupt your conversation."

"What are you doing?" Garth asked quickly.

Wolfe turned to Garth. "Well, I think you were right on track earlier when you said you just ask someone about a rumor instead of believing it."

"What rumor?" Ainsley asked.

"Well, Garth heard that you want me to take you to New York City."

Ainsley laughed. "What? That's absurd. I've never wanted to see that place. It seems like one chaotic nutty bin."

Wolfe smiled. "What about always wanting to be, um…hooked up, as Garth puts it, with a novelist?"

Ainsley's eyebrows rose as she stared at Garth. "Well, I've only known one novelist in my life, and thank the good Lord he's not writing what he used to anymore. So no, I don't guess that's true, either."

Wolfe sighed in relief and turned to Garth. "You're right, Garth. The direct approach is definitely the best."

Garth smiled, but he didn't look happy. Miss Peeple said, "Rumors are nasty old things, aren't they? Where they come from nobody knows. But thank heavens they eventually are stopped in their tracks."

Ainsley smiled and patted Wolfe on the knee. "Well, I'd better go get the dessert ready. Want to help?"

"Sure."

Wolfe followed Ainsley into the kitchen but stopped near a window. The snow was so beautiful, falling in sheets of delicate flakes onto the already white ground. Wolfe suspected the temperature had dropped several degrees in the past hour, and he was thankful for how warm and cozy it was inside the house.

He glanced down and noticed his shoe was untied, but as he bent down to tie it, the engagement ring he had removed from the box and put in his pocket had somehow worked its way up and out. It chimed as it struck the tile, and Wolfe gasped, scooping it up quickly and tucking it away before glancing over his shoulder to see if Ainsley had noticed. She was at the oven, pulling out what smelled like a pecan pie. He stood and sighed with relief.

He turned away from her and nearly knocked Miss Peeple over.

"I'm...I'm so sorry. I didn't see you, I mean I didn't know... How long have you been there?"

She winked at him as she leaned on her cane. "Long enough, deary, long enough. Don't you worry your pretty little self. These lips are sealed. There's nothing worse than a flapping tongue out of control to terrorize the community." She smacked her lips shut.

"Oh, thanks. It's not for sure. It's just in my pocket. I mean, this probably isn't the time, or maybe it is, I don't know—"

She waved her hand at him. "Don't worry. It will work itself out."

Wolfe caught his breath and realized how much he'd babbled and what he'd revealed. He stared at the ground, rubbing his temples.

"Wolfe! Come look at this pecan pie I just pulled out of the oven."

"Excuse me," Wolfe said. He quickly turned to the kitchen, where Ainsley was hovering over her newest pie.

"It'll have to cool for a while, but that will give everyone time to digest round one, and"—she looked at the guests crowded around the pies she'd already set out—"it looks like they've got a good start over there!" She looked at him and frowned. "Are you okay? You're white as a ghost."

He tried to smile. "I'm fine. The pie looks incredible. And the food was incredible. You're incredible."

Ainsley looked surprised and pleased all at once. She set her oven mitts down and stared into his eyes. "I like you more and more every second I get to know you."

"I feel the same about you."

"I have a lot to be thankful for, but most of all that I know a man as sincere, genuine, kind, and honest as you are." She lowered her eyes. "I'm sorry it's taken me this long to get to know you. It should've been sooner."

He grabbed her hands. "Let's just believe the timing is perfect."

"Okay."

"Okay."

A throat cleared, and they turned to find Sheriff Parker and Butch standing near the kitchen counter. "Sorry to interrupt," Butch said with a brotherly smirk on his face.

"You're not," Ainsley said, eyeing both of them carefully. "How's the dessert?"

"Great, as always," her father said.

"Then we'd better try some before it's all gone," Wolfe said, and with boldness that he never knew he had, he took her hand and guided her between Butch and Sheriff Parker to the dessert buffet. She was smiling from ear to ear.

"I love when you do that!" she said.

CHAPTER 27

"IT'S NOT MY FAULT!" Garth exclaimed.

Miss Peeple flapped her hands and said, "Sssshhhh! Keep your voice down, you moron." Luckily everyone was gathered around the dessert buffet.

"I did my job. He didn't bite. Obviously your plan, whatever it was, didn't work either, so stop pointing fingers," he said, pointing his own long, skinny one in her face. "And don't you forget, I've got a certain little recording that I'd be happy to use as entertainment on this wonderful Thanksgiving Day."

"Don't you threaten me, you little beanpole. You have no idea what you're up against."

"You? You're like two hundred years old and your back's curved like that cane of yours. How am I supposed to be frightened of you? I've got evidence of your craftiness that would blow this little town away. And I've made fifteen copies of that tape just in case you get any funny ideas. So don't think you can push me around with that marmy schmarmy 'I'm so wise and deceitful' business. You don't *know* wise and deceitful, Missy."

She shook her head at him and laughed. The poor lad tried hard, but at his best he was just a lot of hot air blowing out a few not-so-impressive words. Sure he was tall and physically much stronger than she. But he was no match for Missy Peeple. Few were. And so for a moment she stood silently, quietly, allowing him to think that in some way he'd affected her. The more she let him float, the bigger the bubble would become. She loved to pop big bubbles.

"Well?" he finally said. "Are you just going to stand there and pout, or are we going to come up with a plan?"

Miss Peeple knew long before this moment that Garth Twyne was a desperate man. And she knew desperate, lovesick men were capable of just about anything. This man's world was about to be turned upside down, and she would count on his desperation to stir up something akin to the storm of the century. But first she was going to have to put him in his place.

"I know about Thief."

Garth's eyes narrowed. "What are you talking about?"

"I know you botched the job. I know Thief, in fact, is *not* neutered."

She actually heard him gulp. "What'd you do? Sneak into my office?" He gasped. "Did you look at my files?"

"It doesn't matter, does it? The truth is, you botched the operation and told the sheriff he was neutered. You and I, dear Garth, know exactly why this town is overly populated with cats. And that's one too many to know such a thing." She smiled sweetly at him.

Garth was processing all this, and Missy let it sink in for a moment before saying, "It's too late, besides." She shook her head. "I'm afraid it's hopeless now."

"What are you talking about?"

In barely a whisper, one that was so quiet she was sure he would only be able to catch every third word, she said, "Boo is going to ask Ainsley to marry him. Today."

He lurched, as if someone had punched him in the gut. Apparently he'd gotten sufficient information from her feeble whisper. She tried not to smile.

"How do you know this?" he asked in a high-pitched squeak.

"Boo told me. And I saw the ring. Beautiful."

"This can't be! They've only dated a few weeks!"

"I'm sorry, Garth. I know how this must break your heart. But listen, you and Melb make a fine couple. At least you won't be alone."

"No!" Garth said, and this time a few people over by the desserts turned around. He smiled and waved, but he was growing pale and looked as if he was going to throw up.

"Oh, honey, listen. It's not as bad as it seems. And Melb is enamored with you. Haven't you seen the way she looks into your eyes?"

Garth's face twisted, and she thought he might scream. But in a low, controlled, and very angry voice he said, "You know Melb hates my guts. She's in love with *Wolfe*." He looked at her with a harried expression. "They're *not* in love. Ainsley is a dreamer. She always has been. One of these days she's going to realize that what she needs is a stable bread-winner like myself. She's too caught up in the lovey-dovey feelings."

Miss Peeple watched as Garth's loathsome eyes roamed the room. He was like a bull looking for some poor soul to gore. He was right where she wanted him. She was a little sad she'd played the Thief card so soon.

"What are you going to do?" she asked.

"I don't know, I don't know," he said. "When did he say he was going to do this awful thing?"

"Sounded like very soon, but he wasn't specific. I'd say soon, though."

Garth slapped his forehead with his hand. "This can't be happening. He knew. He *knew*."

"Knew what?"

"That Ainsley was falling for me. That's the only reason he'd do something so insane as to ask her to marry him *now*. I've got to tell her how I feel about her, tell her how she feels about me. Make her see."

"I doubt that will work. Love can make people blind, Garth." And apparently nonsensical as well.

"You're right." Then he stopped, and by the look on his face, Miss Peeple knew Garth had a plan. "But if I make her see the real Wolfe Boone...expose him for what he truly is..."

"And what exactly is that, dear?"

"I don't know yet. But I'll come up with something."

With dessert over, the crowd had gathered by the fire for a wonderful, creamy pumpkin drink that Ainsley had made. Outside the snow fell more and more heavily, and Wolfe worried for a moment about how people would get home. But as far as he was concerned, getting stranded here was not a bad thing.

Ainsley was busy in the kitchen with something, but Wolfe was, nevertheless, enjoying the fire and the company. Garth's and Alfred's antics aside, he found this crowd fairly amusing. Miss Peeple, whose date was Alfred Tennison, was sitting on a cozy love seat with Mayor Wullisworth listening to him tell war stories about an unspecific war. Alfred seemed content next to Ainsley's friend Marlee, who was wedged between Alfred and Butch and enjoying the close company. Wolfe studied Butch and decided he was the perfect antithesis to himself. His sweater was tied neatly around his neck, his short blond hair perfectly spiked. He seemed to know what his smile did when he flashed it, so he flashed it a lot, laughed heartily, and told jokes with perfect timing. Wolfe didn't hate him, though. In fact, he appreciated him, because with all the attributes also came a sincerity that Wolfe could easily recognize. These all came easily for Butch, and his charismatic personality just liked to show them off.

But Wolfe could only devote half his attention to studying how to be the perfect male. The other half went to a conversation with Melb, whom Wolfe had decided was a lovely lady with a heart of gold. It was rare to find someone as attentive to a conversation as Melb was, and soon he found the conversation shifting from his novel *Black Cats* to his newfound faith. Melb seemed happy to listen, and so they talked about the Lord in front of the roaring fire, sheltered from the storm.

"How's my peach fuzz?"

Melb and Wolfe glanced up to find Garth standing above them, grinning. "Garth."

He scooted her over on the couch and put his arm around her neck, though Melb might have been a football player for all Garth's sensitivity. Melb tried to smile graciously.

"What're you two over here chattin' about?"

"Jesus Christ," Melb said, looking at Wolfe with joy.

"It's true," Wolfe said.

"Oh…for a moment I thought you'd just taken the Lord's name in vain, but you're actually talking about Him, are you?"

"Yep! Wolfe is quite knowledgeable about the Bible."

Wolfe shook his head. "I just know a few things. I have a lot to learn."

Garth turned to Melb. "Your eyes look watery."

"What?"

"Watery. And red. Are you having allergies again?"

Melb blinked. "Allergies?"

"You *are!* Why didn't you say something? Before you know it your face is going to swell like rising bread, and you're going to start coughing. You know how that phlegm tends to gag you. Did you bring your inhaler? Of *course* you didn't." Garth looked at Wolfe. "She's always in denial about this. Her doctor tells her to bring her inhaler everywhere, but does she listen? *Nooooo.*" He pinched her cheek. Melb looked a little dazed. "Wolfe, will you do me a favor?"

"A favor?"

He stood and motioned for Wolfe to do the same. His hand guided Wolfe aside. "Listen, it's the cat. Melb unfortunately loves cats and wouldn't ever mention it, but she's allergic to them. And if she has a full-blown attack, she might have to go to the hospital."

"You're kidding."

"No, I wish I were. Would you mind seeing if you can find Thief and putting him out in the garage?"

Wolfe shifted. "Me? Why me?"

"Well, I have a slight history with this cat. It hates my guts because I neutered it. They sense these things, and it'll claw the crud out of me if I go anywhere near it." He flashed a mild looking scar on the underside of his forearm.

"I just wouldn't feel right about that without asking Ainsley or Sheriff Parker first."

"No, no. Bad idea."

"Why?"

"Thief is practically a kid in this household. The thought of putting that cat out in the garage would break their hearts. As I'm sure you've noticed, there's a cat door in every room of this house, except the garage. That's the only place for him to be where he won't bother Melb."

"I don't think Ainsley's as fond of Thief as you think."

"Well, she's fond of her father, who thinks that cat hung the moon or something. And Butch gave it the name Thief, so there's that attachment." Garth shook his head. "I'm a vet, and I tell you, *I'm* not as attached to animals as these people are. It's a sickness, but I guess everyone has their quirks. Anyway, if we don't get this cat out in the garage, Melb's going to get puffy as a pastry, swell like a water balloon, so what do you say?"

Wolfe sighed. "I'll see if I can find him."

"Great," Garth said with a wink. "Melb and I thank you for it."

"Here, kitty-kitty-kitty." Wolfe had seen a streak of black cross the den and gallop upstairs. He'd followed quietly, hoping not to draw too much attention to himself. From the top of the stairs, though, he had no idea where the cat had gone. "Thief! Thief!" He tried to keep his voice down. "Come here, kitty."

Wolfe strolled the upstairs hallway, peeking into each room carefully, listening for any sound of padded paws on hardwood floors, or perhaps the jingle of collar tags. But all he could hear was laughter from downstairs. He shook his head at the absurdity of the fact that *every* door in the house had a cat door so Thief could roam about as he pleased. Even the bathrooms! Every door but the one leading to the garage.

"Here kitty—" There he was, sitting casually on Sheriff Parker's queen-size bed, purring, his eyes slits, as if he were about to fall asleep.

"There you are," Wolfe said, opening the bedroom door a little wider.

The cat hardly regarded Wolfe but toppled over onto a pillow and lovingly licked his paws. Wolfe tried to get a good look at how long Thief's claws actually were.

"Hey there, Thief." He tried to act casual, though he didn't know whether a cat would pick up on such body language as hands in pockets and head tilted to the side. "What do you say you and I go for a little walk?"

The cat blinked but then went back to licking his hind legs.

"Come here. Come to Wolfey."

"What are you doing?"

Wolfe startled, spun around, and found Reverend Peck standing in the doorway. "Oh, I'm, um…"

The reverend stepped into the room, a concerned look on his face. "I saw you head up this way. This is Sheriff Parker's bedroom."

"Is it? Goodness, I was just looking for, um…for, the uh…"

"Bathroom?"

"Yeah."

The reverend frowned, and Wolfe knew he wasn't buying it. Wolfe also knew that in the Bible God emphasized being honest, and he supposed that meant even when the truth was painful to tell. "No."

"No?"

"No, I'm not looking for the bathroom."

"Son, what are you doing then? The sheriff's a pretty private person, and if he found you snooping around in his bedroom, things might get dicey."

"I'm not snooping… I'm just…" Wolfe sighed heavily. "I'm trying to kidnap Thief."

"Why?"

"Just to the garage. Apparently Melb Cornforth is highly allergic to cats."

"She is?"

"She has trouble breathing, needs an inhaler, and can swell up pretty badly."

"Oh my."

"She's bashful about it, doesn't want to cause any trouble."

"I see."

"And I guess Sheriff Parker wouldn't be too fond of putting the cat in the garage himself, so I offered to sneak him in there for a couple of hours."

"Poor Melb. I had no idea. I'll have to add that to the prayer list."

Wolfe nodded and decided he'd better make his move on Thief while the cat was sitting still. He started to reach out and grab him when the reverend said, "Be careful! That cat's got claws like knives."

"Really?"

"Oh yes. Killed a dog once that got into his territory. At least that's what Sheriff Parker says."

Wolfe stared at the passive cat.

"It was just a little Yorkie, but if you ask me, I think Sheriff Parker may sharpen those claws just to scare people."

Wolfe swallowed. "Well, is he fond of strangers?"

"Couldn't say. I doubt the cat's used to seeing too many strangers in this town. Well, if you'll excuse me, *I* have to find a bathroom." The reverend was gone.

Wolfe sized up the cat, especially the claws. They did look rather sharp, but the cat looked fairly harmless. Wolfe approached him slowly, then pet him, and finally decided it might be okay to pick him up. But as soon as he did, the cat's paws spread dramatically, and he issued a slight hiss, too.

"Why did I volunteer for this?" Wolfe said out loud. Then he had an idea. The cat was sitting on a pillow. He could get another pillow, place it on top of the cat, and hurry downstairs to the garage door, which was just off the stairwell. So without further hesitation, scared to death of turning around to find Sheriff Parker in his face, Wolfe took the other pillow, placed it gently on top of the cat, and picked both pillows up. Surprisingly, the cat hardly flinched, so Wolfe hurried downstairs and rounded the corner. He was just about to the garage when he ran into someone coming out of the small half-bath underneath the stairs. It was Alfred.

"Wolfe! What are you doing with that cat?"

"You don't want to know," Wolfe said with a half-laugh and quickly went into the garage, shutting the door behind him. He released Thief, who looked around the garage and then decided to hop on top of the sheriff's car. It was a little chilly in the garage, but not bad for a cat, and Wolfe decided he'd be fine for an hour or so.

He went back into the house, and Alfred was still standing there.

"Pillows?"

"Long story. Where's your date, by the way?"

Alfred's eyes narrowed. "I don't know. I'm not her nurse. Anyway, I've been looking for you. We've got a lot to talk about, Wolfe. We need to sort some things out."

It was true. Wolfe couldn't avoid talking to Alfred forever, and he did want to run by Alfred some ideas for a book of short dramatic stories about small town life, but this wasn't the time or the place. For one, he had to take Sheriff Parker's pillows back upstairs. Second, he needed a little time alone to decide if now was a good time to ask Ainsley to marry him. When he thought about it, fear pierced his heart. But the thought of not asking her hurt him more.

"Not now. But I do want to talk to you, Al."

"You do?"

"Yes, I've got some ideas."

"Ideas? Ideas! Ideas are good!"

"Excuse me," Wolfe said and hurried back upstairs. He placed the pillows neatly on the bed, smoothed the covers, and rushed out of the room just in time to see the reverend emerge from the bathroom.

"Where's the cat?"

"In the garage, safe and sound."

Reverend Peck smiled. "Good. That was an awfully nice thing you did for Melb."

"Well, she's a nice woman. I just hope she can enjoy the rest of Thanksgiving and not get too sick."

Downstairs the sheriff was calling people into the living room. The reverend said, "Come on. It's time for the toast. This is a wonderful Parker tradition that you won't want to miss!"

Wolfe smiled and followed the reverend, patting the little ring in his pocket all the way down the stairs.

CHAPTER 28

AFTER GARTH HEARTILY thanked Wolfe for helping Melb, Wolfe found Ainsley near the fire, watching her father gather everyone into the living room, and joined her. She squeezed his arm.

"I'm sorry I've been so busy."

"You're a terrific hostess."

"Thank you," she said, and Wolfe knew that compliment meant more to her than most knew. "Besides, the evening's still young, and by the way it's looking outside, I may be here awhile."

She gazed into his eyes, then glanced out the window. "Quite a snowstorm. I hope people can get home okay." Her attention was back on Wolfe. "Did you enjoy dinner?"

"More than you'll ever know."

"I hope you've found some people to talk to."

"I have. Don't worry yourself about me, though. Okay?"

"Okay," she said, smiling and nestling herself into his embrace. She looked up at him. "I'm so glad we're together."

"You are?"

"Yes, aren't you?"

"You have no idea," he said, squeezing her tightly. He studied her eyes. "Ainsley, I'm in love with you."

"You are?"

"Definitely."

She touched his face with her hand. "I'm in love with you too. I've never known anyone like you. You're so genuine, so true. You say what you mean. You have a deep heart. Never in my wildest dreams did I imagine I'd be in your arms, but here I am."

He laughed. "You were always in my wildest dreams."

"Oh?"

He shrugged and was about to say more when the sheriff raised his voice and told everyone to quiet down. In complete obedience the room became quiet and still, the only movement and sound coming from the fire.

"Folks, it's a pretty bad storm outside. Robby Newirth just radioed me, and they've got 31 shut down already." Everyone moaned. "I'm afraid we're all going to be here awhile. I couldn't in good conscience let any of you travel on these roads, at least not alone. I may be able to get the sheriff's truck out here to get some of you back home if needed. The weathermen, God bless 'em, said it should start tapering off in the next two hours. If so, we may be able to travel short distances this evening. Mind you, though, these are the same people who said we'd have a few flurries today." Everyone chuckled. "But folks, we got enough food here to feed an army, so I think we're going to be okay, and definitely in good company!"

Mayor Wullisworth held up his pumpkin drink. "Here's to that!"

"All right, it's time to make some toasts. For those of you who are new, this is a great time to reflect on the year nearly behind us, and the new year that is about to come. It's another time to express how thankful you are, or just to tell someone how much they mean to you. This is usually how we round out our day, but since it looks like you're going to be staying awhile, maybe this will just be the beginning of a really fun evening." Sheriff Parker picked up his drink off the mantel. "Here's to being stranded!"

"Hear, hear!"

Garth, whose absence no one but Wolfe had seemed to notice, came around the corner and said, "Here's to hope in true love!" Everyone expected him to look at Melb, but instead he threw his head back and downed the rest of his pumpkin drink without ever taking a breath.

"Hear, hear!"

Melb, in uncharacteristic confidence, stepped forward, raised her glass, and said, "Here's to great conversations!" She smiled at Wolfe and tipped her glass in his direction.

"Hear, hear!"

Marlee said, "Here's to the Delta Force and our hero Butch!"

"Hear, hear!"

And on they went, everyone in giddy array, cheerfully toasting the evening away. Every toast caused certitude to grow in Wolfe. With Ainsley in his arms, and a crowd full of witnesses, he knew nothing in the world would make him happier than to ask Ainsley to marry him. And as he gazed down at her beautiful face, he was pretty sure she would be just as happy. The ring seemed to dance in his pocket, and as the toasting died down, Wolfe realized it was now or never. Fear quaked in his gut as he looked at the sheriff. But his love for Ainsley seemed to put it to rest.

The sheriff said, "Anyone else?"

Wolfe stepped forward. "I have something to say."

"Well, go ahead," the sheriff said, stepping back.

"First of all, I'd just like to tell all of you how great it's been getting to know you. I've been in this town for a long time, up on my hill, writing my books, and not realizing what I was missing by not getting to know all of you fine people."

"Hear, hear!" came a shout.

"Settle down," muttered the sheriff.

Wolfe swallowed but continued. "Two amazing things have happened to me recently. First of all, I was at a desperate point in my life, knowing inside my heart there had to be a greater purpose in life than writing. I felt so dead inside, and by the grace of God, literally, I walked down the hill and into Reverend Peck's church and made the biggest decision of my life. My heart was changed forever by God. But I also have to say, my heart was changed in another way, too. In fact, my heart was captured by this beautiful young woman." Wolfe looked at Ainsley, who was smiling and tilting her head affectionately. "I've never felt this way about anybody, and I feel honored even knowing her. She's beautiful not only on the outside, but on the inside, too. She does nice things for people, stands up for what she believes, and has more character than anyone I know."

Wolfe turned to her and took her hands. He could feel everyone lean forward in anticipation, and several quiet gasps seemed to suck all the air right out of the room. His brow beaded with nervous sweat, his heart palpitated faster than all the thoughts and words that raced through his mind, and as much as he loved and cared for this woman, he was beginning to find it hard to express what he wanted to in the way he wanted to. So he prayed quietly in his spirit for the Lord to help him. Then he said, "Ainsley, I love you. I'm in love with you. I can't imagine my life without you." He decided it was appropriate to kneel, but just as he was about to bend his knee, something stopped him.

It was a blood-curdling scream, coming from the direction of the garage.

Everyone froze, and then it came again. Sheriff Parker rushed through the room, and people scooted aside as Ainsley followed him, panic seizing her heart. She was right behind her father when he yanked open the garage door. Miss Peeple stood on the first step, trembling and crying, her hand over her mouth. She looked up at Sheriff Parker, tears in her eyes.

"Missy!" he said, taking her arm and pulling her up into the house. He sat her down in the nearest chair. "Are you okay? What's the matter? Are you having chest pains?"

"I'm calling an ambulance," Ainsley said.

"No, no," she said, shaking her head. "It's not that."

"Then what? Why were you screaming?" Sheriff Parker asked. By now, the guests had gathered behind Ainsley, asking questions and whispering. Ainsley motioned for them to settle down.

Miss Peeple shook her head, lowered her eyes, and pointed behind her. Sheriff Parker looked into the garage and gently moved toward the steps. Ainsley tried to stand on tiptoe to see what Miss Peeple was pointing at as her father descended.

Then she heard her father moan. "No," he said. "No!"

"Dad?" Ainsley scooted past Miss Peeple into the garage. There on the floor next to the tool cabinet was her father, hunched over their cat. "Thief!" She joined her father, who had now picked the cat up and was holding him gently. "Dad! Is he okay?"

Her father's expression indicated sadness. "I…I don't know. He's so limp. He's cold…"

Garth suddenly appeared with a stethoscope in his hand. "What happened?"

Sheriff Parker's eyes teared up. "I'm not sure… Miss Peeple found him…"

Garth stared at the cat and then swallowed as he looked at Ainsley. "Well, um, it's freezing out here. Let's at least take him inside, see what we have."

Sheriff Parker cradled the cat as the crowd parted, and he took Thief to the living room, then gently laid the cat in the middle of the coffee table as guests scurried to remove their drink glasses and coasters.

"I don't think he's breathing," Sheriff Parker said in a trembling voice.

"Here," Garth said gently, kneeling beside the table and the cat. "Let me just listen. We'll know more then."

The guests shook their heads and covered their mouths, and Ainsley wrapped one arm around her father's waist. Everyone waited anxiously as Garth listened to the cat's heartbeat. It took what seemed like an eternity before Garth stood, lowered his head, and said, "I'm sorry."

Sheriff Parker's eyes widened. "He's dead?"

"It appears that way."

"It appears that way? Is he dead or not?"

Garth tucked his stethoscope into his back pocket. "I can't find a heartbeat."

Tears pooled in Ainsley's eyes. "I can't believe this. How could this happen?"

The guests offered words of encouragement and condolence, but it was obvious Sheriff Parker was thinking of one thing, and one thing only: Thief was dead.

"How did Thief get into the garage?" the sheriff asked suddenly, breaking the silence.

No one apparently knew, and the sheriff looked down at his shoes.

"It's so cold outside, not fit for man or beast. Thief hates the garage."

Ainsley rubbed his shoulder. "Dad, it was cold out there, but not cold enough to kill Thief. The garage is protected from the elements. He had to have died from natural causes."

"He's only ten. He was in perfectly good health. This just doesn't make sense." Then Sheriff Parker's head rose again, and his gaze found Miss Peeple near the doorway, sipping a glass of water someone had brought her and blotting her forehead with a handkerchief. "Why were you in the garage?"

Glass to her mouth, the handkerchief on her forehead, Missy's eyes widened. "Why?"

"Yes. How did you know he was in the garage?"

"I didn't, dear," she said, handing her glass to Garth and tucking the handkerchief away in her pocket. She steadied herself on her cane. "I was looking for the bathroom."

"The bathroom?"

"Yes. The bathroom."

"You've been in the house many times. You know where all the bathrooms are."

Garth, who was now standing behind the couch, leaned over Sheriff Parker's shoulder and whispered, "She's showing some forgetful signs these days, Sheriff. This is just one of many examples. Plus she's got that incontinence problem, which just makes things worse."

"Oh," Sheriff Parker said.

Wolfe stepped to the center of the room. He was feeling terrible, feeling disbelief. He'd tried to catch Garth's attention several times, but the man avoided his eyes and was obviously not going to speak up. Wolfe knew he was going to have to say something. "Sheriff Parker, I put Thief in the garage."

The sheriff blinked, and now he was staring at Wolfe in disbelief.

"Wolfe, what are you talking about?" Ainsley asked.

"I…um… I was trying to help." He glanced up at Garth, then over to Melb. "Melb's allergic to cats. Really allergic. She can get very sick. And the thought was that if the cat was in the garage, just for an hour or so, Melb could continue to enjoy the day, and then when she left, Thief could come back in."

"So you killed my cat?" the sheriff asked.

"No…no! The cat was fine when I put him in the garage. Perfectly fine." Wolfe stared at Garth, and they exchanged a look that only two men in love with one woman could. In a split second Wolfe knew something very bad was about to happen.

The sound of shattering glass broke the exchange, and everyone turned around. Garth had dropped Miss Peeple's water glass that he was holding. "Oops," Garth said, a slight, nearly undetectable smile on his lips. "I'm sorry. Here, let me clean that up."

Wolfe shuddered. Then he cried, *"No! Don't touch that glass!"*

But before he knew it, Garth had stooped down and scooped up a piece of the glass. Then he squeezed his hand shut, opened it back up, and yelped. "Ouch! I cut myself!" Blood trickled down Garth's hand.

Wolfe felt his head hit the floor.

"Wolfe!" Ainsley rushed to his side as he lay on the carpet in the middle of the living room.

"Is he okay?" the reverend asked, rushing to his side as well.

"He passes out at the sight of blood."

"Doesn't look like he hit his head too hard. I think he's going to be okay, soon as he wakes up."

The sheriff rubbed his brow in fury. Then he looked at Melb, who was sitting in the corner, trembling. "Is it true, Melb? Is what Wolfe says true?"

"Daddy! Wolfe is passed out on the floor!"

"The reverend said he'd be okay."

"He can't even defend himself!"

"Does he *need* to defend himself?" her father asked. He then looked at Melb. "So? Are you allergic?"

Melb's bottom lip was quivering and her eyes widened with every word he spoke. "Um, well…uh…it's just that…"

"What? Is this a hard question?"

"No…no… It's just… You see…"

The sheriff stepped toward her, and the crowd turned with him. "Are you, or are you not, allergic to cats?"

"Am I allergic to cats? No, I mean, yes, I mean…I mean…I…"

"You mean what, exactly?"

"I mean, that…" Melb started to hyperventilate, and her eyes darted between the sheriff, Garth, and Wolfe on the floor. "Goodness, that's not an easy question…I can't say that…I mean I will say…but then…"

"Melb!" the sheriff demanded.

But Melb could do nothing now but sob, and sob she did, as if she were at a funeral.

The sheriff turned around, staring at the crowd. "*What* is going on here?" But no one answered. Ainsley looked down at Wolfe, wondering herself. But Wolfe was still unconscious.

The sheriff marched over to Melb, took her by the arm, stood her to the feet, and guided her quickly to the couch in front of the coffee table, where he ordered her to sit. Melb stared at the cat, lifeless on the table, shaking her head and blotting her nose.

"I guess there's one way to find out if Wolfe Boone is telling the truth, isn't there?" the sheriff said, addressing the guests, eyeing each of them.

"What are you talking about?" Ainsley asked.

"Wolfe said that Melb gets sick when she's around cats. Has allergies, right? Isn't that what he said?"

"That's what I heard," Garth said. "That her eyes start tearing. She swells up and has trouble breathing."

"Perfect. Then there's one way to find out if Wolfe is telling the truth." The sheriff turned to Melb, then walked to the coffee table and picked up the cat. He took a long look at Thief, then attempted to hand the cat to Melb, who drew back in horror.

"Dad!" Ainsley said.

"Put the cat on your lap, Melb."

"What?" Melb asked.

"If you're allergic to cats, then your eyes will water. You'll start sneezing. Then we'll know Wolfe is telling the truth." The sheriff placed the cat on Melb's lap.

"Uh...uh...oh...ooh!" Melb's panicky gasps resonated off the walls of the living room. Then her eyes fluttered, and a collective gasp indicated everyone thought she might pass out.

"Daddy! Stop this!" Ainsley said, but her father held up a stern hand in protest.

Melb lamented, "There's a dead cat on my lap!"

The sheriff was intensely focused, however, and seemed not to care at all what people were thinking or feeling. "Now Melb," he said, "you're going to have to stop crying, or we won't be able to tell if your eyes are watering."

Melb's dazed and glassy eyes blinked at the sheriff, but somehow she obeyed, wiping her tears and taking deep breaths, looking up at the ceiling as if trying not to acknowledge the cat on her lap.

After a few moments, the sheriff said, "Well? I'm not seeing any signs of allergies here. Are you?" *You* wasn't too well defined, so a few people nodded or shook their heads, others stayed perfectly still, and someone mumbled a suggestion from the back, but it wasn't clear who. Sheriff Parker said, "What was that? Did someone say something?"

Oliver stepped forward, clearing his throat. "Uh, I did. I just thought maybe...well, see, I don't get allergic until my cat, Mustang GTE, I call her "Geet" for short, well, until she rubs her fur in my face."

"So what are you suggesting?" asked the sheriff.

"Maybe Melb could...well, she could, um..." Oliver was gesturing with his hands while fumbling along his sentence, and everyone leaned forward, trying to interpret just exactly what it was Oliver was trying to suggest.

"Spit it out, Oliver!"

"Okay, just maybe she could, you know, rub her face in its fur."

Melb whimpered.

Ainsley turned to her father. "Dad. Stop this nonsense."

"Nonsense? Nonsense! Thief is dead, Ainsley. How can you take this so lightly?"

"I'm not taking it lightly. But this is ridiculous. If Wolfe said that he put Thief in the garage to help Melb with her allergies, then I believe him. I don't know what happened to Thief out there, but you can't possibly believe that Wolfe intentionally harmed our cat."

The sheriff's eyebrows cocked. "Oh? Ever since he decided to join the society of Skary and come down off that high hill of his, strange things have been happening. And even *before* that. Cats running all over this town like we're made of catnip. And I don't have to remind you, do I, that Wolfe once *lied* about Thief, said he was frolicking with the lady cats when *everyone* knows Thief is neutered!"

Ainsley could not protest and suddenly felt very confused. Maybe everyone was right. Maybe Wolfe had lied. Maybe he couldn't be trusted. She stared down at his still, peaceful face.

The sheriff continued. "Especially since Melb here hasn't so much as sniffled with Thief on her lap." The sheriff turned to Melb. "Well, Melb, why don't you? Just go ahead and rub your nose in his hair. Then we'll know once and for all. Anybody allergic to cats will react doing that, wouldn't you say, Garth?"

Garth was pale and fidgety but nodded nevertheless. Ainsley expected Garth to protest. What boyfriend would let his girl stick her nose in a dead cat's fur? But she knew her father had a strange influence on people, and most of the time people did whatever he suggested. Oliver, however, rushed to Melb's side to hold her hand.

"Go ahead, Melb. It's okay. He's not going to bite." The sheriff stepped back and waited.

Melb rolled her eyes, teared up again, whimpered, bit her lip, then closed her eyes and stuck her nose down in the fur.

"Rub it around a little, there you go…"

She raised her head, gasping for breath, as if she'd been under water for minutes. Then the room waited. Thirty seconds. Sixty. Two minutes. But Melb didn't swell. Her eyes didn't water. And she never even sniffled. Finally the sheriff turned to Wolfe, pointed his finger at him and said, "He killed my cat!"

Then the reverend stepped forward. "Sheriff Parker, I witnessed Wolfe take the cat."

Sheriff Parker turned to the reverend. "Excuse me?"

"I saw him upstairs when I went to the bathroom. He was in your bedroom; Thief was on the bed."

"Aha!" the sheriff said.

"Wait a minute," Reverend Peck said. "What I'm trying to say is that Wolfe told me exactly what he told you. He said that Melb was having trouble with her allergies, and that he wanted to help out. He said that Melb was a little self-conscious about it, and that she probably wouldn't want to ask." The reverend looked down at Wolfe. "I think you should take him at his word. He was trying to help."

Ainsley watched her father briefly contemplate the reverend's words, but she could tell by the expression on his face that he was thinking over other things, too. He looked around at the room full of people and said, "All right. Well, let's just open this up. Did anyone else see anything? Witness Wolfe 'helping Melb?' " The room was quiet. "Speak up, if you've got something to say."

Alfred cleared his throat, causing everyone to jump and turn. "I saw something."

"Mr. Tennison. Please, tell us what you saw," the sheriff said.

Alfred looked at Wolfe. "I met Wolfe when he was coming down the stairs with the cat."

"And?"

"He was carrying the cat between two pillows."

Surprised gasps.

"The cat was alive then," Alfred quickly added. "I saw its tail swishing."

"And what did Wolfe say to you?"

Alfred's gaze lowered. "I asked him what he was doing, and he said I didn't want to know."

More surprised gasps. Ainsley's stomach tensed.

"I asked about the pillows," Alfred continued, "and he said it was a long story. He put the cat in the garage, and then I said I wanted to talk to him. He said it wasn't a good time, but that he had some 'ideas.'"

"Ideas?"

"Yes, and that's all that happened."

The sheriff looked around the room. "Anyone else?"

Ainsley grabbed her father's arm. "This is crazy. You know Wolfe didn't hurt Thief. Why are you doing this?"

"You're blind, Ainsley. Your feelings for this man are keeping you from seeing what you should."

"No, *your* feelings are blinding *you*. You're being ridiculous. There has to be a reasonable explanation for what has happened."

Garth spoke up suddenly. "It's weird, like a scene out of his book."

Sheriff Parker turned. "Book?"

"Yeah. You know, his latest book. It's called *Black Cats*."

Another round of gasps. The statement even took Ainsley's breath away. She hadn't thought of that.

Garth continued. "I mean, the whole book revolves around black cats and how evil they are, and they rise up against this little town and everyone in the town has to fight for their lives, so they come up with this plan on how to kill off all the black cats."

The startled guests all turned to look at Wolfe, who was slumbering like a baby. Ainsley's heart went out to him, but Garth's words rang in her ears.

"It's a coincidence," Ainsley said.

"He told me he doesn't like cats," Garth said. "I didn't think he meant he'd kill a cat."

Alfred suddenly made a strange noise from where he stood, and as everyone turned to him, they noticed he was laughing, snorting really. "What a great promotional stunt!"

Ainsley said, "What are you talking about?"

"He said he had ideas. Promotional ideas! Of course! He's a genius!" Alfred's exuberant expression faded as his eyes scanned the mortified crowd. "I was just thinking out loud…um…yeah…terrible idea."

But it seemed to be too late. The idea had been planted, and by the look on everyone's face, Ainsley knew there were grave doubts forming in their minds. With tears in her eyes, she said, "All of you, stop it. Please. We don't know what happened, but you can't just stand here and blame someone for this. It's not fair, no matter how it looks. We have to get Wolfe's side of the story."

A few started nodding, and Ainsley thought everyone might come around, until Garth said, "I'm afraid I have more bad news. I didn't know how to say it before, but"—he stepped around the couch to stand by Melb, who still had the cat on her lap—"Thief was poisoned."

"No!" came a collective gasp.

"How do you know he's been poisoned?"

Garth stared at the cat as he said, "By the, um…the way his mouth is closed. Cats tend to die with their mouths open unless they're poisoned." He shrugged. "Don't ask me why. That's just something they teach in medical school."

The mumbling started, and the whispers whipped around the room like a verbal tornado. Even Ainsley felt doubt now. Melb was obviously not allergic to cats. And this all looked like an incredible promotional stunt for his book. And *poison?*

A groan came from Wolfe's throat, and he was coming to. Ainsley bent down over his face. "Are you okay?"

"Yeah. I'm… What happened?"

"Garth cut his hand. You passed out." Ainsley watched as he sat up.

Her father stepped closer to Wolfe and said, "Get up. Get out. Get out of my house."

"Daddy, no. Please. Let's just—"

"He murdered our cat!"

"You don't know that."

"Wolfe was the last person to see him alive! People witnessed him putting Thief in the garage! And Garth says he's poisoned. We arrest people for murder on less evidence than that!" He looked at Wolfe. "Get out of my house!"

Wolfe looked confused and hurt, and Ainsley's heart sank. She had so many questions. So many doubts. She watched as Wolfe carefully looked around the room, making eye contact with every person before standing and straightening his shirt.

"All right," Wolfe sighed. He looked at the reverend. "I didn't do this." Then he looked at Ainsley. "You know I could never do this."

Tears dripped down Ainsley's cheeks. But she could form no words. She watched as he crossed the living room toward the door, but he stopped briefly, stared at Garth, then continued on. From where she stood, she could see him grab his coat and put his hat and gloves on. She turned to her father. "Daddy! There must be a foot of snow on the ground, or more! He's not going to be able to drive his car, and he can't walk in this weather. You know that. You *know* that!"

His eyes, stalwart and steady, stared forward. "Maybe that's what Thief felt like being left out in the garage." And then the sheriff left the room, just as the front door of the house opened and then shut.

Then the only sound in the entire house was Melb, who was still whimpering and staring at the ceiling, the dead cat limp across her knees.

CHAPTER 29

WOLFE WAS TOO cold to cry. But he felt that horrible lump in his throat, the same one that had been there so many years ago when he'd learned his parents had died. How could this happen? It was the only question he was focused enough to ask himself as he trudged through the snow, shivering with each step. The wind chill, he was sure, was below zero.

There would be no driving in this weather, so his only hope was to go by foot. A small forest stood between the Parkers' house and a road that would lead back to Wolfe's. It was the shortest way, but definitely not the best. It was off the beaten path, and if something happened…

He erased the thought from his mind. Why did he care if something happened? He was going to ask the woman of his dreams to marry him today, and now she thought he'd murdered her cat. It seemed the only person who believed in him was the reverend. He had been about to protest, challenge Garth, but he had seen the doubt in Ainsley's eyes. And it had crushed him. His mind spun with the reality of the disastrous day as he stepped forward into the snowy forest.

His skin ached with the cold, and his coat was getting soaked. His emotions swung from grief to anger to confusion. He had just been trying to help Melb! At Garth's request. Why hadn't Garth helped him out? Why had Melb sat on the couch with that dumbfounded look on her face?

He hardly noticed that his steps were becoming more difficult, his breathing more labored, his skin numb. Inside he felt so hot…so angry. He just kept plodding through the snow, one step after another, one thought pushing out another.

Just make it home, he thought to himself as he waded through icy snow and forest brush. Soon, even his anger subsided, and he could concentrate on only one thought, which was putting one foot in front of the other. His body shivered uncontrollably.

Just keep walking. Just keep walking. He repeated the phrase over and over in his mind, delirious, frigid.

Ainsley was crying in the corner of the room, the reverend's arm around one shoulder, her brother's hand resting on her opposite arm. "I can't believe this has happened." Ainsley swiped at hot tears.

The reverend said, "You can't believe Wolfe did this."

"But nothing makes sense. How did Thief die? Who poisoned him? I'm so confused." She crumpled into the reverend's arms, sobbing. "I pray Wolfe is okay."

A commotion in the middle of the living room caused Ainsley to look up. Her father had reentered and was now making his way to the coffee table, where Thief again lay, at Melb's insistence. Oliver had offered to pick up the cat and place him there. But poor Melb was apparently so mortified that she hadn't moved from the couch and still sat in the exact same position as before, her legs pressed together, her arms and hands away from her lap as if the plague sat there.

Her father was holding a blanket. "It's time to say good-bye to Thief," her father said gravely. "What a horrible day. How could this have happened?"

Ainsley noticed Garth looked sick to his stomach, a fretful expression besetting his features. She guessed it was hard to see any animal die if you were a vet.

Her father stood over the cat and shook his head, trying to find words to say. Ainsley moved to his side, but she couldn't console her dad. She was too sad herself, for too many reasons.

"Well, I'm not a man of fancy words," the sheriff said softly, "so I guess all I can say is, good-bye, old friend. We'll miss you."

And with that, he unfolded the blanket and started to put it over the cat, when the most surprising thing happened.

"WWWWWWRRRRRREEEEEEEEOOOOOOOOWWWWWW!"

The room filled with horrified screams as Thief came back to life with a roaring screech. He seemed to fly off the table without ever using his legs, and he landed smack dab in the middle of Melb's lap. Fortunately for Melb, she was passed out cold on the couch, as were three other people at the site of this unlikely resurrection.

Ainsley watched Thief jump around the room and shriek as though he was on speed. He pounced from one piece of furniture to another, causing those who were still conscious to scramble out of the way, screaming and flailing as if they were being attacked.

"It's a miracle!" the reverend exclaimed, just as someone else yelled, "He's possessed! Get outta the way!"

Chaos reigned for many minutes before Thief finally settled down. He paced the room a few times, and then, without further ado, settled into his favorite recliner near the fire, where he yawned.

Sheriff Parker's hands were trembling. Ainsley rushed to him. "He's alive! He's alive!" she said, and her father smiled faintly, still in shock. Butch went to get him water, and everyone else, with trembling knees, either found a place to sit or tried to help those who were still passed out on the floor.

Butch came back in and said, "In all my years of dangerous combat, I've never seen anything like that before!"

Those who could find words just kept repeating how freaked out they were, or, if they were within the sheriff's earshot, how happy they were that the cat was indeed alive.

But dread fell over Ainsley. She looked up at her father. Her voice quivered. "Dad, what about Wolfe?"

She slapped him upside the head as hard as she could. It did nothing more than annoy him, though, and he rubbed the spot and frowned at her.

"What'd you do that for?" Garth asked.

Missy Peeple, who'd steered him out of the chaos and into a quiet corner in the den said, "Keep your voice down!"

"Don't tell me what to do!"

Miss Peeple studied Garth. He was sweating and nervous, and his stupidity was getting to be a huge liability. She grabbed him by the shoulders and shook him, which wasn't hard since he hardly weighed more than feather. "Get a hold of yourself."

He didn't say anything, which was a good sign.

She let go of his shoulders. "What in the world happened in there? Why's that cat alive?"

"Because," Garth breathed, "I didn't kill it."

"Why not?"

"I'm a vet. I have certain moral standards I have to live up to, you know."

Miss Peeple growled. "Well, good grief, what in the world did you think was going to happen when that cat came to?"

Garth swallowed. "I hadn't thought that far, I guess."

"You're an idiot!" she scolded. "And don't you think you could've done this town a favor by putting Romeo the cat out of his misery?"

"Listen to me. I accomplished what I wanted to. Ainsley thinks Wolfe poisoned their cat, and she's going to need a shoulder to cry on. That's where I come in. I'll be there for her, and she'll see that I'm her perfect man."

His expression changed suddenly, and Missy noticed he wasn't looking at her. She turned.

It was Ainsley. Standing in the doorway. With her arms crossed.

It took nearly five minutes for Garth Twyne to explain that he'd not poisoned Thief, but had simply given him a drug to slow down his heartbeat and make him unconscious. Ainsley watched with disgust as Garth fumbled his words, shoved his hands in and out of his pockets, and let his eyes dart around the room as if looking for someone who might feel compassion for him. There was no one.

Ainsley grew so tired of his ramblings that she finally stood up and said, "I can't believe you would do this and let Wolfe take the blame. Why?"

His shoulders straightened, and he looked her directly in the eye. "Because I love you. And I wanted you to see what a terrible mistake you're making by falling for a creep like Boo."

"A *creep like Boo?*" Ainsley's voice rose an octave. "Wolfe would never poison a cat and blame someone else. This isn't love, Garth. This is jealousy. Jealousy does crazy things to people! You're sick, that's what you are. Besides, you're in love with Melb!"

Melb, who was lying on the couch with her feet propped up on a pillow, swallowed hard as the color once again drained from her face.

"Melb's in love with Wolfe," Garth said with exasperation.

"What?"

"We're not in love with each other. We were just trying to"—he looked around sheepishly, then stared at the carpet—"break you up."

Ainsley gave Garth the harshest look she could. She was about to scold him again when she heard Oliver say, "I have something to confess too."

Ainsley turned to him. "What?"

"I've been trying to, well, let's just say I've been hoping Wolfe would go back to who he used to be before he found religion. Ainsley, my intentions were to break you two up as well."

Marlee said, "You're in love with Ainsley too?"

"No." Oliver shifted his attention to Melb. "I'm in love with Melb."

Astonished "oohs!" were only superseded by Melb's cry of surprise. Oliver explained. "I thought Garth and Melb were together, and if Ainsley and Wolfe broke up, I knew Garth would go after Ainsley, and then I could be with Melb. I'm sorry, Melb. That was horrible."

Melb was smiling. "You're in love with *me?*"

"For a long time. I'm sorry I didn't have the guts to tell you sooner." Oliver smiled longingly at Melb from across the room, and their exchange was admired by everyone until Mayor Wullisworth said, "I embezzled money. Okay?"

"What?" the crowd gasped yet again.

"A few years ago. I was in debt. I've almost paid it all back, right, Martin?"

Martin's face grew solemn, and his gaze shifted around the room.

The sheriff said, "You knew about this?"

Martin nodded, and the mayor said, "He was a good enough friend to let me pay it back, but an even better friend for confronting me. Martin's a town treasurer everyone should be proud of."

Martin stepped forward. "But I'm not proud of how I've been acting. I, too, had ill intentions. I've been trying to break them up as well."

"*You're* in love with Ainsley?" Garth nearly shouted.

"No, no. I was afraid. I've done some things I'm not proud of, hoping to put our little town back in place. You see, I thought Ainsley was probably going to be the biggest influence in keeping Wolfe from going back to writing his books. And if he didn't write his horror novels anymore, then Mr. Tennison was going to write his book about Skary, and then everyone would know about the mayor and how I covered up for him." Martin hung his head.

Alfred stepped forward. "There's no book."

Martin and Mayor Wullisworth's jaws dropped. "There's not?"

"No, it was just an excuse to stick around here and try to change Wolfe's mind about becoming a Christian."

"There's no book?" the mayor asked again.

"No."

Ainsley noticed suddenly that nearly everyone's attention had shifted to one person: Miss Missy Peeple. And the little old lady who had looked so feeble and frail moments before was now scowling at the group like a ferocious tiger.

"Miss Peeple?" Ainsley said cautiously.

She narrowed her eyes. "You all are so naive. Sitting in here, talking about your feelings. Getting things off your chest. Are you all going to feel good when Skary ceases to exist?"

"That's nonsense," Ainsley said. "Our town was doing fine before he came."

"Oh? I remember a different version, I guess. I remember when Oliver had to file bankruptcy, when Mayor Wullisworth announced trash would be picked up only once every two weeks, when Marty over here was drinking himself into oblivion every time he did the books."

The room grew quiet.

She continued. "All you people want to be so noble and kind and compassionate, but the truth of the matter is that Wolfe Boone, horror novelist, is the reason Skary exists at all, and the reason all of you are driving newer cars and living in nicer homes and spending the money in your pockets. Before he came we were a speck. We were nothing. Now we mean something. We're known for something."

"But it was wrong," said Oliver. "It was wrong of us to interfere with something like a man finding his faith. And you know what? I have to say I'm inspired by Wolfe. Before, I was going to church every Sunday just because that's what you did on Sunday. But I see a sparkle in Wolfe's eye. I see something there I wish I had."

Martin nodded. "Talking to him today I realized his faith is genuine, that he genuinely loves God. That prayer he said at the table moved me."

All the guests but Missy eagerly agreed.

Oliver said, "I was so adamant about finding out who witnessed to Boo. I don't care who it is now. I'm just glad they did."

Mayor Wullisworth also chimed in. "I thought I could show Wolfe how hard the Christian faith could be. Instead, I've realized how much I need what he has."

"Throw around your religious words and feel better about yourselves," Missy spat. "I'm the only one honest enough to call it the way it is, and if you don't like it, that's too bad."

"So you instigated all this?" Ainsley asked. "All this scheming was your idea?"

"I had a little help from the pig cloner."

Ainsley looked at Garth, then felt her father's hand on her shoulder. "I've made a terrible mistake," he said. "I shouldn't have blamed Wolfe."

"Dad, we have to get to his house. See if he's okay. Please, we have to find a way."

"I agree."

Oliver stepped forward. "I've got a Hummer at the lot. If we can get over there, we can use it."

It took fifteen minutes to travel two miles in Oliver's BMW. They had to have the group push the car out of the snow just to get out of the Parkers' driveway, and after that they slid off the road twice. Oliver's shirt was soaked through with nervous sweat when they arrived at his lot, and it didn't help that Sheriff Parker was yelling instructions to Butch the whole time on how to drive in the snow.

Oliver found the keys to the bright yellow Hummer. Oliver, Butch, Ainsley, Sheriff Parker, and Marty all hopped in. From Oliver's office, Ainsley tried to phone Wolfe, but no one answered. It was five miles from the car lot to Wolfe's house, and Ainsley's heart pounded as she tried to think of the route Wolfe might have taken home. Perhaps he caught a ride from a lone soul brave enough to be out in this weather. Had he stayed on the streets or tried to cut through the trees?

They finally turned onto Dreary Street, which led to the hill on which Wolfe's house sat. It had taken only ten minutes, thanks in part to her brother at the wheel and in part to the Hummer.

"The house looks dark," Ainsley said fearfully as she peered out the window. Butch pulled the Hummer to the side of the street.

"There's a light on in one of the windows," Sheriff Parker said. "Let's hope. Leave the Hummer here. I'm going to have to climb the hill to get to the house. No use in getting stuck. Stay here."

"Daddy, I'm going with you," Ainsley said.

"You're not dressed for this weather," Butch said sternly.

"I don't care." She opened the vehicle's door. "I'm going up to that house." She hopped out and followed her dad and Butch up the hill. She'd been smart enough to grab her snow boots before they left, and though she had her snow jacket, mittens, and a knit hat on, she wouldn't last out here more than a few minutes. She shivered at the thought of Wolfe's being out in this wearing less than she had on, and for longer.

The hill was nearly impossible to climb, and it took a good while to find the path that led to the house. When they finally got there, Ainsley hurriedly rushed to the front door and pounded. "Wolfe! It's Ainsley! Open up! Are you okay? Wolfe!" She listened, but all she could hear were the dogs frantically barking at the door. "Wolfe, please. We know the truth. Garth did it! Please, if you're in there, open the door."

Her father stood behind her, but there was no answer. "I'm going around to the other side, find a way to see in," he said. "You keep trying the door."

Ainsley knocked and pounded, but there was no answer, and her father returned with the news that, as far as he could tell, no one was there. Butch said there were no footprints in the snow. Ainsley leaned against the door and moaned. "This is horrible. Where is he?" She turned to her father, her eyes beckoning a positive answer from him. But he could only shake his head. She grabbed his arm. "We have to find him."

CHAPTER 30

NEWS SPREAD QUICKLY that Wolfe Boone was lost in the storm, and before they knew it, many volunteers had arrived at the community center, dressed for a blizzard, ready to search for Wolfe. Her father and Butch were shouting instructions to everyone, but Ainsley sat in the back of the Hummer, her stomach cramped with worry, praying for Wolfe's well-being. The snow was still falling hard. Where should they search? Maybe he had decided not to go home. Maybe he was at a restaurant. The possibilities were endless, so Ainsley tried not to focus on anything but prayer. But it was not an easy task. She also felt guilty—guilty for believing, even for a second, that Wolfe had killed Thief. It pained her to think of what he must have been feeling when he left the house. All she wanted to do was hold him and tell him she loved him. And ask him to forgive her.

Her father was still giving out instructions on where to search for Wolfe, but by the strain in his voice, she knew he was worried too. It was unsafe for anyone to be out in this storm, and these were untrained searchers. Time was running out. If he was out there somewhere, he wouldn't last long. It was freezing, and night would soon fall. Worry seized her stomach again.

Then an idea struck her. She jumped up from her chair, ran up to her father at the podium, and said, "Dad! I have an idea!"

"What, honey?"

The crowd hushed, and she said, "I know who can find Wolfe."

"Easy…easy…okay, down…good dogs…" Sheriff Parker bent to their level, holding out his hands as the two shepherds barked anxiously.

Butch had skillfully picked the front door lock in order to get the dogs.

"This one is Bunny, that's Goose," Ainsley said, and just the sound of her voice calmed the dogs. The barking turned to worried whines. "They know something's wrong."

"Shepherds are smart. I think we need to get our volunteers in the forest, behind the dogs." He said that to Deputy Kinard, who nodded and then quickly left his side. "He must've cut through the forest." She watched her dad shake his head at the thought. "Poor guy."

"They'll find him if he's out there," Ainsley said, rubbing their necks. She looked at them. "You'll find him, right?"

They both barked enthusiastically. After five minutes, the volunteers were ready to be led by the dogs, and Sheriff Parker put both of them on leashes. "Kinard. Bledsoe. You two are strong. You'll have the leashes. Keep the dogs under control. We don't want to lose them. And let's just send out a few volunteers behind you. We don't need the whole town in this forest, or we could have a disaster on our hands." He looked at Butch. "Lead 'em, son."

Kinard and Bledsoe took the dogs, restraining them as best they could as they scrambled down the back steps of the house. Butch marched forward like a soldier off to war. His father followed them, looking back once. Ainsley waved and prayed, *Please, God, help us find Wolfe.*

It was spring, and thousands of flowers dotted the field where they were married. Reverend Peck was there, and others: Oliver, Melb, Martin, Butch, the mayor. The sheriff. The sky was as blue as it had ever been, not a cloud to be seen, and a slight breeze tickled their necks as they held hands and listened to Reverend Peck talk about love. He talked a lot about God's love and how a man and a wife should mimic it. His heart swelled with each passing word. It was a dream come true.

A dream. Dreaming.

Wolfe raised his head and opened his eyes. He was in the snow. He managed to move his arm, but he couldn't feel the rest of his body. He tried to roll over but couldn't. It was hard to breathe, and he was conscious enough to know he was in trouble. He didn't know how long he'd been out in the storm, but he felt snow on his back. He groaned and let his head fall back into the snow, thankful he had enough feeling in his cheek that the cold actually stung a little.

He closed his eyes, wondering what he would dream of next. Goose and Bunny. He smiled a little, listening to their barking as he greeted them at the door. He sat down with them in front of the fireplace and rubbed their tummies. Those dogs were going to miss him. He prayed they would find a good home. There was so much to pray for, so little time, so little strength...

He heard their barks again and tried to push the sad thoughts of where they might end up out of his mind. No use worrying. There was nothing he could do. Barking again. He opened his eyes, hoping the dream would go away. But with his eyes open, the barking came again, and again, until finally Wolfe realized he wasn't dreaming. He heard men's voices, shouts, more voices, and then barking again.

"Here," Wolfe whispered. His vocals cords refused his mental command to shout. "Here..."

If he could just sit up, he might actually be able to see someone, or let someone see him. But he was covered in snow, hardly able to move or speak. How would they find him?

He could tell the dogs were only a few yards away, and he tried again. "Here. Goose. Bunny. Here." He was merely mouthing the words, though, and his strength was ebbing quickly. His head hit the snow, and his eyes closed involuntarily. "Here..."

Then his face felt warm. Very warm. And wet. He couldn't open his eyes, but he knew it was them. Licking his cheek and whining. He felt strong hands on his body rolling him over, and then everything went black.

The hospital room was quiet and serene. Ainsley sat perfectly still, watching for any movement, but there was nothing. Her throat ached with fear; her heart beat with expectation.

"*We found him!*" She played those words over and over in her head. It had come over the radio of one of the deputies as she paced the floors of his home, waiting. He was alive when they found him, but the doctors at the hospital were cautious.

"Give it some time," one had told her. "He was out there a long while."

She covered her mouth as more tears drained from her eyes. Though he was being warmed with heating blankets, his hands were still cold. He looked peaceful, though, and she tried to concentrate on his face.

"I'm so sorry," she cried, squeezing his hand, hoping to see his eyes open. "I'm so sorry all this happened. This was supposed to be a wonderful day for you. Now it's awful. The worst day of your life. All because I didn't believe you. I didn't stand up for you. It's my fault." She cried harder, then gathered herself, looking him over, waiting for movement. There was nothing.

"Wolfe," she said, "I love you. And all this time, the whole time I've gotten to know you, I guess I've been a self-righteous pig. Yes, that's right. A pig. I always thought of how much I could teach you, how much I would show you about the faith. In a way, you becoming a Christian was for me like payback. I thought of it as a sort of revenge…the man that destroyed my town became a Christian. But I don't think that's what happened at all. In fact, *you're* the one who taught me things. You're the one that showed me what true faith is. I guess I made it complicated. But you made it simple. I made it a standard. But you made it life. And now—" She choked on her words and squeezed his hand, but he didn't squeeze back.

If the circumstances hadn't been so dire, Reverend Peck would've started dancing on the platform. Still, he couldn't help but marvel at the crowd that now packed his tiny church. In weather that wasn't fit for a dog, treacherous weather in fact, the small town of Skary had gathered to pray. He couldn't remember his church ever being this full. On a sunny day in June, hardly anyone would show up. Most of the time, more people showed up for weddings or funerals than for a Sunday morning service. And the four times a year when he promoted a Saturday of prayer for people to sign up and come pray, he usually filled most of the time slots himself.

What had happened to his little town? He looked into the faces of compassion, love, concern, mercy. It was like nothing he'd ever seen. Some were already bowing their heads in prayer. Others were in silent pondering. All for a man many of them hardly knew. He had a deep feeling that they weren't there to pray for Wolfe Boone, horror novelist. They were there to pray for Wolfe Boone, resident of Skary and brother in Christ.

Sheriff Parker, his uniform damp from the search, stood silently with the crowd, his arms folded in front of him. The mayor, Butch, and Marlee sat on the third row, clinging to each other and waiting for the reverend's lead. Oliver, Melb, Martin, and even his new acquaintance Alfred Tennison, were all there in his church.

He'd imagined all the things he would say if he ever got to preach in front of a large crowd. He loved to watch the Billy Graham crusades, imagine himself on the stage with George Beverly Shea, singing the hymns, preaching the Word, praying over the lost. This wasn't a stadium full of people, but by Skary standards, it could be considered a packed house. He smiled as he looked out across the crowd and saw people he'd prayed for over the years, those who'd stopped going to church for one reason or another. All of them, standing side by side, ready to give rather than receive, ready to pray for a man who desperately needed a touch from God.

The already quiet crowd became motionless as Reverend Peck

assumed his position behind the lectern. He held his Bible tightly in one hand and steadied himself with the other. He prayed for God to speak through him and to answer the prayers of the people that had gathered. And then he said, "'Where two or more are gathered, I am in your midst.' Those are the words of Jesus. He is here. Waiting for us to pray to Him for Wolfe."

And so Reverend Peck led the congregation in a prayer for Wolfe. When he paused, someone else picked up the prayer. One after another, people offered their prayers to God, and Reverend Peck was touched by each one. There was so much depth and feeling and sincerity that he knew, beyond a shadow of a doubt, that not only was the Lord listening to the prayers, but He was in them, speaking through the people as they obediently stood in the church and prayed for someone in need.

Reverend Peck prayed along with all of them, and never in his life had he felt the presence of God the way he did now. It was as if time didn't exist, and he wasn't exactly sure how much time was passing. For once he didn't care.

It wasn't until he felt a firm hand on his shoulder that he opened his eyes and looked up. The congregation was still there, and standing next to him was Sheriff Parker. He hadn't even realized the sheriff had joined him on the platform.

"I just got a call from the hospital," the sheriff said into the tiny microphone on the lectern. "Wolfe is awake. Looks like he's going to make it."

CHAPTER 31

"HERE YOU GO," Ainsley said, delivering the hot chocolate to Wolfe, who sat in his favorite leather chair by the fire. "Fresh hot cocoa with whipped cream and chocolate sprinkles."

Wolfe smiled at her and sipped the cocoa. "Perfect."

She joined him in the living room and sat on the couch next to the chair. "You're feeling okay?"

He laughed. "Stop it. You've been asking me that for three weeks. I'm good as new."

"The doctor says you should take it easy."

"Sitting in a chair drinking hot chocolate by the fire isn't taking it easy?"

She smiled at him. "I just want to make sure."

"I feel great. I have all my fingers and toes. I'm fine."

"I know, I know," Ainsley said, shaking her head. "I'm being over-protective. I'm sorry." She looked at him. "I think I still feel guilty. Wolfe, I'm so sorry about what happened."

"Stop apologizing. Please. It wasn't your fault."

"I should've—"

"Don't. Things worked out the way they were supposed to. I'm kind of enjoying all the attention. How else would I get someone to make me hot cocoa with sprinkles? Huh?"

"I'm just glad the truth was exposed. It was a rotten thing Garth Twyne did."

"Yeah, but he did it because he cares for you."

"That's no excuse." She leaned forward, propping her elbows on her knees. "There is one question I have to ask. And I have to admit, I'm not the only curious one."

"Okay, look, it's true. I'm not a big fan of cats, but fifty percent of the population hates cats. However, I can understand why you might've thought—"

"No, no," she laughed. "That's not what I was going to ask."

"Oh."

"The question is, who shared the gospel with you?"

"What?"

"Who witnessed to you, as they say? Who got you to convert?"

"That's the question?"

She nodded. "Everyone wants to know."

He shook his head, smiled, and set down his mug. "I guess that ranks up there with the question, 'Who was Deep Throat?' eh?"

"In a town this size it does. So who was it?"

He paused, then said, "You."

"Me?" She laughed. "Me? How could it be me? I never even spoke to you before that day in The Haunted Mansion."

"True."

"In fact, I was kind of mean to you."

"Also true."

"So how is it me?"

He shrugged. "I watched you a lot. I was attracted to you the first time I saw you. But one of the first things I noticed about you was how you treated people. You were kind to old people. You took the time to talk to those who seemed lonely. You were patient with those who were needy. More than once I saw you put your tip in that bottle for the orphanage at the front counter."

Ainsley frowned. "But I never talked to you."

"I know. But when I saw you doing all those things, in a way, you did. You weren't doing it for attention, but that's where I saw your heart. In what you did, not what you said. You lived out your faith instead of talking about it. And I knew, deep in my heart, that's what I wanted to do and be."

"I still don't understand. It was no secret that I wasn't your biggest fan."

"True. But you were sticking to your convictions, and I admired that about you."

Ainsley leaned back into the couch, trying to absorb what Wolfe was telling her. All this time everyone thought there was some conspiracy to convert Wolfe, and in reality just living out the gospel gave God room to do His own work.

When she looked back at him, he was beside her, kneeling. He took her hand, and she closed her eyes. She loved how this man prayed. When was the last time she had knelt to pray? Or offered up a prayer to God in the middle of the day for no apparent reason? She took so many things for granted in the Christian faith, even got lazy about them, but Wolfe showed her after peeling away all the layers what it was really about.

She longed to hear him pray again. The prayer he'd prayed at Thanksgiving was one of the most beautiful she'd ever heard. There was a poet somewhere deep inside this man… She'd have to figure out how to bring him out. She waited patiently for him to begin praying, wondering what he would thank God for, how he would offer up praises, or what he would ask for. But suddenly she wasn't hearing a prayer. She was hearing laughter. She smiled herself, figuring he was just filled with pure joy—something she longed to reacquaint herself with. But the laughter continued, and Ainsley had to open her eyes to learn the reason for it.

"What's so funny?" she asked.

"You are."

"Me?"

"You."

"Why? I'm just waiting for you to pray."

"But I'm not praying."

"You're not?"

"I'm asking you to marry me."

Ainsley's heart stopped as she watched Wolfe hold up a ring in front of her. "A ring."

"My mother's." He locked eyes with her. "That's why I'm kneeling. To ask you to marry me. Your father, by the way, has already said yes."

Ainsley had cried many tears of frustration, heartache, and fear recently, but the tears that flowed from her now were nothing less than pure joy. "Oh, Wolfe."

"Say yes. Make my dreams come true."

"Yes. Yes! I'll marry you!" She didn't wait for him to slip the ring on. Instead she fell into his embrace and threw her arms around his neck. They kissed, and then he put the ring on her finger, and it fit perfectly. It was so dainty, yet so beautiful.

"I love you," she said to him.

"I love you, too. I have for more years than you know. Your yes is like the warmth from a sun that I've only been able to observe from far away. Your rays have finally reached me."

She took his face in her hands. "You should write poetry."

"Oh? I'm not sure Alfred would go for that."

"You're eloquent with words. Your heart is deep. And you see things that others don't."

He smiled at her, kissed her again and said, "Maybe I'll give it a try someday."

Missy Peeple stood silently behind her screen door, looking out at her once glorious town. Things were already changing. She could sense it. Soon there would be no tourists. No fame. Nothing out of the ordinary except their name, and that was even spelled wrong. Cute when attached to the hometown of a horror novelist. Dumb for any other reason.

Skary, Indiana. Just another little town nobody's ever heard of.

For a few long moments Missy watched cars go back and forth on her street, thinking briefly of Mayor Wullisworth and love lost. But her eyes suddenly caught something on the corner of her porch. Something black. She wrapped her shawl around her bony shoulders, unlatched the screen door, and stepped into the cold.

There, sitting on the rail of her small porch, was a black cat—its tail swishing, its eyes narrow and perceptive.

"Well, well, well. If it isn't the feline who is single-handedly responsible for the despicable cat population in this town. Hello, Thief."

The cat meowed and hopped over an empty flower pot to come closer. He sat and stared at her.

Missy looked around and then at the cat. "Worried about whether your secret is safe with me, eh?" She smiled a little. "What would you do with your days, dear Thief, if things were 'fixed,' as they say?" His attention was fully on her, and she regarded him with a cocked eyebrow. "Driving around with the sheriff all day long with nothing more to do than observe the man at work. What a torturous life."

Then something struck Missy Peeple. And it wasn't lightning. No, it was an idea. A brilliantly clever idea. An idea that would put her little town back on the map! She clutched her cane and laughed excitedly. Thief's ears flicked with perky awareness.

"Of course," she said. "Of course!" If this town couldn't be known for the gory and the gruesome, then by golly it was going to be known for something. Cats. Cats! It would be a phenomenon that nobody could explain. People from all over the country—no, the world!—would come to buy cats from a place that seemed to birth them from the bowels of the earth. She winked at Thief. Of course, she knew all the better. There could be theater productions of the play *Cats,* and they could run *That Darn Cat!* all day long at the movie theater. There could be merchandise. They could rename all the streets for every breed of cat. *Arsenic and Old Lace* could become *The Cat's Meow,* a bed and breakfast just for cats and cat lovers!

Yes. Yes! Once again, Missy Peeple would save the town of Skary.

She turned to the cat and looked him in his golden eyes. "I think you will come in handy. Very handy indeed."

ACKNOWLEDGMENTS

IT IS UNFORTUNATE that only one name is on the cover of a book, as there are so many people who contribute to the process of its creation and production. Thankfully, God knows and sees everything. I thank all of you who contributed to *Boo*. May God richly reward and bless you.

I want to especially acknowledge Erin Healy, whose creative additions to this novel have made it more than I could imagine; Dudley Delffs, too, for your continuous encouragement, contribution, leadership, and behind-the-scenes work; Laura Wright, for helping finish up this package by studying every last detail; and finally, the entire WaterBrook Press team, where I most definitely feel part of a large loving family.

I'm also so thankful for a loving church family, who supports me and cheers me on, but most of all teaches me what it means to be like Jesus. WCC, the Flock That Rocks, I'm your biggest fan!

Speaking of family, I am incredibly blessed to have a talented, wonderful, handsome husband, who is such a delight to his wife and children. Sean, thank you for your sacrifice. Only I know what terrific things you do so that I can do this. And kids, I love you so much too. Thank you to the rest of my family for always being supportive and happy to help however you can.

I'd also like to acknowledge Judy Secrist, Patty Pace, and Sandy Bourquin, who are continuous supporters and loving contributors to my work.

And finally, how can one not acknowledge our Father? He is the One who gives me a mind filled with imagination, a heart to tell a story, and hands to form the words on the page. Lord, every day I get to do this is a gift straight from You. Thank You with all my heart.